MW00880190

LITTLE
Blue
Whistle

MARK LAGES

authorHOUSE®

AuthorHouse™
1663 Liberty Drive
Bloomington, IN 47403
www.authorhouse.com
Phone: 1 (800) 839-8640

Published by AuthorHouse 11/16/2018

ISBN: 978-1-5462-6930-4 (sc)
ISBN: 978-1-5462-6929-8 (e)

Library of Congress Control Number: 2018913803

Print information available on the last page.

This book is printed on acid-free paper.

CONTENTS

Soaked to the Bone

n a week, my son, Paul, and his boyfriend will arrive here at our new home in South Carolina for Thanksgiving. Paul's boyfriend's name is Terrance. This will be the first time I have met Terrance. If you haven't already figured the situation out, Paul has just come out of the closet and told us he's gay. According to Paul, this is the first time in his life that he's been honest with us. It doesn't seem fair, does it? Why does he get to be so soul-searchingly honest when I'm not allowed to return the favor? Why do I have to walk on eggshells? Why can't I respond to his announcement by saying, "What—are you out of your fucking mind?" But I didn't say anything like that. I held my tongue.

I am Robert Ashcroft, a sixty-three-year-old heterosexual father and husband, married to Veronica, who is fifty-nine. We are as decent and old-fashioned as ice cream and apple pie. For example, we were both virgins until our wedding night, and how many people can say that? And not that there's any way we can prove this, but our lovemaking ever since then has been as tame as a little girl's tea party. There has never been any oral sex, nor fancy sex toys, nor screaming and hollering, nor off-the-wall gymnastic-style stand-on-your-head positions. It's just been a lot of decent and straightforward sex the way the good Lord intended—quiet, clean, and wonderful. I'm not trying to brag about our wholesomeness; I'm only saying that as parents, we set a good example, and if Paul picked up any perversions, he didn't learn them from us.

I'm not allowed to be honest with Paul, but I will be honest with you. But I have a question. Why am I allowed to bare my soul to complete strangers when I'm not allowed to be honest with my own flesh and blood? It's the same old game I'm forced to play with Veronica. She asks, "Tell me the truth, Robert. Do these jeans make me look fat? Do they make my butt look big?" If I tell a lie, I can make her feel great. But if I tell the truth, I'm rotten to the core. Am I rotten to the core? Is there something wrong with me?

In any event, I've got just seven short days to come to terms with Paul's lifestyle, and seven days isn't a very long time. When you consider the fact that Paul is thirty years old, seven days is the blink of an eye. For the past thirty years I've thought my son was as normal as a box of Cracker Jack at a baseball game. He did go out with some girls. He was even married for a few years, so what the heck happened? When he was a kid, we never caught him wearing any of Veronica's clothes, and he never played with Barbie dolls or showed an interest in riding horses. He was a good ice skater, but never a figure skater. He did like daffodils, but I don't remember him ever making flower arrangements out of them. For thirty years, in my eyes he's been a character out of a Norman Rockwell painting, a red-blooded American boy who matured into a man. As queer as a three-dollar bill? No, never.

I can trace Paul's life back to the exact date and time of his conception. Not many people can say that about any of their children, but I can say it about Paul. It's not because I'm right but because I want *to be* right. It could only be the evening I'm thinking of because it was by far the best evening nine months prior to his birth. It's also because my memories of that night are so vivid. To this day, I can close my eyes and see exactly where we were and what we were doing just hours before we participated in the lovemaking that set all the wheels into motion, resulting in the little mucous-and-blood-drenched infant we named Paul.

We were in Barbados, getting ready to order dinner at a restaurant called The Purple Dog. It's true that we could've taken a taxi that night, but we decided to walk and enjoy the balmy evening air. We had called and made reservations for a table for two and had plenty of time to get there on foot. They sat us at a table with a marvelous view of the adjacent beach, and we were looking at our dinner menus, trying to decide what to order. When I say *we*, I am referring, of course, to me and Veronica. I was thirty-two years old at the time, and Veronica was twenty-eight. The year? It was 1987, the same year that Ray Bolger died. Do you remember Ray? "I don't know," he said, "but some people without brains do an awful lot of talking." Yes, that Ray Bolger. The dude hit the nail on the head. Veronica and I were staying in Barbados for a well-deserved two-week vacation away from the rat race in Southern California. As fate would have it, we wound up at The Purple Dog.

Like I said, my memories of this evening are sharp and vivid, and if I close my eyes right now, it's like watching a brilliant old Technicolor movie. If I had any talent as an artist, I would sit and paint you a wonderfully detailed picture of The Purple Dog on canvas, accurate inside and out. My painting would be true from the corny Coke bottle salt and pepper shakers on the tables, to our waiter's ill-fitting hairpiece, to the little green bug the man sitting next to us found crawling in his salad. He almost ate the damn thing! I didn't feel sorry for the man. I felt sorry for the poor bug, scrambling to get out of that slippery salad bowl before the man devoured it with his big, toothy mouth. What a horrible way to go.

Our waiter's name was Omar. Have you ever met people who are simply happy to have a job? Do you know the kind of people I mean? You don't meet a lot of these people in Southern California. Where I lived, people actually seemed aggravated to have a job. Like they felt put upon when you asked them to do something, feeling degraded and wrongly taken advantage of. For some reason, people in Southern California all seemed to think they should be rich and famous, wearing solid-gold Rolex watches, driving around in the backs of limos, and dodging the paparazzi. You won't meet many people like Omar in Southern California. At least, that has been my experience. Of course, as they like to say, your mileage may vary.

Omar had but one thing in mind when he took our dinner orders, which was to see to it that we were happy with our experience at The Purple Dog. Not since the morning after my ugly sister first got laid in high school have I seen a person smile so much. You would think Omar had just won the lottery, but he was happy to be working and making himself useful to others, bringing home a paycheck, and having a purpose in life.

"Are you ready to order?" he chirped like a little bird, and Veronica told him we needed a few more minutes. Well, she's the one who needed the extra time. I was ready to order, but I've learned that when Veronica needs something, we both need it. I think this is a female thing, and it was fine. She always did this, and I was used to it.

"I don't know what to get," she said to me.

"What are you thinking of?" I asked.

"Well, either the swordfish or the pork chop."

"You haven't ordered swordfish for a while," I said. "But you've had good luck with pork chops lately."

"That doesn't help much."

"Which sounds better to you?"

"The swordfish sounds good."

"The last time you ordered swordfish, you said you didn't like it. I think that was at that little restaurant in Laguna Beach."

"But that was their swordfish, and not the swordfish here at The Purple Dog. I like good swordfish. And I feel like having swordfish tonight."

"Then order the swordfish."

"How do I know if their swordfish is any good?"

"You're asking *me*?"

"Well, which would you order? The swordfish or the pork chop?"

"I wouldn't order either of them."

"So what are you getting?"

"I'm getting a hamburger and fries."

"I had a hamburger for lunch. I don't want to have the same thing for dinner as I had for lunch."

"Then order the swordfish or the pork chop."

Veronica looked back down and stared at her menu. I was not going to get frustrated with her, because I knew exactly what she was doing. She wanted the night to be perfect, and she wanted to order just the right dish. She wanted our experience at this restaurant to be a night we would both remember forever. We were, after all, spending a small fortune on this vacation, and we might as well get some good memories out of it. I let her stare at her menu for about a minute. Then I asked, "What do you think you're going to get?"

"I've decided," she said. "Call the waiter over."

"Omar," I said, and the man's face lit up. He was so looking forward to serving us.

"Yes, sir," Omar said.

"I think we're ready."

"Ma'am?" Omar said to Veronica with his pen poised and ready for action.

"I'll have the halibut," she said.

"Yes, ma'am. That's a great choice. Our halibut is delicious."

"I'll have the burger and fries," I said. "And bring me a bottle of catsup. And bring us a couple more drinks from the bar."

So she ordered the halibut. Yes, even I was a little surprised, and I thought I knew my wife pretty well.

But it all turned out great. There we were, husband and wife, four thousand miles from home on a Caribbean island surrounded by water, ordering dinner and drinks from a man named Omar in a place called The Purple Dog. We'd been in the sun all day, and our faces were a little raw, but not burnt. As you get older, you forget what it was like to soak up all that sun and not worry about how it might damage your skin. To be so young! And to be so in love! There's nothing like it in the world. You should know that it turned out Veronica loved her halibut. Maybe the halibut really was good, or maybe Veronica just wanted it to be good. I didn't ask her. The truth was that my hamburger was fantastic. Omar said the beef came from the island locally, but I suspected he was making that up. What difference did it make?

During dinner, we are talking about our family to be. We were trying to have our first baby. Veronica asked me if I wanted a boy or a girl, and I told her I would be happy with either. "So long as the baby is healthy," I said. "That's all that really matters." Isn't that what people always say? But the real truth was that I wanted a boy. I had plans for a boy. I had hopes and dreams for my boy before he was even born. I can tell you precisely what was going through my head as I sat there eating my hamburger and watching Veronica eat her halibut. I was living the first thirty years of my son's life, from the day he first came into the world to the day he and his wife would decide to have their own children.

Forget all the baby years. Those years didn't really interest me, the years Paul would be drooling and crawling around on the kitchen floor at his mother's feet, filling his diaper, guzzling down bottles of warm formula, and chewing on rubber teething rings. Those were really the precious years for the mother, when she could rock her little baby to sleep, sing it sweet lullabies, and burp it over her shoulder. The years that interested me were those after-the-baby years, the years we could call Paul a boy. Yes, I wanted a rough and tumble, messy-haired, card-carrying little boy.

The Paul I dreamed about was no sissy. This Paul was an expert at catching frogs, lizards, and grasshoppers, and he'd bring them into the house, causing poor Veronica to stand up on the beds and scream for her life. This Paul always had dirt under his little fingernails and grime behind his ears. This Paul wore holes in the knees of his grass-stained jeans faster than he would grow out of them. He would be master of his skateboard and bicycle, and he'd own a pocketknife I bought for him, a knife I told him he could never, ever take to school. School was for the birds, right? Classrooms and offices full of old fuddy-duddies with no sense of humor and a penchant for making life miserable. My Paul would be sent to see the principal a few times, not all the time like a problem child, but often enough to prove he was a boy. Maybe he would get caught opening his sack lunch early and eating a Twinkie during class, or maybe he would get in a schoolyard fight with some loud-mouthed boy. But he wouldn't get in trouble for anything really serious.

My Paul would love to play sports. Doesn't every all-American kid love sports? Paul would be a holy terror with a baseball bat in his hands, standing in front of the other team's catcher with his bat on his shoulder and his eye on the ball, capable of knocking that ball clear over the fence, capable of putting the wood to almost any kind of pitch. Pitchers would fear him, and they'd duck when he hit the ball to keep from getting hit. Fielders would fall on their faces trying to get him out, and the coaches on the other teams would smack their foreheads with the palms of their hands. When Paul was in the outfield playing defense, there wouldn't be a corner of the grass that'd be safe from his trusty glove. The boy could catch anything, and the coaches on the other teams would plead with their hitters not to hit the ball toward Paul, yet they'd do it anyway.

Or maybe Paul would be into football. Football is a great sport, isn't it? Maybe he'd be a running back, or even a quarterback. Or maybe he'd be a sure-handed wide receiver with legs like Mercury. Who knew? The opposing teams would fear him, and their coaches would spend hours and hours talking to their players, trying to figure out ways to slow Paul down and keep him from inflicting too much damage. From Pop Warner he'd move on to high school football, and all the students, teachers, and parents would be cheering him on. The girls at school would be hog-crazy for him, and they'd all envy the lucky girl Paul finally set his sights on. His girl would be the cream of the crop, the cat's pajamas, the loveliest and sweetest piece of candy in the bag.

After graduating from high school, Paul would go on to college, and after college he'd get a job—not just any old job, but a job that paid well and had a great future. Paul would have the world on the end of a string. My boy. My wonderful boy named Paul. So, yes, I wanted a boy, a boy who would grow into a fine young man with a future as big and promising as a Montana sky. I wanted to name him Paul after my grandfather, and I wanted Paul to be all the things I never was. My Paul would have everything. Paul would be loved, and Paul would get the girl.

But back to Barbados and my evening with Veronica at The Purple Dog. Apparently, all this daydreaming about my son at the dinner table had made me hungry, because I devoured my burger and fries like I hadn't eaten anything for a month. Veronica was still picking at her food, and I looked at her. I remember it hit me just how beautiful this girl was. I realized this feeling influenced by my love for her, but what I saw was so real, and so palpable, that I actually felt light-headed, the way you feel when you stand up too fast. It's amazing how a woman can do this to a man, stealing all rational thought from him and making him feel like a giddy schoolgirl experiencing her first crush. Right then and there I would've done anything for Veronica. I would've broken into the Tower of London and grabbed the Crown Jewels, or slayed a fire-breathing dragon, or even climbed to the top of Mount Everest in shorts and bare feet. All she had to do was name it, and I would've done it. Or at least I would've given it a college try.

On our way back to the hotel, it rained. I don't mean as in a little drizzle or a few drops, but it was quite a downpour. What is it about tropical rainstorms that make one feel so romantic? God, we were laughing and holding hands like idiots, soaked to the bone, dripping all over the place and sloshing wet like fools. I remember the clerks and bellboys laughing at us as we returned to our hotel. "Do you like our island rain?" one of them asked, and Veronica shouted, "I love it! I love it!" We stepped to the elevator and pressed the button on the wall. When we finally got inside of the elevator, and when the elevator started moving up, Veronica fell into my arms and laughed like a little girl. We were dripping water all over the floor, and we were dripping water on each other. I looked down at Veronica's face, and she looked up at me like she was posing for a picture. With her wet hair, and lovely brown eyes, and a smile that could melt all the glaciers in Alaska, she looked up at me, and honest to God, I couldn't believe that this girl was mine!

When we got to our room, we shed our wet clothing and made love that evening with the patio door wide open, with the rain pouring down and splattering all over the outside deck and patio furniture. And that, I'm quite sure, is exactly when Paul was conceived. He was created out of the love between a young man and woman breathing heavily on a creaky hotel bed, rainstorm beating down outside, our wet clothes strewn all over the floor, and the rest of the world put on hold.

Now I keep telling myself over and over, "Paul is gay. Paul is gay. Paul is gay." It makes no sense to me. Does it make any sense to you? It's like mixing blue and yellow paints and coming up with orange.

Hello There, Little Man

When Veronica was eight months pregnant, she looked like she was carrying a baby elephant. Honestly, the woman was huge, like one of those character balloons they guide with ropes down Central Park West during the Macy's Thanksgiving Day Parade. And they say women glow when they're pregnant, but Veronica was positively on fire. Her skin was a hot and bloody shade of red, especially her cheeks. It was like she had a terrible sunburn, but she was always indoors. And she was always out of breath, huffing and puffing everywhere she went like she'd just climbed several flights of stairs with a piano strapped to her back. I felt so sorry for her. I had no idea that our idyllic little lovemaking escapade in that Barbados hotel room eight months earlier would have such a powerful effect on her.

But Veronica was a trooper. She certainly could've stood there like a victim and angrily said, "Look what you did to me!" She could've done that, but she never did. Instead she did her due diligence, buying every book about pregnancy and childbirth she could get her hands on. It was her intention to bring to term the healthiest baby ever to draw a first breath in Southern California. No baby was ever pampered and nurtured more in its mother's womb than Paul was. For Veronica, it was all about providing the baby with proper nourishment. You should've seen the all meals they ate together. I've never seen Veronica spend so much time in our kitchen, not in all the years we've been married. She'd begin each dinner with large epicurean salads filled with healthy greens, sliced fruits, and raw nuts. Then she'd serve up

9

big broiled steaks, pork chops, lamb chops, fatty slabs of boiled corned beef, and big, juicy pot roasts. She'd also make mashed potatoes and gravy, hot dinner rolls dripping with butter, baked potatoes with sour cream and chives, boiled baby potatoes, french fries, onion rings, and every kind of cooked vegetable dish you can imagine. Serving platters, plates, and bowls of food crowded every square inch of our dining room table as though a sultan and his entire retinue were dining with us every night.

How much weight did she actually gain during her pregnancy? Veronica has never revealed her weight to me for as long as I've known her, not even when she was at her leanest, so I have no idea how many pounds she put on. But it was substantial. She didn't need maternity clothes; she needed a full-size Barnum and Bailey circus tent. Now, I'm exaggerating, of course, but you probably get the picture.

Right now, I'm standing in the family room of our new home in South Carolina. I'm standing by the fireplace, and as you can see there are many framed family pictures on the mantel. There are photos of the three of us together on our vacations to Europe, the Caribbean, and Hawaii, and a few solo shots taken of Paul in Southern California during various stages of his childhood. There are also pictures of the grandparents, a picture of my sister, and one of my aunt and uncle, but nowhere in this group of photographs are there any of Veronica when she was pregnant with Paul. The pregnancy pictures mysteriously disappeared about fifteen years ago. I have no idea where they are, but I know who took them. Obviously, it was Veronica who absconded with the pictures, and she either destroyed them or hid them where none of us could find them. And I now wonder if Paul noticed this. And if he did, would he have interpreted Veronica's actions the wrong way? The reason Veronica purged the pictures had nothing to do with her wishing that she'd never been pregnant, and certainly it had nothing to do with her regretting having brought Paul into the world. The reason had to do with Veronica's vanity.

It was simple, really. Veronica just didn't want to be reminded day after day that she was once as large as Holstein cow. This is something you should know about her—she's very aware of how she looks. She takes very good care of herself, and she's proud of her appearance.

She eats all the right things, and she doesn't smoke. She works out in the gym regularly. She hardly ever drinks alcohol, and she gets plenty of sleep. People often say she looks ten years younger than she actually is. Anyway, all of this is important to Veronica, and having pictures around the house of her pregnancy sort of defeats the aura she's trying to sustain. Which brings me back to Paul. Do you think he noticed that all the pregnancy photos were taken away? Do you think he might have taken it the wrong way? I'm certainly no shrink, but don't they say that male homosexuality has something to do with boys and their relationships with their mothers? I've heard that before, but I don't remember where.

When Veronica was finally due to have Paul, I really began to feel for her. The poor girl looked like she was going to explode. If I hadn't seen the ultrasound for myself, I would've sworn she was carrying sextuplets. In my imagination, I pictured the litter squirting out of her on delivery day, one after the other, with her obstetrician catching them out of the air with a baseball mitt while the nurse kept score. But I saw the ultrasound for myself. It was only one male baby, our little boy who we were going to name Paul.

Days went by, one after the other, past Veronica's due date. The doctor grew concerned and told us they were going to induce labor. He said they could do this with a certain drug, and the doctor assured us it was done all the time and that it was a perfectly safe procedure. So into the hospital we trotted, hoping to finally get Paul out of Veronica's body. I don't think Veronica would object to me telling you that she was terrified.

Now, I'm going to recount some of the details of how Paul came into this world. I was nervous when it happened, and when I get nervous, I tend to forget things and mix events up, so my account may not be completely accurate. It was also thirty years ago, so you have to take that into consideration. A lot of time has passed since I saw Paul being born, and time tends to warp memories. But you'll get the general idea.

Veronica's obstetrician's name was Dr. Stanley. If I remember right, one of the first things Dr. Stanley did, besides getting Veronica on her back and up on the stirrups, was to break her water. I have no idea how he did this. I assume he had to lance some kind of membrane. He stuck his head under Veronica's gown while the nurse held the gown up over his head, and he performed the ritualistic task. If I remember right, the water was supposed to run into some kind of a pan. It was supposed to be a rather routine procedure, them filling the pan and then disposing of the fluid. No doubt this doctor had performed this water-breaking ceremony hundreds of times before. But I told you Veronica was large, and apparently her size was made up largely of the water. I mean, Jesus, it was actually embarrassing the way this stuff gushed out. The pan, or whatever it was they used to collect it, overflowed within seconds so that water was running everywhere, and it was dripping and splashing all over the floor. Soon, there was a puddle at the foot of the bed large enough for a small child to swim in, and they had to bring in a mop and pail to clean the mess up. "I've never seen so much water," Dr. Stanley said. He seemed bewildered, but he was also smiling when he said this, so I assumed it wasn't a problem.

This was going to be no ordinary delivery, I thought to myself. After the water breaking, we had to deal with the contractions. They weren't coming naturally. They were coming from chemical drip into Veronica's IV line, and the doctor kept timing the contracts and then increasing the drip. Then he'd get his head under Veronica's robe again to check things out, and he'd read off some numbers to the nurse, who would write them down. "You're not quite ready yet," the doctor would say, and then he'd leave the room. He'd come back later to do the exact same thing. "Not quite yet," he'd say. "But we're getting closer." Well, each hour that passed became more painful for my wife than the last. I could tell she was in great discomfort, and she kept asking the nurse to give her more drugs for the pain. She tried the breathing exercises they taught in her Lamaze class, but the whole breathing thing was a joke. It did nothing to help. After about ten hours of this IV-induced torture, Veronica was beginning to panic. I could see it in her eyes.

The doctor got his head under her robe again for the umpteenth examination, and this time when he pulled out his head, he said, "This isn't going to work. The baby is too large for the birth canal."

"What does that mean?" Veronica asked.

"It means we need to do a C-section."

I knew it, I thought. She overfed the little monster, and now he's too big to come out.

They wheeled Veronica into an operating room, and they told me I could come and watch. I'd been to Lamaze classes to prepare myself for all of this. This was something Veronica wanted me to do, and I remembered our Lamaze teacher stressed that I was to be Veronica's partner, no matter what. This was even if it meant watching a doctor cut into her belly. So, yes, I went into the operating room, and they provided me with a stool to sit on up near the head of the bed. They had Veronica on her back, and they pulled up a sheet so she couldn't see what they were doing to her. But I could see everything from where I was sitting—the blood, guts, and the whole nine yards. It looked like she'd been in a terrible car accident or fallen through a plate glass window. Then, without any warning at all, Dr. Stanley reached into Veronica's shiny gray insides and pulled out a living baby! It was so utterly bizarre and so disconcerting that the blood rushed from my head and I nearly fell off my stool. "What does it look like?" Veronica asked me.

"It, uh, looks good," I said. What a stupid thing to say! It was a sticky, bloody mess.

Dr. Stanley raised Paul into the air, holding him by his legs. There was no need to slap his bottom, since he was crying already.

The rest of this experience in the operating room is lost. I don't remember if I stuck around to watch them staple Veronica's stomach or if I left right away. The next thing I recall is standing in another hospital room where Veronica was in bed with the baby in her arms. The baby was swaddled in a warm blanket and wearing a cloth cap. "Hello there, little man," I said to Paul. He just stared back at me, trying to figure out what the heck was going on and who the heck I was. He looked so content to be in his mother's arms. He was a clean slate, a newborn babe, a little mind just starting out. New, new, new! He was as new as a car right off the showroom floor that had only a couple of miles on it. There's nothing like the smell of a new car, am I right? And there's nothing like the smell of a new baby. He was my son, my own flesh and blood, and just a few hours old.

The grandparents came to visit. They wanted to see the baby, and they wanted to know how Veronica was doing after her experience. Veronica's parents were the first to enter the room, and then my parents. They were all cackling and clucking like a henhouse full of excited chickens, but I could tell Veronica was happy that they came.

Veronica described the entire experience for them, including her abundance of water. "You were so big," her mother said. "So I guess that makes sense." I could tell her mother was a little embarrassed, not wanting her daughter to seem like some sort of freak full of too much water. I think it's funny the things people worry about. Her father was concerned over the fact that she had to have a C-section to get Paul out, as if this meant she wasn't strong or brave enough to push the baby out on her own.

"Maybe next time you won't need to do that," he said. I pointed out that Paul was just too big to fit through the birth canal, and this seemed to appease everyone. The bigger the better, right? "Maybe he'll be a linebacker," Veronica's father said, and everyone liked the idea of Paul becoming a football player.

Showdown at the Back Forty

The year was 1963, and I was in the third grade. I'm going to tell you a story about myself, and I'll try to be as honest as possible. I've noticed that when most men describe their years as kids, they paint a picture of themselves as being faster, smarter, stronger, braver, better looking, and more adept at sports than they ever were. Usually there's no one around from their past to contradict their lies and exaggerations, so they can get away with it. But what is the point of this? To prove that they have great imaginations? To prove that they can lie? To prove that they're delusional? I already know that I have a great imagination and that I can lie. And I know there are times when I'm delusional. I mean, aren't we all delusional at one time or the other? No, I'm going to try to be honest with you, mainly because without my honesty the story I'm about to tell you has no meaning. And if the story has no meaning, there's no point in my telling it.

In 1963 I was eight years old. I was the son of an architect and his lovely wife. They were known formally as Mr. and Mrs. Edwin Ashcroft, and this was how people addressed their letters and packages to them. But Mom's first name was Elaine, not Mrs. Edwin Ashcroft. I liked the name Elaine, and it didn't seem right to call her by my father's name. She was sweet, good-looking, and always well-mannered. She always smelled so clean, not like perfume, but more like a bar of deodorant soap. She did whatever my dad told her. I mean, if Dad told her to jump off a bridge, she'd ask, "Which one?" No kidding, it was that bad. I also had an older sister. She was in the sixth grade and was about as pretty as a rattlesnake. Her name was Betty, and she had as much interest in me as she would have had in reading Aristotle's *Nicomachean Ethics*. Betty and I went to the same school, but we saw very little of each other. I think she avoided me because she thought I was immature. All in all, I'd say we had a very normal family. We lived in a tidy little three-bedroom ranch-style house, with two big cars, a large front lawn, an automatic Kenmore washer and dryer, a dog named Ralphie, two lazy short-haired cats named Whiskers and Sleepy, and a pet albino rat named Edward who I kept in a cage in my bedroom.

Let's be honest about this; as a kid I was nothing to write home about. It's true that my mom always told me I was special, and I think she meant well. And I really did want to believe her. But the fact was that I was rather boring and ordinary. You know how some kids have talents or attributes that set them apart from others? Some kids are good in sports, or good at art, or good at music. Some kids are especially good-looking. Some kids can do magic tricks, some can imitate the sounds of wild animals, and others can calculate complicated math problems in their heads. But me? I was just black-haired, brown-eyed Robert Ashcroft, an ordinary tinfoil-wrapped peanut butter and jelly sandwich of a boy if ever there was one. Throw me in with the rest of the peanut butter and jelly sandwiches, and you'd never be able to pick me out.

I was at school playing a game of basketball during morning recess with some friends when along came Frankie McGuire. God, how I hated this kid. Up until this day, I never had anything to do with him, but I hated him. The boy made me sick with his feminine affectations, the way he used his long-fingered hands when he talked, and the way he walked up on his toes like a freaking ballerina. Back then we didn't call boys like Frankie gay, because back then to be gay actually meant to be happy or joyful. We called boys like Frankie fags, fairies, homos, sissies, pansies, or queers. I didn't know that much about Frankie, but I'd heard he was being raised by his old grandmother. No wonder he was such a fag, being brought up some little old gray-haired lady who probably knew as much about raising boys as she knew about the latest rock 'n roll artists playing on her dusty old RCA Victor radio. In a way I felt sorry for the kid, not being raised by a regular mom and dad. Where were his mom and dad? No one seemed to know or even care.

But I wouldn't feel sorry for Frankie long, not after he opened his big mouth during our game. I'd just missed a jump shot, and Frankie laughed out loud and pointed at me. "You missed the basket, stupid," he said. "In case no one told you, the basket is the metal hoop with the net on it. You're supposed to put the ball through the hoop."

"Pardon?" I said. "Were you talking to me?"

"You did just try to make a shot, didn't you? Isn't that what you were doing?"

"What about it?"

"You missed."

"So maybe I did. What about it?"

"My grandmother could've made that shot."

"Piss off," I said.

Frankie gave me the weirdest look, like he was intent on getting even with me for something I'd done to him. He seemed angry with me, but I never had done anything to him. I simply knew who he was. There were kids who picked on him, but I wasn't one of them. "The truth hurts, doesn't it?" he said.

"What truth?"

"The truth that you stink at basketball."

One of my friends said, "Are you going to let him talk to you that way?"

"Make him take it back," another kid said.

"Yeah," a third kid said. "Make him take it back."

I walked up to Frankie and gave him a little shove in the chest. "Take it back," I said.

"Take it back yourself," he replied, and he pushed me back. I stood there and stared at him. I was confused at first. What was this little fairy hoping to accomplish by challenging me?

"Back off, fairy," I said.

"Back off or what?"

"Or I'll pound your face in." There, I said it. I didn't want to say it, but I did.

"You're the fairy," he said. "I can take you in a fight anytime, anywhere."

Some of my friends were now laughing.

"Fight him," a kid said.

"Yeah, fight him," another kid said.

I was being backed into a corner. It was the weirdest thing, how this kid decided to come right out of the blue and pick a fight with me. I thought for a moment he might be kidding, but when he stayed in front of me, staring me down, I had to figure he was serious.

"How about after school," I said.

"Name the place," Frankie said.

"The Back Forty."

"Right after school," he confirmed.

"I'll be there," I said.

"Then so will I," Frankie said. Then he walked away, talking to himself and laughing.

The school bell rang, and it was time for us to return to class. I remember wondering what had just happened? One minute I was minding my own business, shooting hoops with my buddies, and now I had made a date for a fight with Frankie McGuire after school.

Nothing travels faster among elementary school kids than news of an afterschool fight. Halfway through our lunch recess, it seemed everyone had learned about Frankie and me, and when afternoon recess came, it was the only thing the kids in the playground were talking about. The reaction to the prospect of this fight was mixed. I'd say most of the kids at school looked forward to it, the same way they look forward to a good TV show. They wanted to be entertained, and it was always entertaining to see two kids throwing punches at each other, no matter who they were. Hopefully there would be some blood. Hopefully there would be a black eye. Hopefully one of the boys would make a fool of himself and cry. And most hopefully of all, there wouldn't be an adult arriving at the scene to break things up. Adults could ruin everything. It didn't matter who won, so long as there was a fight.

It was true that most of the kids at school didn't care who won or lost, but there *were* certain groups who were taking sides. For one reason or the other, some would be rooting for one of us to win. My friends were on my side, of course. They wanted to see me beat the living daylights out of Frankie the homo, not so much because they hated Frankie, but because a victory for me meant a victory for our group, and for each of them it would be a victory by association. Same thing held true for Frankie's small group of friends. They'd root for him to win for the same reason.

There was another school of thought. Some kids just thought the fight was lame. It wasn't because they didn't like fights in general; in fact, many of these kids were known as good fighters. They just thought a showdown between a confirmed fairy like Frankie and a virtual nobody like me wasn't worth all the attention it was getting. "One fairy verses another," I heard one of these kids say. "Who wants to watch two fags go at it in a bitch-slapping contest?" another said. I'll be honest. These comments hurt my feelings.

The fight became a big deal for me. It was a big deal because I was so sure I would win. But, as the afternoon went by, I noticed something strange happening to me. My confidence was eroding, and I began to wonder what I'd gotten myself into. I asked myself, for example, *Why did Frankie pick on me?* Of all the kids he could've pestered on the playground, he specifically sought me out. Why was this? How calculated of a move was it? We were both about the same height and build, so maybe that was part of it. It made sense that he wouldn't pick someone bigger than him, someone who might knock him silly. And it also made sense that he wouldn't have picked on someone smaller. Beating up a kid smaller than him would just make him look bad, like he was a bully. No, it had to be someone like me, similar in size. But why me? There were plenty of other kids who were similar to us. In fact, there were lots of them.

Then I figured he must have noticed something about me that convinced him he would have a chance. Yes, there was something about me, a chink in my armor. But what the heck was it? Did I really come off as the sort of kid Frankie could handle in a fight? It's a terrible thing to suddenly doubt yourself, but now, instead of feeling confident, I felt vulnerable. I wished I'd never agreed to the stupid fight to begin with. I could picture myself losing, and that was a problem. It was not just a minor problem. It was a huge problem. Losing to Frankie the fairy was the worst thing that could happen to me!

The Back Forty was to be our venue. It was a vacant lot several blocks from our school. The lot was surrounded by the fenced backyards of houses, creating a space that couldn't be seen from the street. No one knew who owned the lot or why it was vacant. It just happened to be one of those odd pieces of land that kids claimed and called their own. It was all dirt, weeds, and litter. There was an old car engine off to the side, probably dumped there years ago by the owner of the lot. There were always empty beer cans, left there by high school kids. Once we found a dirty magazine there with pages and pages of naked women. We never did figure out who left it there or why, but we enjoyed looking at all the pictures.

The Back Forty was far enough away from the school to be perfect for fights. Adults at the school knew about the lot, but they seldom went there. The place got its name well before our time. No one knew who first called it the Back Forty. Probably some adult. None of us even knew what back forty meant.

When school was dismissed, I began to feel ill, and there was a knot in my stomach the size of a medicine ball. My friends met me in the hall, and we walked toward the Back Forty like we were marching off to war. There was no way I'd be able to back out of this. The line had been drawn in the sand, and it had been crossed. As they say in a poker game, I was all in. I had pushed all my chips to the center of the table. When we got to the lot, I was surprised at the number of kids who had shown up to see us fight. I wasn't exactly popular at school and neither was Frankie. But everyone had heard about the fight and wanted to see it.

How many kids actually showed up? I don't know. I would guess there were about a hundred. They formed a big circle, leaving room in the middle for Frankie and me to conduct our business. Frankie was the first to step into this open space. He took off his glasses, handing them to a friend in the front row of the crowd. He then undid the top button of his shirt and rolled his head around to limber up his neck and shoulders. I figured he must have seen someone do this on TV. "Go get that stupid fag," one of my friends said, and he pushed me into open area with Frankie. I mimicked Frankie, rolling my head around and loosening up. Then a boy named Cam stepped out and stood between us. Cam was acting as the ring announcer, and he was making quite a show of it. The kids in the crowd loved every minute of his performance. It was like watching Jimmy Lennon on the TV, except this Jimmy didn't have a microphone. "In this corner, we have our own Robert Ashcroft," Cam shouted. "And in the other corner we have your Frankie McGuire. This will be a one-round bout until one of the fighters gives up and runs home. There are no rules. There's no referee and no time limit. Are you both ready? On your mark, get set, and fight!"

It was on.

At first, I had to laugh. Frankie stepped up so that he was about five feet from me, holding his arms and fists out like he was a nineteenth-century English pugilist. This made me feel a little better, for Frankie looked like an idiot. Some of the kids in the crowd were laughing at him. The way he stood, it looked like he had a bad case of hemorrhoids.

I put up my own fists like a modern American boxer, like I'd seen it done on TV. "Hit him!" someone in the audience yelled.

"Yeah, hit him!" yelled another.

"Knock his lights out!" someone said.

So I did it. What I mean to say is that I threw my first punch. I happened to miss Frankie's head completely, and he responded with a painful left jab to my nose. I could feel my head snap back when the punch landed, and my eyes began to water from being hit in the nose. Then I threw another punch. This one grazed Frankie's cheek, but again he responded with a stiff jab. This time the jab landed right on my chin. For a second my eyes went out of focus, and then I seemed to be okay. Then Frankie began to throw punches at me in succession. This was not what I'd expected. I held up my hands to defend myself. He was landing one blow after the other, and all I could do was hold up my arms. I was now so busy trying to block his punches that my own punches were nonexistent. Then, like a bolt of lightning, he smacked me hard in the ear, and my head began to ring like a fire engine siren. He smacked me again in my temple, and I felt my legs buckling. He hit me again on my nose, and my eyes watered. I tried throwing a few punches back, but they missed badly. It was like trying to hit a fly out of midair. He kept buzzing around me, throwing one punch after the other, and the fight was turning into everything I feared it would be. I didn't know what to do. "You're losing!" one of my friends yelled, and suddenly I was terrified. How could I possibly lose a fight to the biggest sissy in school? If I lost this fight, I'd never be able to live it down. I'd be a laughingstock. I had to do something, so I cocked my right arm way back. The with every ounce of strength in my body I threw my right fist toward Frankie's head, and *kaboom!* The punch landed square on his nose. I could feel his cartilage buckle from the blow, and I saw his head jerk backward. "Ouch!" he cried, and he stepped back. I dropped my guard and looked at him. Blood was now gushing out of his nostrils, and he had his hand up to his crooked nose. "I think you broke my nose!" he cried. "You broke my nose!"

"His nose is broken!" someone shouted.

"Look at all the blood!" another kid yelled.

Frankie looked at his hands, which were now bloody from having been around his nose. The blood from his nose was now running off his chin and dribbling all over the front of his shirt. He looked like he'd been hit with a baseball bat. There was no way he could continue.

"The winner!" Cam announced. He had come out of the crowd and was holding my right hand up in the air. "The winner by technical knockout!"

Some of the kids in the crowd clapped and cheered, as though they got their money's worth. Of course, none of them had paid anything. Others groaned, disappointed that the fight was now over. Frankie ran into the crowd and pushed his way through all the bodies. The last I saw of him, he was holding his broken nose and running home. I had won the fight. One very lucky punch and the nightmare was finally over.

When I got home that day, I had to explain things to my mom. I wouldn't have said anything at all, except for my face. My eye was swollen shut, my cheeks were red, and I had a fat lip. Mom wanted to know what happened. I didn't tell her much of anything about Frankie, only that he'd goaded me into a fight that I couldn't back down from. She wasn't at all happy that I'd been fighting, yet she didn't make a big deal of it. But she did say I'd have to explain things to my father.

That night at dinner, I explained the situation to Dad. I told him the truth, more or less. Let's just say I told him what he needed to know. I told him a kid was picking on me in the schoolyard, making cracks about my basketball game. So I stood up for myself. I told Dad I challenged the kid to a fight after school in the Back Forty. I told him I broke the kid's nose, and you should have seen the look on Dad's face. It was like I'd just brought home a math test with an A+, only ten times better. "I had my share of scuffles when I was your age," he said happily. "No broken noses, though." Dad then laughed and shook his head. "I'll bet you won't have any more trouble with that kid picking on you. Once you show a bully you're not afraid, you take away all his power."

Dad was right, of course. But who was the bully? I didn't have a good answer for that.

And They're Off!

This is the perfect house. When Veronica and I moved here to South Carolina, we made sure our new home would be big enough to accommodate not just Paul as a visitor, but also any friends he brought along. So even though it would be just the two of us living here 99 percent of the time, we bought a four-bedroom house. There's a master bedroom for Veronica and me, and we furnished the second bedroom for Paul. We turned the third bedroom into a guest room and outfitted the fourth as a home office. When Paul visits this Thanksgiving, he'll have his room to himself, and hopefully he'll ask Terrance sleep in the guest room. If Terrance and Paul sleep in the same room, it's going to be a little weird. Although this whole thing is weird, isn't it? I guess it's going to be weird no matter who's sleeping where.

I put a lot of effort into setting up Paul's room, and I hope he likes what I did with it. We want him to feel comfortable when he comes to visit, like this is his home away from home. I installed some shelving on Paul's walls, and on them I placed some items from his childhood, things I'd dug out of the boxes of stuff we'd saved over the years. We saved his favorite toys, books, board games, and stuffed animals. We also kept a pair of his shoes. These were very special shoes, the Teenage Mutant Ninja Turtle sneakers we bought at Target and that Paul wore on the day he first walked. I showed the shoes to Veronica and asked her, "Do you remember these?"

"Of course I do," she said.

"The park," I said.

"Yes, I remember the park."

Paul took his first steps at the public park down the street from our house in Anaheim. Veronica and I went to this park for picnics every now and again. It had a great grassy field surrounded by large, healthy oak trees, wooden picnic tables, and sooty old barbecues. We always ate on the lawn and not at the tables. And we never used the barbecues. We'd spread out a blanket, and Veronica would organize all the cold food she'd prepared. She'd always bring a bottle of wine and a corkscrew, for while neither of us were big drinkers, it was nice to have a glass of wine to go along with our meal. I remember the day Paul wore those sneakers.

Veronica made some ham and cheese sandwiches, and she brought along some raw vegetables and homemade ranch dip. The ranch dip was good, but eating the raw vegetables was like eating dirt clods. I know raw vegetables are supposed to be good for you, but they've never been my thing. Veronica brought a bottle of Chardonnay, and I opened it with our corkscrew and poured each of us a half glass. There were some green pimento-stuffed olives, a hunk of soft Camembert cheese, a box of Triscuits, and a Tupperware container filled with potato salad. Of course, there was also food for Paul. I can't remember if Veronica brought him baby food or yogurt, but it would've been one of the two.

It was one of those spring days when you were glad you lived in Southern California. The skies were clear, and the air temperature was just right. The grass was warm and freshly mowed, and the birds were singing in the trees like they were auditioning for roles in a movie musical. Once in a while a noisy plane would fly overhead, but even the sound of planes was somehow soothing and lazy. Paul was sitting on his corner of the blanket, busy playing with one of his Fisher-Price toys, stacking colorful plastic donuts up on a little plastic pole. It was interesting how much pleasure he got out of doing this. Veronica and I were eating and talking about Jeff and Amber, friends of ours who lived down the street.

Jeff was a real estate broker, and Amber was a stay-at-home mom. They were nice people, and we got along well with them. We met them at a Christmas party thrown by one of the other neighbors, and we were talking to them at the party about movies and television shows.

They said they didn't like the fact that sexual scenes and innuendos had become so popular, and we agreed with them. "I don't find it entertaining at all," Veronica said. "I just find it annoying."

"Same here," Amber said.

"I find it childish," I said.

"It's like watching a bunch of teenagers trying to impress each other," Amber said.

"Sophomoric," Jeff said.

"Yes, exactly," I said.

"That doesn't mean I believe in censorship," Jeff said.

"No, no," I said. "Me either."

It was after this very agreeable exchange that we became good friends. We got to know Jeff and Amber pretty well, and we also got to know their children. They had two kids, both boys. Their ten-year-old was named Adam, and their eleven-year-old was Taylor. Taylor was a great kid, just the sort of boy you'd expect Jeff and Amber to be raising. But Adam? Well, Adam was another story. Paul was stacking his plastic donuts when Amber brought up the subject of Adam.

"Have you heard the latest about Adam from Jeff?" Veronica asked me.

"I haven't talked to Jeff for a while," I said.

"Adam was suspended from school."

"They suspend fifth graders?"

"Apparently they do."

"What'd the poor kid do this time?"

"He broke a boy's arm."

"At school?"

"On the playground."

"You mean, he broke it on purpose?" I asked. I was laughing a little, but Veronica was serious.

"Yes, he did it on purpose."

"What happened?"

"Well, according to Amber, Adam came up to Jeff six months ago and asked him if he could take martial arts classes. At first Jeff and Amber were going to say no, but then they thought about it and changed their minds. They figured it might be good for Adam to

LITTLE BLUE WHISTLE

get involved in some kind of organized sport. They thought it would be a healthy way for him to expend some of his energy in a positive way, and they figured the discipline would be good for him. In fact, the more they thought about it, the better the idea sounded, and Jeff looked into it. He found a Muay Thai school nearby and took Adam in to sign up."

"So Adam went for it?"

"Amber said he loved it. Jeff drove him to classes three times a week for about six months, and Adam took the classes seriously. She said Adam was determined to do his best."

"And?"

"Well, there was the incident at school."

"The broken arm," I said.

"Yes, the broken arm. Adam got in a fight with a kid in the sixth grade, and Adam broke his arm."

"Do they know what the fight was about?"

"At first Adam said the boy called Adam a fag. That's what everyone thought happened for about a week, until the truth finally came out."

"The truth?"

"It turned out Adam had given the boy twenty dollars to buy some marijuana, and the boy decided to keep the money without delivering the product. I guess he figured because Adam was a year younger, and because he was a lot smaller, he wouldn't have the guts to do anything about it. But he figured wrong. I guess Adam beat the boy up pretty bad, and in doing so he broke the boy's arm."

"I didn't know Adam was smoking marijuana."

"There are probably a lot of things we don't know about Adam."

"Did the police get involved?"

"I don't think so."

"Well, I guess that's good."

"But the sixth grader's parents said they're going to sue Jeff and Amber for the doctor bills. They're also suing for pain and suffering."

"Are they going to pay Adam back his twenty dollars?" I asked, chuckling.

"It isn't really funny, you know."

27

"No, of course not."

"Amber says Jeff is thinking about taking Adam to see a psychiatrist."

"That should thrill Adam."

Veronica thought for a moment and then said, "You know what they say about kids, don't you?"

"What do they say?" I asked.

"What you've found out about them is probably only a tenth of what there actually is to know."

"How's Taylor doing?" I asked. I changed the subject because, after all, Jeff and Amber did have two sons, not just Adam. Taylor seemed to get so little attention.

"Taylor is doing great," Veronica said.

"No problems at school?"

"None that I know of."

"Still gets good grades?"

"According to Amber, all A's and B's."

"Does he still play baseball?"

"Yes, of course."

"Don't you think it's weird how Jeff and Amber have two boys approximately the same age, raised by the same parents under the same roof, and yet they're so completely different?"

"It *is* weird."

"You know what I think?"

"What do you think?"

"I think maybe no matter what you do, what you say, or how you behave, your kids are basically what they are right out of the starting gate."

"So parenting doesn't matter?"

"It matters. But maybe it matters a lot less than we would like to believe."

While Veronica was thinking about this, I turned to look at Paul. I expected to seem him playing with his plastic donuts, but he was gone! We were so busy talking about Jeff and Amber that we didn't notice our own son had stood and walked away. And now he was wobbling, barely balancing, walking about fifty feet away from us!

"Jesus!" I exclaimed.

"Weren't you watching him?" Veronica asked.

"I thought you were watching him."

"Well, go get him!"

I set my sandwich down and ran toward Paul. He was still walking. It was an amazing thing to see, his first real steps. He was grinning from ear to ear, moving his clumsy feet as fast as he could. I reached down and grabbed him under his arms, lifting him up to me, giving him a big congratulatory bear hug. I then set him down so he was standing again, and I aimed him toward Veronica. "Now, go to Mommy," I said. He giggled, and his legs carried him forward.

"And they're off!" I shouted.

Paul then stopped, turned to his left, and walked away from both of us. "Now where's he going?" Veronica asked.

"Who knows," I said.

Spit in the Ocean

ncluding me, there were five of us. We'd meet the first Tuesday of every month for poker, beer, and hot pastrami sandwiches at my house. Veronica would take Paul to her parents' house for the evening where they'd eat dinner and watch TV. It was nice having the house all to ourselves. We could cuss, tell off-color jokes, belch, and gamble, and there'd be no women or children around to cramp our style. We'd sit around the dining room table like a collection of card-playing ne'er-do-wells in a dusty old western saloon, betting, drawing, raising, and hitting the brass spittoon from fifteen feet.

Of course, I'm kidding about the brass spittoon. But bet, raise, and draw we did.

Are you ready for me to introduce you to this motley crew? I'll go around the table one by one and introduce you to the boys, starting with me. You already know my name, and you've already met my wife and son. It'd been almost thirty years since my third-grade fight with Frankie McGuire. So how much had changed? There was nothing special about me back then, and there was nothing special about me now. I'd developed no remarkable talents or skills. In the looks department I was still entirely forgettable. If I robbed a bank without a disguise, I'd never be arrested because no one would be able to recall my face. It was true that my body had filled out since I was an eight-year-old, but I was hardly an athlete. I didn't exercise or play sports. Heck, I even avoided stairs whenever possible. So was I smart instead of athletic? I'd say I was certainly smart enough to get by. No one ever called me dumb, because I wasn't. But I was definitely no

Albert Einstein, and generally speaking, math and science were still my archenemies.

But you know enough about me. Let's move to the rest of our group. To my immediate left was Jeff Carlisle. I've already told you about Jeff and his wife, Amber, and their two sons, Taylor and Adam. And I think I told you Jeff was a real estate broker, but what I haven't told you about Jeff is that he was a closet atheist. Have you ever met a closet atheist? They go to church every Sunday, and they say grace before dinner. When times get tough they're known to say a prayer or two in public to get things to go their way, and when a loved on dies they sigh and say the person is probably in a better place, namely heaven. But the truth is that they don't believe in God and heaven any more than they believe that jolly old Santa Claus carries a sack full of presents down our chimneys. And they don't believe in the tooth fairy, or the Easter bunny, or Linus's Great Pumpkin.

Here's the crazy thing. If you were to put Jeff on the spot and ask for his opinion of Paul telling the world he was gay, he would defer to his Bible. He would voice the truth taught to him as a child. Jeff would look you in the eye and read the verse from Leviticus that says, "If a man lies with a male as with a woman, both of them have committed an abomination; they shall surely be put to death; their blood is upon them." Jeff would read this verse to you with a straight face.

In his public life, Jeff was a devout Christian. When he voiced his Christian opinions, you'd never guess what he was actually thinking, and you'd never suspect the doubt about God's existence that stirred his soul. You'd never guess that the words that left his mouth had so little to do with the feelings he had in his heart. How did I know this about Jeff? I think it was because I was the same in a way. True, I wasn't a Bible-thumper, but I did blabber opinions I knew in my heart were wrong, opinions that had been taught to me by my parents, and taught to my parents by their parents, and so on. Intuition told me that Jeff and I were in the same boat.

But enough about Jeff for now. To Jeff's left sat our good friend Andrew Goodman, all two hundred and seventy pounds of him. I think you would've liked Andrew. He was a general building contractor, a real nuts-and-bolts type of guy. He was a riot, and he often kept us entertained with his stories. The man talked and talked, and he never met a cuss word he didn't like. Andrew wasn't particularly religious, but he was a moral man. He knew the difference between right and wrong, and if he saw a wrong, he stood up and did something about it without quoting anything from the Bible. When you've met as many religious people as I have, it's refreshing to know a few people who have faith in their own moral compass.

I'll tell you a story about Andrew that I think is revealing. He had three sons, all of them in high school. The oldest son wanted to start working to earn some extra spending money, so Andrew got him a job working for a carpenter he knew named Ernie. Everything went fine for a few weeks, until one day Ernie was robbed. Someone took all his tools from his truck in the middle of the night. With no tools, Ernie had to walk off his jobs and let Andrew's son go. Then a week later, Andrew caught wind of some news. His son had been selling tools to workers on other jobs, and Andrew quickly put two and two together, knowing there was only one place he son could've acquired so many tools to sell. He confronted his son, and the boy fessed up to taking the tools from Ernie's truck. Andrew took his son over to Ernie's house that same night. He knocked on Ernie's door, and when Ernie answered, Andrew said, "Here's the kid who took your tools, and here's the money he got for them. He's going to apologize to you. You can do whatever you want to him. I'm not going to stop you. I'm just here to make sure you don't kill him."

To Andrew's left was Tim Ashbury. I've known Tim since high school. We came to know each other because our last names are so similar. Whenever we were told to form lines in alphabetical order, I always found myself standing right behind him. Kids called him Tiny Tim, not because he bore any resemblance to that stringy-haired weirdo on TV who played the ukulele and sang "Tiptoe Through the Tulips," but just because he was small for his age. He was still small when we graduated from high school, but we stopped calling him Tiny Tim. He's an adult, and now we just call him Tim.

Tim became a certified public accountant. He married a girl he met during his junior year in college named Lucy Greenbriar. Lucy was at least foot taller than Tim and must have outweighed him by fifty or sixty pounds. She was a strong woman, and I don't mean strong as in able to bench press hundreds of pounds or tear phonebooks in half, but strong as in determined to get her way. Behind her back people would say she was probably a lesbian and that she married poor Tim just to make it appear like she wasn't. Tim and Lucy never did have any children, which added fuel to the fire of these lesbian rumors. I used to feel sorry for Tim, being married to a woman everyone figured to be a dyke. I ran into Tim recently, and he is still happily married to Lucy, which kind of flies in the face of all the things people said about them. Most of the people who were spreading those rumors are now either divorced or stuck in unhappy marriages.

Seated to Tim's left and completing the circle was Chet Branson. Chet was a private investigator. He came into our group by way of Andrew. The story went that Andrew was building a large project in Santa Ana, and he contracted with a roofer named Jason Trimble to install the roof. Andrew said he paid Jason a large cash deposit to buy materials. Several days went by, and no materials were delivered to the job. Then a week went by, and then two weeks. Andrew was very busy at the time, or he would've caught on to the scam sooner. It turned out that Jason simply cashed Andrew's check and made a run for it. Andrew tried to call him, but the number was disconnected. He then checked Jason's license number with the state, and the number actually belonged to a plumber in Yucaipa. He checked Jason's street address, and it belonged to a liquor store. He went to the police, but they said there wasn't much they could do. He then called around and got Chet's phone number from a friend who faced a similar problem. Andrew hired Chet, and Chet found Jason hiding out in Phoenix. He gave Andrew the information. Andrew contacted the police again, and between the police in Santa Ana and the police in Phoenix, they arrested Jason and brought him back to face charges. During this fiasco, Andrew came to like Chet, and vice versa, and the two men became friends. It turned out the Chet liked to play poker.

I don't know about you, but I'd always thought of private dicks as being kind of sleazy. I pictured them hiding behind bushes with cameras, breaking into people's bedrooms, and recording private conversations. Actually, Chet seemed like a very decent guy. He was married and had two children, a boy and a girl. The kids went to a private Catholic school, and the wife stayed home to take care of them when they weren't in school. They lived in a community where the cheapest homes sold for a million dollars, and Chet drove a Lexus that couldn't have been more than a year old. His wife drove a large SUV, large enough to take the kids and their friends to sporting events, after-school activities, and birthday parties. No, he wasn't a black-and-white Sam Spade with a crappy little office and a whiskey bottle in his desk drawer. Chet was as suburban as they came.

So there you have it, five relatively good friends playing poker and nursing beers. I think we got along pretty well. We were like the five musketeers, one for all, and all for one. We were never put to any test, but if we were, I think we would've stuck together.

On the night I want to tell you about, Veronica didn't go to her parents' house. Instead, she went to a friend's house without Paul. The friend had a horrible fight with her husband, and the woman needed someone to talk to. It wasn't appropriate to bring Paul along, so he stayed home with me. He was to be in his bedroom while the five of us played poker in the dining room. Paul had plenty to keep himself busy. If there was one thing this kid didn't lack for it was toys, children's books, and art supplies. He even had his own TV and video player.

I don't remember how the five of us got on the subject of homosexuals, but I remember Tim saying, "I've heard the same thing about Rock Hudson."

"I can picture him on top of Doris Day," Andrew said. "But it's hard for me to picture him with some dude's dick in his mouth."

Everyone laughed at this.

"It's your deal, Robert," Tim said. He pushed the cards toward me.

"What's the game?" Andrew asked.

"Spit in the ocean," I said.

"You know how to get four fags on a barstool?" Chet asked the group.

"How?" Tim said.

"You turn it upside down."

There was more laughter.

"I've got a good one," Andrew said. "Have you heard the one about the three Labrador retrievers at the vet's office?"

34

Everyone shook their heads.

"Three Labrador retrievers are talking in a vet's office," Andrew said. "There's a yellow Lab, a brown Lab, and a black one. The yellow Lab asks the black one, 'Why are you here?' The black Lab says, 'I'm a pisser. I piss on everything in sight. I piss on my master's floor. I piss on his bed. I piss on the rest of the furniture. I was brought here to be cured.' The yellow Lab asks what the doctor did, and the black Lab says, 'He's prescribing me Prozac. They say Prozac works for everything.' Then the yellow Lab turns to the brown one and asks, 'Why are you in here?' The brown Lab says, 'I'm a digger. I dig up everything. I dig up the flowers, and I dig holes in the lawn. I always dig under the fences.' When the yellow Lab asks what the doctor did, the brown Lab says, 'He's giving me Prozac too. They say it works for everything.' Then the brown Lab looks at the yellow one and says, 'So what are *you* doing in here?" The yellow lab says, 'My master is a fag.' The brown and black Labs looks at the yellow Lab, puzzled, and the yellow Lab explains to them, 'I'm a humper. I hump my master's cat. When my master's guests come over, I hump their legs. When my master was bending over to dry himself after a shower last night, I jumped up and started humping *him*.' The brown lab says, 'So I suppose they're giving you Prozac too?' The yellow Lab says, 'No, I'm here to have my nails clipped.'"

Everyone laughed again.

"You know," Tim said. "You not supposed to use the word fag anymore. It's insensitive. You're supposed to say gay."

I began dealing the cards, four each facedown and one card up.

"They're all fags to me," Andrew said.

"Do you gents even know where the word fag comes from?" Chet asked.

"Don't the Brits call their cigarettes fags?" Tim asked. "I heard that from someone."

"I'm not talking about cigarettes," Chet said.

"Then what?" Andrew asked.

"Long ago, fags or fag were bundles of sticks used to start fires."

"So what does that have to do with queers?" Andrew asked.

"When they burned people at the stake, sometimes they would

grab a queer and toss him on the fire. Just for the hell of it. Just because he was a queer. So queers came to be known as fags."

"No kidding?" Tim said. "Is that true?"

"Where'd you hear that?" Andrew asked.

"I read it in a book."

"Too funny," I said. I mean, it was cruel, but it was kind of funny.

Everyone picked up their cards and looked them over. I loved playing spit in the ocean. It was my favorite poker game. We continued to play and talk about fags and queers for another half hour. Andrew knew a couple more jokes. Then we started talking about football, and then about baseball. Finally, it was time to call it a night. Veronica was still at her friend's house, but my friends counted up their chips, and we converted the chips into cash.

They left the house, and I went to the table to clean things up. I carried the sandwich wrappers and empty beer bottles into the kitchen, and that's when he caught my eye. It was Paul! He hadn't been in his room at all. In fact, he'd been sitting in the hallway at the foot of the stairs, eavesdropping on our game. He was sound asleep now, curled up on the floor. I leaned over and picked him up, carrying him to his bed. I tucked him in and turned off his light. As I left his room, I laughed under my breath. It was just the sort of thing I would've done when I was his age.

I didn't think much of it then, but now I wonder. How much of our conversation did Paul hear? How much of it did he understand? What would he remember? He was only four years old, but I think kids understand a lot more than we give them credit for.

When Veronica got home, I was watching David Letterman in the family room, and she sat beside me on the couch. I noticed that she smelled like cigarettes. Her friend must have been smoking up a storm while crying on her shoulder all night.

Her friend's name was Rosie, and Rosie's husband was named Arnie. Veronica told me their whole story even though I would rather have been watching Letterman. The truth is that I didn't even like Letterman that much, but I liked hearing relationship stories even less. Veronica turned down the volume with the remote, and then she recounted the entire affair. God, what an awful bore! But I was too

36

tired to fight back, and I loved my wife too much to tell her I had no interest. So I sat and listened like a good husband, throwing in an occasional, "Oh, really?" or a lively, "Oh, wow!"

It turned out that Arnie had been seeing another woman who he met at work. This had been going on for several months. Long story short, things came to a head when Arnie decided to take this woman out to dinner on Rosie and Arnie's anniversary night. The nerve of this guy, right? I wanted to laugh, but I didn't. Veronica went on and on about their relationship and all the problems they seemed to be having. She talked to me about Rosie's needs, and about Arnie's childhood, and about Rosie's mother, and about their finances, and about the remodel they did to their kitchen last spring, and about the fact that they hadn't been on a vacation for the last two years. But I knew exactly what was happening. It didn't take a genius to figure it out. The truth was that Rosie had been letting herself go the way some women do after ten years of marriage, and by letting herself go, I mean to say she'd gained about sixty pounds. She really looked awful. I thought to myself, *If that pig hadn't gained all that weight, maybe she'd have a husband who was interested in her.* But what I said was, "Gee, honey, that's really a shame that they're having problems. I hope they can work things out."

The Three Bell Tour

had the strangest dream last night. Or maybe it wasn't strange at all. I guess what's really strange is how much of the dream I could recall. Usually when I wake up in the morning, I can recall only scattered bits and pieces of my dreams. Some details are there, yet they aren't. But the dream I had this morning was so amazingly vivid and real that my mind had no problem remembering all of it.

In this dream I was a tourist. Yes, I was definitely a tourist, dressed in a striped tank top, a baggy pair of hibiscus-patterned swim trunks, and rubber flip-flops. I was flip-flopping my way down old Whitehead Street, down in Key West, viewing the historic homes. I was alone, and I didn't know where Veronica was. Maybe she was back at the hotel reading a book and taking a break from the sun, or maybe she was still at the beach. It really didn't matter where she was, because this dream had nothing to do with her. It wasn't that kind of dream.

It was late afternoon and storm clouds were beginning to darken the sky. As the clouds gradually swallowed up the sun, the winds picked up, blowing through the trees and creating an eerie whistling sound. It was as though the trees were whistling a tune for me, a familiar tune, yet I didn't know what it was. I think it had something to do with a boy's love for a girl, but I could be wrong. Then the sky grew even darker, and the winds blew much harder. The windy music began to blast from the trees like from the horn section of a big band, and then *boom!* An enormous thunderclap exploded overhead and sent a chill up my spine. There was more thunder, some white flashes of lightning, and a lot more of the strange music. Then out of nowhere it began to rain. I mean, it wasn't just raining. It was absolutely pouring toads and lily pads. The wind was whipping the rain into a frenzy, and I was getting drenched. I had no parka or umbrella on hand, but I don't think either would've helped. My hair was soaked. My clothes were soaked. Rivulets of water were running down my face and arms and dripping off my chin and elbows.

Genius that I was, I sought shelter. I looked around, but all I could see was rain. So I kept walking. I guess I figured I'd bump into something sooner or later. Then suddenly, through the heavy downpour, I saw the outline of a rectangular structure. It was a house to my right, a boxy little two-story home with an upstairs veranda and lot of arched windows. I made my way closer, so I could see. There was a cement walkway through the landscaping that led up to an arched front door, and I could see that the door was open. I fought the rain and howling winds and made my way up the path to the doorway. When I reached the porch, I stepped inside the house, and everything was suddenly calm. An elderly woman closed the door behind me, hiding away the storm. She smiled sweetly and handed me a towel. "Wipe yourself off with this," she said, and I used the towel to dry my face and hair. Then I looked more carefully at the woman, and she was no longer elderly. She appeared to be in her forties or fifties, and I was sure I recognized her. She had short, sandy hair and big chocolate-brown eyes. She was wearing makeup that made her cheeks appear rosy and warm. In her own, weird, middle-age, pedestrian way, she was stunning.

"Do I know you?" I asked. I would've sworn I'd seen her someplace before.

"You should," she replied.

"From where?"

"From the grocery store."

"From what grocery store?"

"The only grocery store you go to. I'm the cashier in the express lane."

"The express lane?"

"Fifteen items or less. Last time you were there you bought cat food, milk, and a carton of eggs."

"Yes," I said. "And some coffee filters."

"If you say so. I ring up an awful lot of customers. I can't be expected to remember everything that everyone buys."

"What are you doing here?" I asked.

"I'm working."

"I mean, what do you do?"

"I'm a greeter. I'm here to greet the visitors, like a hostess at a fancy restaurant. Are you here to take a tour?"

"Actually," I said, "I was just hoping to get out of the rain."

"It is quite a storm," she said, and she looked out the window. "But now that you're here, now that you're inside, why not?"

"Why not what?"

"Why not take a tour? There's a lot to see and a lot to learn. Everyone says this is the most rewarding bit of history in all the Keys."

"Is the tour free?"

"Of course not. It requires a lot money to keep this place up. Trimming the landscaping. Keeping the woodwork painted. Feeding all the damn cats."

"How much is the tour?"

"Well, that depends."

"Depends on what?" I asked.

"It depends on what you came here to do. Everyone comes here for something different. You'd be surprised at what some people want. Some people don't even know where they are. I had a man in here last week who thought this was Hunter S. Thompson's beach house."

"That's weird."

"He'd been drinking," the woman said. "I could smell it on his breath."

"I seldom drink," I said.

"Just a little wine now and again? Or maybe a beer or two?"

"Something like that."

"So, tell me, what exactly do you want? What do you expect to get out of your visit? Are you a casual fan? An ardent fan? A student of American literature? No, you look too old to be a student. Maybe you just came by to visit the gift shop?"

"There's a gift shop here?"

"Yes, there's a gift shop," the woman said. "We'd have a riot on our hands if we didn't have a gift shop."

"So what are my choices?"

"Choices for what?"

"The tours you offer. You asked me what I wanted to do. So what are my choices?"

"Yes, yes, the tours," the woman said. This made her smile. I could tell she really wanted to tell me about the tours. She cleared her throat and said, "There are three basic tours to pick from. The first tour is our One Bell Tour. It's our cheapest and most popular choice. For five dollars we show you where the restrooms are, give you a complimentary bottled water, and then guide you to the gift shop. This tour is highly recommended for those who just came here to shop."

"And the next tour?" I asked.

"The next is the Two Bell Tour. For ten dollars, you get everything included in the One Bell Tour plus five full minutes in our outdoor smoking area, a bag of treats to feed the cats, and three complimentary bottled waters instead of one. This tour is popular with smokers and cat lovers."

"Or people who are thirsty."

"Yes, that too."

"And the third tour?"

"The third is our Three Bell Tour. This tour is fifty dollars. You get everything from the One Bell Tour and the Two Bell Tour, plus you have free rein of the house, both upstairs and downstairs, for precisely an hour and fifteen minutes."

This was a no-brainer for me. "I'll take the fifty-dollar tour," I said.

"The Three Bell Tour?"

"Yes," I said. I reached into my pocket and removed my wallet. I pulled the money out of my wallet and handed it to the woman.

"You'll need this," she said. She pinned a little tag on my shirt to show that I'd paid the admission."

"Where's the typewriter?" I asked.

"The typewriter?"

"Yes, I want to see the typewriter. I want to see it for myself."

"Go up the elevator and to the left."

41

"That's it?" I asked.

"You can't miss it."

Some newly arrived tourists opened the front door and stepped into the house. The woman smiled at me and then went to greet them. I walked to the elevator and pressed the up button, watching the doors open for me. I stepped into the elevator and was immediately lifted to the second floor. When the elevator doors opened, I stepped out and to my left.

Now, I'm not sure exactly what happened, but I wound up in a long hallway that led to a junk room, that led to a bedroom, that led to a walk-in closet, that finally led to the man's private office. There was no typewriter in the office, but there was a small stack of papers on the desk. I was curious, so I picked up the papers. On the top sheet was typed the title *Dirty Face*. That's all it said. I set this page facedown on the desk and started reading the story that began on the next page.

It was the tale of a sad young man named Ricardo Jose Alejandro Lopez who lived in a small fishing village on the northern coast of Venezuela. The residents of this village were a proud people. They were not proud of their work ethic, or honesty, or skills at catching fish, but, oddly enough, they were proud of their clear complexions. They were a beautiful people with the most enviable, coffee-colored skin in all of Venezuela. Then, early one spring morning, the boy named Ricardo Jose Alejandro Lopez was born.

The boy had an ugly dark-brown birthmark on his face that marred his countenance from the upper left corner of his mouth to just below his left eye. The midwife, Maria, tried to rub it off with a towel right after he was born, and his father tried to wipe it away using alcohol and a strong soap. But they had no luck, and the mother cried and cried. The father, who was furious with the baby for causing his wife so much distress, gave him the nickname *Cara Sucia*, or Dirty Face. The nickname was not meant to be complimentary.

Word quickly got around in the village about the blemished child. One man who had seen the baby said it looked like a large bird had relieved itself on his face. "Truly disgusting," he said. "They ought to put a sack over his head." Some of the villagers said the birthmark was a bad omen, and they felt enormous pity for the mother. Some said it

42

had to be the mark of the devil and that the boy was evil. The father continued to be angry, and the mother continued to cry. "What did I do wrong?" the mother asked her best friend. They both agreed she'd been a good woman with a fine complexion, and they could not come up with an answer.

I set the papers down for a moment. What in the world was I reading? There was a large chair at the desk, and I pulled it closer and sat down. I looked at the manuscript in my hands again, and I decided I had to read more. Was this bizarre story actually written by you-know-who? It was a little hard to believe, but I seemed to have stumbled upon some unknown and unpublished work kept secret by the famous author. Was I the first person to read this? Were there others? I leaned back in the chair, and putting my feet up on the desk, I continued to read.

The story went on by recounting the boy's difficult childhood years. The nickname *Cara Sucia* stuck with him as indelibly as his ugly birthmark. Most often he was called Cara for short. No one ever called him by any part of his long and beautiful given name. The people in the village could've called him Ricardo, or Jose, or even Alejandro. Those were all nice names, weren't they? But no, he was the boy with the dirty face, *Cara Sucia*.

School was rough for Cara. We all know that children can be cruel, and the kids at Cara's small village school were no exception. None of the kids wanted him on their playground teams. No one would eat with him during lunch, or talk to him while waiting in lines, or voluntarily sit next to him in class. They told jokes about Cara behind his back. "Cara is so ugly that he has to sneak up on his mirror!" Or, "When Cara plays in the sand, his cat tries to bury him!" Or, "When Cara was born, the doctor slapped his mother!" The joke telling was relentless, and it went on from the time he was a small boy until the time he matured. Did Cara do well in school? He was an average student, of average intelligence, and he earned average marks. And that's all he ever wanted to be. He wanted to be an average boy at an average school getting average grades and doing the sorts of thing average boys did at that age. But no one could bring themselves to ignore the birthmark.

Then it happened on a day in July. It was the morning of July twenty-third. Cara was walking along the beach, thinking about what he was going to do with his life now that he was out of school. No one wanted him. There were plenty of respectable jobs in the village, but no one had any desire to hire the boy. He was a pariah, an outcast, and worst of all, he was unemployed. His father had thrown him out of the house just a few days earlier, telling him to fend for himself. "It's time you grew up and supported yourself," his father said. But what was he going to do? Would he live in a leaky hut in the jungle with the snakes, monkeys, and bugs, eating whatever sustenance he could get his hands on, drinking murky swamp water, wearing the same clothes day after day?

While walking along the beach, Cara came upon a crowd of villagers. Now this is where the story I was reading really got kind of weird. It made little sense. But then, dreams are often weird, aren't they? I mean, they're weird after you've been awake and had time to think about them, even though they made perfect sense while you were asleep. Anyway, this crowd of villagers had formed a large circle on the beach. They were circled around an angry alligator and a small village girl named Isabella. The alligator was face-to-face with Isabella, and the girl was on her knees, sobbing. The alligator snapped his powerful jaws several times and moved closer to her, threatening to chew her up and eat her. No one did anything to help. It was believed by the villagers that when an alligator has a small child cornered, the only way to save the child was to substitute one's own life for the life of the child. And no one in the crowd wanted to give up their life.

Cara pushed his way to the front, and he got down on his knees. He looked the alligator right in its cold and merciless eyes. "Take me," he said to the alligator, and the gator stared at him. Like the rest of the villagers, the alligator was well aware of the rules. It took one last threatening snap at Isabella, and then it wriggled into place so that it was now face-to-face with Cara. "Take me, you bastard," Cara said. The alligator smiled, baring its rows of yellow prehistoric teeth. Just as the gator smiled at Cara, Isabella's mother reached in and grabbed the girl, pulling her out of harm's way. Then in a violent frenzy, the alligator attacked Cara right there on the beach. It was unholy and vicious. It was bloody and messy, and the horrified villagers watched the fatal attack, doing nothing. The alligator ripped Cara into pieces and devoured him like it hadn't had a meal for weeks, gulping down his flesh, bone, cartilage, curly hair, and birthmark until there was nothing left but a puddle of blood on the sand.

Like I said, this happened on July twenty-third. The villagers talked about this date on the calendar for years. And finally, after several years had passed, one of these clear-skinned villagers suggested they label July twenty-third a village holiday. They would call it *Dia De La Cara Sucia*, and from that day forward, everyone would take the special day off and remember the brave young man with the birthmark. They would remember Isabella and the evil alligator and the puddle of blood on the sand that was once Cara. And in honor of Cara, everyone in the village would smear a splotch of mud across their left cheek, mimicking the boy's birthmark. They would go about their business for the rest of the day with the mud on their faces.

"Are you done?" a voice asked.

I turned around to look. It was the woman who had sold me the tour, the woman who worked at the grocery store. "Done with what?" I asked.

"Done reading?"

"I suppose I am," I said.

"That's good. Your hour and fifteen minutes are up. I'm going to have to ask you to leave."

And that was the end of my dream. I set the papers down on the desk and stood up. I started to walk out of the room, and the next thing I knew I was opening my eyes and waking up in bed.

Little Blue Whistle

no longer have seven days to prepare. Now, in six short days, Paul will arrive at the Augusta Regional Airport with his boyfriend, and we will drive them to our house in South Carolina. It's like we got the hell out of California, and now California is coming to us.

It's midmorning, and Veronica is riding her horses. I have the house to myself, and I'm sitting at the kitchen table, enjoying my fifth cup of coffee and thinking about Paul. His little blue whistle is on the table next to my cup of coffee. I pick it up and carry it into the family room. I place it on a shelf beside our fireplace, next to a framed picture of Paul and Veronica at Disneyland. The picture was taken in 1994, the same year that we got the whistle.

I was thinking earlier this morning about the dream I had about Cara and the alligator, and then I was thinking about the years Veronica, Paul, and I lived in California. I could remember the day Paul moved out of our California house. He was eighteen when he left for his first year in college. He'd been accepted to USC, just like I was, and just like my father was. It seemed like such a long time ago that Paul left, and I remembered what a total wreck I was. I remembered all the gut-wrenching worry, the unbearable sorrow, and the feeling that my heart was being ripped out of my chest. It was so utterly hard for me to fathom that something that had brought so much joy could come to such an abrupt and painful end. It was like someone slammed a door in my face, but what the heck did I expect? I mean, did I think that Paul would live with us forever? No, I had known that he would eventually have to pack his bags, gas up his car, and move on with his life. I knew it was the natural order of things. It was birth, infancy, childhood, adolescence, and then adulthood. Like a butterfly breaking out of its chrysalis, it was Paul's turn to open his wings and fly away.

Just prior to moving out, Paul cleaned his room and boxed up all the junk from his childhood that he wanted to save, but that he couldn't take with him to college. He had no place to put the boxes, so he left them with us. That was twelve years ago. We've held on to these boxes all this time, and they're now in the closet of his room here at the new house. He still says he doesn't have a place to put them, so he wants us to keep them for a few more years, which is fine with me.

I'll admit that this morning my curiosity got the best of me. I never have opened any of Paul's boxes. I've never known what they contained, and I always thought it was best to respect Paul's privacy by leaving the boxes alone. An hour ago, however, I picked up my cup of coffee and carried it into Paul's room. I guess this is what happens when you don't have to go to work, when you have a little free time on your hands. Retirement can make you nosey. I set my coffee on Paul's dresser and opened the closet door. I then pulled out the top box, carrying it over to his bed. It wasn't very heavy, but it did feel full. I set the box down and gave the matter some more thought. Should I just put it back where I got it? Then I said, "Oh, what the hell," and I tore off the packing tape and opened the top of the box. When I looked inside, I was relieved to see that there was nothing especially gay. There were no Barbie dolls, or lipstick tubes, or photographs of shirtless boys, or French cookbooks, or little toy ponies or unicorns.

So what was in the box? It was filled with the kinds of things you'd expect any normal boy to save. There was an old baseball mitt, a couple of grass-stained baseballs, and the first marble-based trophy Paul won for being on a winning baseball team. He was so proud of that trophy that you'd have thought he won the World Series. There was also an old deck of Bicycle playing cards, a plastic squirt gun, and a metal sheriff's badge that had his first name etched on the star. To my surprise, Paul had saved my dad's old fishing knife. I guess Dad gave him the old knife after he bought his new one. There was a Beanie Baby of a little dinosaur that looked like it'd been to Mars and back, and there was a Hohner Marine Band harmonica. Ha, I remembered the harmonica. Paul learned to play only one song on it, and that was "Oh! Susanna". I don't think he ever played it without hitting at least ten wrong notes, and he played it over and over. I have no idea why he didn't learn any other songs. But, come to think of it, maybe it was good that he stopped at "Oh! Susanna." One lousy song was enough for all of us.

It was down on the bottom of the box that I found the blue whistle. I couldn't believe he'd actually saved it, and it made me smile. After all these years, there it was, just as blue and shiny as it was the day we bought it. We got the whistle from the toy section at the grocery store when Paul was six. It was on his very first day of school, the morning he was to start first grade. Why the whistle? I'll get to that.

But first, the fishing knife. Finding the knife did surprise me. It's true my father and I would take Paul fishing. My father loved to fish the ocean, and I loved it too, probably because my father loved it so much. When I was a kid, Dad would take me out and we'd sit for hours on a stinky old chartered boat, watching our lines sit in the seawater, waiting for the fish to bite. We'd literally spend hours sitting on our rear ends, doing absolutely nothing. I don't even remember talking much. You'd think we would've at least talked. I know it doesn't sound like much fun when I describe it this way, but I enjoyed those hours with my dad immensely.

When Paul was finally old enough, we'd take him with us and make it a men-of-the-family affair. It would be the three of us on a stinky charter boat, three generations of Ashcrofts, the grandfather, father, and son. Dad would always be in charge. He'd attach the lures to our lines and cast them toward the water. He'd crack open a couple of beers, one for him and one for me. He'd give Paul a Coke, and we'd all share from a big bag of pretzels. Then the boat would slowly move forward, and we'd sit and wait for the fish to bite. Sometimes we'd talk, but most often we would sit quietly and mind our own business. Then a line would pull taut. "You've got one!" Dad would shout, and the fishing pole would arch like it was going to break in two. The fish would tug and fight for its life. "Reel it in!" Dad would shout. "Be careful not to lose it! Not too slow, and not too fast! Here, let me do it." Dad would take the pole and show us how it was done. He'd lift the poor fish out of the water, so it was dangling in the air, and then he'd swing it over the boat to cut the line. "We got the little bastard!" he would exclaim.

I remember watching Paul during all of this. I didn't get the impression he ever enjoyed himself. He'd have the strangest look on his face when we caught a fish, like he was experiencing something awful. I could see it in his eyes. It was a look of horror and disgust. You know, I truly think most boys his age would've been jumping up and down with joy seeing a dumb fish struggling for its life. "I finally got you!" Dad would say. He'd hold the fish tight with one hand, and he'd grab his fisherman's knife with the other. "This is how you kill a fish," he'd say to Paul, and he'd poke the end of the knife into the fish's head and twist it. "You scramble up their little brains. Just watch how I do this. A couple of twists, and he'll be as good as dead." The fish would wriggle and twitch as Dad turned the knife, and finally it would lay still. "So how about that? Do you want to kill the next one? I'll give you my knife and let you have the honors."

"No, thanks, Grandpa," Paul would say. "I'd rather you did it."

"Suit yourself. But one of these days you're going to need to do this for yourself, or you won't be much of a fisherman."

I put myself in Paul's shoes. I remembered when I was his age. I would've been overjoyed at the chance to kill an animal by poking a knife into its living brains. For most of us little boys, fish, birds, squirrels, and rabbits were all fair game. Shoot them, stab them, and show them who's the boss. Then cook them and eat them if they're edible. Goddamn little Daniel Boones we were, fishing, hunting, and living off the land. I think boys thrived on this, but not my son, Paul. I think for Paul, pulling a fish out of its home in the water, killing it, and eating it was just not something he would ever see as great fun. Paul loved his grandpa, and I know he loved me too, so he tolerated us. He didn't raise a fuss about going with us, but deep down I think he hated our fishing trips. I think he hated everything about them, including the Coke and pretzels.

Was this a sign that my son would be gay? I don't know. I mean, what the hell do I know about homosexuality? But it could've been a sign, right? Maybe the clues were there early on, and I was just too ignorant to see what they were.

And maybe there were other signs. Ronnie Rosenblatt comes to mind. Ronnie was a boy who lived on our street, and he was the same age as Paul. Was Paul's relationship with Ronnie another sign that I missed? The boy was picked on relentlessly by the other kids in the neighborhood. He was something like my own Frankie McGuire, except Ronnie had no spirit and no desire to fight back. You could spit on him, pull his hair, trip him, or throw rocks at him, and he'd never stand up for himself and fight back. You never had to worry about Ronnie. He might say, "Please stop it," or, "Leave me alone." But that was all he'd ever do to defend himself.

No, I didn't like Ronnie Rosenblatt, but I knew Paul had feelings for the kid. I knew this because he told me he did. And when I explained that it wasn't his job to look after boys like Ronnie, Paul told me, "I don't have to look after him, but I can be his friend." So, against my wishes, he did become Ronnie's friend. They weren't close friends, but they did things together. And Paul took a lot of teasing from the other kids because of it. This didn't seem right to me. Then Ronnie and his parents packed up their things and moved, and that was the last anyone saw of Ronnie. Paul probably wouldn't like to hear me say this, but I was relieved when the boy moved away. I didn't like Ronnie, and I didn't like Paul hanging around with him. Why would I want my boy hanging out with a weirdo like Ronnie Rosenblatt? Birds of a feather, isn't that what they say? Many kids don't realize how important it is to hang out with the right people. It's a fact that you're judged by the company you keep, and keeping company with losers is no way to go through life. Was this a gay thing, befriending a boy like Ronnie? You tell me. I really don't know.

I think part of the problem may have been that before Paul entered the first grade, he spent an awful lot of time with his grandparents. I'm not talking about my parents, but Veronica's. They were good people, but I think they were better suited for raising girls. They did a fine job with Veronica and her sister, but boys were different. Did we make a big mistake? Before he was old enough to go to school, Paul spent his mornings with Veronica's parents while Veronica worked part time at keeping books for a local construction company. She trusted her parents, and why shouldn't she? I remember we debated whether to take Paul to a preschool during these years, but we decided against it. We both felt he'd be better off with family. And Veronica's parents were good people and they definitely loved Paul. I'm not questioning any of that. I just wonder now if they should have been spending so much time with him.

You know, you can easily overthink all these different factors, mulling over the past and getting muddled up in hindsight. Yes, there were all the fishing trips with my father, and there was that oddball, Ronnie Rosenblatt, and then there were Veronica's parents. But do any of these things really account for much, or am I just grasping at straws? I've noticed something about myself ever since Paul decided to come out of the closet and tell the world he was gay. I have this strange desire to take the blame for not having done something sooner, for not having stood up for my son and fought for his manhood when there was still a fighting chance. But was there ever a fighting chance? I just don't know.

Confusing, isn't it?

I was going on earlier about my son's blue whistle. I told you when we bought it, and where we bought it, but I didn't tell you why.

On the morning Paul was to start first grade, Veronica had to be at work early, so it was my job to take Paul to the school. You should've seen the kid. Veronica had gone all out. She had taken Paul to the mall the week before and bought him all new clothes. He was wearing a new shirt, new belt, new pants, new socks, and a brand-new pair of shoes. He had a new backpack, every pocket filled with school supplies. Honestly, he looked like he should be standing in a kid's back-to-school clothing store window display.

Paul seemed excited about the whole school thing. That morning, he ate a heck of a breakfast, about fifty pancakes and a hundred bacon strips. I'm obviously exaggerating, but his appetite was good, and his mood was elevated. He couldn't seem to stop smiling. I gulped down my coffee, and I asked him, "Are you ready to go?"

"I'm ready," he said.

"Are you nervous?"

"A little," he said.

"Just remember that everyone there is in the same boat. It a first day for everyone."

We hopped in the car and drove to the school. When we got there, I said goodbye to Paul. He sat there looking at me, not opening the door or saying goodbye back.

"What's wrong?" I asked.

"Can you come in with me?" he asked.

"Sure, I can do that. I don't see anything wrong with that."

"I don't want to go by myself."

"Don't worry about it," I said.

I found a place to park the car, and we walked to his classroom. It was just about time for class to start, and the room was filled with kids. There were only a couple of open seats left, and Paul hesitated at the doorway.

"Go on in," I said.

"Do I have to?" Paul asked.

"You do," I said. "This is what you've been looking forward to."

"Can you stay here?"

"No, I can't stay here," I said, laughing.

"Don't go," Paul said, and he grabbed my hand."

"Paul," I said. "It's going to be fine. Just take a seat with the other kids. Everything will be fine."

"I want to go home."

"You can't go home. You're in first grade now. You're a student."

"I don't want to be a student."

"Come on, Paul," I said. "Just take a seat with the others. Mom will be here to pick you up as soon as school is over."

"Come on in," the teacher said. She noticed Paul hesitating in the doorway, and she wanted him to feel welcome.

"See, your teacher wants you."

"No," Paul said.

I looked at the teacher and shrugged my shoulders. I felt kind of embarrassed. The teacher said, "Come on in, young man. No one is going to bite."

I tried to push Paul forward, but the harder I pushed, the more he resisted. "I won't go in!" he suddenly shouted, and now the other kids were all staring at us. I'm sure this wasn't helping. The last thing Paul needed was for all the kids to be looking at him.

"Class starts in one minute," the teacher said. She was smiling and pointing to the clock on the wall. Suddenly Paul burst into tears.

"Come on, Paul," I said.

"No!" Paul shrieked. Now he was bawling, and tears were rolling down his cheeks.

"We'll be back in a minute," I said to the teacher, and I took Paul outside, away from the door, so we could have some privacy.

"I can't go in there," Paul said. He had stopped crying but was now sniffing and rubbing his eyes. "I can't go in there, and I'm not going to go in there."

"I have an idea," I said.

"What kind of idea?" Paul said.

"I should've thought of this earlier. We should've done this to begin with."

"Done what?"

"You need a good luck charm," I said.

"A what?"

"A good luck charm," I said. "I felt exactly like you when I first went to school. But my dad gave me a good luck charm, and it protected me. It gave me courage. And it took away all my fear."

Of course, this was a lie. My dad never gave me any such thing, but I had to do something to get Paul into the classroom.

"Where do we get a good luck charm?" Paul asked.

"I know the perfect place," I said.

"Where?"

"We'll go to the grocery store."

"The grocery store?"

"Don't they have a toy section? I'm sure they do. We've bought stuff there before. It's the perfect place. They have a ton of good luck charms, all ripe for the picking."

"They just have toys."

"But any toy will do," I said. "Don't you see? You just pick something out, and then you make it your charm. It's like magic. And toys make the best good luck charms, because toys are for kids, and kids are the ones who need good luck charms."

Paul didn't ask any more questions or argue with my logic. I think he so desperately wanted to go to school that he would've believed in anything. We got in the car and went to the grocery store, where we found the toy section. Paul looked at all the toys, trying to decide which to pick. "Any of these will work?" he asked.

"Just pick one," I said.

"I want this," Paul said, and he grabbed a package containing a little blue whistle.

"Good choice," I said.

"Do you really think it will work?"

"I know it will," I said.

We bought the toy whistle and went back to the school. Paul put the whistle in his pocket. When we went back to the class, I opened the door. The teacher was talking to the class, but she stopped when she saw us. I told Paul to go on in, and he kept his hand on his pocket as he walked in and took a seat. He was keeping his hand on his pocket to make sure he had the whistle with him. "Welcome to class, young man," the teacher said.

"Thank you," Paul replied.

Paul then looked toward me. I waved goodbye to him, and he smiled. I closed the door and walked back to my car.

Paul brought that whistle with him to school every day for the next two weeks, keeping it safe in his pocket. Then after two weeks I noticed he left it on his dresser in his bedroom. He no longer needed it. It was kind of sad, seeing the whistle sitting there all by itself. It no longer had a job to do.

And now, twenty-four years later, Paul's whistle sits on a shelf in our family room as a reminder that I had my moments. I mean, none of us are perfect, but sometimes we do perfect things. A good luck charm? How did a mediocre father like me ever come up with such a great idea?

The Double Play

P aul loved playing baseball. When he was nine years old, it was all he cared about. If he had things his way, he would've been playing baseball morning, noon, and night. He would've said to hell with school, to hell with all his after-school chores, and to hell with eating meals, bathing, or getting any sleep. He was only nine, and already life seemed too short. There just weren't enough hours in the day.

Paul had been playing organized ball since he was six, and the team he was now on called themselves the Orioles. All the teams in his kid's league were named after big league teams; the season before he was on the Dodgers. The Orioles was a pretty good collection of ballplayers, and considering their age and general immaturity, they seemed to know what they were doing. They were winning a lot of games, many more than they were losing, and the parents were patting themselves on the back for having such talented children. I could go through the players one by one and describe them to you, but I'm not going to do that. You want to know who was even more interesting than the kids? It was the parents. Maybe it just seemed this way to me because I spent so much time in the bleachers with them. I wouldn't go so far as to say we were like family, but we were all part of the team. We were the other side of the equation. We were the adults. We were the ones who wrote the checks, provided the rides, brought all the postgame snacks and drinks, and cheered and booed from the stands. There were fifteen bright-eyed kids, and sure each of them was indispensable, but us parents were the real good, bad, and ugly of the team.

One of the dads was a fellow by the name of Bradford Collins. He was the ugly. I say that with conviction and from experience. Funny thing about this man is that he wanted everyone to call him Brad, but he made sure we all knew his actual name was Brad*ford*. Don't ask me why this distinction was important to him, because I never did know. I *did* know what Brad did for a living because I'd seen his face begging for business on all his late-night TV ads. He owned a garage door company in Costa Mesa that served all of Southern California "with a smile." He apparently did pretty well for himself installing these garage doors, because he drove a brand-new black Mercedes and wore a gaudy Rolex watch that you couldn't help but notice. When I say a gaudy Rolex, I mean that it was solid gold and loaded with a ridiculous number of little cut diamonds and rubies, like it had been dipped in jewel sauce. To me, it was the sort of watch a gas station cashier who just won the lottery would buy to impress his friends. But that was just me. I'm sure there were people on the team who were in awe of Brad's watch.

I want to describe Brad to you in a fair and unbiased way, but how do I do that? How do I remain impartial? I mean, how do you describe a belligerent orangutan without describing a belligerent orangutan? It's tricky, because I generally like giving people the benefit of the doubt, and I don't like being mean or insulting. But let's be honest. Brad, for all intents and purposes, was a complete ass and a loudmouth. I always sat as far away from him as possible, so I wouldn't have to hear the vitriol that gushed from his lips during our games. I wasn't the only parent to keep his distance; in fact, I noticed that the only person who deliberately sat near him game after game was his ever-faithful wife. She was an interesting woman. She seemed like a decent person when you talked to her casually, but she couldn't have been all that decent, right? After all, she's the one who married Brad the loudmouth. No one I knew of had twisted her arm. Maybe she was actually as big of an ass as her husband, but just did a better job hiding it in public.

The first time I heard Brad yelling from the bleachers was during the second game of our season. I didn't hear him during the first game because he wasn't there. He had some kind of garage door emergency to attend to. When I first heard Brad yelling, I thought his raucous brand of heckling was amusing. And it was at first. I'd never heard a parent letting the other team have it quite like Brad. The guy was relentless. We were playing the Astros, and the word was that they had the best pitcher in the league. I was told the rest of their team wasn't so great, but their pitcher was phenomenal. This pitcher was a boy named Alan McKenzie, a daddy longlegs of a boy with a crazy windup and a fastball that struck fear into the hearts of all the boys who had to face him. It was clear to Brad that we would never beat the Astros unless we got some hits, and we weren't going to get any hits so long as this phenom was on his game. So what did Brad do? He did what Brad did so well. I don't have an accurate list of every insult and disparaging word that Brad shouted that afternoon, and if I tried to reconstruct his words, it's doubtful I would be able to convey just how disturbing his heckling was. It was hurtful, demeaning, and embarrassing. At times, it was crude. It certainly wasn't appropriate for a youth league baseball game being played by nine-year-old boys.

I think the heckling took all of us by surprise. None of the other adults, including myself, knew quite what to do. It was true that parents often yelled from the stands, didn't they? So what was wrong with Brad doing a little old-fashioned heckling? But was he going too far? No one seemed to know for sure. Between pitches Alan would glance at our bleachers. It was obvious that he heard Brad, and it was obvious that he was trying to ignore him. But Brad and his big mouth were impossible for anyone to ignore. In retrospect I'm surprised that no one on our team told Brad to tone it down, but no one did. And sure enough, after several innings of Brad's barking, Alan began to lose his cool. Brad obviously got into the boy's head. One of the mothers from the other team shouted at Brad, telling him to stop badgering their player. But Brad just smiled when she yelled at him, and he responded by heckling the boy even more. I think he liked the attention he was getting. I think he saw himself as a team player, as an integral part of our effort to win. And this poor kid on the mound was now thoroughly rattled and throwing pitches all over the place.

So far, neither team had scored a single run after five innings. In the beginning of the sixth, Alan walked three batters in a row so that now the bases were loaded. Up to the plate came our own Bobby Hancock, arguably the best hitter on our team. He stood there with his bat in his hands, staring at Alan, wondering what kind of pitch he was going to get. Alan did his crazy windup and threw the ball, but it was way outside. It wasn't even close to home plate. Bobby would've had to have had eight-foot arms just to touch the thing with the tip of his bat. The boys in the Orioles dugout began to join in with Brad and shout at the pitcher. Then the second pitch came in across the plate, but it was high, way up and about even with Bobby's chin. The third pitch wasn't any better than the first two, so there were now three balls. Alan knew he had to get his fourth pitch over the plate, or he'd be walking in a run. So he slowed things down. He wound up like he was in slow motion, and he tossed a nice and easy lollipop right over the plate, and *whack!* Bobby swung his bat and practically knocked the ball into pieces. It sailed high in the air, over the outfielders' heads, and about ten feet beyond the outfield fence. It was a home run! A grand slam! And Brad was now on his feet shouting, "Atta boy, Bobby! Atta boy! Way to show that pitcher who's the boss!"

I felt sorry for Alan. He was letting his team down. The coach from his team walked out to the mound to visit with the boy before our next player came to bat. He had his hand on Alan's shoulder, and Alan looked like he was going to cry. I think I could read the coach's lips. I think he said, "Don't worry about it, son. It's only a game." It's probably the worst thing you can tell a nine-year-old, that it's only a game. These kids had no jobs, or careers, or marriages, or military enlistments. For these boys, their games were everything.

Anyway, the game went on, and we wound up beating the Astros 9-3. They never were able to recover from Bobby's grand slam. It was nice to win, but I'll be honest. I was disturbed by what happened that day. And I was angry with myself for not saying something to Brad about his behavior. I talked to Veronica about this, and she said I was smart to keep quiet. "Let him dig his own grave," she said. "You're better off just keeping your mouth shut. You did the right thing." I thought about this, and I remembered a little postcard my dad bought for me years ago. I tacked the postcard to my bulletin board in my bedroom. The postcard was a drawing of two ugly men, nose to nose in profile, shouting at each other. The postcard said, "Never argue with a fool because people won't be able to tell you apart."

During our third game, Brad didn't go after anyone on the opposing team like he'd done with Alan. He was shouting at the players a lot, but it wasn't a big deal. But then the strangest thing happened. During the fifth inning, he went after one of our own players! The boy's name was Steven Driscoll, and his dad's name was Arthur. Steven was a cute kid with scruffy red hair and freckles. He was small for his age, and he wasn't particularly athletic. But he did want to play baseball, and he showed up to all the team practices and games religiously. I would not say he was crazy about the sport like my son was, but he certainly wasn't a slacker or detriment to the team. The kid tried awful hard, and what more can you ask for? The coach put Steven in the outfield. We were playing the Cardinals that day, and their batter hit a fly ball right toward Steven. It was a high fly ball, and it seemed to hang in the air forever. We all stood up and watched, waiting for the ball to come down into Steven's trusty glove. Had he caught the ball, it would've ended the inning. But Steven did not catch the ball. It landed in his glove, was there for a second, and then rolled out and fell to the grass. The other team scored two runs.

Well, Brad came unglued. At first, he started yelling at Steven. I wasn't sure if Steven could even hear him, way out in the outfield. But then Brad turned around and started in on Steven's father. I could tell Arthur was surprised by the attack. You would've thought Steven had just lost the most important game of the season. The truth was that we were still ahead by two runs, so it wasn't really a big deal. "Jesus Christ," Brad said. "When are you going to teach that son of yours how to catch a fly ball? It was right in his mitt, wasn't it? All he had to do was squeeze it. I don't think I've ever seen anything like that. You know what they say, don't you? They say a team can only be as good as its weakest player. It makes our team pretty weak when our damn outfielders can't even catch routine fly balls. It was right to him, for crying out loud. It was right in his goddamn mitt."

Arthur just sat there, staring at Brad. He didn't say anything.

Finally, Brad sat down in a huff. His wife put her hand on the back of his neck and massaged it, trying to calm him down. The poor guy. All he wanted was for our team to win.

We went on to endure an entire season with Brad in the bleachers, and no one ever grabbed him by his collar and told him to shut the hell up. No one did anything. No, we all learned to put up with him and his big mouth. And why was this? Why would a group of rational, well-behaved adults put up with such an obnoxious man? I think there were a couple of reasons, the first being that, like me, they didn't want to get into shouting match with a man who obviously had no intention of changing his ways. What would be the point? It would be like complaining about the weather or the stock market. Some things in life are just beyond our control. The second reason was that I think some of the parents secretly liked what Brad was doing. There are a lot of people in the world who wish they could be more outspoken, but who haven't got the nerve for it. They condone the behavior of men like Brad because he's doing what they wish they had the guts to do, namely speak their minds. I was definitely not one of these people, but I could see how some of these parents might be. They were probably the same people who were impressed with Brad's Rolex watch.

I did finally stand up and speak my mind to Brad after the last game of the season. Well, I didn't exactly speak my mind. I let my pizza do the talking for me. Sometimes you can say more with a couple slices of pizza than you can with all the words in the English language.

Our last game of the season was against the Marlins, and no one thought we had a chance against this team. They had some of the best players in the league, and even their worst players were pretty darn good. They hadn't lost a single game all season. So what was our coach's advice to our boys during practice? He said, "The Marlins are a very tough team. Just do you best. That's all anyone can ask of you." It was like the coach was conceding the game before it had even started.

But Paul was conceding nothing. He was all fired up for this game. He went to be early the night before, so he could get plenty of sleep. When he woke up, he ate a big breakfast, not so big that it would slow him down, but big enough to give him the energy he would need to play his best game. After breakfast he spent the morning throwing a tennis ball against the garage door and catching it. He performed this ritual for several hours. He kept coming into the house to check the clock, to be sure we'd leave on time. When it finally was time, we piled into the car and drove to the park. Veronica came with us to this game. She didn't make all the games, but because this one was so important to Paul, she made sure she'd be there to watch. After the game, the team planned to meet at Nick's Pizza for an end-of-the-season pizza party. Nick's was the place where all the teams went to celebrate.

We arrived at the game about fifteen minutes early, in time for the coach's pep talk to the boys, and in time for Veronica and me to get a decent pair of seats in the stands. Then the Marlins took the field, and our team was up to bat. We started the batting order with a boy named Freddie Sanchez. Freddie was a good hitter, and we all had high hopes. The first pitch to Freddie was a strike, but Freddie didn't let it bother him. He stood there in the batter's box with a look of determination on his face that was impressive. Somehow, I knew that Freddie was going to get a hit, and he did. He smacked the ball right over the pitcher's head and into center field. Everyone cheered, and we were off to a good start.

Honestly, it was a terrific game, much closer than anyone expected. The teams were always within a couple runs of each other, and there were several lead changes. Neither team was beating the pants off the other, and the boys on both teams were playing well with a minimum of mistakes. And here was the weird thing. Loudmouthed Brad was keeping his heckling to a minimum. I mean, he was still shouting at the players, but most of what he was shouting was positive. He was telling our boys how good they were doing and encouraging them to keep it up. "Way to go, boys," he'd say. "Good play. Good eye. Way to play the ball. Way to swing that bat. Keep it up, and we might just win this game!"

Sound too good to be true? Well, it was. Brad did finally break down and show his true colors. Because Brad was Brad, right? It's like I said earlier, a belligerent orangutan is a belligerent orangutan. I'll tell you what I finally did to Brad at the pizza restaurant, but first let me describe the ninth inning of this game. The Marlins were ahead 5-3 at the top of the inning, and little Steven Driscoll stepped up to the plate for us. Like I said earlier, Steven was not a big kid, but the bat he brought to the plate was huge. It looked like he was holding a wooden telephone pole. "Why didn't he pick a smaller bat?" I whispered to Veronica. She shrugged her shoulders and watched. The first pitch to Steven was a ball, and the second pitch was a strike. The boy just stood there, watching the pitches go by. Then on the third pitch he swung the big bat in front of him and showed bunt. It couldn't have been a more perfect pitch, and Steven laid down a bunt that had the catcher tripping over his own feet. By the time he finally threw the ball to first, Steven had stepped on the bag and he was safe. Everyone in our side of the bleachers jumped up and cheered. We had a man on base!

Next to bat was Paul. Paul had been having a good game so far, with two base hits and a walk under his belt. "Cross your fingers," I said to Veronica. The Marlin's pitcher started his windup, and I couldn't watch. I closed my eyes and listened. The whole place was quiet as a church on a Monday morning. It was eerie how quiet the place was. Then I heard the umpire yell strike. *Damn it,* I thought. I waited, still with my eyes closed, and then I heard him yell strike a second time. I waited again, but this time, after a couple minutes, I heard the crack of the bat against the ball, and the parents in the stands went crazy. When I opened my eyes, Paul was safe at first, and Steven was standing on second. We now had two men on base and no outs. We were in good shape. The next boy to bat for our team was Joey Ohms. "This is our chance," I said to Veronica. "This boy can do it."

Here was the thing about Joey. He always swung for the stars, meaning he always tried to hit a home run. He had a lousy batting average as a result, and his strikeouts were often disappointing. But when he did finally connect with the ball, look out! He could hit that ball clear to the next town. Could he deliver in this game, now in the ninth inning? Again, the stands were quiet as the pitcher did his windup. Then I couldn't believe my eyes! The pitcher threw the ball right down the middle of the strike zone on the very first pitch, and Joey swung at it with all his might. The sound of the ball hitting the bat confirmed everything. I don't think I'd ever seen a nine-year-old wallop a ball so far, and now everyone on our team was hysterical. The boys all rounded the bases, giving one another high fives. We were winning 6-5, and we were winning in the ninth inning!

Our next three at bats were uneventful. The first boy struck out swinging, and the second boy struck out looking. The third boy hit a ground ball straight to first, and he didn't even bother to run. So now it was the Marlin' turn to bat. It was the bottom of the ninth.

It was the most stressful inning of baseball I'd ever watched. The Marlins' first batter struck out, so that was good. There was one out. Their second batter hit a ground ball through our infield, and he made it safely to first base. Now there was one out and a man on first. Are you following me? What happens next is important. The third batter came to the plate and took a strike and two balls. Then on the fourth pitch, he hit the ball straight to Paul at second base! It was an easy double play, and Paul stepped on second base and then fired the ball to first. Unfortunately, the ball sailed on Paul, and it flew over the first baseman's head. The double play was blown! The runner continued on to second and stopped there. The inning should've been over, but it wasn't. Our team had to face another batter because of Paul's error.

My heart sank. The next batter for the Marlins hit a homer, scored two runs, and the game was over. It was a walk-off home run, and just like that, the Marlins won the game 7-6.

After the game everyone met at Nick's Pizza for our end-of-the-year celebration. We might have lost our last game to the Marlins, but it had been a terrific season. There was plenty to celebrate, and everyone was in a great mood despite the loss that day. The coach and his wife ordered a pile of pizzas and several pitchers of Coke. People were sitting and standing, talking to one another, having a good time. Some of the boys were a little wild, and their parents had to settle them down. I was sitting with Veronica, and we were talking to Arthur Driscoll about his son's amazing bunt. It was then that I heard Brad running off at the mouth to the coach and his wife. Brad was talking about my son! "The kid throws like a girl," Brad said. "He's thrown like a girl all season. He's just been lucky we have a good first baseman."

"Paul's one of our better players," the coach said, defending Paul. "What happened this afternoon could've happened to anyone."

"I still say he throws like a damn girl," Brad said. "Always has."

I couldn't sit still for it. I stood and walked right up to Brad. "Are you talking about my Paul?"

"He should've made that double play," Brad said. "It was a routine double play."

"The ball got away from him," I said.

"It could happen to anyone," the coach said.

"Your kid throws like a goddamn girl. Everyone on the team knows it. I'm just calling a spade a spade."

"You're an ass," I said.

Brad stared at me for a moment. "What'd you just say to me?" he asked, and he gave me a little shove.

I had my slice of pizza in my hand. I also noticed that Paul had walked up to us to see what was being said about him. I didn't know how long Paul had been there or how much he'd heard. I was suddenly overwhelmed with an impulse to defend my son and let this loudmouth have it once and for all. And by have it, I mean have my pizza, the whole slice of it. I lifted the pizza up and smashed it into Brad's face. I took him completely by surprise. You should've seen the idiot, pizza sauce and cheese and pepperonis sliding down his face from his hairline to his chin.

"What do you think you're doing?" his wife shrieked.

"I'll show you what I'm doing," I said. I reached over to the table and picked up a fresh slice of pizza. I held it up and looked Brad's wife in the eye.

"You wouldn't dare," she said.

"Oh, but I would," I said, and I went to smash the slice of pizza in her face. She tried to duck, but I did get the top of her head. Sauce, cheese, and pepperonis were now smeared all over her forehead and hair, and everyone in the restaurant was staring at us. "A double play!" I exclaimed.

"You're both out!" Paul said.

As Brad and his wife wiped the pizza from their heads, the coach looked at me and sighed. He was disappointed in me. "Jeez, Robert," he said. "I think you should probably leave."

I nodded my head and said, "You're right."

"Asshole," Brad said to me.

"Come on, Paul," I said.

"Do we have to go?"

"Yes," I said. "Go get your mom."

Paul reached and grabbed another slice of pizza from the table for the road. He then went to get Veronica, but she was already standing with her purse, ready to go. My wife and son followed me out of the restaurant. No one said a word. We got into the car and put on our seatbelts. Then when I started the engine, I noticed Paul staring at me from the backseat through the rearview mirror.

"What is it?" I asked.

"I'm glad you did what you did," Paul said. "In fact, it would've been fine with me if you'd punched them both right in the face."

"Don't say that," Veronica said.

Punch them in the face? So now what do you think of my nine-year-old boy? He was talking about punching people in the face. A broken nose. A broken jaw. Maybe a pair of big black eyes. He didn't sound very gay to me. My son was no kind of sissy. And no, he did *not* throw like a girl.

Sleepover

When Paul was ten, he made friends with a boy from school named Donald Farber. He met Donald in his fifth-grade class. I thought it was interesting these two boys became pals, because Donald didn't play a lick of baseball, and all of Paul's more recent friends were boys he'd met on his teams. I don't think Donald played any sports at all. He just wasn't that kind of kid. He was shorter than Paul, and he was frail. By frail, he wasn't necessarily a sissy, but honestly looked like the sort of boy who'd have serious difficulty wrestling anything stronger than a moth. Donald had sandy brown hair and hazel eyes, and his thin lips were always wet and shiny. His skin was a milky white color, like he spent no time in the outdoors at all. There was a good component to this friendship. Veronica and I agreed it was encouraging that Donald did so exceptionally well in school, and we were hoping some of his studiousness would rub off on our son. To date, Paul did just okay in school, and in our opinion, he could've been doing better.

I had a terrific evening planned for the boys. After picking up Donald at his house, we'd stop at Blockbuster and rent a movie. Then I'd take them to an Angels baseball game where we'd eat hot dogs, cotton candy, and peanuts until our stomachs couldn't take anymore. We'd sit together and watch the game, standing up and hollering every time an Angel got a hit and booing every time the ump made a bad call. We'd come home when the game was over, where the boys would watch their movie on the family room TV while Veronica and I watched TV upstairs in the master bedroom. We'd let the boys watch

TV until late, and we'd let them sleep on the floor. They could stay up all night watching TV for all we cared.

When we finally did pick up Donald at his house, he was wearing a brand-new Angels baseball cap. The tag was still on the cap, hanging from the side of the visor. "Donald has never been to a ballgame before," his mother said. "I picked the cap up for him last night at a sporting goods store. He's been so looking forward to going with you. It's all he's talked about for the past two days."

"He'll have a great time," I said.

"There are some things I need you to know. First, make sure Donald doesn't eat anything with peanuts. He's allergic to peanuts."

"No problem," I said.

"And here's his inhaler. He has a slight asthmatic condition, and sometimes he needs this thing to help him breathe. I'd have him keep it on him, but he's always losing things. It's like there are holes in every one of his pockets."

"Okay," I said, and I took the inhaler. "I'll hang onto it for him."

"And here's a twenty-dollar bill so he can buy a souvenir. But I told him not to spend the whole thing. Make sure he doesn't spend the whole twenty. That's why I'm giving it to you."

"Okay," I said.

"And don't let him have any candy. Last month he had two cavities at the dentist."

"No candy," I said.

"And make sure he brushes his teeth before he goes to bed. His toothbrush and toothpaste are in his backpack along with his pajamas."

"I'll be sure he brushes his teeth."

"Finally, if possible, try to leave a light on while he's sleeping. Sometimes he has nightmares, but I find a night light helps."

"Got it," I said. "I think we have a night-light in our house somewhere."

"His dad's out of town. But he'll be back tomorrow afternoon, and then he'll pick Donald up."

"Sounds good," I said.

Donald's mom knelt down to her son and said, "Be a good boy, Donald."

"Yes, Mom."

"And mind your manners."

"I will, I will," Donald said. His mom gave him a big, wet kiss on his forehead, and he wiped it off with the back of his hand.

"We'll take good care of him," I said. "We'll treat him like he's one of our own."

"Let's hurry up," Paul said. "We're going to be late."

We said goodbye to Donald's mom, and off we went. We climbed into my car, and I sped off.

Our first stop was Blockbuster. Do you remember all those Blockbusters? They used to be everywhere, and then *boom!* They were gone. Anyway, the store wasn't very busy, which was good. Ordinarily, this particular store was packed with people, and there was always a long, annoying line at the cash registers. Paul knew exactly what he wanted, and he went straight to the horror section, holding Donald by the hand and dragging the boy along with him. It was pretty funny. You should've seen the look on Donald's face when they got there. It was like he'd been dragged into a back room filled with porno movies. He looked like he wanted to cover his eyes with his hands. "What's the matter?" Paul asked, noticing Donald's behavior. "Don't you like movies?"

"I'm not allowed to watch horror movies."

"You're not?"

"My mom says they'll give me nightmares."

"I watch them all the time. They don't give me any nightmares. I've been watching them ever since I was a little kid."

"They look scary."

"They're just movies, Donald. They're not for real, you know. None of this stuff actually happens."

"I guess that's true."

"Let me do the picking. I'll pick one out for us. It won't be too scary."

I put my hand on Donald's shoulder. "You'll be fine, son" I said. "Paul will pick a good one."

"Here's one I haven't seen," Paul said. "This one looks cool."

"What's it about?"

"A friend of mine saw this. It's about giant worms that eat people."

"It's not too scary?"

"Are you scared of worms?" Paul asked.

"No, I suppose not."

"There, you see? It's just about a bunch of worms. Except they're really big, and they eat people. There's no such thing in real life. You know that, right?"

"Yeah, I know that."

"It's just a movie," Paul said. "You'll like it. I promise that you'll like it." Then Paul handed the movie to me.

I took the box from Paul's hand and carried it to the cashier. After charging it to my credit card, we were off to the baseball game. I had to chuckle. I knew Donald was stewing over this movie. He would stew a while, but I knew he was going to be fine.

When we got to Anaheim Stadium, it was a little after eight. I figured the game was probably now in the second inning. But something was wrong. I drove clear around the stadium just to be sure. The parking lot was empty, and as I looked at all the vacant parking spaces, I said, "I was sure the newspaper said there was a game tonight at seven-thirty."

"No one is here," Paul said.

"Obviously, there is no game."

"You must have read the paper wrong."

"Or they printed it wrong. Sometimes the paper makes mistakes."

"So now what do we do?" Paul asked.

I thought about this. This was a problem. I had two young boys in my car, and I'd promised them a night of fun. Donald's mom even went out of her way and bought him that Angels cap for the occasion. Then a light bulb went off over my head, and I asked, "How would you boys like to go to Disneyland?"

"Disneyland is for little kids," Paul said.

"I like Disneyland," Donald said.

"Well, if Donald likes it, I guess it'd be okay. We could go on some of the rides."

"Sure," I said. "They have some great rides. And we can get something to eat there. They have plenty of good places for dinner.

We'll go to their best restaurant, and I'll let you guys order anything you want off the menu."

"To Disneyland," Paul said.

"Yeah, to Disneyland!" Donald exclaimed. Now we had Donald excited.

I drove to Disneyland, and it wasn't a long drive. The traffic wasn't as bad as I thought it would be. But by the time we got to the Happiest Place on Earth, everyone was leaving. "What the fuck?" I said angrily. Then I looked in the rearview mirror and saw Donald looking at me. "I mean, what the heck, of course. I should've said what the heck."

"They're closing," Paul said.

"I can see that."

"This kind of sucks."

"It does," I said. "I didn't realize they closed so early this time of year." I drove away from the park, thinking like mad, trying to figure out something for the boys to do.

Then it hit me like a thunderbolt. Have you ever had an inspiration that amazes you with its brilliance? It does actually hit you like a thunderbolt, doesn't it? In my opinion, this idea of mine was nothing short of pure and unadulterated fatherly genius. "Have either of you boys ever gone on a shopping spree?" I asked.

"What's a shopping spree?"

"Ah, I'm glad you asked that," I said. "Now, here's what we're going to do. I'm going to take you boys to the grocery store. I *know* the damn store is open. They stay open every night until midnight. We'll get each of you a shopping cart, and I'm going to time you. When I say go, you can roll your carts up and down the aisles and fill them with anything you want. Cookies, ice cream, chips, dip, soft drinks, frozen pizza, popcorn, candy bars, and anything else that looks good. Grab whatever you want and take whatever you can get your hands on. I'll give you ten minutes. At the end of the ten minutes, we'll roll up to the cashier and buy all the food you put in your carts. We'll take it all home with us, and you can feast in front of the television and watch your movie. You can eat and drink until your belt buckles pop off."

Paul looked at Donald, smiling. "What do you say to that?"

"Is it really okay for us to do this?" Donald asked.

"If I say it's okay, then it's okay."

"What if someone in the store tries to stop us?"

"I'll be there the whole time."

Donald thought about this. Then he said, "I've never done anything like this before."

"There's a first time for everything," I said. "And first times are always the best."

We drove to the grocery store. We stepped up to the entrance, and each boy grabbed a shopping cart. They lined up beside each other like race horses in a starting gate. I looked at my watch and raised my hand. I waited for the second hand to hit the twelve, and then I dropped my hand and shouted, "Go!"

You should've seen these two kids! They were off and running. I followed them and watched them loading up their carts. Donald was very careful about what he picked, while Paul was just grabbing everything he could get his hands on. It turned out that ten minutes was a lot of time, because when the minutes were finally up, their carts were nearly filled. I wish I'd had a camera with me. It was funny as hell.

We went to the checkout line, waited behind a couple of moms doing their grocery shopping, and then put the goods on the conveyor belt. The cashier began to ring it up, and she gave me a disapproving look. She asked, "Are their mothers here?"

"No," I said.

"Where are they?"

"They're at home."

"So this is all your doing?"

"Disneyland was closed," I explained.

"They have a grocery store at Disneyland?"

"No," I said. I was thinking of explaining the situation to the lady, but then I said, "Never mind."

The woman shook her head and continued to ring up the items. "I have to be honest," she said. "I've never seen anything quite like this."

I felt like saying, "Just do your damn job and mind your own business," but I said nothing.

When everything was bagged and loaded in the carts, I paid the cashier with a credit card. We then pushed the carts to my car and loaded the stuff into the trunk. We drove home, and when we started bringing the bags into the house, Veronica appeared. You should've seen the look on her face. "What the heck is all this?" she asked. "It looks like you went to the store. I thought you boys were going to a ballgame."

"We went on a shopping spree," Paul said. He plopped a bag down on the kitchen counter and then ran out of the house to get another.

"A shopping spree?"

"There was no ballgame," I said.

"No ballgame?"

"The paper must've printed it wrong. No one was there. Then we tried to go to Disneyland, but they were closing the place up. So we chose the prize behind door number three, which was a ten-minute shopping spree at the grocery store."

Veronica just stared at me.

"They had a ball."

"I'm sure they did. Who's going to eat all of this garbage?"

"They are."

"It's going to make them sick."

"They'll be fine," I said. "They're ten-year-old boys. They can eat anything."

"Look what else we got," Paul said to Veronica. He was holding up the movie.

"What movie did you get?" Veronica asked.

"It's about giant worms," Paul said.

"They eat people," Donald said. He was smiling when he said this. I was glad to see that Donald was getting into it.

"Good Lord," Veronica said. "You should've called me. I would've come up with something better for the boys to do than eat junk food and watch a movie about giant worms."

"That's why I didn't call you," I said.

Sure, she would've come up with something. Veronica probably would've had them making zoo animals out of pipe cleaners and watching *Barney*. No thanks to that. These two boys were going to have the time of their lives, thanks to me.

Once they brought everything in the house, the boys spread their booty out across the family room floor, and Paul stuck the movie into the video player. Veronica brought out some blankets and pillows for the boys, so they could get comfortable and sleep on the floor. I turned off the lights, so it would be dark in the room, and Veronica and I then went upstairs to leave the boys alone. We went to our bedroom to watch some TV before sleeping.

After a couple hours I went downstairs to check on the boys. They were still watching the TV, surrounded by empty cookie boxes, candy wrappers, and drained soft drink cans. The light from the television was glowing on their wide-awake faces. They were watching the movie for the second time. I figured they had enough sugar in their blood to stay awake at watch the movie another five times, if that's what they wanted to do.

"How's the movie?" I asked.

"It's great," Paul said.

"I'm not going to have any nightmares," Donald said confidently.

"Of course you're not," I said. Then I leaned over and asked Donald, "Can I have a few of your Oreos?"

"Help yourself," Donald said.

I grabbed a handful of cookies. I said goodnight to the boys and carried the cookies upstairs, climbing back in bed with Veronica.

"How are the boys doing?"

"They're having the time of their lives."

"Turn off your light. I want to sleep."

"Okay," I said, and I turned off the light. I was eating my cookies.

"Are you eating something?"

"Oreos," I said.

"You're a child," Veronica said. Then a minute or so later, she was sound asleep. Our TV was still on, and the remote was on my nightstand. I grabbed the remote and changed the channel. I found an old black-and-white movie from the 1930s about a family in the Midwest. There was a mother and father, two daughters, and a younger son. The father was an inventor, and the daughters, of course, were chaste and beautiful. The son was a boy's boy. Do you know what I mean by a boy's boy? Think Norman Rockwell. Think fishing holes and bare feet. It didn't strike me so hard then, but it strikes me now just how wonderful these old movies were. Sometimes I think I was born into the wrong era.

I fell asleep halfway through the movie. I was in a dream when there was someone knocking on our bedroom door. The knocking woke me up. I checked the time, and it was nearly two in the morning. "Who could that be?" Veronica asked. She was awake too.

I climbed out of bed to open the door. It was Donald with his backpack on. "Can you take me home?" he asked.

"You want to go home now?"

"Yes, please."

"Is there something wrong?"

"I just want to go home."

"Where's Paul?" I asked.

"He's downstairs."

"Is he awake too?"

"Yeah, he's awake. Will you take me home?"

"Sure," I said. "Just let me get dressed."

"Thanks," Donald said.

I put on some clothes and then Donald and I stepped downstairs. Paul was still in front of the TV, watching an infomercial about cooking utensils. "I'm taking Donald home," I said to Paul.

"I know."

"Are you going to say goodbye?"

"Bye," Paul said.

Donald and I went outside and got into my car, and I drove him to his house. When we got there, the front door was open, and the porch light was on. His mom was standing on the porch. "Donald called me," she explained.

"He was welcome to stay longer," I said.

"It's better this way," she said.

Donald walked into the house, and I said, "He's a good kid. We liked having him over."

"Thanks for bringing him home. I would've come to get him myself, but I have the baby to look after. And my husband is out of town."

"It's no problem."

"Have a good evening."

"You too," I said, and Donald's mom closed the front door. I walked to my car, thinking about this situation. What a strange woman Mrs. Farber was, and what an odd kid Donald turned out to be, knocking on our bedroom door in the middle of the night. He seemed to be having so much fun with Paul. Were the man-eating worms too much for him? Was it all the junk food? Was the floor too hard? Should I have found a night-light? Maybe the kid just wasn't cut out for sleepovers. That had to be it.

When Paul told us last week he was gay, it changed everything. Now I sit here in our South Carolina home, wondering. Do you want to know what I'm wondering? I'm wondering about that evening, and I hate where my mind is taking me. But I have to be honest, right?

I now have questions about what really happened. Why did Donald want to leave so abruptly? Was it something Paul said or did? This certainly could've been the case. Did Paul do something inappropriate? Did he try to touch the boy? Or did he lean over and try to kiss him? Maybe he did! Maybe he misread the signals Donald was sending and made an unwanted advance. It happens. I mean, even straight couples can misread signals. It happens all the time.

Maybe ten was way too young for anything like this to occur between the boys. Or maybe it was the perfect age. I can remember being very interested in young girls when I was ten, interested in all kinds of ways. You want to know how this whole thing makes me feel? I'm not angry, or hurt, or embarrassed, or even offended. I just feel sad. I feel sad for my son and sorry that he has to be gay. I shouldn't have to think like this about Paul. A father should be able to look back on his son's childhood and remember baseball games, cotton candy, toads, lizards, skateboards, and fishing trips. He should not be wondering about the nonsense that is now crossing my mind.

Dinner at Claude's

like the weather in South Carolina. We didn't get much rain in Southern California, but here it rains often. I'm sitting on our covered back porch this afternoon, and the storm clouds have rolled in. Thunder is booming, lightning is flashing, and the heavy rain is falling from the sky in buckets.

I'm thinking back to a time when I was twenty-six and Veronica was twenty-two. This was several years before Paul was born. Veronica and I were having dinner out at a restaurant called Claude's with one of my old high school friends and his wife. My friend's name was Chuck Harper, and his wife's name was Maureen. I hadn't seen Chuck for years, but I ran into him a couple weeks earlier at Home Depot where he was buying a garden hose and where I was picking up a roll of duct tape. It was nice seeing Chuck again, and it was his idea for us to have dinner together at Claude's.

During this time, I was working for the architectural firm of Waxman & Smothers. They had an office in downtown Santa Ana, and I'd been working there since I graduated from college. I think I told you earlier that my dad was an architect. I looked up to him when I was young, and I wanted to follow in his footsteps. But you know what? I hated my job at Waxman & Smothers with a passion. It was no wonder architects had the fifth highest suicide rate in the nation. I looked forward to going to work each day almost as much as I looked forward to my next root canal. Day after miserable day I sat at a drafting table in a stuffy drafting room, drinking black coffee and laboring under the fluorescent lighting, drawing, erasing, and drawing again. I was like Sisyphus pushing a boulder up a hill, except I didn't even have the benefits of working out in the fresh air or getting any exercise. If ever there was an employee in Orange County ready to make a career change, it was me.

Then along came Chuck Harper. You could call it the best kind of kismet. He was tan, physically fit, and happy as lark. He adored his wife, Maureen, and he loved his job. You're not going to believe what this guy did for a living, but keep an open mind, because it wouldn't be long before I'd quit my job at Waxman & Smothers to do the very same thing. Who would've thought that a casual dinner with an old high school chum would have such an impact on my life? Chuck started the evening off by striking up a conversation with Veronica. "So Robert tells me you're an accountant," he said.

"A bookkeeper, actually," Veronica said.

"At a construction company?"

"Part time. They don't need anyone full time. It's a small company."

"What kind of projects do they build?"

"All sorts. Right now, they're building a small medical complex."

"So you're working for doctors?"

"Yes," Veronica said.

"I've worked for a number of doctors. Some of them can be a real pain. But some are pretty cool."

"These doctors are a pain."

"What kind of doctors are they?"

"They're all pediatricians. I think they spend too much time with kids. It's like working for a bunch of third-graders."

"I worked for a proctologist once. Great guy. He had a great sense of humor."

"Tell them the joke," Maureen said.

"Which one?"

"The one about the glass eye."

"Oh, yeah," Chuck said. "Do you guys like jokes?"

"Who doesn't like jokes?" I said.

"This is a good one. I think you'll like it. My proctologist customer told it to me. It made me laugh when I first heard it."

"Good, let's hear it."

"Okay, there was once a guy who had a glass eye. He liked to amuse the kids in his neighborhood by popping the eye out and pretending to eat it. The kids would go crazy over this stupid stunt. One day he popped out the eye and put it in his mouth as usual. But this time, by accident, he actually swallowed the thing. Days went by, and he hadn't had a bowel movement. He figured the eye must have got lodged in his digestive system so that it was blocking the way. He waited a few more days, thinking he would pass the eye, but it never came out. Finally, he went to see a proctologist, and the doctor had him drop his pants and bend over the examination table. The doctor put on his latex gloves and spread the man's cheeks. He looked, and there was the eye, lodged in the man's anus, looking right back at him. The doctor smiled and said, 'What's the matter, pal, don't you trust me?'"

We laughed. Well, all of us laughed except for my wife. Veronica would tell me later that she thought the joke was dumb.

As if from thin air, the waiter suddenly appeared at our table to take our beverage orders. He also told us about the specials that were not listed on the menu. We ordered our cocktails, and the waiter left us alone for a while. "How's *your* job going?" Chuck asked me. "To tell you the truth, you could've knocked me over with a feather when you filled me in at Home Depot, when you told me you were an architect."

"I'm not an architect yet," I said. "I still need to take the state exam."

"You always seemed to have a nice way with people. I always thought of you as a people person. If someone were to ask me what I thought you were doing with your life, I'd have guessed you were a salesman or some kind of manager, not some dude who spends all his time bent over a drafting table."

"My father is an architect. I guess I followed in his footsteps."

"But is your father like you?"

"Not really," I said.

"There, you see?"

"See what?"

"You did what most people do when they finish high school or college. You didn't pay attention to the wise little voice in your head. Instead, you took the path of least resistance and followed the road you knew others expected you to take. Tell me, are you happy being an architect?"

"Not at all."

"It's like they say, isn't it? To thine own self be true? Shakespeare hit the nail on the head when he put those words in Polonius's mouth."

"You've read Shakespeare?"

"I went to college, you know. I've read and studied all sorts of interesting stuff."

"I didn't know you went to college."

"Graduated from UCLA. You thought because of what I do for a living, that I didn't go to college?"

"Well, yes," I said.

"Listen, college was important to me. Without it, I would never have become what I am today."

"That's true," Maureen said.

"College helped me to understand who I was and what I would be best at."

"I guess my undergraduate experience was different from yours," I said. "College educated me to be something that makes me miserable."

"That's because you went there for the wrong reason. You went to college to learn how to do something. I went to college to learn what *not* to do."

I thought about this, and then I said, "That doesn't make much sense."

"Well, it does if you think about it."

"If college taught you what not to be, then where did you get the inspiration to do what you're now doing?"

"Ah, that came from Henry."

"Henry who?"

"Henry Windom."

"And who is he?"

"He sold me my first new car."

Just as I was about to ask Chuck another question, our tricky waiter materialized out of thin air again, holding our cocktails on a plastic tray. He set the drinks down before us, one by one, and then asked if we were ready to order our meals. Everyone was ready, and as we rattled off our choices, the waiter wrote everything down on his little pad of paper. When this was done, he smiled and walked away. For the record, Veronica ordered the pork chop. It was either that or the swordfish.

"Tell me more about Henry," I said to Chuck. "How did he enlighten you?"

"Henry was different from anyone I'd ever met. And do you know how he was different?"

"How was he different?"

"He was happy. I mean, he seemed to be an honest-to-God, genuinely happy man. He seemed to truly enjoy what he was doing, and he did everything he could to make my car buying experience a good one. Prior to meeting Henry, when I told my friends I was going to buy a new car, they all warned me that I was in for a dreadful experience. But it wasn't so with Henry. It was not at all what I'd expected."

"What did he do that was so different?"

"The answer to that is so simple. He went about his business with me like he loved every minute of it, like it was his passion, like it was his calling, like there was nothing in the world he would rather have been doing."

I thought about this. The man Chuck was describing was a car salesman, for Christ's sake. What was so special about being a car salesman? I was about to say something to Chuck when our waiter brought out our salads and began placing them on our table. The service at this place was annoyingly fast. I wanted to talk to Chuck, and now I was supposed to eat a salad? "Anyone want some ground pepper?" the waiter asked. Chuck and Maureen had the pepper, but Veronica and I said no. The waiter asked us if we wanted another round of drinks, and everyone said yes.

"So it was because of Henry that you became a car salesman?" I asked Chuck. He was eating his salad, and he replied with his mouth full.

"I became a car salesman just as soon as I possibly could. I didn't waste a minute."

"And you've been doing this for how long?"

"For three years."

"And are you as happy as Henry?"

"I'm as happy as a clam in saltwater." Chuck stuffed another leafy forkful of salad into his mouth.

"Tell me what you love about your work," I said. It sounded like I was making small talk, but I actually wanted to learn how a college-educated man could find such happiness selling cars. The idea of it intrigued me, and I had questions.

"First and foremost, I love selling cars because it requires me to be honest." Chuck swallowed his mouthful of salad and continued. "In fact, that's precisely what I do for people. I tell them the truth. I always tell the truth to my customers. You don't know what a relief it is not to be a liar, not to make things up, not to have to bend and stretch the facts. Being honest with others makes life so simple and pleasant." I must have been smiling, because Chuck said, "I can see you find this amusing. I suppose like most people, you don't associate selling cars with honesty."

"I didn't actually say that."

"But you were thinking it?"

"Maybe a little."

Chuck set down his salad fork. Then he leaned toward me. "Let's say you came to me, and I sold you a car. What would you do if you discovered down the road that I'd been less than honest with you? Would you come back to me a few years later when you were in the market for another car? No, of course you wouldn't. The business of car sales is all about building up a base of satisfied customers who keep coming back to you, time and time again. You need to be in this game for the long haul if you want to do well, and if you want your customers to keep coming back, you have to earn their trust. And to earn their trust, you have to be honest."

"I guess that makes sense," I said. I couldn't argue with Chuck's logic.

"Which brings me to another thing I love about selling cars. I love the idea that I am helping people. I help them to make good decisions. Most people need to own cars, don't they? Owning a car isn't like owning an artwork or a piece of jewelry. These days, a car is a necessity, not a luxury, and picking the right car for the right price is imperative. I help people find what they need, giving them my expertise and sound advice. I'm not just honest. I'm also well-informed. My customers depend on me, and I don't take my responsibility lightly. People go to doctors for medical advice and to lawyers for legal advice. But where do they go when they're buying a car? I'd like them to come to me. I want to be their expert. I want to be their confidant."

Chuck picked up his fork and dug into his salad again. He poked some of it into his mouth. He was looking at me, smiling and chewing at the same time. "Do you ever get bored?" I asked.

"Bored? Do you have any idea how many different kinds of people I deal with every month?" he asked me.

"Not really," I said.

"I sell cars to everyone. I sell them to construction workers, doctors, firemen, police officers, lawyers, school teachers, corporate executives, rock musicians, grocery store cashiers, and psychologists. I've never been bored, not once. It's fascinating and challenging work. I mean, think of it! A guy like me always has to stay on his toes and be well-read in every topic in order to have any chance at keeping up. Do you know what a game changer it is when you know something about your customers, when you share some common interests? It makes all the difference in the world. So I read, study, and investigate, and I'll bet I've learned more about the world and the seven and a half billion people who inhabit it over the past three years as a car salesman than the average Joe learns over the course of his entire life."

"I never thought of that," I said.

"Selling cars isn't for slouches."

"I believe you."

Our waiter showed up to take away our salad plates and deliver our dinners. I have to say that I felt a little guilty. I'd made Chuck do so much talking about his job that he'd barely touched his salad. Everyone else had finished theirs, right down to the last crouton and crumble of feta cheese. "This food looks great," I said, looking at the dinner that was now before me. "More drinks?" the waiter asked. Everyone but me said no. I definitely wanted a third drink.

"I'm not saying I want to sell cars," I said to Chuck. "But if I wanted to do it, how would I go about getting a job? Would I need experience?"

"Some experience helps."

"But some dealerships will train?"

"Some will. It depends on if they think you're worth investing their time in."

"So a recommendation from someone such as yourself would probably help?"

"I'm sure it would."

The waiter returned and delivered my third drink to me. I think I've told you before that I'm not much of a drinker. Three drinks are a lot for me, but I gulped this third drink down like a pro. Sure enough, the booze went straight to my head. I wasn't sure I liked the way it made me feel, for I was suddenly strangely disconnected from the others. I could hear our dinner group talking, but they were no longer talking about Chuck selling cars. Instead, they were talking about how Coca Cola had changed its recipe, and Maureen was predicting the collapse of the company. She said something to the effect that people often embraced change, but that some things just didn't need to be changed, and that some things just couldn't be changed, and Coke was one of them. "Coke has got to be Coke," she said. Coke? Seriously? Who gave a shit about Coke?

But everyone continued to talk, and while they were talking I ordered a fourth drink, and then a fifth. When I downed the fifth drink, Veronica put her hand on mine. "What's up with the drinking?" she asked. "This isn't like you." She was right.

Have you ever seen the old Harold Lloyd movie about Mr. Diddlebock? Well, that was me. I was Mr. Diddlebock, and I was about to look up at the ceiling and howl. Like a madman, I suddenly slammed my fist down on the restaurant table, and everyone looked at me, wondering what the heck I was doing.

"Goddamn it!" I shouted. "I'm going to sell cars. I'm going to quit my job tomorrow and become a fucking car salesman!"

At first no one said anything. I had taken them quite by surprise with my outburst. You should've seen the look on Veronica's face.

"No more drinks for you," she said.

"I think he's serious," Chuck said. "I think the old boy wants to sell some cars."

83

"Don't be ridiculous," Veronica said. "He's just had too much to drink. He doesn't know what he's talking about."

You know, I don't think I said anything the rest of the evening. I had made kind of a fool of myself, and I knew it.

But I would prove Veronica wrong. Later that week I called Chuck, and he arranged for me to have an interview with the sales manager at his car dealership. He said there was an opening in sales. He said they were looking for someone with experience, but he thought they might hire me if Chuck promised to take me under his wing. And just like that, it happened. Two days after the interview, they offered me a position. I quit my job at Waxman & Smothers, and a week later I was working side by side with Chuck. It was like the oppressive weight of the world had been lifted from my shoulders. Suddenly, there was a joyful skip in my gait and a smile on my face. Even Veronica was in on the optimism. True, she was wary at first, but gradually she warmed up to the idea of her husband selling cars for a living. She took me to the mall to shop for clothes. "If you're going to be a success, you need to look your best," she said. Veronica also convinced me to get a stylish haircut and a manicure. By the time she was done jazzing me up, I looked like a showcase mannequin at in the men's department of Macy's. No more T-shirts and sweatpants. No more shaggy hair. No more bending over a drafting table all day.

There was only one thing that remained to be done. I needed to tell my parents. I went over to their house and told them in person, and it went as I expected. Mom was immediately supportive, but Dad was quiet, like his doctor had just given two months to live. In fact, Dad barely spoke to me for the next two months. I knew he'd get over it, and so I gave him time to get used to the idea. He did eventually come to terms with it, and we were friends again.

I've never had any regrets about what I did, and I've never had any desire to go back to architecture. I made the right decision. I was a car salesman for over thirty years until I retired eight months ago. I loved my job. I made good money at it, and I did a great job taking care of my family. How did Chuck put it? I was happy as a clam in saltwater.

This brings me back to my porch in South Carolina and the storm I've been watching. The rain is letting up, but the thunder is still clapping and pounding. It's funny how the mind wanders in a storm. I find myself thinking about Paul. He called my father yesterday and gave him the news. I wasn't present to hear either of them talking, so I have no idea how the conversation went. This morning I called Dad and asked what he thought of Paul, and he laughed and said, "I honestly don't know which is worse, being told your grandson is gay, or being told your son is a car salesman."

I had to laugh. It figured Dad would say something like that. After all these years, he's as sharp as a tack. He's ninety-five years old, and he still has a sense of humor. Good for him.

Matilda

P aul turned thirteen when he was in seventh grade, and I remember it was around this time that he brought his first girlfriend to our house. She was a pretty little twelve-year-old named Matilda Manchester. Matilda was in Paul's biology class, and she lived with her parents and sisters in our neighborhood, on the street behind ours in a two-story house that always had a large American flag flying next to the front door. Actually, it was a *huge* American flag. There was no way you could miss it.

Veronica and I met with Matilda's parents. I'll tell you all about that very interesting meeting, but first let me tell you a few more things about Matilda. I remember that we liked everything about this girl. She was several inches shorter than Paul, and she always wore her light-brown hair tied back in a ponytail. She had big hazel eyes, and she would bat them while she talked to you, like she was flirting. But I decided she wasn't actually flirting, because she did this no matter who she was looking at. I thought she was a good-looking kid, that her face was nicely put together, everything right where it belonged. I wouldn't go so far as to say she was glamorous like a beauty pageant contestant, but she was definitely very cute. And she was one of those young people who enjoyed her life and loved people. Veronica and I were in complete agreement on this. We thought Matilda was good for our son.

Paul needed someone like Matilda. At this age he was getting moody, something we attributed to his adolescence. He would be fine one day, and then the next day he would seem quiet and withdrawn.

Baseball, which used to be his joy and number-one passion, was no longer bringing him the same happiness. He still played on teams, and he was still a good player. But it was obvious that he now had things on his mind other than getting hits, stealing bases, and making double plays. When Matilda came into his life, his moods definitely improved. So what do you make of this? When Paul told us he was gay, he said he'd always been gay. I assume this included seventh grade. So now I wonder why he chose Matilda and why not some boy? Did he think he needed a girlfriend to keep us from discovering his secret? Or did he truly care for her? I think he was fond of her, just not in the way we thought.

Every winter our family would take an annual three-day trip to Big Bear to enjoy the snow. We'd always bring along one of Paul's friends, usually a kid from his baseball team. But this year, since he'd been seeing Matilda, Paul wanted to bring her instead. I guess we should've expected it, but it caught us completely off guard. It was so different, this idea of bringing along a girl and having her spend time with us in the intimate confines of a cabin. We'd be breathing the same air and sleeping under the same snow-covered roof. It would change the complexion of everything, wouldn't it? I mean, it was one thing for Paul to spend time with the girl after school and on weekends, but it was wholly another to have her living with us during our vacation. Yes, we liked her. In fact, we liked her a lot. But having her come with us to Big Bear? Veronica and I didn't know quite what to say.

We weren't alone. I turned out that Matilda's parents were also concerned. They wanted to know more about our family, and could you blame them? Sure, they knew Paul because he'd been over to their house many times, but they didn't know Veronica or me from Adam. They decided it was time for the parents to meet, and when they invited us over to their home, I said yes, absolutely, that Veronica and I would be there. A couple nights later we were standing on their doorstep beside their American flag. The flag looked even bigger up close than it did from the street, and for a moment I imagined I was back in school, holding my hand over my heart and reciting the Pledge of Allegiance. I snapped out of it and pressed the doorbell. I heard it ring inside the house, and Mrs. Manchester opened the door. "Oh, how wonderful," she said. "You must be the Ashcrofts. You must be Robert and Veronica."

"Yes," I said.

"Come in, come in," she said. "Barry will be down in a minute. He's been in the shower, and now he's getting dressed. He just got home from work, and I told him to clean up before you got here. My name is Edwina. No one likes the name Edwina, so everyone calls me Ed."

"Okay," I said, and Veronica and I stepped into the house. Ed closed the door behind us.

"What a lovely home," Veronica said, looking around at the furnishings.

"Oh, thank you."

I knew Veronica was just being polite. It wasn't that the house was shabby, or dirty, or even disorderly, because it wasn't. It was as clean as a whistle and was obviously meticulously maintained. Everything was in its intended place, dusted, polished, and wiped down. It was just kind of bizarre. I don't know how else to describe it.

"What an interesting painting," Veronica said. She was looking at a picture of a flower bouquet. It wasn't ugly, but it didn't go with any of the other furnishings. Of course, nothing went with anything here. Like I said, it was bizarre.

"That's our Jack Lord," Ed said. "It's a limited-edition serigraph."

"A serigraph?"

"A silkscreen. We bought it in Hawaii when we were there on vacation. We just fell in love with it. We had it shipped here to our house."

"It's so colorful," Veronica said.

"Isn't it?"

"Book 'em, Dano," I said, trying to be funny.

"Yes, yes," Ed said. She laughed, and her laughter made me laugh. "Barry loves that show. Oh, yes, he just loves that show. Jack Lord is one of his favorite actors of all time. They told us all about him when we bought the serigraph. He's such an interesting man. Did you know they were planning to have Jack play Captain Kirk on *Star Trek*?"

"I didn't know that," I said, and I tried to imagine Steve McGarrett on the bridge of the *Enterprise*. It wasn't working for me.

"Can I get you something to drink? A glass of wine? A bottle of beer? A soft drink?"

"A beer would be good," I said.

"If you have any chardonnay, I'll have a splash," Veronica said.

"I think we have that. Follow me. Let's go to the kitchen."

We followed Ed to the kitchen. Like the rest of the house, the kitchen was spotless. There was a hunk of soft cheese and some crackers on the counter, and Ed told us to help ourselves. "Help yourselves," she said. "Please, help yourselves."

"Thank you," I said.

"Ah, there they are," Barry said. "There they are." He was walking into the kitchen. His hair was still wet from the shower.

In case you haven't already figured it out, Barry and Ed both had a habit of saying things twice. Who knows how they picked up this habit. I noticed it right away. It took a while for Veronica to notice, but once she caught on, she looked over at me every time one of them did it. I didn't laugh, but it was kind of funny.

"Here, sweetheart," Ed said, and she handed her husband a beer.

"So you're Paul's parents," Barry said.

"Yes," I said.

"He's a good kid, good kid. We like Paul a lot."

"That's good to hear. We like Matilda too."

"They're both good kids."

"Yes," I agreed.

"So," Barry said seriously. He wasn't going to beat around the bush. "What's this about our daughter going with your family to Big Bear?"

"Paul would like her to come," Veronica said.

"I see."

"The kids kind of sprung this on us."

"Yes, I see."

"Obviously, we need to think about it."

"So is this idea is okay with you?" Barry asked. "I just want to understand where you stand."

Veronica and I looked at each other. Then I looked at Barry and said, "We like your daughter a lot."

"So that's a yes?"

"I guess it is," I said. "I mean, I don't know. It would be nice if she came. I think the kids would have a good time."

"A good time, a good time."

"Of course, you'll have to trust us to look after your daughter."

"Can I show you something?" Barry asked.

"Of course," I said.

"Wait right here." Barry walked out of the room and then came back with a glass jar. "I want you to look at this."

"Okay," I said, and I looked at the jar. Inside was a small piece of jagged metal about the size of a quarter.

"Did you go to Vietnam?" Barry asked me. The question caught me a little off guard.

"I didn't. I missed it by a year."

"You were lucky."

"Yes, I was. Did you go?" The answer to this was obvious, but I asked anyway.

"One year in country."

"How old were you?"

"I was eighteen. It was the worst year of my life."

"I heard it was bad."

"It was hell on earth. Do you know what this is?" Barry was now shaking the glass jar so that the piece of metal rattled inside.

"I don't," I said.

"It's the shrapnel our family doctor removed from my thigh three months after I'd returned to the States. I caught it in my leg two months into my tour of duty. The field medic said he'd removed it, and he sewed my leg up and sent me back into action. For ten months I had this damn thing in my leg, and do you know where it was? It was lodged right up against my femoral artery like a knife. Our doctor here in the States said it was a miracle this thing didn't work its way into the artery. Do you know what would've happened if it had cut the artery? I probably would've bled to death. No doubt about it; it would've been a disaster. But did that medic care? No, his job was to patch us boys up, tell us not to be pussies, and shove us back into action. And into action for what, to kill people who just wanted their independence? Didn't we once go to war to secure our own independence? You want to know what my dad said to me when I was drafted? He believed what he was told. He said, 'You'll be in good hands. They'll look after you. They'll take good care of you.' It's a miracle I lived through that nightmare, and it was no thanks to the US military. Do you know why I have that American flag at our front porch? It isn't because I love our government or it's military. No, not at all. It's there to show my support for all the young people the military puts in harm's way while telling gullible parents that they'll look after their kids. Sure, they'll look after them, just like they looked after me, marching me around that jungle with a piece of shrapnel against my artery. Bastards, all of them. Bastards and liars. Sew them up and push them back into action. Now when I hear someone tell me that they'll look after one of my daughters, I have to wonder, am I being told the truth, or am I being lied to again? It's a nice thing to say, that you'll look after another man's child. But do you really mean it? Do you have any skin in the game? And will you really take full responsibility for doing all it entails?"

I wasn't sure what to say to Barry. Clearly the man had serious issues with trusting others.

"We'll look after Matilda in the same way as we look after Paul," Veronica said.

"Will you?"

"We will," I said.

"Help me here," Barry said to his wife.

"They seem honest to me," Ed said.

"They do, they do," Barry said.

"And they've raised a nice boy. Paul is a good boy, so they must've been doing something right."

"Something right," Barry said, thinking this over as if this wasn't the first time he'd thought about it. Then to me he said, "It's hell, you know. You want your kids to be independent, yet you don't want to let them out of the house. The world can be such an ugly and dangerous place. Yet it's the only world we've got. And I can't very well keep our daughters at my side for the rest of their lives, can I?"

"No," I said.

"I think we should let her go to Big Bear," Ed said. "It's only for three days."

Ed set the jar with the shrapnel down on the kitchen counter, and

Barry looked into my eyes. "Ed is usually right about these kinds of things," he said. "She has good intuition. So, yes, goddamn it, Matilda has my permission to go with you to Big Bear. So long as I have your word that you'll take care of her."

"You have my word," I said. I said it emphatically, like I was taking an oath.

What was wrong with me? Do you see what just happened here? Before Veronica and I came over, we were wondering if we even wanted Matilda to come along, and now I was giving my word to her father that I'd look after her. Or what? What would this war veteran do to me if something happened to his beloved daughter? I didn't even want to think about it. The guy probably knew how to kill a man with his bare hands as easily as he could crack his knuckles or tie a shoe.

But there we were just a couple of weeks after this meeting, the four of us in my car and driving to Big Bear. Veronica and I were in the front, and the kids were in the back. When we arrived at the cabin, we all got out and carried our suitcases inside. The first thing the kids wanted to do was hike outdoors through all the snow and pine trees. Who could blame them? Didn't we come there to enjoy the mountains? But all I could think of was the promise I'd made to Matilda's father. Hiking seemed like a great thing to do, but what if the kids got lost? What if they went too far and couldn't find their way back, and what if a storm blew in? It would be just my luck to lose them in a blizzard. I could see them freezing to death, shivering until their teeth chattered, eating pine needles to keep their stomachs full, and getting frostbitten toes, fingers, and noses. How the hell would I ever explain all *that* to Matilda's father?

"We'll be back in a couple hours," Paul said.

"Don't wander off too far."

"I'll have dinner ready at six," Veronica said.

"We'll be back before then."

They left, and they were gone a little over an hour. Of course, they found their way back. But that's not to say I didn't worry the whole time they were gone. And it will give you some idea of what this vacation was like for me. I spent almost the whole time fretting over things I wouldn't have thought twice about if Paul had just been with one of his male buddies. Except this trip involved Barry Manchester's daughter. Veronica told me to relax, but all I could think about was that piece of metal shrapnel in Barry's jar, the American flag on his porch, and what Barry would do to me with his bare hands if something happened to his daughter.

Veronica and I spent our last night in the cabin, with a fire in the fireplace and an episode of *American Idol* on the TV. A couple hours had passed since we'd returned from dinner out, and the kids were upstairs. Veronica was sitting upright on the sofa, and I was laying with my head in her lap. A commercial came on, and I turned down the TV volume. "It's awful quiet up there," I said. "What do you think they're doing?"

"I'm sure they're fine," Veronica said.

"I think it's too quiet."

"Honestly, you worry so much."

"I'm going to go check on them."

"They're probably asleep. They've been up since five this morning. If they're sleeping, leave them be."

"I don't think they're sleeping. I'm going to check on them."

"Go ahead."

"You never know with kids," I said. "They need to know we're keeping an eye on them, or they'll think they can get away with anything."

I stood up from the sofa and walked to the staircase. I then climbed the stairs to the hall above. I looked in Matilda's bedroom, but she wasn't there. Then I looked in Paul's bedroom, and they weren't there either. I heard some giggling coming from the bathroom, but the bathroom door was closed. Jesus, the bathroom? What the hell were they doing in the bathroom? I walked to down the hall and opened the door.

That should have been my first clue, right? As you know, I've been racking my brain over the past two days, trying to recall what I missed. There had to be clues. A boy isn't gay for thirty years of his life without leaving a clue or two, or three. What kind of father was I? How did I overlook it all? I was like Inspector Cousteau, a bumbling idiot, a moron's moron, tripping over evidence right and left, yet not seeing the truth until it got dumped in my lap. Idiot, idiot, idiot! I honestly don't know what I was thinking.

So what did I find in the bathroom? Paul and Matilda were standing in front of the mirror. Matilda's makeup case was sitting open on the counter, and she was putting the finishes touches on Paul's face.

He was a girl! Well, he wasn't actually a girl, but Matilda had made up his face with her mascara, eyeliner, rouge, lipstick, and whatever else girls use. It was eerie. It was really strange. He didn't look like a boy with makeup on. He actually looked like a young and attractive girl. Put him in a dress with a wig, and he could've fooled anyone.

"What the hell?" I said.

"What do you think?" Matilda asked. "Isn't he gorgeous!"

Paul laughed. "Judging by the look on his face, I don't think my dad wants a daughter."

"What's going on up here?" Veronica asked. She had climbed the stairs. She was in the hall, trying to see over my shoulder.

"See for yourself," I said. I moved out of her way, so she could see Paul.

"Oh, my," Veronica said.

"Isn't he gorgeous?" Matilda asked.

"He's beautiful," Veronica said.

I don't remember what I did after that. I don't think I said anything. I think I just sighed and went downstairs to watch the rest of our *American Idol* show. Veronica stayed with the kids for a few minutes. I could hear them talking and laughing. Seeing Paul this way didn't seem to bother her at all. "They were just having fun," she told me when she finally came downstairs. "Don't be such a stick in the mud."

I guess they *were* having fun.

But I had it all wrong, didn't I? What an idiot I'd been. All this time I was worried about Matilda, when it was Paul I should've been worried about. Chalk one up for me, the clueless father.

The Return of Frankie McGuire

S igmund Freud wrote, "Dreams are often most profound when they seem the most crazy."

I feel asleep early last night. For some reason I was exhausted, and I passed out on the couch at about nine. At ten-thirty Veronica woke me up, and we went to the bedroom. I slept soundly until early this morning when the craziest dream woke me up. I got out of bed and put on my bathrobe. Now I'm sitting at the kitchen table eating a sandwich and washing it down with a tall glass of cold milk. I haven't made a sandwich like this for myself for years. When I was in my forties and fifties, I often had trouble sleeping, and you would find me up late at night in the kitchen making a sandwich like this. I was a bathrobe-clad incarnation of the Sunday funnies' Dagwood Bumstead piling everything onto my sandwich except for our family dog. I've never been very handy in the kitchen, but I'm an expert at making these sandwiches.

I look at the clock on the wall, and it's three-forty. I sigh and take a bite of my sandwich. Before I tell you about my dream, I should preface the dream by recalling a conversation I recently had with Veronica. This was before Paul broke his news to us about being gay. Veronica and I were eating dinner in our home, and I'm not sure what came over me that night. I swallowed my meatloaf and said, "I'm not leaving any fingerprints."

"Fingerprints on what?" Veronica asked, laughing a little. "Did you commit a crime?"

"That's not what I mean. I'm not talking about those kinds of fingerprints."

"Then what are you talking about."

"Fingerprints," I said.

"Fingerprints on what?"

"On anything. On anything at all. Proof that I've been here. Proof that I've made some sort of contribution to the world. Proof that I've existed."

"Of course you've made a contribution."

"Have I really?"

"Think of all the cars you've sold. Think of all your happy customers, cruising around in their brand-new cars, washing them, filling them with gas."

"That's hardly making a mark on the world."

"We all do our share," she said. "That's the way it works."

"Maybe we do. But what will I actually leave behind when I die? After my heart stops beating, after I've been pronounced dead, and after my body has been buried, no one will even know I was here. I'll have been plucked from the world of the living, and it will be like removing a grain of sand from the beach."

"What is it that you want?"

"I want to be remembered. I want to be well-known for something other than selling cars. I want to leave behind my fingerprints. You know, maybe I should've stuck with architecture. My father has left pieces of himself over the years that are sewn indelibly into the physical world, real things made of wood, concrete, and glass. That has to be a wonderful feeling, knowing that the world will go on living in your buildings, walking in your gardens, and mending your roofs. But me? What will remain of me? It's like I am invisible. So I sold some cars. Or maybe even a whole lot of cars. That hardly qualifies as any kind of legacy."

"But you hated architecture."

"Maybe I did, but what did I actually hate? I think I hated paying my dues. I was never really an architect. I was a young man learning a trade, doing the grunt work, and climbing the ladder. I think I may have given up too soon. I only got my foot on the first rung. I didn't really give architecture a chance, did I? Not really. I never got to play ball. I quit because I didn't like to practice, but maybe if I'd stuck it out and played a few actual games, I would've loved it like my father did. And then I would've had a chance to leave my mark. Or forget architecture for a moment. It didn't have to be architecture. It could've been something else. Maybe I should've become something completely different, like a writer, or musician, or some other kind of artist."

"An artist?"

"Think of it, Veronica. Think what amazing lives they lead. They leave behind *huge* fingerprints, don't they? They leave behind whole handprints. They leave behind all sorts of books, poems, paintings, sculptures, symphonies, popular songs, and even a few gaudy serigraphs. They live on forever in libraries, museums, and concert halls. They live on people's walls, on their bookshelves, and in their LP collections. We know who these people are, and we will always know. With only the slightest effort, you can pick up a book written by an ancient author and be transported to his specific universe of thoughts, plots, characters, dialogues, and settings like the ink on his paper hasn't even dried. You can wade through the waters of his life, smell his air, and feel his seasons. He is immortal in a way. He will never die. He is interesting, and he is always alive. But me? I sell cars for a living. My mark on the world can be described accurately as 'Who gives a shit?' When I die, you may as well chisel these four words on my headstone right below the years I wasted my time being alive.

Veronica was listening to me patiently, eating her own meatloaf. She swallowed and then spoke. "You're forgetting one thing," she said.

"Am I?"

"You are forgetting one very important fingerprint you will be leaving behind. I'm talking about your mark on the world. I'm talking about *your* immortality."

"And, it is?"

"It's your son."

The blood rushed from my head. Of course, there was Paul! It was so obvious. He was *my* mark on the world. I'd raised him from the day he was swaddled in a blanket and scrubbed clean by the nurses at the hospital. How could I have forgotten my own boy? He was *my* fingerprint, living, breathing, and making his way through the world as large as life, all 98.6 degrees of him.

I guess that made me feel better. Yes, it did make me feel a lot better. But now to the dream. I take another bite from my sandwich. I chew it up and wash it down with the milk.

You know, I'm taking a risk here. The truth is that listening to another talk about a dream he had can be brutally boring business. Whenever someone tells me, "I had the strangest dream last night," I always buckle my seatbelt and prepare myself to be bored to tears. But you've gotten to know me now, and you know something about my situation. In light of this, I think you'll find my recollection of this particular dream to be entertaining. Maybe even a little revealing. Or maybe a lot revealing. And maybe you'll even hear elements of this dream that can be applied to your own life. That would be ideal, wouldn't it? Maybe this entire very personal story is relevant to your own life.

It began while I was at work, while I was standing in the showroom, watching a man look at one of our cars. I was the only salesman on duty, so I took my time before approaching the man. There was no need to beat anyone to the punch. I was letting him look at the car on his own, letting him get his feet wet. He opened the driver's door, and he climbed into the car, sitting in the driver's seat. He took a deep breath through his nose to experience that new-car smell. Then he held onto the steering wheel with both hands and pretended he was driving, looking through the windshield, and then at the dashboard to see how fast he was going. I stepped up to introduce myself. "My name is Robert," I said, and I reached for a handshake. The man grasped my hand. I remember he had long, slender fingers, kind of creepy.

"I'm Harmon," he said.

It was funny; he looked very familiar, but I'd never known anyone by the name of Harmon. I rolled the name around in my mind, thinking, *Harmon, Harmon, Harmon.* No, there was no Harmon in my memories, and I was usually pretty good at remembering names. I was drawing a blank. I'll describe this guy for you, and maybe you'll be able to place him. He had a very gentle face and fine, brown hair. His nose was pointy but crooked, as though it had been broken some time ago. He had pale green eyes, thin lips, and a string of small pearls for teeth. He didn't look anything like a woman, but he was strangely effeminate. "I'm looking for a sports car like this," he said. "In fact, I want to buy two of them. This exact model. I want one car to be red and the other yellow."

"Who are they for?" I asked.

"They're for my daughters. They're identical twins. They're turning sixteen this month."

"I see."

"I want to surprise them."

"A new car like this is a nice surprise."

"It's not like I can't afford it."

"Of course not."

"Can you get the colors I need?"

"I can get you any color you want."

"The colors are important. I want to match the colors of their hair. One is a golden blonde, and the other is a redhead."

"I thought you said they were identical twins."

"They dye their hair. They want people to be able to tell them apart. They've been dying their hair since they were eight."

"What are their names?"

"Rachael."

"Just Rachael?"

"We gave each of them the same name. You know, since they were identical twins, we thought they ought to have an identical name. Since then, we've come to the conclusion that might have been a mistake."

"Yes," I said.

"But our hearts were in the right place."

"I'm sure they were."

"So when can I pick up the cars?"

"How does tomorrow morning sound?"

"I play tennis in the mornings."

"How about the afternoon?"

"Not sure what's on my schedule. Can you just deliver them to me?"

"I can probably do that."

"I'll write my name and address down on this piece of paper. I live about twenty minutes from here."

He handed me a small piece of paper, and I looked it over. "It says here that your first name is Howard," I said.

"That's right. Is there a problem?"

"You told me your name was Harmon."

"Did I? I wonder why I did that. My name is Howard. I certainly ought to know my own name."

"Howard it is," I said.

"What's your name again?" he asked me.

"I'm Robert," I said.

"Ah, Robert. That's a nice name. I had a German shepherd named Robert. We had to put him to sleep."

"I'm sorry," I said.

"No need to apologize. He was a terrible dog. Peed on everything we owned. Made our house smell like a kennel."

"They say vinegar gets the smell out."

"We tried that. It made our house smell like vinegar. It was like living in an Italian salad. I think I liked the dog urine better."

Just then my sales manager at the time, Roger Burke, appeared from around a corner. I stopped him, so he could say hi to my customer. "This is Mr. Burke, our sales manager," I said to Howard. Howard smiled and reached out to shake Roger's hand.

"Pleasure to meet you, sir," Howard said.

"Good to meet you."

"I'm going to buy two cars. They're for my daughters, for their birthdays."

"That's great. I hope Robert is taking care of you. What did you say your name was?"

"My name is Gilbert."

"Gilbert?" I said, interrupting the two men. "I thought your name was Howard."

"Where on earth did you get that idea?"

"Isn't that what you told me?"

"Why would I tell you my name is Howard when my name is Gilbert?"

"The customer is always right," Roger said, putting his hand on my shoulder. "If the man says his name is Gilbert, then we'll call him Gilbert."

"That's right," Gilbert said. "The customer is always right." Roger and Gilbert suddenly laughed like they were privy to an inside joke.

"I gotta run," Roger said. "Keep up the good work, Robert. Make our friend happy."

"I'll do my best," I said.

"I almost forgot," Gilbert said to me. "I have two birthday cards that I want you to put in the cars. One goes in Cynthia's car, and the other goes in Rebecca's."

"Who are Cynthia and Rebecca?" I asked.

"They're my daughters."

"I thought they were both named Rachael."

Gilbert laughed and said, "Why would I give them the same name? There'd be no way to tell them apart. Didn't I tell you they were identical twins? Besides, I don't even like the name Rachael. I knew a girl back in high school who was named Rachael. She spit in my milk carton during lunch when I wasn't looking. Everyone knew about it except for me, and I drank the whole thing. One of the kids told me about it after school, and I nearly puked. Has anyone ever spit in your drink or food?"

"Not that I know of."

"It's really gross."

"I can imagine."

"I used to get picked on a lot in high school. Maybe you remember me?"

"You do look familiar."

"They called me a fag, a fairy, a weirdo."

"I'm sorry."

"You keep apologizing for things. You don't have to apologize. My life has turned out fine. Those high school days are far behind me. Now I'm a very wealthy man. You should see where I live. And you should see my wife. She's gorgeous."

"I'm sure she is."

"She's sixteen years younger than me."

"Wow," I said.

"My daughters take after their mother. They're the best-looking girls at their high school. The other girls at school all wish they looked like them, and the boys all want to go out with them. They're both planning on marrying medical doctors or lawyers. They're going to be secure, happy, and admired. Do you have any kids?"

"I have a son."

"What's his name?"

"We named him Paul."

"How old is he?"

"He's thirty."

"Is he married?"

"Not yet."

"He's probably fighting the girls off, am I right? He's waiting for just the right one? You know, you want to make sure he's using condoms."

"We've had that talk."

"I wish I had a son."

"Kids are kids," I said.

"Not really. A son could've carried on my name. A son could've completed my legacy. With a son, I could've put my fingerprint on the world. My unique fingerprint and no one else's."

"I understand that."

"Of course you do. You're a father, right? All fathers understand that. All fathers are acutely aware of fingerprints."

"But what if one's son is, well, different?"

"Different?"

"What if a father's son is gay?"

"Gay? Are you kidding? Don't even think that way. That would be the worst thing ever. I can't even imagine it. No, no, never."

"Damn!" I exclaimed. Now I know who you are. Your name isn't Harmon, or Howard, or Gilbert. I'd recognize your voice anywhere. I have no idea why it took me so long to figure this out."

"And just who do you think I am?"

"You're Frankie," I said. "You're Frankie McGuire."

"Are you sure about that?"

"I'm positive."

"I owe you something," Frankie said.

"You do?"

"It's been a long time coming."

What happened next took me completely by surprise. It was completely unexpected. Frankie cocked his arm back and let his fist fly directly into my face in one head-spinning motion. He hit me right in the nose! "So, how does that feel?" he asked. My face throbbed like I'd been hit with a frying pan, and blood began to spurt from my nostrils. And that's when I woke up. Veronica said it sounded like I was crying in my sleep, but I doubted it. I was not a crier. No, goddamn it, I was not a crier.

I told you the dream was crazy. And it was weird how the last two nights I had such detailed recollections of my dreams. But back to my sandwich. I have put on too many pickles. I lift up the bread and peel three of the pickles off. I drop them into the sink, turn on the water, and run the garbage disposer. There's an art to making and eating these sandwiches, and I'll admit to being a little out of practice. Too many pickles? That was definitely a rookie mistake.

Summer Friends

When Paul turned fifteen, we were very concerned. He was no longer seeing Matilda, who Veronica and I both thought was so good for him, and he also stopped playing baseball. We could understand Matilda in a way, but baseball? For years baseball had been his passion. It seemed to us that he abandoned the two things that had been bringing most of the joy to his life.

So, if he wasn't playing baseball with his friends or spending time with Matilda, what *did* he do? His new path took us completely by surprise. Looking back, I can put my finger right on the date Paul changed his life, and it was Miss Newcomb who had really gotten the ball rolling. She was Paul's ninth grade creative writing teacher, and she gave Paul his first A+. It was his first A+ ever, in any grade, and in any class. She gave him the mark for a short story he wrote about a boy his age who lost his dog to cancer, a subject about which he knew nothing. True, we had a dog, a Boston terrier named Lucy, who we brought home from the pet store when Paul was ten. But Lucy never had cancer, and Paul never was very close to her. He liked her, but it was hard to imagine him falling apart over losing her. But this story he wrote? It was amazing. It was a real tearjerker.

The second short story Paul wrote for this class also earned him an A+. It was about a teenage boy whose parents were getting divorced. Again, Paul had no real-life experience with divorces, but he wrote the story as though he was right there with his main character, being pulled apart by the parents in a selfish and contentious divorce. When I read this story, I was amazed at what our son could do with words, and I was impressed with his insights into complex human relationships and emotions. His writing was quite good, on par with published authors ten or twenty years his senior. If you'd asked me a year earlier if our son had any talent as a writer, I would've slapped my knee and laughed out loud. Our son, Paul? A writer? Maybe when hell froze over. But the kid could write. If you lived anywhere near hell, it was time to buy a pair of ice skates.

I remember when Veronica and I sat down with Paul for a Sunday dinner a month or so after he received his second A+. Paul told us his plans. He wasn't the slightest bit shy about it, and he wasn't asking for our approval. He was simply telling us what he was going to be. "I'm going to be a writer," he said.

"I liked reading both of your stories," I said. "They were quite good."

"I liked them too," Veronica said.

"What suddenly made you want to be a writer?"

"I don't know," Paul said.

"I don't remember you ever wanting to write when you were younger. In fact, you always seemed to hate writing assignments. Something must have changed and inspired you."

"I don't know how to explain it. When I sat down to write that first story for Miss Newcomb's class, the words just poured out of me. It was like I was in a ballgame and hitting one home run after the other. Every time I stepped up to the plate, I just knew I was going to hit it over the fence, over and over again, every letter, word, sentence, and paragraph, right over the outfield fence."

"That's talent," I said to Veronica.

Then Paul really surprised us. "I'm going to write a whole novel," he said. "I'm not going to waste my time with any more of these short stories."

"A novel?"

"That's quite an undertaking," Veronica said.

"I have it all mapped out in my head. It's just a matter of typing it onto my keyboard."

"What's it going to be about?" I asked.

"Do you really want to know?"

"Of course I do."

"Same here," Veronica said. "What are you going to write about?"

"It's going to be about two friends, a pair of boys about my age who, once upon a time, became friends during their summer vacation. I'm going to title the book, *Summer Friends*."

"The title makes sense," I said.

"These two boys were never friendly in school. They had little to do with each other. One boy socialized with all the popular kids, while the other boy was studious but kind of a social outcast. The book is going to be written in the first person by the more studious boy. I figured this made the most sense, since it would be unlikely that a less studious boy would ever write a novel."

"That does make sense," I said.

"How did the boys meet?" Veronica asked.

"They lived in the same neighborhood. In fact, they lived six houses down from each other."

"But how did they meet?"

"I'm getting to that. The more popular kid was Andy Pratt, and the other kid was Nigel Chatsworth. Andy had two older sisters, while Nigel was an only child. They were the same height, although Andy had a more athletic build. Nigel was an odd-looking boy, with a large nose; small, dark eyes; and a head full of perpetually unkempt brown hair. Andy, on the other hand, was handsome with green eyes, a smattering of freckles, and neatly trimmed red hair. You asked how they met, and the fact was that they always knew each other. After all, they lived on the same street. It was just that they weren't friends. I guess you could have called them acquaintances."

"Then how did they become friends?"

"It was during the summer after their freshman year that they become pals. This friendship began on an afternoon when Andy was in his front yard with nothing to do, throwing a football up in the air and catching it. Nigel was riding by on his bicycle, and he noticed Andy in his front yard. He turned his head to look at him, and when their eyes met, he smiled. He took one hand off his handlebars to wave, not paying attention to where he was going. Then *wham!* He crashed right into a parked car. He went flying off the bike and onto the hood of the car. Nigel was terribly humiliated by this blunder, but rather than laugh at Nigel's mishap, Andy ran over to see if he could help."

"So then what happened?"

"Andy asked Nigel if he was okay, and Nigel told him not to worry about it. Andy picked up the bicycle and set it on the sidewalk while Nigel checked his body for cuts and scrapes. 'Do you want to play a little catch with the football?' Andy asked. 'I'm getting tired of throwing it to myself.' Nigel looked at Andy, and then he said, 'I'd like that.' So they went to Andy's front yard and threw the ball back and forth for a while, talking and laughing about some of the students and teachers they both knew at school. And that's how their friendship began, tossing that ball and talking."

"It sounds like you've already thought a lot about this," I said.

"I've got the whole thing in my head. Like I said, it's just a matter of typing it up."

It's one thing you could say about Paul, that when he set his mind to do something, he gave it his all. For days, then weeks, then months, he hunkered down in his room at his computer, typing page after page of this remarkable novel. If you've ever lived with a writer, then you'll know what I'm talking about when I say that Paul was off in another world. You could talk to him, but he wouldn't really be paying attention to you. All he could think about was his story and what was happening in it. Veronica and I both felt at times that it was getting out of hand. The kid seldom showered and often wore the same clothes days in a row. He never combed his hair, and sometimes he skipped his meals. He ignored his chores and his schoolwork. It was like pulling teeth just to get him to do anything other than write, but we were patient. Despite all his rather annoying behaviors, we were glad to see him so dedicated to something constructive. And he did seem happy, like he was doing something he wanted to do.

I asked him several times during all this if I could read what he'd written, but his answer was always no. He didn't want me to read any of it until I could sit down and read the whole thing. So I waited and I waited. When he finally finished the novel, he was sixteen. He was now old enough to get a license and drive a car, but he couldn't have cared less. What did he want? He wanted to get his novel published.

He wanted others to read it and tell him what they thought. He wanted people to read from cover to cover and tell him, "This is the most amazing thing I've ever read!"

Veronica and I were the very first to read it. Paul emailed his writing file to a printer and had them run off a couple paper copies for us. I remember sitting at the dining room table and reading page after page of Paul's manuscript. It took me a couple of days to finish it. So what did I think of the thing? Did I think it was worth Paul giving up a year of his life, hunkered down in his bedroom day after day in front of his computer? Before I give you my opinion of the manuscript, I'll tell you about my favorite chapter. I think it epitomizes the rest of the book.

Paul titled all his chapters, and the title of this chapter was Free Ice Cream. When I read it, it really made me laugh. Much of it reminded me of my own childhood. The chapter began with Andy and Nigel riding their bikes on a hot summer day, not necessarily going anywhere. They were just riding around, the way kids do. They found themselves in a small shopping center, and in the shopping center was a free-standing Dairy Queen. Around the side of the Dairy Queen, some construction work was being done, and a part of this construction work involved installing new concrete sidewalks. The boys wheeled up to the construction work. All the workmen had apparently gone home for the day. They had put up some yellow caution tape to keep people out of the construction area. "Do you see what I see?" Andy asked Nigel.

"See what?"

"The sidewalks."

"What about them?"

"The concrete is still wet. They must've just poured them."

"I see them," Nigel said.

"Are you thinking what I'm thinking?"

"I don't know. I mean, I don't think I know what you're thinking."

"Do you see anything sharp around? Like a nail or a stick?"

"There's a box of nails," Nigel said. He pointed to the box sitting in the shade.

"Oh, man," Andy said. "It's like they're just asking for it."

"Asking for what?"

"For us to write something in their concrete."

"We're going to write in their concrete?"

"Do you see anyone around to stop us?"

Nigel looked around and then he looked at Andy. "I don't see anyone."

"Grab me one of those nails."

Nigel set his bike down and walked to the box of nails. He removed a nail and handed it to Andy, who was now kneeling in front of the wet concrete. "What are we going to write?"

"I don't know."

"Maybe we shouldn't do this."

"Don't wuss out on me, Nigel."

"I was just saying."

"We could write our names. Not our last names, of course, but our first names."

"Someone might still be able to figure out who we are. How many kids around here are named Nigel?"

"Then how about our initials?" Andy said.

"I still don't like this."

"I'll write your initials for you. If we get caught, you can say you didn't do it. And it wouldn't be a lie. You keep guard. Let me know right away if you see anyone coming."

"Okay," Nigel said.

Andy proceeded to write the initials into the wet concrete with the nail while Nigel kept his eyes open. "Take a look," Andy said.

"Oh, wow," Nigel said. "You made them so big. I didn't think you were going to write so big."

"Now we're famous."

"Well, we're something."

Suddenly, and at first for no apparent reason, Andy began rubbing over the initials with the palm of his hand, smearing them back into the wet concrete. Out of the corner of his eye, he had seen a workman approaching. Nigel then saw the same man as second or so later, and his first inclination was to jump on his bike and ride away. But he stayed there with Andy. "What the hell do you boys think you're doing?" the man asked.

"We're cleaning up your sidewalk," Andy said.

"You're what?"

"We saw some kids over here. It looked like they were writing something into your concrete. After they left, we came over to see what they wrote."

"And what did they write?"

"Their initials, it looked like. I was trying to rub them out."

"Spoiled little brats," the man said, referring to Andy's imaginary kids.

"Yes, sir," Andy said.

"What's your names?" the man asked.

"My name is Andy, and this is my friend, Nigel."

"You're a couple of good eggs," the man said.

"Sir?"

"I've got a couple of boys of my own. They're a few years younger than you, but I always try to teach them to do the right thing. It's not easy, with all the idiots in the world these days, running around and behaving so badly, setting so many bad examples. You must have good parents. I'll bet they'd be proud of you. I'll tell you what I'm going to do. Do you boys like ice cream?"

"Sure we do."

The man reached into his back pocket and removed his wallet. He then took out several dollars and handed them to Andy. "Go into the Dairy Queen here and buy yourselves a couple of chocolate-dipped ice-cream cones. That ought to hit the spot."

I was by myself in our dining room, but I laughed out loud when I read this chapter. What a great little tale Paul had created from his imagination! Or maybe he didn't make it up at all. Maybe it was something that actually happened to him, something he never told us about. Who knew with kids? Anyway, everyone walked away happy. No harm, no foul.

The rest of Paul's book was filled with many similar stories. It was great piece of nostalgic writing from top to bottom. Well, except for the very bottom. The ending to Paul's novel really surprised me, and I didn't like it. It seemed like a shame to write such an upbeat book, only to drive it right into a brick wall. The ending made me worry a little about my son. I thought you could tell a lot about a writer by the way he ended his stories. If only I'd had a little more insight.

When Veronica read the ending, she said, "Oh my God, this is a love story." I had no idea what she was talking about. It was just the sort of stupid thing a woman would say, and I ignored it. To my way of thinking, the story had little to do with love and more to do with two boys who were just friends. Lots of boys were friends, right? So what *did* happen at the end? I'll tell you. When the boys' high school started back up in fall, Andy was immediately faced with peer pressure from his old social circle of friends. He gave into the pressure and snubbed Nigel. He kept his distance from the boy and had nothing to do with him. He wouldn't even say hi when they passed in the halls. This sudden change of heart was more than Nigel could bear, and one afternoon after school he went into his bedroom closet and hung himself with his belt from the clothes pole. When he parents found him, he was stone cold dead. Can you believe it? *That's* where Paul ended the book, with Nigel's parents undoing the belt around his neck and laying his corpse on his bed. Summer was over, and so was Nigel.

Following the date Paul completed his novel, the rush was on to get it published. He must have contacted near to a hundred publishers and agents, sending out letters and sample chapters from the book. This went on for months, and then the replies started coming in. Sadly, not a single publisher or agent anywhere in the country was interested in Paul's novel. It was awful. Paul fell into a depression, and for months he just sat on the family room sofa eating potato chips or cookies and watching TV. Veronica and I had no idea what we should do. We tried to talk to him, but it was like talking to an empty room. We finally convinced him to see a psychiatrist, and the time Paul spent with his shrink was a story unto itself. I remember thinking I should've sent Miss Newcomb an invoice to reimburse us for the cost of the sessions. Without the A+ on that first short story, none of this would ever have happened. Anyway, that's how I saw things then.

This morning I was having breakfast with Veronica at our kitchen table. There was a pot of coffee in the middle of the table for us to share. I was having a bowl of Captain Crunch and milk and a couple slices of toast with butter. Veronica was having a soft-boiled egg and a half of a grapefruit. I brought up the subject of Paul's short-lived career as a writer. Veronica stuck her spoon into her grapefruit and said something interesting. She said it wasn't the act of writing that had caused Paul so much distress. I had always blamed the novel, but she said he was headed for trouble years earlier. Not months earlier, but years earlier. She also said, "When I first read that novel, I suspected Paul was gay."

"Why didn't you say something?" I asked.

She replied, "Because you wouldn't have been able to handle it."

She was probably right. And she was probably right when she said the novel was a love story. I have a copy of the old manuscript here at our house. I remember coming across it while organizing the garage, when we first moved here. It's in a cardboard box that hasn't been opened for fifteen years.

I think for a moment and wonder, *Should I get the box and read the manuscript again?* I might see things differently, knowing what I now know, but I tell myself no. Why would I want my nose rubbed in it? Sometimes it's best to just leave certain things alone, and some boxes are best left unopened.

How Wet I'll Be

When Paul was a senior in high school, he befriended a boy named Marty Michelson. We heard some bad things about Marty, primarily that he was a troublemaker. In fact, I knew of several parents who wouldn't allow their kids to have anything to do with the boy.

Veronica and I were curious, so we asked around about Marty's parents. We found out that his mom's first name was Barbara and that she divorced the father when Marty was ten. It turned out that Marty's father was one of those dumbbells who was always at odds with the law. I found out that he was serving three years for forging a check on his employer's account and trying to cash it using a stolen ID and wearing a wig and a pair of dark glasses. They say he looked nothing at all like the man on the stolen ID, and supposedly the bank teller could tell he was disguising himself because his wig was crooked. I thought the fact Barbara chose this man to be her husband said a lot about her as a person—not that she was a criminal herself, but that she had really bad taste in men. Have you even met any women like this? It's like they *want* to live with idiots.

Anyway, those were Marty's parents—a woman with bad taste in men and an idiot husband. They were not exactly what Veronica and I were hoping for. We talked about Paul getting involved with Marty and his family, and we almost stopped things. But then we decided rather than forbid Paul to see Marty, we would let the boys continue to be friends. We believed that Paul needed to learn to size people up for himself, and how was he going to do this if we interfered every time we thought he was making a wrong move? I'm sure there were those who thought we were crazy to do this, but we felt we were doing the right thing. We were trying to raise Paul into a young man who could think for himself.

I guess I wasn't all that surprised when we got a call from the Anaheim Police Department. The man who called introduced himself as Officer Jackson. It was three in the morning on a night when Marty was sleeping over at our house. Marty's mom was on a skiing trip in Mammoth with one of her ne'er-do-well boyfriends, and she had asked if Marty could stay with us over the weekend. We said okay, and to the best of our knowledge, the boys went to bed at ten. But what they actually did was to stay up until Veronica and I went to bed and then they left the house. Marty had a quart of whiskey he'd acquired from his mom's liquor supply, and the boys went to the park to drink it. It was the same park at which Paul first learned to walk, the one with the big oak trees. When Officer Jackson called, he said he had found the boys up in one of the trees, drunk and singing loudly. One of the neighbors who lived near the park heard the boys and called the police. They were singing a song Paul used to sing as a small boy. The lyrics went, "How dry I am; how wet I'll be, if I don't find the bathroom key." They sang that stupid verse over and over, like a pair of drunken mockingbirds, waking up the entire neighborhood.

The officer turned out to be a pretty nice guy. He said over the phone that he could take the boys to jail on a number of minor charges, but that he was okay with me just coming over to pick them up. He didn't want to get them in trouble with the law. I drove to the park, and by the time I got there, Officer Jackson had talked the boys down from the tree. They were no longer singing. Instead, they were sitting on one of the park benches, their hands cuffed behind their backs. "Didn't want them making a run for it," the officer said, referring to the handcuffs. He then took me aside to give some advice. "This isn't the first time I've had some trouble with Marty. I hate to say this, but the kid is kind of a bad seed. I didn't know if you knew that. Your son seems like a nice kid, and you'd probably be wise to keep him away from Marty."

"Thanks," I said.

"I don't want to tell you how to raise your boy. I'm just giving a little friendly advice."

"I understand," I said.

As I watched the officer unlock the handcuffs from the boys' wrists, I couldn't help but think back to when I was Paul's age. This incident with Paul and Marty reminded me of the first time I was caught drunk. I too was with a friend, and the boy's name was Nathan Cox. Nathan had an older brother, Mike, who was twenty-two, and we talked Mike into buying a quart of tequila for us on a Saturday night. We started drinking at around eight, and by eleven we were falling-down drunk. In between eight and eleven, we took turns drinking from our bottle and wandered around town, looking for things to do. First, we went to the movie theater, where we bought a pair of tickets and went inside. Nathan kept the tequila bottle hidden in his wadded-up jacket. I don't remember the name of the movie, but it starred Brigitte Bardot. I'd never seen her before. I remember I thought her lips were too large, but Nathan was crazy over her. Every time she appeared on the screen, he would stand up and howl like a love-starved wolf. The man seated behind us would tell Nathan to sit down and be quiet. "Sit down and shut up, you idiot," the man would say. Finally, Nathan turned around and said, "What are you, a homo?" As soon as he said this, the man stood up and Nathan realized he'd made a big mistake. This guy was twice our combined size, and we could tell from the look on his face that he planned to let us have it. Nathan looked up toward the ceiling and cupped his hand to his ear. "I think he hear my mother calling for me," he said, and he quickly made through the row of seats and out of the theater. I was right behind him. "Jeez," Nathan said to me. "You really pissed that guy off." He was kidding, of course.

After running from the man in the movie theater, we drank more tequila and walked several blocks to a little Italian restaurant. This time Nathan stashed our bottle in some bushes by the front door because keeping the bottle in his coat while trying to eat dinner would have been too difficult. We sat at a table by the window, looked over the menus, and the waitress came and took our orders. I ordered a small pizza, and Nathan ordered a jumbo seashell pasta dish. We must've been talking too loudly, because people in the restaurant were staring at us. We were both way too drunk. Nathan said to them, "Haven't any of you ever seen teenagers before?" When the waitress brought our meals, Nathan gazed at his pasta. "How much do you want to bet?" he asked.

"Bet for what?" I said.

"I bet I can eat this whole bowl of pasta without chewing any of it."

"Why would you want to do that?" I asked.

"Why not?"

"I don't know."

"I'll bet you ten bucks. If I eat this whole bowl of pasta without chewing, you owe me ten bucks."

"And if I see you chew?"

"Then I'll pay you the ten bucks."

"No gimmicks?" I said.

"No, this is fair and square. I'll swallow down the whole freaking bowl. No chewing, right down to the last jumbo seashell."

"Okay, you're on," I said. "It'll be an easy win. No one can eat a whole dinner without chewing."

Boy, was I ever wrong. I watched in awe as Nathan poked the jumbo seashells into his mouth, swallowing every spoonful without chewing. His jaw stayed perfectly still the entire time. Meanwhile, I ate my pizza. When we were done, Nathan asked the waitress for our check, and she brought it to us on a little plastic tray. Nathan picked up the bill and looked at it. "How much have you got?" he asked.

"I've got a five-dollar bill," I said.

"That's it?"

"Why?" I asked. "How much do you have?"

Nathan rummaged through his pockets and then put a few wadded dollar bills on the table. "We don't even have half of what we need."

I checked my own pockets, but I had nothing more to offer. "Five is all I have."

"Give me your five," Nathan said. I gave it to him, and he added it to his ones and made a small stack of bills. Then he placed the money on top of the check, and he slid the plastic tray to the center of the table, so it looked like we were paying. "Now we need to get out of here," he said. "Before they count it."

"What if they stop us?"

"Don't worry," Nathan said. "Just act normal, like nothing is wrong."

I looked over at the waitress, and she saw that we'd put our money in the middle of the table. She smiled at us, not knowing we were shorting her. "Excellent meal," Nathan said to her loudly. "Give our compliments to the chef." A man seated near to us rolled his eyes.

"Thanks," she said. She was obviously in a hurry. She rushed back to the kitchen to get a dinner order for another table.

"Move it," Nathan said. "Let's get out of here before she gets back." We stood up and headed for the door. I'm not sure who started it, but by the time we reached the door we were both laughing our heads off.

When we got outside, we retrieved our bottle from the bushes, and we got the hell out of there. "I guess we won't be eating there again," Nathan said.

Eventually, we wound up in a park, sitting on a bench. We were passing the bottle back and forth, finishing off the rest of the tequila. No one else was in the park, and we had the place to ourselves until two girls approached. I think they were about our age. It was hard telling for sure, because both of us were now so drunk. "Do you guys have any more booze?" one of the girls asked. Our bottle was empty, and Nathan was holding it by the neck, swinging it like a pendulum between his knees.

"This is all we had," Nathan said.

"You guys drank that whole thing?"

"We did," Nathan said, and he belched loudly,

"Do you have any money?"

"No," Nathan said. "Do you?"

"No," the girl said, and she now seemed a lot less interested in us, learning that we had no money and no booze.

"Have a seat," Nathan said, and he patted the bench with his hand.

"I think we'll pass," the girl said.

"Let's get out of here," the second girl said to the first one.

"Oh man, I think I'm in love with you," Nathan said. "Did anyone ever tell you that you look like Brigitte Bardot?"

"They're drunk," the second girl said.

The next thing we knew they were gone, and Nathan and I were by ourselves again.

Everything we did after the encounter with the girls was a blur. I remember we crossed a busy street, and someone honked a horn. I remember peeing on a fence and hearing a woman yell at me. What I don't remember is how we wound up back in my neighborhood, but that's where we were. One of my mom's friends saw us sprawled in the gutter down the street from her house as she was driving home. She called my mom, and my mom came to get us. I recall very little about the drive home, but I do remember on the way to Nathan's house, he puked all over the back seat. I remember Mom saying to me angrily, "You'll be cleaning that up in the morning, young man."

The next morning, I woke up with a horrible hangover. My eyes ached like I'd been in a fistfight, and my head was pounding like a drum. For the first hour, I must've puked five or six times. Then, when my stomach settled down, Mom gave me a roll of paper towels and a bottle of Windex. She told me to go clean her car. It was disgusting. Nathan had thrown up all over the back seat, not just in one spot, but all over the place, like he couldn't keep his head still. Since he hadn't chewed any of his jumbo seashells, the puke didn't look that much different from what he'd been served at the restaurant, except now it smelled like vomit. I tore off several paper towels, and as I did, my mom's Irish setter jumped into the car. Before I could stop her, she began licking the seat and eating the jumbo seashells. She didn't just eat a little. She gobbled it all up like she hadn't been fed for days. It was gross and funny at the same time. I knew I should've stopped her, but I really didn't want to clean up the puke myself. And I never did tell Mom what happened that morning. If I'd told her, she would've killed me. "You let her *what?*" she would've said. Sometimes I thought she loved that stupid dog more than she loved me.

Anyway, that was the first and last time I got drunk with anyone. I learned my lesson, and I never got falling-down drunk again. But now, back to Marty and Paul at the park. I put the boys in the back seat of my car. I recall thanking Officer Jackson for his patience, and I took the boys home in my car. They went directly to Paul's room to sleep. Veronica watched them stagger past her and shook her head. "How much did they drink?" she asked, and I told her it appeared that they polished off a quart of whiskey. "Good Lord," she said. "That's an awful lot of alcohol." We went back to bed when we heard Paul's bedroom door open and the bathroom door slam shut. One of the boys was throwing up, and we could hear him coughing and gagging through the wall. "I hope he's getting it in the toilet," Veronica said.

For the next hour, the doors kept opening and closing, and the toilet kept flushing. It was like trying to sleep next to a nightclub restroom. Finally, at about five in the morning, the boys fell asleep. Veronica and I woke up at seven, but we barely slept a wink. We let the boys sleep in, and they didn't come out of Paul's bedroom until two in the afternoon. Meanwhile, Marty's mom had called to see how he was doing. "I just called to be sure Marty was behaving himself," she said. I told her about what had happened at the park, and she was very upset. "I just don't know what I'm going to do with that boy," she said. "Do you want me to come and pick him up? We can leave here early, and I can be at your place in about six hours. I'm so sorry this happened."

"Don't worry about it," I said. "Boys will be boys. I think they'll be fine."

It was easy to blame that night on Marty rather than on our son. Even Officer Jackson knew about the kid. It wasn't until last year that Paul told us what actually happened. Veronica, Paul, and I were eating dinner out together at restaurant, talking about some of the dumb things we did when we were in high school. I brought up the time I got caught letting the air out of my English teacher's tires. Veronica told us about the time she put itching powder in her friend's bra and panties while she was showering in the gym. And Paul brought up the night that he and Marty got drunk and climbed the tree in the park. "That kid had problems," Veronica said. "We should have listened. We shouldn't have let you hang out with that boy."

Paul laughed at this, and Veronica asked him what was so funny. "It's funny that you would blame that night on Marty."

"Why is that funny?"

"Because the whole thing was my idea. I talked Marty into stealing the whiskey from his mom's kitchen. Marty didn't want to do it, but I wouldn't leave him alone. It was my idea to sneak out that night and go to the park, and it was my idea to climb the tree."

"Well," I said. "I'll be damned."

"He was still a first-class troublemaker," Veronica said, not wanting to let go of the idea that Paul was superior to Marty.

"You should give the guy a break," Paul said. "He wasn't really so bad. We were all just kids, and we did a lot of dumb things. All kids do dumb things, don't they? It was true that Marty got caught acting stupid more than the rest of us, but maybe he wanted to get caught. Did you think of that? He didn't have much of a dad, and his mom was always busy with her boyfriends. Maybe he just wanted someone to pay attention to him."

"I wonder what ever happened to him," I said.

"He's a car mechanic."

"You've seen him?"

"I heard it from a friend."

"Does he still live around here?"

"He has a shop in downtown Santa Ana. I heard he has three or four mechanics working for him. I guess he's doing well for himself. I mean, he's independent and has his own business."

"That's good to hear."

"Did he go to college?" Veronica asked.

"No, no," Paul said. "I think he went to a trade school."

"Have you heard anything about his mom?"

"She passed away a couple years ago from lung cancer. She was a chain-smoker."

"Too bad," I said.

I imagined someone asking Marty about Paul, the same way we were asking Paul about Marty. What would he say? Would he know anything about our son? Would a friend of a friend have filled him in? Marty would probably say, "I heard he was gay." That would kind of sum everything up, wouldn't it?

Off to College

I was proud, excited, and monstrously sad. Those are the words I'd use to describe how I felt when Paul went off to college. There are days in your life that you just never forget, and this was one of mine. I had more than one of them. There was the day Kennedy was assassinated, the day Elvis died, the day John Lennon was murdered, and the day the World Trade Center collapsed. And now there was the day Paul packed up his things and left our home. On the surface I was calm, mature, and encouraging, but beneath that well-acted and regulated exterior, I was a mess. I didn't know whether to laugh or cry. I didn't know whether to wish Paul luck and give him a firm see-you-later handshake or fall to my knees and beg him to stay a little longer. It was only an hour's drive to USC, and he could have stayed at the house and commuted. He didn't really have to live in LA, did he? But we'd all talked about this. We decided it was best for Paul to move out and live on campus where he'd be able to take part in school activities, make new friends, and hopefully meet a nice girl. It was all a part of the college experience, part of Paul growing up and becoming a man.

Fortunately, Paul would not have to face this new life in college alone. A longtime friend of his was also going to USC, and we made some calls arranged for the boys to be roommates at their dormitory. This kid's name was Jonathan Keller, and he came from a good, respectable Orange County family. His father, Burt, was a dentist who had an office in Newport Beach, where he specialized in perfecting smiles. There was a lot of money to be made providing this service, and Burt did well for himself. He only had to work three days out of the week, and he occupied the rest of his time with tennis and golf. He was fit as a teenage athlete and exercised regularly using the fully equipped gym they had added on to their house. He was always tan, and he had a smile so bright that it could light up the Grand Canyon on a moonless night. I'm not exaggerating. You practically had to wear a pair of dark glasses and a quart of sunscreen just to talk to the guy.

Burt's wife was named Molly, and she too had a perfect smile. But she was also one of those women who had spent too many hours of her youth in the sun, and the rays had done a number on her skin. Even though they were close to the same age, she looked ten or fifteen years older than Burt because of all her wrinkles. And she still sunbathed on a regular basis despite the damage the sun had done to her skin, figuring, I guess, that a tan and wrinkled face looked better than a pasty one. She always wanted to look her best for Burt. She was a dental hygienist, and she was Burt's second wife. Burt divorced his first wife to marry Molly six months after she was hired to work in his office. She still worked for Burt, but not because she needed any extra money. It was more likely that she was afraid Burt would run off with whoever he hired to replace her.

Burt and Molly had two children. Of course, there was Jonathan, but they also had a daughter named Sheri. The girl was two years older than Jonathan, and everyone said she looked like Molly without the wrinkles. Sheri also went to USC, where she was studying to become a registered nurse. She wasn't really all that interested in nursing, but she was interested in meeting doctors. Her dream was to marry a wealthy surgeon and become his wife. If a college degree was required to make this happen, then by God, she would go to college. I know I'm making her out to sound shallow, but actually she was a very nice girl. I'd only met her a couple of times, but I liked her a lot. Any doctor would be lucky to snag himself such a bright and lively wife.

When Paul was packed and ready to leave our house, I was sitting at our dining room table. I was drinking a cup of coffee and counting down the minutes until I would have to say goodbye to my son. I realized he was only moving an hour away, but it may as well have been clear across the country. It was symbolic more than it was literal. It was the act of moving out of our house, of saying goodbye, and of no longer sleeping in his bedroom. We would no longer all have dinner together each night. Veronica wouldn't be nagging him to wash his clothes, or clean his room, or do his fair share of the household chores. For sure, things were going to be different, and I had never been a big fan of change.

It was a good thing that Paul had Jonathan. The boys had been good friends ever since grade school. They knew each other well, and they liked each other. They played on some of the same baseball teams, and they were in several of the same classes together at school. I remember when Paul was writing his novel, Jonathan was the only kid who consistently stopped by to see how he was doing. And when Paul was depressed after no one wanted the novel, Jonathan was there to support him. As far as I know, Jonathan was the only kid who knew Paul went to see a psychiatrist. It was not something Paul wanted kids to learn about, but he didn't mind that Jonathan knew. If Paul had a best friend in his youth, I guess you could say Jonathan was that boy. More than any other kid, he fit the bill.

As I waited at the dining room table, I recalled the day I left for college. The morning I packed up my things and got ready to leave, Dad broke down and started sobbing like a teenage girl. Back then I didn't really get it, and the truth is, I was a little angry with him for being so emotional. Then he said something odd that really struck me. He said, "For all these years, we've lived in the same house, and under the same roof, and now you're leaving. You know, I feel as though I barely know you. You're going to be gone, and I don't even know who you are."

Well, of course he knew me. What was the old fool even talking about?

But those were the sort of words you never forget. I kept the words in the back of my mind during all the first eighteen years I was Paul's father, and I swore to myself when Paul packed his things and moved out of our house, the words would never leave my lips. I wouldn't even think them privately. I would *know* my son, from the top of his bushy hair to the calloused bottoms of his bare feet. There'd be no regrets, no fretting over lost time or missed opportunities.

Yes, Dad was upset when I moved out of the house, and Mom

was probably sad too. But me? Hell, I wasn't upset at all. I was as about as sad as a five-year-old on a summer day with a double-scoop chocolate ice-cream cone and a ticket for the merry-go-round. Why should I have been sad? There was so much to look forward to! I remember feeling like a dog unleashed, like I was a songbird being freed from its cage. Now I could sing, fly, and go wherever I wanted to go. I wouldn't have to ask anyone's permission to do anything, and if I wanted to return at three, four, or five o'clock in the morning, there would be no one waiting at the front door to slap my hand. If I wanted to walk around in my boxer shorts, I could walk around in my boxer shorts. If I didn't feel like doing my laundry, I could wear the same shirt three days in a row. If I wanted to eat my soup out of the pan, all I'd need was a spoon. I knew when I said goodbye to my grieving parents and climbed into my car that my college years were going to be the best of my life.

I truly loved going to college. I wasn't a terrific student, and I never made the honor roll. But I was thrilled to be there. I went to parties, football games, and movie showings. I met more different kids than I had imagined possible; not the sort of dopey kids you meet in high school, but kids who had futures, kids who could speak other languages, kids who could draw and paint and sculpt, kids who could argue about philosophers, kids who could play the piano like Arthur Rubinstein and sing like Billie Holiday. Jesus, the talent in college was astonishing. At least it was to me. It made me feel special to be among all these amazing people, as if I was one of them, as if I too had some kind of talent. And then came the best thing to *ever* happen to me. I was at a party, when I saw her. It was Veronica, standing across the room, the loveliest thing I'd ever laid eyes upon.

When he went off to college, I wished for many things for my son. I wished he would be happy. I wished he would find a field of study that intrigued him, something he was passionate about, something he could sink his teeth into. I hoped he would have a handful of good professors, kind-hearted and intelligent adults who cared about young people and would take him under their wings and help him to grow not just as a student, but as a man. And I wanted him to make many new friends. I pictured him staying up all night talking with them about philosophy, politics, cinema, literature, art, and science. I was hoping the great big world we live in would open up for him in college like a sweet, giant flower. There would be so much for him to learn and take in. But wait! Do you know what my biggest wish for Paul was? Forget everything I just mentioned. More than anything, I wanted him to discover the love of *his* special girl. I wanted him to stumble as I did upon the girl of his dreams. She was there somewhere around that campus, and I knew it. She would love him with all her heart, and he would be proud to have her at his side. No, not just proud. He would be ecstatic.

Have I told you how Veronica and I met? I don't think I have, so I'll tell you now. I was pushing twenty, and she was just sixteen. She was still in high school, while I was a college student. But I can tell you for a fact that it was love at first sight. I saw her at a party being thrown by a friend where she was standing across the room with her big sister, a frizzy-haired beast of a girl who you'd never in a million years guess was related in any way to Veronica. Her name was Scarlett. She was named after Scarlett O'Hara from *Gone with the Wind*, but she looked more like an old Tara plantation plow horse than she did like Vivian Leigh. Veronica's father was sort of funny about his daughters and their names. I couldn't tell if he wanted them to be spoiled brats or strong and independent women. Veronica was named after Veronica Lodge, the rich girl from the *Archie* comics. I was never quite sure what the old man was trying to accomplish when he named his daughters. And make no mistake about it, *he* picked the names. There was no doubt in my mind that Veronica's mom had nothing to do with it.

Veronica Lodge? Not even close. My Veronica was a sweet, thoughtful, and loving young woman with big hazel eyes, long auburn hair, and a pair of lips made to be kissed only by the man she loved. I identified these attributes during the first few minutes we talked. And we did talk up a storm at that party. In fact, we talked so much that her sister took notice of my interest and came over to point out that Veronica was still only sixteen, just in case I was getting ideas. "I brought her to the party," Scarlett said. "And she's coming home with me." But her protective sister didn't stop Veronica from writing down her name and number on a piece of paper she found in her purse. She folded the paper in half and handed it to me right before they left. "It's my own number," she said. "I have my own phone. Daddy got tired of us tying up the main phone, so he got us our own lines. Call me any time." I guess I should point out that this was before the advent of cellphones.

It wasn't asking too much, was it? Was I being lame and unreasonable, hoping Paul would meet a girl like I had? I didn't think so. I didn't think I was hoping against all odds for anything that any other loving father would've wanted for his son. But weeks went by, and then months, and Paul never mentioned a single girl he'd met when we talked to him. It was always Jonathan and I did this, and Jonathan and I did that. They went to ballgames together, out to dinner for pizza, to music concerts, and to parties on the weekends. I figured Paul was just shy. And maybe Jonathan was too. I mean, there are lots of boys who have trouble talking to girls. I told Veronica that Paul would probably grow out of it. "Some boys just mature earlier than others do," I told her. I believed this, and why wouldn't I believe it? It was true, wasn't it? I knew guys at work who didn't marry until they were in their thirties.

Then came the shocker. I don't think anyone expected it. The boys were nearly done with their freshman year at USC when Jonathan came out of the closet. That's what they called it then, coming out of the closet, when you throw all caution to the wind and announce to the world that you're a boy who loves other boys, or a man who loves other men. I was appalled, and I remember talking to Veronica about it right after we heard. "That rotten little homo," I said. "He's betrayed us."

"Why the anger?" Veronica asked. "He can't help what he is."

"Don't you see what this does?"

"What does it do?

"It makes *our* son look like a homosexual."

"You think so?"

"Of course it does. They've been living in the same room together for nearly a year. By choice, I might add. I *asked* the school to put them in the same room. It's not like it was an accident."

"But you didn't know."

"Obviously, I didn't know. If I knew Jonathan was a queer, I would never have let the creep in our house, and I sure as hell wouldn't have asked the school to put him in the same room with my son."

"But you liked Jonathan."

"Past tense, Veronica."

"Do you hear yourself?"

"I can hear myself just fine."

"And?"

"Jesus, do I have to draw a diagram? This is awful. What about Burt and Molly? Can you imagine if Paul had done this to us? How's Burt going to face his patients, and what will Molly say to their friends? And what about Sheri? Did Jonathan even think of how this might affect his sister? I don't care what Jonathan is, or why he is, or when he first was. I don't care if it's in his DNA, or something in the air, or if he despises girls because he has issues with Molly. In my opinion, he should've kept his mouth shut."

Well, well, well. Just goes to show you, doesn't it? I had no idea what I was talking about. I was clueless as a chimpanzee in a math class.

So Paul and Terrance will be here for Thanksgiving. It will be interesting. My guess is that they'll want to give Veronica a hand in the kitchen. I can picture them now, having the time of their lives. A dash of this, and a pinch of that. And where will I be? Well, I'll be right there as always. I'll be searching the house for hidden cameras and looking for Allen Funt. "Smile, Robert," he'll finally say, coming out from around a corner. "You're on *Candid Camera*."

And I'll hug the little bald man and say, "Thank God! Thank God, you're finally here!"

For Ten Bucks

"Ten bucks, fartface," Lewis said. "Ten bucks or you can forget it."

"Where am I supposed to get ten bucks?" I asked. "My weekly allowance is only a quarter."

"That's your problem. I'm just telling you how much it'll cost you. The price is ten bucks."

I was a nine-year-old boy when this conversation took place. The porcine and heavily freckled kid who just called me fartface was two years older than me, and his name was Lewis Hickman. He lived eight houses down the street in a quasidilapidated two-story hovel with a weed-infested front lawn. Their front yard consisted of the lawn, three badly neglected bottlebrush shrubs, and a spindly pine tree. At first glance, you'd have thought the house had been abandoned. But then most of the time you'd see there were cars parked on the cracked and oil-stained driveway, and the cars were always showroom clean. There was Mr. Hickman's big red Cadillac Coupe Deville and Mrs. Hickman's blue and white convertible Thunderbird. What the Hickmans saved on paying for yard upkeep, they apparently put into their cars.

I enjoyed growing up on our street. There were a lot of kids to play with. I knew who all the kids were, but I wasn't friends with all of them. For example, I knew who Lewis was, but I wouldn't have called him my friend. He wasn't my type. Never mind his off-putting looks—he was also the sort of kid who got his kicks out of badgering younger kids and girls, and as a rule I avoided bullies. It wasn't because I was morally superior or better than Lewis. It was more because bullies like Lewis Hickman terrified me. You never knew where you stood with a guy like Lewis. You didn't know how he was going to behave from one hour to the next, if he was going to be your good friend or if he was going to do a sudden about-face and make you eat something like a live caterpillar. I would never forget poor Joey Campbell. I saw Lewis throw the little guy to the ground and then sit down on him with all his weight. As if the crushing weight wasn't punishment enough, he dropped a live caterpillar into Joey's mouth and told him to swallow it, or else. Or else what? Who knew? This was the Lewis we were talking about. No, I had no intention of being his next victim.

But now here I was doing business with Lewis. He had something I wanted. You know, back in the day, ten dollars was an awful lot of money, but there was no way Lewis would settle for anything less. The problem was that I had no access to ten dollars. I knew after talking to Lewis that I'd have to come up with a clever plan that got the funds from multiple sources. Yes, multiple sources. Welcome to a nine-year-old's world of high finance. I thought J. Paul Getty would've been proud of me. I met in secret with my three-man board of directors, namely me, myself, and I, and we decided the first order of business was to destroy Mr. Carlos. I'm not talking about Mr. Carlos, a man. I'm talking about Mr. Carlos, my *hencho en Mexico* clay pottery piggy bank.

My parents bought me the handmade ceramic bank for the previous Christmas, thinking it would motivate me to be thrifty and teach me to save my money. To date, the bank had been the recipient mostly of what I didn't spend of my weekly allowance. I was given a quarter each week, so if I spent a dime that week, I would put fifteen cents into the bank. If I didn't spend any money, it would get the whole quarter. I picked up the bank, gave it a shake, and it rattled nicely. I then waited until my parents were both out of the house, since I didn't want them to know what I was doing. The afternoon turned out to be the perfect time, and while Dad was at work and Mom was visiting with a friend across the street, I got my dad's hammer from his workbench in the garage. I laid Mr. Carlos on his side on my bedroom floor. "Sorry, old fella," I said, and I dropped the hammer on him. He broke into pieces without saying a word. And there in the shards of shattered, painted pottery was my glorious booty.

I picked through the pieces to count the money. The total came to $3.57. For some reason I thought there'd be more, and I'd be lying if I said I wasn't disappointed. But money was money, right? I would get the rest of what I needed somewhere else. I went to the kitchen pantry and grabbed the broom and dustpan. I then swept Mr. Carlos up and carried his pieces to the kitchen. I was about to dump the remains in the trash when I realized this wouldn't do. No, no, this was all wrong. I couldn't let my mom or dad see the broken pieces in the trash. They couldn't know that I'd destroyed Mr. Carlos, because they would've asked what I needed the money for, and what would I say? If I told them the truth, well, let's just say there was no way I'd ever tell them the truth. So I took the dustpan to the side of the house. I removed the lid from the outside trash can and burrowed a hole into the trash. I poured the shards into the hole and carefully covered it. When I was done, you wouldn't have guessed poor old Mr. Carlos was in there with the banana peels, empty cans, junk mail, and old coffee grounds.

I went back to my room and counted the change again. I came up with the same total. I was $6.43 short of the ten dollars I needed, and this was a significant shortfall. It was time for another board meeting, and that's when we put our three heads together and came up with plan number two. The target of this plan was Bobby Hardy, and he lived with his parents across the street. Bobby was a year younger than me, and about eight inches shorter. He was kind of a nuisance, always following me around and trying to be my buddy. For some reason, he looked up to me. He was one of those kids who seemed to have a difficult time making friends. He was a small boy, kind of frail, and he wore a pair of very thick corrective glasses. Without his glasses Bobby was as blind as a bat, so he wore an elastic band around the back of his head that held the glasses to his face and kept them from falling off no matter what he happened to be doing.

I went to Bobby's house that afternoon, and I pressed my finger on the doorbell. I knew Bobby had received a birthday card from his grandma a few days ago, and I knew she'd put a five-dollar bill in the card. Bobby told me all about it, thinking I'd be interested. Bobby always told me stuff like this, thinking I would care. But now I *was* interested. If Bobby would loan me the five dollars, I would only need another $1.43. And there was a very good chance he would make the loan, hoping that by making such a loan he would confirm our friendship.

Bobby's mom answered the door, and she was elated to see me. She was wearing a colorful floral dress with a string of pearls around her neck and bright-white modern wristwatch. Her red hair was spun into a beehive atop her head, and I honestly would've have been surprised to see a few honey bees nearby, either coming in and out of their hive or pollinating the flowers printed on her dress. She had bad eyes like Bobby, and she too wore thick glasses. The glasses made her eyes appear too big for her face. I felt kind of sorry for the woman, in part because of the way she looked, but also because she was so desperate for her son to have a playmate. And I also felt guilty for deceiving her, making her think I was there because I liked Bobby, when I was actually just there to get my hands on his money.

I followed Bobby's mom to his room, where we found him sitting at his desk and pressing together Legos. Bobby's mom left the two of us alone. I remember there were Legos everywhere, all over the top of the desk, on the floor, and even spread out on Bobby's bed. He appeared to be making a large spaceship. I moved some of the Legos out of the way and took a seat on his bed. I then got right to the point, asking Bobby if he remembered getting five dollars from his grandma. "Of course I do," he said, still working on his spaceship.

"I'm here to ask a big favor," I said.

"A favor?"

"Can you loan it to me?"

"You need money?"

"I do," I said. "I'll pay you back. I promise I can pay you back."

"What do you need the money for?"

I couldn't tell Bobby why I needed the money. He was too young to know the real reason. At least I thought he was too young. I didn't know how much he knew about these things, so I said, "I want to buy my mom a present for her birthday. Her birthday is coming up next week."

"What are you going to get her?"

"I haven't decided yet."

"Can I come shopping with you?"

"No," I said. "It's kind of a private thing, you know. It might be kind of embarrassing."

"Why would it be embarrassing?"

"I don't know. I just want to do it by myself."

"Okay," Bobby said. He then started looking on the floor. "Do you see one of these in black?" he asked, holding up a red Lego piece. "Look on the bed. There might be one on the bed."

"So will you lend me the money?" I asked while looking for his Lego piece.

"Aha!" he said, finding his black piece and sitting back down at his desk.

"Will you?" I asked again.

"Will I what?"

"Lend me the money?"

"Well, there's kind of a problem with that."

"A problem?"

"I don't have it."

"What do you mean, you don't have it?"

"Well, not all of it."

"What does that mean?" I asked.

"I spent most of it on more Legos."

"Legos?" I said. Jesus, this kid needed more Legos like he needed someone to step on his glasses. "You bought more Legos? Why would you buy more Legos? You've got enough of them here to build a house."

"I think I have a little over a dollar left."

"A dollar?"

"Do you want to borrow it? I can loan it to you. I have a dollar and some change."

"I guess if that's all you have."

"I have more in the bank, in my savings account. But my dad won't let me touch it. He wants me to hang on to it for college."

"I'll take the dollar."

"It's in here," Bobby said, and he opened his desk drawer. He removed a dollar bill and some coins. He then handed them to me. I stuffed the money into my pocket and stood up.

"I have to go," I said.

"Already?"

"I really have to go."

"We don't have to play with Legos. We can do something else."

"Maybe tomorrow."

"I see."

Now I was feeling guilty again. "For sure tomorrow," I said. "I'll come over tomorrow afternoon."

"That would be great," Bobby said.

I left Bobby's house. "Going so soon?" Bobby's mother said as I stepped out the front door. I swear to God I saw a bee come in through the door, looking for the woman's hairdo. I pretended not to see it.

"I just remembered I have to do something," I said. "I'm coming back tomorrow."

"Oh, I see. I guess we'll see you tomorrow then," Bobby's mother said, smiling.

When I got home, I went straight to my bedroom to count up my money. I now had $4.86. I thought long and hard about where I could get the rest and decided on the only course of action that made sense. It would be risky, wrong, and dishonest. I suppose you could even call it a crime. Yes, I decided to cross the line and steal the money from my mom's purse.

Believe it or not, I'd never done anything like this before. I would commit the crime that evening while Mom was preparing dinner. She would be busy in the kitchen, and my dad wouldn't be home yet from work. Mom always kept her purse in the master bathroom, on her side of the counter. I tip-toed into the room and carefully unsnapped the top. I then looked inside for the wallet, and I found it between a hairbrush and a tampon. I removed the wallet, and then looked for the cash. There was about sixty bucks, but all I needed was six. With great care, I pulled out a five and a one. Just as I was doing this, I heard my mom's voice.

"Robert," she said. "What are you doing?"

"I'm, uh, taking some money."

"You're stealing from me?"

"I needed six dollars."

"What on earth for?"

"I need the money to get you a birthday present. I wanted it to be a surprise."

"A birthday present?"

"Your birthday is next week. I wanted to get you something, and I don't have any money."

Mom thought about this, and then she said, "Give me back what you took. How much did you take?"

"Six dollars," I said, handing her the bills. She put the six dollars back into her wallet and then removed a ten.

"Here, take this ten. Get me something nice. What you have left over from the ten you can put into Mr. Carlos."

"Thanks," I said.

"We won't say anything to your father about this."

"No, he might get mad."

"There's no reason he has to know."

"No," I said.

"But next time you need some money, ask me for it. Don't just take it out of my purse. I don't want you to think I'm saying it's okay for you to steal. Because it's not okay."

"No, I know that."

"Fine, run along then. Dinner will be ready in thirty minutes."

"Thanks, Mom."

Jeez, I loved that woman. Did she really believe my story about the birthday present, or was she just allowing me a way out? I never did find out, but what I did know is that my problems were solved. I now had enough money to give Lewis *and* to buy my mom a present. That evening after dinner I rode my bike to Lewis's house. He was in the front yard with Eddie Taylor, and they were playing catch with a baseball. "Well, if it isn't fartface," Lewis said when he saw me.

I ignored his insult and said, "I got the money."

"You got the ten dollars?"

I reach into my pocket and pulled out the ten my mom gave me, showing it to Lewis. "It's right here."

"Well, I'll be damned."

"So when can I see?"

"How about tomorrow?"

"That suits me fine."

"Four o'clock, here at my house. My parents will both be gone. But just in case something goes wrong, and you see one of their cars in the driveway, don't knock on the door. Come only if both cars are gone."

"Got it," I said.

"I'll give you fifteen minutes."

"That's all?"

"Take it or leave it."

"I'll take it," I said.

"You won't be disappointed. Ask Eddie. He's seen them all. Will he be disappointed, Eddie?"

"Nope," Eddie said.

"Now get the hell out of here before someone thinks we're friends."

"Okay," I said, and I rode back toward home on my bicycle.

I arrived at Lewis's house at exactly four o'clock the following day. His parents' cars were gone, so the coast was clear. I stepped up to the front door and knocked. Lewis opened the door and stuck his hand out. "The ten bucks first," he said. I reached into my pocket and removed the ten-dollar bill, putting it into Lewis' hand. He then folded it and stuffed it into his pocket. "Follow me," he said, and the two of us walked through the strangely furnished house until we reached his father's study. The house looked like it had been furnished for a Vincent Price horror movie. There was a carved wooden desk in the middle of his father's study, and Lewis opened the top drawer. From this drawer he removed a small key, which he used to unlock one of the side drawers. He opened the side drawer and reached into it, pulling out a stack of magazines which he plopped down on the surface of the desk. "Have a seat," he said, so I sat down at the desk in a big leather chair. Lewis looked toward a pendulum clock on the wall and said, "It's five after four. You have until four twenty, and then the magazines go back into the drawer. Then you go home and forget we ever did this."

"Okay," I said.

So what were they? It was his father's pornography collection, a stack of weird magazines I'd never heard of. Forget your run-of-the-mill issues of *Playboy*, these were the real McCoy. Maybe they were from Europe? I didn't know, and I didn't care. I turned the pages and looked at the pictures. Most of them were in black and white, but many were in living color. The pages were glossy, and the subject matter was beyond my wildest dreams. There were women of all nationalities, of all hair colors, of all skin tones, posing like I'd never seen women pose. Some were wearing unbuttoned shirts, unzipped pants, skimpy nightclothes, stockings with garters and garter belts, but most of them were wearing nothing at all. It was unbelievable! Page after page, they were worth every penny of the ten dollars I paid. There were breasts, big versus petit, nice and round versus pointy. There were vaginas of all kinds. There were arms, legs, and lots of rear ends. Some of the women were skinny, and some were heavy. And the faces! These were *real* women, smiling for the camera. I had honestly never seen a collection of women so alluring in all my young life. And I wanted all of them. I wanted to live with them, to hold them, and to kiss them. I wanted each of them to speak into my ear with their warm and sultry voices, "Oh Robert, I love you."

Before I knew it, Lewis said, "Time's up." He grabbed the magazines and put them back in the desk drawer. It was disappointing that the time went by so fast, but I left his house and got back on my bike. As I rode home past all the houses, I couldn't get the images out of my mind. I was a changed man. Well, I wasn't really a man. But what was I? I was no longer the same. I was a boy whose eyes had been opened, seeing what every red-blooded male sees at one time or the other for the first time in his life, the mind-numbing marvel of that creature we all so casually call a woman. They were so different from us. They were special, and they all deserved to be treated like goddesses. Pity the men who loved other men. Homos, queers, fags, and gays, what the heck was wrong with them? How in God's name did they not see what I saw? Even as a nine-year-old boy, I could see. Even as a nine-year-old, I could feel. Even as a nine-year-old, I knew there was only one way things were meant to be! Women and men were made for each other. Nothing else made any sense.

Meeting Crystal

I remember when Paul called. He was a twenty-year-old sophomore. It was around seven in the evening, and Paula and I were sitting down at our dining room table for dinner. For some reason I remember what we were having; Veronica had made us a couple of pork chops, asparagus spears, rice, zucchini bread, and salads. We were just about to dig in when the phone rang, and as Veronica went to answer it, she said, "I wonder who that is?" She always said this when the phone rang, even if she knew who was calling.

"Tell them to call back in an hour," I said. "I'd like to eat dinner."

Then I heard Veronica talking into the phone in the kitchen. "Oh, hi, Paul," she said. "We're right in the middle of dinner now. Oh, yes. Okay. Uh-huh. Wednesday night would be perfect. What do you want me to make? Okay. Sure. I can do that. Six o'clock is fine. That sounds great. We can't wait to meet her. Okay. Good. Love you too." Veronica then ended the call and returned to the dining room table, smiling. "That was Paul," she said.

"I gathered as much," I said. "So what'd he have to say?

"He's coming down for dinner Wednesday night."

"That's good," I said. It was always great when Paul came down to visit.

"He's bringing a girl with him."

"A girl?"

"He wants us to meet her."

"What's her name?"

"Her name is Crystal."

"Well, I'll be damned," I said.

So was Paul dating girls? Maybe he was. This was welcome news, and I looked forward to meeting Crystal. I wondered what the girl would be like. Would she be quiet, maybe a little shy, or was she going to be talkative and outgoing? Would she be loveable or obnoxious? What color was her hair, and what color were her eyes? Did she have any freckles? Was she a tiny little thing like Peter Pan's Tinker Bell, or was she tall and stout enough to hold her own in a men's basketball game? It was like getting a surprise gift for no special occasion, and I had no idea what was going to be in the box.

Veronica was funny. She really made me laugh. You would've thought we were going to be entertaining a famous princess or movie star. She had the maid service come that afternoon to make sure every square inch of the house was spotless. She had the gardener mow the front lawn and trim all the bushes. She even told him to add some flowers by the porch. Then she made me wash both of our cars, which was pointless since we kept them parked in the garage. For dinner she prepared beef stroganoff, salads, dinner rolls, and a vegetable dish. I don't remember what the vegetable was, but I remember that she purchased a cheese cake for dessert. She used all our good dishes, expensive flatware, and linen napkins. There were silver candleholders with brand-new candles, and she brought out the little antique silver salt and pepper shakers we'd purchased when we visited England. When six o'clock rolled around, Veronica had me light the candles.

You should've seen her. She had done up her hair, put on her makeup, and slipped into one of her favorite red dresses. There was an art to this. She didn't look like she was going out to the opera, but she did look very nice. In fact, she looked terrific. When I saw her, I realized I was slightly underdressed, so I went to our bedroom to change clothes. I put on a new plaid shirt, slacks, and my dress shoes. In the bathroom, I trimmed my fingernails and scrubbed my hands clean. I gave my face a quick once-over with my electric razor. I looked again at myself in our mirror. There was something missing. What was it? After a few seconds it hit me. I needed to be wearing my watch. I had a nice Seiko watch that Veronica had given to me for Christmas several years ago, but I seldom wore it. I didn't like being reminded every minute of the day that my life was ticking away, but tonight I would wear it for our guest.

They arrived at six on the button. Veronica and I met them at the front door. I didn't know what to expect, but it would be accurate to say I was surprised. Crystal was not what I thought we'd be getting. Hopefully I didn't gasp or have a look of surprise on my face when I first saw her. That would've been rude. "So you must be Crystal," Veronica said. She reached out to shake the girl's hand, and Crystal shook it for her. I then reached out my hand, and Crystal took a hold of it.

"Nice to meet you," I said.

"It's nice to meet both of you," Crystal said. Then she let go of my hand.

"Please come in," Veronica said. The kids stepped inside the house, and Veronica closed the door. "Follow me," she said, and she walked to the kitchen with the rest of us walking behind her. "Dinner is almost ready."

"It smells great," Crystal said.

"It's beef stroganoff," Veronica said. "Paul told me you liked it."

"I love it."

"Would you like a glass of wine?"

"That'd be great."

"Red or white?"

"Chardonnay if you have it."

"I do happen to have that," Veronica said.

We all made small talk in the kitchen until Veronica said she was ready to serve the salads. Then we went to the dining room.

I can sum up my first impression of Crystal quickly by telling you that she looked a lot like one of those girls who used to stand up and dance Grateful Dead concerts, a joint between the fingers of one hand and a can of beer in the other. Do you know the kind of girl I'm talking about? I sized her up. She had long, thick, light-brown hair she wore in a braid that fell down the middle of her back. She had a fresh hibiscus flower in her hair, which I figured she picked from the bush alongside the driveway. Or maybe Paul picked it for her? Her face was lovely, accentuated by the flower in her hair. Her skin was clear and tan, and her eyes were a striking emerald shade of green. I guess the most noticeable thing about her face was her mouth, or more precisely, her teeth, which were white and perfect. Honest to God, I didn't think I'd ever seen anyone with such perfect teeth. I guessed her parents must have shelled out a small fortune on braces.

It turned out there was no reason for me to worry over my clothing. Crystal looked like she'd just returned from that Grateful Dead concert. She reminded me of a girl I knew in high school who I used to stare at while she ate her lunch on the school front lawn. Crystal was wearing a white tank top without a bra, and her breasts were ample. Hell, I'll just say it. Her breasts were large, just like that girl's in high school. Crystal reached up to be sure the flower in her hair wasn't falling off, and I noticed she didn't shave under her arms. She wasn't hairy like a man, but there was some hair. And she wasn't wearing any jewelry except for some leather thongs with beads around her wrists. It was no surprise to me that she didn't wear a watch. She was wearing a snug pair of jeans that looked like they'd been to the Himalayas and back, worn and full of frayed holes. Her belt was a brown leather strap with a substantial silver buckle that looked like a Navajo Indian piece. On her feet were a pair of thin-soled sandals made of leather and colorful beads, like the thong bracelets on her wrists. All in all, she looked like a hippie, but we all know hippies disappeared from college campuses around the same time as slide rules. So what the heck was she? Veronica seemed as curious as I was, and as we took our seats at the dining room table, she said, "Tell us about yourself."

Crystal laughed and said, "I wouldn't even know where to begin."

"Are you a sophomore like Paul?"

"Yes, I'm a sophomore."

"Do you have a major?"

"She's a poet," Paul said.

"Ah," I said. "A poet."

"How interesting," Veronica said. She then turned to me. "Don't you think that's interesting?"

"Yeah," I said.

"To answer you, I'm an English major."

"Do you plant to teach?"

"Oh, no. I'm afraid I'd make a terrible teacher. I plan to write."

"She's already had some of her poems published," Paul said.

"No kidding?"

"Probably not anywhere you'd see. They were published in some small poetry journals, and one was in our school paper."

"I'd like to read them," Veronica said.

"So would I," I said, which was not really true. I liked reading poetry about as much as I liked going to the dentist. Maybe less. Poetry just had never been my cup of tea.

There was a lull in our conversation, and then Paul blurted out, "We're living together."

It took Veronica a while to process what he just said, and then she said, "You're *what?*"

"We're living together. In the apartment. Crystal now lives with me."

"What happened to Abe?" Abe was the kid Paul had been rooming with ever since the fiasco with Jonathan. We liked Abe, and his father always made sure his half of the rent was paid.

"Abe moved out two weeks ago."

"Abe moved out?" I asked. "He didn't drop out of school, did he?"

"No, of course not. He's living with his girlfriend in their own apartment. They got a place right down the street. That left me in the apartment by myself, and Crystal was commuting to and from her parents' house in Santa Monica. We had been good friends, and she was tired of the drive. So we said, what the heck, why not? She moved in last week. Her dad is paying me her half of the rent, so nothing's changed. I mean, moneywise. We've covered the bases."

"I see," I said.

"What do your parents think of this?" Veronica asked Crystal.

"They've been wanting me to move out of the house for the past year. Dad says I'm too old to live at home."

"How old are you?"

"I'm twenty-eight."

You should've seen the look on Veronica's face. Now not only was her son living with a girl who didn't shave her underarms, but he was living with a girl who was eight years older than him. This wasn't a girl. This was a woman. "Isn't twenty-eight a little old to be just a sophomore college?" Veronica asked.

"Not at all," Paul said defensively.

"I took a few years off after high school," Crystal explained. "I wanted to find myself before I jumped into college. I wanted to learn who I was."

"What'd you do?"

"I discovered America."

"I thought Christopher Columbus did that," I said. I thought this was funny, but no one laughed.

"She means she got in her car and travelled around the country to discover America," Paul said. "She did it all by herself."

"For eight years?"

"Where'd you go?"

"Everywhere," Crystal said. "From the redwood forest to the gulf stream waters."

"What'd you do for money?"

"My dad sent it to me as I needed it."

"He must be a generous man."

"Daddy has more money than he knows what to do with. It was nice of him, but it didn't really put him out."

"You must have a lot of interesting stories to tell," Veronica said.

"I have some good stories."

"So did you find yourself?"

"Did I find myself where?"

"I thought you went off to find yourself."

"Oh, yes, that. I suppose I did. I found out that I was who I always thought I was, that I was a poet. I've always written poetry, ever since I was a little girl. I don't know what made me question this as a teenager, but there was something about graduating from high school that caused me to second-guess myself. I thought maybe poetry was just a childhood diversion. I thought maybe I was meant for other things. You know, I'd lived my entire life here in Southern California. What did I know? The truth was that I knew very little. The world was a great big mystery to me, so I bought a little Volkswagen, a sleeping bag, and some other necessities, and off I went. I was eighteen when I left, and twenty-six when I returned home. Dad said if I wanted to keep getting my allowance, I'd have to go to college. So I sat down and sent in several applications, and USC accepted me. The others didn't."

"Tell us something you learned," I said. I was genuinely curious.

"Learned?"

"During this trek all around this great country of ours. What did you learn?"

"Oh, of course. What I learned. Well, I learned that my Volkswagen went 334 miles on a single tank of gas and no further. I learned that pickup truck drivers were the most likely to pull over and help you out when you were stranded on the side of the road. I learned that cops are of no help at all. As one cop in Nevada told me, 'Do you see a AAA decal on the side of my car?' In fairness he did help me out, but I think he would rather have been writing me a ticket. I learned that skies really are different sizes in different states, and when they say Montana is big sky country, they say it for a reason. Eventually, I learned the difference between Idaho and Iowa. One is famous for potatoes, and the other for corn. Corn as far as the eye can see. I stopped at a little restaurant in Iowa and ordered corn on the cob. They told me they were out of corn, and looked around and I said, 'You've got to be kidding.' I learned the world's largest ball of string was in Cawker City, Kansas, while the world's largest ball of string *rolled by one man* was in Darwin, Minnesota. I learned that restaurant service in New York City wasn't any faster than it was in Chicago. I learned they really do say ma'am and sir in the South. One lady told me her son was suspended from school for three days because he refused to call his teacher ma'am. I learned that grits are not all the same. They were prepared different everywhere I ordered them. There was no quality control at all. I learned that outside of California, politicians, not movie stars, are the real celebrities. This was an eye-opener for me. It never occurred to me someone would run for a government office just so they could become famous and be asked for autographs. I saw the Gateway Arch in St. Louis, the Grand Canyon in Arizona, and the presidents' heads at Mount Rushmore. They say Rushmore will last millions of years. I learned that the mountain was named after a New York attorney named Charlie Rushmore, who was checking titles of mining properties. He came upon the mountain, and when he asked the guide what it was called, the guide said, 'I don't know. Let's call the damn thing Rushmore, ha, ha.' I learned a lot about people in this country. I learned that most Mormons are not polygamists, and that most whites in the South do not belong to the KKK, and that most blacks in New Orleans don't play the trumpet. But, true to common belief, I learned that most Texans do own at least one cowboy hat. I could go on and on. Wahoo! Howdy and top of the morning to you, ma'am.

Crystal laughed and then stopped talking, and we were all staring at her. I was trying to figure out what any of this had to do with the girl finding herself when Veronica stood up and said, "I guess I'll go get the salads."

"Yes," I said. "Let's eat."

"I'd like to help," Crystal said, and she stood up and followed Veronica into the kitchen. They weren't gone long, and when they returned they put the full salad bowls on the table.

Everyone was quietly eating their salads. There was an occasional clink of a fork against a bowl, but that was the only sound in the room. Then Crystal finally set her fork down and spoke up. "We're not having sex, if that's what you're worried about," she said. I nearly spit my mouthful of salad across the room.

"I wasn't actually thinking about that," Veronica said. She was lying, of course.

"I just wanted to clear the air."

"She's telling the truth," Paul said.

"We're just good friends."

"You know what Oscar Wilde said about men and women being friends, don't you?"

"Actually," Crystal said. "I know he said a lot of things.

"He said between men and women, there is no friendship possible."

Crystal thought about this and then said, "I think he was wrong. Maybe that was true while he was alive, but platonic relationships are now quite common. This is the twenty-first century."

"So it is," I said.

And that was fine with me. I hoped she was right. I wanted Paul to meet a nice girl, and Crystal was a nice girl. But seriously, what was with the hairy armpits? And the age difference? It would never do.

I never even considered the idea that Paul might be gay. The thought never crossed my mind. What I thought was that he needed a girl to come into his life and light the sparkler of love in his heart the way Veronica had lit mine. Not Crystal, but a girl he could fall head over heels in love with. I was sure she was out there and that she was as much in need of him as he was of her. It was just a matter of time.

One Professor Down

I n my imagination, it was pouring all day in Los Angeles, and the rainstorm showed no signs of letting up. Dramatic music played in the background. The streets, rooftops, and palm trees were soaked with water, and it was evening. Cars passed in the street, cutting through the downpour with their yellow high beams, wipers swatting water from their windshields. It was supposedly a full moon on this night, but there was no trace of the orb anywhere in the sky. The storm clouds were black, thick, and impregnable. There was nothing but falling rain, everywhere.

Paul was outside a window in his raincoat, fedora hat, and muddy galoshes, standing in a flowerbed. This house happened to be in Beverly Hills. It was a nice house, the kind of nice house that movie stars, directors, successful businessmen, or attorneys lived in. The drapes were pulled open, and Paul could see into the brightly lit home. There was a sofa, several chairs, a coffee table, a chest of drawers, a grand piano, and a variety of vases, statues, books, and lamps. And there were people. Paul counted the people, three men and one woman, all well-groomed and nicely dressed like they'd just been out socializing at a cocktail party.

This was my vision. I imagined Paul could hear only bits and pieces of the group's conversation. Because the window was closed, their voices were muffled, like they were underwater. Paul could make out some words and sentences, so he removed a small notepad and ballpoint pen from his pocket. He began to take notes, and he held the notepad close to his chest, trying to keep the rain from landing on the pages. There was a sudden explosion of white light and a crack of thunder that startled the woman. It made her jump, but it didn't matter to the men. Then the woman began to plead for her life. The men were listening to her, but they didn't seem to be buying her story. And that's when it happened.

One of the men pulled a revolver from his jacket pocket, and he aimed it at the woman's chest. The woman held her hands in front of her, between herself and the gun, and she started to cry. She was shaking her head and saying, "No, no, please!" Paul then heard on of the men say, "Once last chance, sister." The woman said, "I've told you everything I know!" It wasn't what the men wanted to hear. "Fold her up," one of the men said, and *pop!* The gun fired. A dark red spot appeared on the woman's chest, and she fell backward and crumpled to the floor. Then *pop, pop, pop!* Three more shots and finally the woman was still and lifeless. "Let's scram out of this joint," the first man said.

I suppose you could say I've watched too many black-and-white movies in my life, and you might be right. But this is what went through my head when Paul called from college and gave us the news. He was now a junior at USC, twenty-one years old, and he had decided what he wanted to do with his life. He didn't want to be an architect like his grandfather, or a smooth-talking automobile salesman like his old man. He wanted to study journalism. More specifically, he wanted to be an investigative reporter, uncovering crimes, digging up dirt on bad guys, and exposing injustices. He wanted to be the guy wearing the wet fedora hat and shiny raincoat, writing on his notepad by the window in the rain.

"More power to him," I said to Veronica. It was the morning after Paul had called us, and we were sitting down to eat breakfast. "I'm just glad he finally has some kind of life path in mind."

"I guess he did always want to be a writer."

"Hell, yes, he wants to be a writer. How many kids do you know of who have written an entire novel before they even graduated from high school?"

"Do you think this line of work is dangerous?"

"I'm sure he'll be careful."

"He sounds so determined. He could make some people very angry."

"That's true," I said. "But he could also be a good guy and a hero."

"A hero," Veronica scoffed. I didn't get the feeling that she wanted her son to be a hero.

"Don't try to talk him out of it."

"Why not?"

"He needs this. Men need a purpose in life. Men need to know they count for something."

"Men are idiots."

"*Men* won World War II," I said. "*Men* stopped Adolph Hitler and Hirohito." Okay, this was a pretty dumb thing to say, but it was first thing in the morning, and I'd had only one cup of coffee.

Veronica didn't try to talk him out of it, and Paul didn't waste any time. He changed his major to journalism and signed up for the required classes. He also went to work investigating one of his professors. To his way of thinking, there was no sense in waiting until he graduated to get the ball rolling. "I'm going to bring this bastard down," he told me. When I said this might not be such a good idea, he said, "Listen, either you're behind me or you're not." Against my better judgment, I said yes, I was behind him.

I told Veronica about Paul's plan, and she sighed and said, "Here we go."

The professor Paul was interested in was a fifty-six-year-old math teacher named Aaron Jeffries. He was not a very handsome man. He always looked like he'd just bit into a lemon. What I'm going to tell you about this story was either told to me directly by Paul, or it comes from what I read in Paul's articles in the newspaper.

Paul first came to know Jeffries when he was in the professor's calculus class. Paul was a freshman, and he was having a lot of difficulty with the class, not because he was particularly slow but because he was immature. Paul will be the first to admit this. He started off the class without enthusiasm, and his lack of effort quickly put him behind the eight ball. During the second half of this course, Paul realized he might not get a passing grade. He arranged a meeting with Professor Jeffries to discuss his situation, and they got together in the professor's office. As Paul was entering the office, a girl was leaving. She was a very attractive girl. And she was smiling from ear to ear. It was obvious to Paul she was not failing.

Paul told the professor he was worried about passing his class, and the professor listened to Paul patiently. Then the professor began to talk, and as he talked, Paul's eyes were drawn to a large poster on the professor's wall. The poster was a black-and-white photo of a barefoot blonde at the beach, dressed in a two-piece swimsuit, dripping wet with ocean water. Scotch taped to her crotch was the word "if," cutout from some newspaper or magazine. What did that mean? Why would this professor tape a cut-out word on the girl's vagina? It was weird. No, it was weird and a little disturbing.

"You kids kill me," the professor said. "You screw around and ignore me until midterms, and then you suddenly realize you're about to fail my class. You come into my office crying like babies, asking me to give you a break. I'll do for you exactly what I do for the rest of your friends, which is nothing. You made your bed, and now you can lie in it. If you need a tutor, I'll give you some phone numbers. But that's all I'll do." Paul thanked the professor for his time, and he went back to his dorm room. He stretched out on his bed and looked up at the ceiling. The professor was right. All of this was Paul's fault, yet, yet what? That *girl*. Paul couldn't get her out of his mind, that smiling, self-confident blonde who very likely knew as much about calculus as she did about arc welding. What grade was *she* getting?

Eventually, Paul did pass the class. It wasn't easy, but he did it. But he never could get that professor out of his mind. The man had belittled Paul. And that girl! That beautiful blond-haired girl who was smiling when she came waltzing out of his office. She looked like a cat who had just dined on the family canary. Why was she so self-confident? Was she promised an A? Did she have to do any work at all? Or did she just have to take a shot at it, to make it look like she was doing something? Wasn't this guy afraid he'd get caught? It was all so obvious to Paul, what the professor was doing. The girl, the poster, the whole nine yards.

Here's the thing about Paul. You may have already noticed that when he decides he's going to do something, he's usually in all the way. When he played baseball as a boy, he didn't just play a game here and there. He played every chance he had. Then when he decided to write his novel, he dropped everything. He spent hours and hours at his desk in his room, typing on his keyboard. That's all he did for months. And granted, for a few years after his manuscript was rejected by every publisher in America, he lost his way. But now he was as determined as ever. He was on the warpath again. He wanted to be an investigative reporter. He wanted to be *the* investigative reporter, and he wanted to knock everyone's socks off. And yes, he would start with Professor Jeffries, maybe in part because of the way the professor treated him, but primarily because he knew the bastard was trading grades for sex with young and naïve female students. What could be more despicable? It had to stop.

The way Paul had it figured, he had to do one of two things. He had to either catch the professor in the act with one of his students and prove he was giving them good grades because of it, or he had to get one of the girls to go public with what had happened. Neither would be easy. But catching the professor in the act? Surely, if the man was smart enough to be a college math professor, no doubt he was smart enough to hide what he was doing. And Paul was taking a full load of classes, so it wasn't like he had time to follow the professor around everywhere he went, day and night. And proving that the professor was changing the actual grades? How would he even be able to do that? No, it made much more sense to get one of the professor's girls to turn on him.

He would start with the girl from his freshmen class, that girl who ate the canary. Paul remembered exactly what she looked like. But who the heck was she? Paul never did learn the girl's name. He had no idea where she lived, or who any of her friends were, or if she was still at the university. But like all great reporters, he came up with an angle. Maybe it would work, and maybe it wouldn't, but it was worth a try. "You never know until you give it a shot," Paul told me, and he called the school newspaper and ran a quarter page ad. He composed the ad, describing the girl from his memory and then listing the details of the class they were in. "If you think you're this girl, or if you know anything about her, please call me," Paul said in the ad.

"It's important that I talk to you immediately." Paul listed his name and phone number, and then we waited for the calls.

Paul received five calls from the ad. Two of them were prank calls from male students who obviously had too much to drink. One of the prank calls said they were holding the girl hostage, but that they would release her if Paul would send ten thousand dollars and a case of beer. The other said the girl had died in a freak car accident. "She plowed into a car full of freaks, ha, ha." The third call was from a young man who said he thought the girl had transferred to UCLA, but he couldn't remember her name. "Are you sure she was a blonde?" the caller asked. "I remember her as a brunette." The fourth call was from a girl who gave her name and phone number in case Paul couldn't find the girl and just wanted someone to chat with. She said she was a good listener. But the fifth call was from a girl who claimed to be a friend of the mystery girl. "I know for sure my friend is the girl you're looking for," she said. "Her name is April Tanner. She dropped out of school at the end of her sophomore year and now lives down in Long Beach with her parents. She's working as a waitress." Paul called back and got the name of the restaurant.

Paul immediately drove down to Long Beach to check the lead out. He saw her, and at first he wasn't sure. He said it was her, and yet it wasn't, meaning that the girl looked different. She had put on about forty pounds and cut off her long blond hair. But yes, yes! She was definitely the girl! Paul was sure of it. He sat down at one of her tables and ordered lunch and a cup of coffee. When April approached him at the end of the meal with his check, Paul told her, "I need to talk to you about USC. Can you talk after work?"

"Talk about what?"

"About Professor Jeffries."

"Oh, him." She sounded disappointed.

"Will you talk to me?"

"Who are you?"

"I'm a journalism student at USC. I'm investigating the professor."

"I'm not sure what you're doing here, but if it has anything to do with Professor Jeffries, I'd rather be left out of it."

"I need to talk to you."

April stared at Paul for a moment. Then surprisingly she said. "I get off work at eight."

"Can I meet you here then?"

"I suppose."

"Is there a place where we can talk?"

"You can take me out to dinner."

"I can do that."

"You're paying. I don't have any money."

"Yes, I'll pay for it."

"I'll be ready to go at a little after eight." The girl then walked away to tend to her other tables.

Paul picked up April when she got off work, and they went to a restaurant in Seal Beach for dinner. They were there for nearly two hours, and she told Paul everything. Once she had made her mind up to talk, it was like she couldn't find the brakes, and she remembered it all in astonishing detail, beginning when she was a bright-eyed freshman and ending when she dropped out of school. "He ruined me," she said. "I never got over it. I guess I'm still not over it. I mean, I am and I'm not." She didn't cry. There was a toughness about her that Paul admired. When she was done telling her story, Paul told her that he wanted to write a newspaper article about her experience. He asked if he could use her name in the story, and she said, "You've got to be kidding. My life isn't exactly over, and I still have *some* self-respect."

"It's a story that should be told," Paul said.

"But in a newspaper?"

"What better place?"

"No way," April said. "It would be too embarrassing, and it would destroy my parents. They're upset enough that I dropped out of school. No, no, I just can't let you do that."

Paul thought about this and then said, "What if I write the article without any names. We won't use your name, or the professor's. We won't even say what class it was. We'll just say it happened in a random class in a random subject, but at USC."

"You could do that?"

"You'd be my source. But I wouldn't tell anyone who you were, except maybe the editor. He'd probably have to be convinced that the story was true."

April went along with this. She wanted the story to be told. She just didn't want to be personally associated with it. So later that week they got together, and April recounted her story again, but slowly this time, so Paul could get it all down on paper. Paul then wrote his article and took it to the paper, where an editor named Ralph Masters approved the story and promised to print it. Two weeks later the story appeared, not buried in the back, but on the front page.

Paul was surprised by the fact that the story was on the front page. He was also surprised at how everyone reacted to the story. It was picked up by other papers. It was mentioned on the TV news. The next thing he knew, everyone was talking about the anonymous girl at USC. Then came trouble. Some alumni got together, and they demanded that the girl's name be released. They took out a full-page ad in the newspaper. "Anyone can make up a story like this besmirching a college's reputation," the ad said in a letter to the public. "But we want names! Either come out of the shadows and identify yourself and the professor or shut the hell up." The ad served its purpose, and the feeling began to build that if someone was going to make accusations like this, they ought not do it anonymously. Otherwise, like the alumni's letter said, anyone could say anything about anyone.

Paul got a call from April three weeks after the alumni placed their ad. "They're winning this game," she said. "They're making my story look like a fabrication."

"The public is wary."

"So the truth wasn't good enough?"

"Unfortunately, no."

"Then fuck it," April said. "Print my name. And print the professor's name. Let's get all our cards on the table. Let's see what the alumni does with that."

"Are you sure?" Paul asked.

"I'm positive."

So the paper published a second article written by Paul about the alumni's challenge and revealing the names of April and the professor. It was like whacking a beehive with a baseball bat. All hell broke loose at the school. First, the professor threatened to sue the paper. Then he threatened to sue Paul. Fortunately, the school didn't want to get involved in lawsuits. The alumni, who were amazed at the girl's nerve, took out another newspaper ad, this time claiming outright that April was a liar. They said she had a schoolgirl crush on the professor. He had appropriately rejected her lame advances, and now she was getting even. By now, everyone had a different opinion. It just depended on who you talked to. That was the case until the whole issue exploded. Along came the match to the fuse. Or should I say matches. Four former female students stepped forward and told the press that the exact same thing had happened to them when they were in the professor's class. The parents and friends of these women got together and took out their own full-page ad in the newspaper. They were demanding that the professor be fired without delay and that the alumni group provide a public apology to April. For a few days nothing happened. Then Professor Jeffries turned in his resignation.

The Saturday after the professor resigned, Paul held a celebration dinner at a restaurant in Pasadena. Many of the people involved in exposing the professor showed up to pat one another on the back. Of course, I was there, and so was Veronica. We watched our son when he stood up to make a toast. "That's one professor down," he said. "And a whole world of rotten apples to go."

Don't get me wrong. The professor had it coming. The man was a veritable rat. And Paul only did what should've been done years ago. But I could sense something, and so could Veronica. There was now something different about our son. He wasn't just a news reporter in a fedora hat, standing outside that window in the rain. He wasn't just looking for a scoop or trying to get his name on the front page. No, it was much more personal than that. It was as if he was trying to get even with the world for something it had done to him.

The Home Improvement Bug

t's midmorning. There is a low gray fog hanging in the trees. In California, this would mean cooler temperatures, but here in South Carolina the fog means nothing. It just means you can see the humidity that you already know is there.

I was dreaming like a wild man before I woke up this morning. I try to remember the dream, but I don't have much to go by. I'll tell you what I do remember. I was on my way to the airport to catch a plane, but I wound up walking through Disneyland. There was a tall, gangly man dancing in the middle of Main Street and wearing a tight-fitting Grinch costume, and I had a dog with me who kept running away from me and coming back. What kind of dog was it? I'm not exactly sure, but it was a small dog, about the size of a cat. I think the dog had brown fur. Suddenly there was a ruckus, and a parade filled the street from curb to curb. A group of knee-high cartoonlike creatures passed me with paper notes pinned to their backs. I wasn't sure if they were dancing or marching, and I couldn't read what was written on the notes. Then I realized I was missing my flight, and in a sudden panic I woke up.

I've told you about my dream on Key West and my dream selling a pair of cars to Frankie McGuire, and now you know about my most recent dream at Disneyland. That's three dream-filled nights under my belt, making it four more days until Terrance and Paul arrive here in South Carolina. I make myself a cup of coffee and step to the bookshelves in the family room where I left Paul's blue whistle. Veronica is gone riding her horses, and she won't be back until the afternoon. I have the house to myself. I always have the house to myself in the mornings. I reach and pick up the blue whistle, and I blow into it. It's louder and shriller than I remember. I look at it for a moment and then put it back down on the shelf.

On the next shelf down is a framed photograph of Paul and Marie at Paul's college graduation dinner. I pick the photo up and look at it. It's hard to believe this picture was taken eight years ago. It seems like only yesterday that Paul was graduating from USC, and it doesn't seem like that long ago that Marie was in our family. It's amazing how much things can change in one's life. But now that I'm thinking about it, I have a question for you. Do things really change at all? Maybe it isn't a matter of change, but rather a process of things coming into focus. As life marches forward, the blurred edges sharpen. The final view we enjoy, if we're lucky enough to live a good long life, is of the same vista we started with, but now without all the wavy lines and distortions.

I guess I should tell you about Marie. I liked Marie. She was a year younger than Paul, and a year behind him in school. She was going to Long Beach State while Paul was at USC. It was amazing how pretty this girl actually was. If her IQ was about twenty points lower, she could've been a model for cosmetics or hair products. Her eyes were her most noticeable feature—large, wet, and crystalline brown. When you looked into them, they spoke to you. They said, "I'm loving, empathetic, and very intelligent, and I'm paying close attention to you." God, how I loved looking into this girl's remarkable eyes. It was fun just making conversation as an excuse to connect with them. God built the rest of her face around her eyes—a small nose, full lips, and an interesting mouthful of teeth. And she had other features, but it was the eyes. Everything about Marie revolved around her eyes.

Marie and Paul went way back. Paul had known of her since they were in grade school. They didn't become good friends until they were both in college. They were paired at a party thrown by an old high school friend, and Paul liked her right away. She wasn't vain or superficial like so many other girls her age. She was a psychology major at Long Beach State. She planned to be a psychologist after she finished college, and she wanted to go into marriage counseling.

She thought couples were fascinating, and she thought she could help people out. She told us she admired the way Veronica and I seemed to get along so well. She said, "You're nothing like my own parents. My mom and dad should've called it quits years ago." As I came to know her parents, I agreed with Marie. Never mind love. Her parents didn't even seem to *like* each other much, not even on a good day.

Marie and Paul were boyfriend and girlfriend for two years before they got married. During the two years prior to their marriage, they both graduated from college. During this time Paul got a job at the paper, and Marie enrolled in graduate school at Pepperdine University to get her PhD. Once they were married, they had no plans to have children, thank God. They did purchase a modest house using money they borrowed from us and Marie's parents. By modest, I mean to say the house was kind of a dump. It was all they could afford on Paul's salary, but it was theirs, a place they could call home.

During the first months they were married, we had no reason to suspect anything was wrong. They were just two relatively inexperienced kids who had recently said their wedding vows and moved into a home. One was working, and the other was going to school. They seemed to love each other. I mean, it certainly seemed that way to me. I had no idea the marriage was all wrong for Paul. I honestly thought he had found the life he wanted.

After about four months of marriage, Paul was bitten by the home improvement bug. I never quite understood the forces behind this. But he was insistent that their house had to be refurbished and remodeled. He was obsessed with the idea just like he was obsessed with baseball as a kid, just like he was obsessed with writing that novel, and just like he was obsessed with bringing down Professor Jeffries. The first thing he did was to hire an architect. Well, Paul didn't actually find a real architect. The man he hired had no license, no office, and no formal training. He worked at a lumberyard during the day doing takeoffs for material bids. He drew remodel and addition plans in his spare time at home to earn extra money. This guy's name was Richard Stokes.

Paul met with Richard many times at the house, so he could describe his vision. I don't think Marie had much to do with it. "Whatever you want to do is fine with me," she probably said. She had her hands full at school getting her PhD and didn't need the diversion. She loved Paul and trusted him.

Once Richard and Paul had completed the plans, Paul sent them out to several local contractors to get some prices. He had a budget in mind but had no idea what the actual prices would be. When the prices started coming in, Paul quickly grew discouraged. I asked him what kinds of prices he was receiving, and he told me, "Jesus, Dad, I don't know if I'll ever be able to afford the kind of house I want." I felt sorry for him, but I also felt that maybe he was trying to do too much, too fast. Then Paul got a lower price from a contractor Richard recommended. This price was half the others. This was a number Paul could work with, and he was back in the game. When Paul told me about the bid, I told him that something didn't sound right. "He's a fully licensed and insured contractor," Paul said to me. "And he has references. And Richard recommends him."

Even though I was wary at first, Paul wanted to move forward with the cheap contractor. His name was Ernie Smiley, and he'd been in business for about two years. He was a kid. I mean, he couldn't have been over twenty-four, about Paul's age. But he managed to do and say all the right things. Paul got me involved, asking for my opinion. After seeing the proposal, talking to Ernie on the phone, and calling his two references, even I was convinced that he'd probably do a satisfactory job. He explained the price difference to me this way. He said, "I'm just starting out in the business, and I need to get a list of good-size projects under my belt. I have no overhead to speak of, and I supervise all my own jobs. Sometimes I do some of the work myself, which saves a lot of money. I just need a chance to prove myself, so I'm willing to do your son's job at cost, with nothing added for supervision, overhead, or profit. This is a huge savings. This makes my price about half of what other contractors would charge."

Obviously, Paul did not have the money to pay for the work with his own cash. The plan from the very beginning was to get a home improvement loan from a bank, but I don't think Paul realized how stingy banks were when it came to lending money. He went to several banks and was politely turned down by all of them. Then Paul came to me. It's not like I was surprised. A little voice in the back of my head said, "If the banks think this is a lousy risk, it probably is." But I ignored the little voice, and the next thing I knew I was funding a construction project for my kid son and his kid contractor. Veronica seemed to be happy that I was doing this. She obviously had not experienced any voice in the back of her own head.

So the gate opened, and our race horse was off and running. Right off the bat the job went over the budget. I couldn't believe it. The permit was going to cost about five times what Ernie figured. "There's nothing I can do about permits," Ernie said. "All the cities are unique, and their fee structures are all different. If we were building the project somewhere else, my estimate would probably have been right on the money." What I said to myself was *What a load of crap.* But what I said to Ernie was "I guess we'll just have to add that to the cost." Something told me this wasn't going to be the first time we'd have an overage, so I added a column to my spreadsheet for unexpected costs.

The demolition proceeded, and true to his word, Ernie was there with a sledgehammer performing a lot of the labor himself. He also had a Mexican kid working for him by the name of Salvador. Things seemed to be going well. Then on the third day of demolition, Salvador got his finger caught on a nail while he was pulled out a stud, and it broke his bone. Ernie immediately took him to a walk-in clinic, and I got a call from Ernie while I was at work. He told me about Salvador's injury and asked if I'd give the clinic a credit card number over the phone to pay for putting the finger in a cast. "I don't have enough money to pay for this," he said.

"Put it on your insurance," I said.

"I can't."

"Why not?"

"I don't have insurance right now."

"I thought you said you carried worker's compensation insurance."

"I did carry worker's compensation."

"And?"

"I just don't have it now."

"I don't understand," I said.

"Between the time I told you I had the insurance and now, I wasn't able to pay the premium."

"You let your policy lapse?"

"Just temporarily. After you give me my demolition draw, I'll have the insurance reinstated."

What I wanted to say was "What a load of crap." But what I said was "Okay, put them on the phone, and I'll give them a credit card number."

When I got home that night, I added the cost of the broken finger to my spreadsheet. One day later Ernie was done with the demolition, and he brought me his invoice for his draw. The invoice was for about twice the amount specified in the contract, and I looked at it closer. There were charges on the invoice for removal of dry rot caused by old roof leaks that could not have been foreseen until the demolition took place. They refer to these kinds of charges in the construction business as "extras." I got on the phone with Ernie and made it clear I didn't want Paul to be nickeled and dimed throughout the project with a steady flow of extras. I told Ernie we expected him to know what he was doing and knowing what he was doing meant anticipating such work rather than charging extra for it. "You should've included this in your original price," I told him.

"There's just no way I could've known," Ernie said. "You don't know what's in a wall until you start tearing it apart."

I wanted to say, "What a load of crap." But I said, "I suppose you're right."

Then came the rainstorm. I had paid Ernie everything he asked for with his demolition invoice. I also told him not to forget to pay his worker's compensation premium. He said he'd already paid it. The rain came just a couple of days after I paid the invoice. It started at about five o'clock in the evening. It was a light rain at first, just a few drops here and there. But the news said the rain would be heavy overnight. I knew that Ernie had torn apart the roof in many areas of Paul's house, and I was concerned about the rain. I called Paul and told him to get a hold of Ernie as soon as possible to cover the open areas with some plastic sheeting. Paul tried to call him, but his cell phone kept going straight to voicemail. Paul said he didn't think it was going to rain that hard. "The news always says it's going to rain, and then nothing happens. Last time they predicted a rainstorm, it didn't even drizzle." He was right about this, but I told him to keep calling Ernie, just in case. When I talked to Paul at seven, he still hadn't been able to reach Ernie, and at eight o'clock it began to pour.

I called Paul when the rain started coming down and asked him to call Ernie again. He said there was no need, that Ernie just showed up with Salvador. The men carried several rolls of plastic sheeting up to the roof, and they began to cover the open areas. By the time they finally started, the rain was coming down in buckets and the wind was blowing like crazy. Marie went to spend the night at her parents' while Paul stayed in case Ernie needed help. According to Paul they got about half of the roof openings covered when Ernie slipped on the wet roof shingles and fell through the plastic, right into the living room. He landed on the coffee table and cut open his back. There was no way he'd be able to continue, and blood was now running down his pantleg and all over the floor. Ernie would need a ride to the walk-in clinic. Salvador had no driver's license, so that left Paul to do the driving. By the time they reached the clinic, it was nearly nine. And that's when I got the call from Paul. He wanted me to give the clinic my credit card number again so that they could pay for Ernie's stitches. I was pretty angry. "I thought that idiot had his worker's compensation insurance in force," I said.

"It only covers his workers."

"You mean, he has no insurance for himself?"

"No, not for himself."

You can imagine what I wanted to say, but instead I asked Paul to put the hospital on the phone so that I could give them a credit card number.

Meanwhile, I didn't realize it, but Paul's house had still not been properly covered and was getting drenched inside and out.

I got a call from Paul the next morning. He said I should come by and look at the damage to the house, so I drove over to see. It was beyond belief. The furniture, carpet, doors, hardwood flooring, and everything else you can think of had been soaked by the rainstorm. It looked like a hurricane had swept through the house. Ernie was there with a big gauze bandage on his back, trying to clean up with a soaking wet push broom. Salvador was taking the day off, being as that it was a Mexican holiday. "This is a fucking disaster," I said to Ernie.

"I tried," he said. "I really tried."

"They did their best," Paul said. Like a dope, he was sticking up for Ernie.

"What's all this going to cost?" I asked.

"I'll have to figure a price."

"I suppose this will be another extra."

"It's an act of God," Ernie said. "I can't be held responsible for acts of God."

Well, what do you think? What I've described was just the first week. Hell, the week wasn't even over! You can imagine how the rest of this crazy job went. When it was all done, I looked over my spreadsheet, and the column for unexpected costs was twice as long as the column for the original budget. It was a joke. I don't even want to tell you what the total cost of the job came to.

Once Ernie was paid in full, we had to figure out a way for Paul to pay me back. Paul barely made enough money to make the original payment we had figured. So I sat down and came up with a payment plan that would delay the bulk of the payments until Marie had earned her PhD and was bringing home a paycheck. I remember that she wasn't very happy to hear this. In fact, from what Veronica told me, she was now very frustrated with Paul and the entire remodeling project. Poor Marie. She probably shouldn't have left things up to Paul. I think she would've been fine with some minor improvements here and there, just enough to make the house more livable.

I always thought it was the house remodel that caused Paul and Marie to get divorced. That would make the most sense, right? Everything else in their lives seemed fine at the time. But two years after the divorce I ran into Marie at the post office. I was mailing a car part to one of my customers, and we passed as I came through the entry doors. "Marie!" I said.

"Oh, hi," she said.

"You're looking good."

"Thanks," she said.

"Are you still living here in town?"

"I'm living with my parents."

"Ah," I said. I thought for a moment and then said, "I'm here to mail a car part."

"I just sent a birthday gift to my niece. She lives in Arizona."

"Say, I never did get a chance to tell you how sorry I was about everything."

"Sorry?"

"About the divorce. You know, about you and Paul and that awful house remodel."

"House remodel?"

"Isn't that why you got divorced?"

"No, of course not."

"No?"

"It had nothing to do with remodeling the house. That was nothing."

"Then what was it?" I asked.

Marie was about to say something, but the words didn't leave her mouth. She had stopped herself from answering my nosy question. Instead she said, "You should ask Paul. It really isn't my place to say."

"Well, I'm still sorry," I said.

"So am I," Marie said. "I loved your son."

I made a mistake. I should've followed Marie's advice and asked Paul what she was talking about, but I never did. I should've asked Paul what had happened. I just didn't think it was any of my business. It was like my dad always said, "Don't be afraid to ask questions. How else will you ever learn?"

What's That Spell?

" Give me an F, give me a U, give me a C, give me a K, and what's that spell?"

How old are you? Do you remember that song? Do you remember those days? Things were so much different then. They were *much* different. When I was in eighth grade, the Vietnam War was where I was expected to go in a few years to do my duty for God and my country. I was to help stop the evil advance of communism. I was to learn how to shoot a gun, learn how to toss grenades, and learn how to kill lots and lots of gooks. *Pop, pop, pop!* Watch them fall out of the trees. Watch them die, the bastards. And watch my buddies die. And watch my friends lose their fingers, eyes, arms, and legs. This was no joke. This was the game conjured up by the nutty adults of the United States for their beloved children. This is what they were giving us for our eighteenth birthdays, and we damn well better have said thank you and appreciated it. God help the cowards who burned their draft cards or packed their things and moved to Canada.

I got to know Eric Childs during this era, when I was in the eighth grade. I don't remember exactly how we met. Maybe it was in our civics class, since the two of us were in the same third period class with Mr. Tuttle. But it's hard to imagine we became friends in the actual class, since we were seated at the opposite ends of the room. My desk was near the door, and Eric was seated clear across the room by the windows. Eric was one of those kids who always stood out from the others because of the way he looked. You couldn't miss him. His curly hair and shiny, bulbous nose made him look like there was always a bright spotlight aimed down on him. I'd never seen a boy with such curly hair or with such a large and mature nose. For several months, Eric was my friend, and we would hang out together during lunch breaks, sitting on the grassy field behind the gym, eating our sack lunches, and talking. I also went over to his house a few times after school, and we would hang out in his bedroom.

Eric lived with his mom. His parents were divorced, and his dad had moved back east to Boston. I liked Eric's mom. She wouldn't let me call her Mrs. Childs. She politely insisted that I call her by her first name, Lisa. I thought it was kind of cool, being on a first name basis with an adult. I guess you could say Lisa was kind of a hippie. She wore her sandy hair in two long braids that fell forward over her chest, and she was always had big silver hoop earrings that nearly touched the tops of her shoulders. She had kind of a natural beauty that required no makeup, and I remember she always smelled like she showered in patchouli oil. The first thing you noticed when you walked into Lisa's home was that paisley was her favorite pattern. She was a paisley fanatic. The curious designs were printed on her loose-fitting dresses, on her sofa throw pillows, and all over her window curtains. They were on her tablecloth, placemats, napkins, and even on some of Eric's shirts.

Eric was an interesting kid, to say the least. He had all kinds of creative ideas about God, the universe, and the meaning of life. I loved listening to him talk. I was also a little surprised when I learned that this son of a peace-loving, patchouli-oiled mom was an ardent sports fanatic, and can you guess which sport he followed? It wasn't baseball, or football, or basketball. It wasn't even soccer or rugby. It was boxing. It was bloody, face-pounding, knock-your-opponent-unconscious boxing. And can you guess who his idol was? Maybe you can. It was none other than the self-proclaimed greatest boxer of all time, Muhammad Ali. Eric had photos of Ali tacked up all over his bedroom walls. It was amazing. He had magazine and newspaper clippings next to the pictures. He had several letters Ali had written to him in response to fan letters he had sent to the champ. "Wow," I said when I first stepped into his room. "I didn't know you were a fan of Muhammad Ali."

"Of course I'm a fan," Eric said. "Who doesn't love Ali? He's the greatest."

"So he says."

"How much do you know about him? I know everything worth knowing. I know, for example, that he was the youngest boxer ever to take the title away from a reigning heavyweight champ."

"How old was he?"

"He was twenty-two."

"Who'd he beat?"

"He beat Sonny Liston. Have you ever heard of Sonny Liston? The guy was an intimidating, head-bashing beast, and no one thought Ali had a prayer when he stepped into the ring with him. The odds for the fight were seven to one against Ali, but he beat on that ugly monster until he gave up and refused to come out of his corner. Ali ran over to the press at the side of the ring and shouted, 'Eat your words. I am the greatest. I shook up the world. I'm the prettiest thing that ever lived!' And believe me, he was all that. Listen, Sonny tried every trick in the book to win that fight. Thumbs, elbows, and rabbit punches. He even smeared some kind of weird ointment on his gloves that that would get in Ali's eyes and temporarily blind him. But it didn't work."

"And now Ali can no longer fight."

"You're right, he can't. Not in a sanctioned bout, anyway."

"They stripped him of his title."

"The completely screwed him over. And for what?" Eric asked.

"For refusing to fight in Vietnam."

Eric glared at me, like I was the one who stripped Ali of his title. "Would *you* fight in Vietnam?"

"I don't know," I said.

"Would you go to jail?"

"My mom doesn't think I should have to go to the war," I said. "She doesn't even think we should be over there. She argues with my dad about it."

"Your mom is right."

"Maybe she is, maybe she isn't. But I don't want to go to jail. And I don't want to move to Canada."

"You want to kill the Viet Cong instead? You want to *get* killed?

Ask yourself this, Robert. What did the Viet Cong ever do to you? Like Ali said, he has nothing against those people. No Viet Cong ever called him nigger. It's so true, isn't it? And I can't think of anything the Viet Cong have ever done to me. Not a single thing. All they wanted was their freedom from the French, and now they want their independence from us. They just want the bullies to leave them alone. Tell me, why don't we just leave them alone? Why is their country our business? What the hell are we doing over there?"

"Preventing communism."

"Why?"

"Because we have to stop communism."

"But why?" Eric asked.

"Because," I said. "It's because communism threatens our way of life."

Eric laughed. "Communism isn't a threat," he said. "It's a fad."

"A fad?"

"It's a fad, and I'm not going to kill for a fad. And I'm certainly not going to die for one."

"Don't you believe in democracy?"

"Of course I believe in democracy. Why would you even ask me that?"

"Don't you think the Vietnamese deserve to have a shot at democracy?"

Eric laughed again.

"What's so funny?" I asked.

"You've been brainwashed. You're talking without even thinking. Let's say Vietnam did have a democracy. Let's say they had a democratic government from north to south. And say they say, 'Let's hold a democratic election right now and put an end to all this fighting. Let's give the people exactly what they want, a government for the people and by the people, just like our friends in the United States.' What do you think would happen?"

"I don't know."

"They'd vote to become communist."

"How do you know that?"

"Because Eisenhower said it himself. He said eighty percent of the citizens in Vietnam *want* communism. We're the problem over there. We're the cause of the war. We don't want them to have what they want. We don't believe in democracy unless people vote the way we want them to vote. We don't *really* believe in democracy. We believe in people agreeing with us. And if you have the audacity not to agree with us, we turn your country into a wall-to-wall war zone."

"Did Eisenhower really say that?"

"It's a matter of public record. He said it was about eighty percent. That's exactly what he said. We claim to be fighting for democracy, but real democracy is the one thing we won't let the Vietnamese have. The whole war is a farce. We're not fighting for democracy at all, and just because the men waging the war are all experienced generals and leaders, it doesn't mean they aren't phenomenally dumb. Or corrupt. Or just plain evil. Or maybe they're all of the above."

I thought about what Eric just said. I didn't know how to respond. The war had never been described to me quite this way. Then I looked around at all the pictures of Muhammad Ali on his walls and said, "My dad says Ali is a hypocrite."

"Does he?"

"He says it doesn't make sense for a man who makes his living beating the holy crap out of others to suddenly have a conscience about hurting people."

"I don't think Ali has anything against hurting other people. I think he just doesn't see why he should have to hurt people who aren't doing anything to hurt him. If you aim a gun at his forehead and try to kill him, he'll very likely pick up his own gun and try to kill you first. But if you're just minding your own business, growing rice and eating with chopsticks, most likely he'll leave you alone. I don't see anything hypocritical about that."

"You're probably right," I said.

"I am right."

A war halfway around the world? A heavyweight boxer? You're probably wondering what all this talk about Vietnam and Muhammad Ali has to do with my son, Paul. Am I right? In fact, Vietnam and Muhammad Ali have a lot to do with him. In fact, you'll soon see they have everything to do with what Paul did.

Fast-forward to my eighth-grade civics class with Mr. Tuttle, where Eric sat over by the windows and where I sat near the door. I could see Eric from where I was seated, and he could see me. "There is a price we must pay for democracy," Mr. Tuttle said. "It's a price that has to be paid over and over. It's infuriating, heartbreaking, and frustrating, but it's a fact of life. We have to be ready to defend our way of life *with* our lives. Each of us must be prepared to make the ultimate sacrifice, especially young people, for there are those in the world who would like nothing more than to rule over us with an iron fist, tell us all what to do with our lives, and take away our freedoms. Some of these men are evil, and some are just misguided, but the results are the same if we don't stand up and fight. Everything our forefathers worked so hard to create for us will be destroyed, razed, and burned to the ground, and we'll be nothing more than slaves in our own land. How many of you want to be slaves?"

Of course, no one in the class raised a hand. These kids didn't really understand freedom, but they knew they didn't want to be slaves. Who in their right mind wanted to be a slave?

"We must be prepared to fight tooth and nail for everything we have," Mr. Tuttle said. "And by tooth and nail, I mean we must be ready to kill, or be killed. We must be ready to maim or be maimed. We must not be afraid of our enemies. No, no, let them be afraid of us. We must be brave, steadfast, and resolved to win every skirmish and battle at all costs. We must be on one another's side, and we must have one another's backs. We must follow the orders handed down to us by our leaders, confident that they know what's best for us and our country. Together, and only together, we can keep our democracy intact for ourselves, for our loved ones, for our children, and for all our children's children. United we stand, and divided we fall, isn't that what they say? Give me liberty or give me death. Is there anyone in this room who doesn't get what I'm saying?"

Mr. Tuttle stopped speaking again. And again, no one raised a hand. His little pep talk was going over well with his kids. One thing you have to understand, however, is that this talk was taking place in an Orange County school, and Orange County during 1968 was about as white and conservative as you could ever imagine. I mean, hell, Orange County? Trying to find a Democrat in Orange County was like searching for an ice cube in the middle of the Mohave Desert.

"It saddens me," Mr. Tuttle said. "I keep reading in the paper about these misguided youngsters burning their draft cards and moving north to Canada. Meanwhile, the dominoes are toppling. You can practically hear them falling. One by one, it'll be Vietnam, Cambodia, and Laos. And the next thing you know, they'll be on our California coast, managing our government, teaching in our schools, and telling us what color of shirt to wear in the morning. It sickens me to think about it."

Eric suddenly raised his hand, and everyone in the class stared at him. "I'd like to say something," Eric said.

"Go ahead, Eric," Mr. Tuttle said.

"I think any American male who signs up for military service and goes to Vietnam to pull a trigger or throw a grenade is the *real* enemy of democracy. In fact, I say they're an enemy of basic human intelligence, because only an idiot would feel there's honor in killing people who are doing nothing more than fighting for the freedom and independence of their country."

"I beg your pardon?"

"And by the way, your domino theory is crap."

"Pussy!" one of the boys said.

"Commie," another said.

Then someone threw a pencil, and it bounced off Eric's forehead. "Chicken," a kid said, then he made clucking sounds.

"The war is a farce," Eric said to them.

"*You're* a farce," a girl said.

"And you're a moron," Eric said to the girl. "You don't even know what you're talking about."

"Alright, that's enough," Mr. Tuttle said. Then to the class he said the obligatory, "This is a free country, and Eric has a right to his opinions." I think it's funny to watch people say things when they don't really mean them, but I didn't laugh.

I didn't have lunch with Eric that day. Instead, I sat at one of the picnic tables near the basketball courts with another group of boys, but I could see Eric on the grass behind the gym. The boys I was sitting with were talking about Eric and what he said in our civics class. Then one of them said to me, "You're his friend, aren't you?"

"I wouldn't really say we're friends."

"Don't you usually have lunch with him?"

"Sometimes I do."

"What's his problem?"

"I don't know," I said.

Then Jason Trumbull, one of the school's star football players, appeared at our table with his friends. Jason was one of those kids who the others looked up to, not because he got good grades, and not because he was kind to anyone, but because he played football. Everyone at the table knew that Jason's older brother was in Vietnam, and Jason felt this gave him a right to be outraged by Eric's statements in our class. "So Eric the pussy-cat-hearted thinks the war is a farce," Jason said to us.

"He's a traitor," one of the boys said.

"No, he's just a wuss," said another.

"I'm going to show him what we do to traitors and wusses," Jason said. "Anyone coming?"

"What are you going to do?"

"Not sure yet," Jason said.

"This ought to be good," the kid next to me said, and he stood up. "You coming?" he asked me.

"I'll come," I said.

"All of you should come," Jason said.

The next thing I knew, we were following Jason toward Eric. My friend was sitting on the grass, and he'd seen us approaching. But he didn't stand up or try to leave. What would be the point? Everyone would just follow him.

"What's up?" Eric asked when we got there.

"We're trying to figure out what to do with you," Jason said.

"Do for what?"

"For being a coward."

"I'm hardly a coward."

"My brother would disagree with you."

"If your brother had half a brain, he'd tell you it took a lot of guts for me to disagree with Mr. Tuttle. It took courage to do what I did."

Jason laughed, and the rest of the boys laughed along with him. "Stand up," Jason said.

"Piss off," Eric said.

This lack of cooperation angered Jason, and he said, "You know what you are?"

"What am I," Eric said.

"You're an F-A-G. You know what that spells? I'll tell you what it spells. It spells Eric. Turns out you can spell Eric with only three letters." Again, the boys all laughed. It wasn't very funny, but the boys laughed anyway.

"Very clever," Eric said.

"Let's see you spell this," Jason said. He cleared his throat and then spit right on Eric's leg. Eric scowled at Jason, but he didn't do anything. What would be the point, with all the kids there?

Then another boy spit on Eric, and this time the spit landed in his curly hair. "You made your point," Eric said, trying to brush the spit from his hair. But this wasn't the end of it. A third boy spit, and then a fourth, and then a fifth, so that the next thing I knew they were all clearing their throats and spitting on Eric, over and over. He just sat there on the grass doing nothing to defend himself. He was covered with wads of disgusting saliva. It was in his hair and all over his body. What the heck could he do about it? He knew if he stood up, he'd just be pushed back down. If he tried to run, they'd just grab him and throw him to the ground. So he just sat there, taking it, until Jason finally said, "This is the last one." He leaned down and spit in Eric's eye. The boys all laughed, looking at Eric, and then they all began to walk away. They were laughing as they walked. They laughed all the way back to the picnic table.

I stood there staring at Eric right after Jason spit in his eye. He refused to look at me or say anything to anyone. I hadn't spit on him, but I did watch the whole thing without coming to his defense. I probably should've felt sorry for him, but I didn't. I didn't feel sorry for him at all. I remember being disappointed. In fact, I was angry at Eric. He had put me in a very awkward position, the two of us having been friends. He had destroyed this friendship, and why? Just so he could be honest about his unpopular ideas? Who cared what he really thought, or what he really was?

And now my son seems to be doing the very same thing. I used to ask myself why people like Paul and Eric didn't just keep their mouths shut. Don't they say, "Silence is golden"? Maybe it is, and maybe it isn't. But here's the really interesting thing. I now see exactly what Eric was talking about, and I think he was right. Yes, goddamn it, he hit the nail right on the head. The war in Vietnam was every bit of the farce he said it was.

Wake Up, America

Are you surprised that Paul got married? You want to know what I think? I don't think Paul ever really wanted to be gay. I think if there was anything he could've done to put an end to his homosexuality, he would've done it in a heartbeat. I think when he married Marie, he thought the marriage might turn his life around. It'd be like getting over a phobia by jumping into your fear with your eyes wide open and facing the fear like a man. That's how my son was raised, to tackle things head-on, and not to back down from challenges just because they seemed too tough. And I liked Marie a lot, but I think that maybe if she had been more of a wife and less of a career girl chasing after her PhD and dreams to become a psychologist, then maybe Paul wouldn't be where he is today.

But it's all water under the bridge, right? The two divorced, and once the divorce was final, Paul and Marie put their remodeled house up for sale. Marie moved back in with her parents, while Paul stayed in the house until it sold. The house was on the market for six months, and the final sales price covered the mortgage as well as what they owed to me and Marie's parents. I'll tell you the truth. I was relieved to get my money back, every last dime of it. It was one of the few good things to come from the divorce. It was like busting open Mr. Carlos and finding thousands of dollars.

It was shortly after the sale of the house that Paul got the Jeremy Foster assignment. It was the first high-profile story he'd been given since he started work at the paper. It was about time, right? Prior to this he was covering mind-numbing zoning battles, petitions for traffic signals needed at intersections, some heated neighborhood squabbles, and a few minor celebrity weddings. His boss, Mr. Edwards, thought he was now ready to handle a *real* story, and he called Paul into a meeting. They were in the conference room, and a secretary brought in a pot of coffee and some cups. Paul liked this. He told me you could tell that a meeting was important when the secretary brought in coffee. Sometimes I forgot how young he was. I mean, in some ways Paul was wise beyond his years, but in other ways he could be surprisingly naïve.

Mr. Edwards was in the room along with two other men. One of the men was a middle-age attorney wearing a three-piece suit and polished leather shoes. He had a square jaw, thins lips, and hair in his ears. His briefcase was open, and his legal pad was on the table, so he could take notes if necessary. The second man, if you could call him a man, was actually just a kid. He was obviously in his early twenties with bushy blond hair, a boyish face, and a pair of striking blue eyes. He was dressed in a loud Hawaiian shirt, board shorts, and sandals. He looked like your typical Southern California surfer; however, Paul would learn later that this kid had never surfed a day in his life. In fact, he didn't even like the ocean. He simply liked the way surfers dressed.

Mr. Edwards started things off by introducing Paul to the two men. The attorney's name was Thomas Parker, and the kid's name was Billy Gabriel. It was Billy who had the story to tell, and Thomas was there at the instruction of Billy's father to manage the situation and protect his son. Billy's father was also an attorney, and Thomas was his partner. The four sat quietly for a moment, and then Mr. Edwards cleared his throat to say, "Paul has experience in these kinds of situations. You might remember his big USC sex-for-grades story that appeared in the paper several years ago. In fact, that was the reason we hired him. He knows the ropes."

"Hell, he doesn't look much older than Billy," Thomas said.

"Trust me, he'll be perfect."

Thomas stared at Paul, then at Mr. Edwards. He said, "But *you'll* be in charge?"

"All the way," Mr. Edwards said. "I'll be in charge of Billy's story from the starting gate to the finish line."

"Well, I guess that's okay with me." Then to Billy, Thomas said, "Any objections?"

"None from me," Billy said.

"Then let's get on with it," Mr. Edwards said. He looked at Billy. "Now, tell us all exactly what you told me yesterday. Tell the whole story, and don't leave anything out."

"Do I have your permission to record?" Paul asked, and he removed a recorder from his pocket.

"I guess that'll be okay," Thomas said.

"It's okay with me," Billy said. "Fire it up. Let's get this show on the road."

Paul turned on the recorder and set it on the table. "The floor is yours," he said to Billy.

Billy drew a breath, preparing to speak.

Before I tell you any of Billy's remarkable story, I need to tell you a little about Jeremy Foster. You've surely heard of Jeremy, and maybe you've even listened to his radio show. Just about everyone in the country knows who the man is. In Southern California he comes on the air at nine in the morning. I've listened to him many times, not because I agree with everything he says, but because I happen to think he's entertaining. Love him or hate him, you have to admit the guy has a way with words. Of course, he's not for everyone. Veronica thinks he's an idiot, and she doesn't listen to him at all. She tells me every time I listen to his radio show, my IQ probably falls three or four points.

The first time I heard his show, *Wake Up, America*, it was right after Obama was elected president for his first term. He didn't spout off the usual dire predictions for the country the way his fellow conservative talk-show hosts were doing. Honestly, to listen to these other guys you'd think the world was coming to an end. No, Jeremy was more amused than he was fearful. I remember he said, "You're all about to see a change in this country. For all these years we've had white presidents, and now, finally, a black man has taken office. It's an historical event to be sure, and maybe you're expecting some drastic changes, and maybe you're nervous about what's going to happen next. I say that unless you're black, not much is going to change in our country. If you are black, and if you voted for Obama, you're going to notice a *huge* change. First, let me tell you all the things that will not change if you're black. Your salary isn't going to go up, and those bigoted, cigar-chewing cops aren't going to leave you alone. Your racists neighbors are still going to glare at you and keep their children away from yours. The minimum wage will still be as unlivable as it is today. There are still going to be ignorant bosses who won't hire you, and there will still be landlords who refuse to rent to you. So what huge change is going to take place for blacks in our country? I say *you're* going to change. You're going to learn something, and it's something white people have known for years. I'm talking about something we've known since the first candidates were running for office, standing on soapboxes and spewing out campaign promises. You're going to learn that no matter what color a politician's skin is, or what his religion is, or what kind of accent he has, or what he did for a living before he ran for office, he's still a politician. And make no mistake about it, politicians are politicians. You can put lipstick on your pig, but it's still a pig. So, to all you Obama-loving black voters, I say howdy and welcome one and all to mainstream America. You've finally made it! And now you get to be as jaded as the rest of us."

I laughed out loud when I heard this. There was a lot of truth to the words, without a doubt. You know, I read an in-depth biographical magazine article several years ago about Jeremy that was very interesting. Somehow, over the years he had become the voice of American conservatism, but before Jeremy got into radio, do you know what he wanted to be? He wanted to be a stand-up comic. For the longest time he tried to make a name for himself in stand-up, but without success. What he eventually discovered was that most people who go to comedy clubs are liberals. You can disagree with this assessment, but you'd be dead wrong. Stand-up comedy audiences are a liberal as they come. I don't think it's because liberals have a better sense of humor. Rather, I think it has more to do with the fact that they're more comfortable with listening to people say "shit" and "fuck," and they like hearing people talking explicitly about sex and acting cool and cavalier about illicit drug use.

So, if he wanted to be a stand-up comedian, how did Jeremy happen to get into radio? According to the article I read, his radio career started at a restaurant in Beverly Hills. Jeremy was eating dinner and drinking with several of his male friends, and they were celebrating one of their birthdays. As usual, Jeremy was telling jokes and poking fun at the world. The other men were laughing up a storm. A few of the patrons had their waiter move them to tables further away to distance themselves from the ruckus. One man, however, who was eating alone, asked his waiter to move him closer to the men's table. He wanted to hear more of Jeremy. He was interested in what he was saying, and for the next thirty minutes the man sat by himself, eating his veal cordon bleu in close proximity to Jeremy and his rowdy friends. He listened to Jeremy go on and on. He smiled the whole way through his dinner, and he laughed out loud several times. When the man was done eating, he put his napkin on the table and paid his bill. Then he removed a business card from his wallet. He stuffed the wallet back into his pocket and walked up to Jeremy. "I want you to call me tomorrow," he said, and he handed Jeremy the card. "You're a funny man. Just call me. You and I need to talk."

Jeremy had no clue what the man wanted, but he called him the next day. They agreed to meet that afternoon at the man's office in Burbank. It turned out the guy was the program director for KPLA, the popular talk radio station. The man's name was Justin Whalen, and he had a proposal for Jeremy. He said he'd give Jeremy a full hour on the radio between three and four in the morning. When Jeremy asked what he was supposed to do with the hour, Justin said, "You just talk. That's all you have to do. I heard you talking at dinner last night, and I'm convinced you won't have any trouble filling an hour. You're a natural talker, and you're funny. And best of all, you're not an annoying blowhard liberal. You're actually able to entertain people without acting like an ass. Radio personalities like you are few and far between. That's how I see it, young man. You can go places. So what do you say?"

Jeremy didn't even have to think about it. He didn't even ask how much he'd be paid. He showed up at the studio that night, and the sound engineer showed him how to operate the equipment. He was a fast learner, and when it was time to go on the air, Jeremy put on his headphones and spoke into the microphone like he'd been doing it all his life. He started off his hour of air time by saying, "My name is Jeremy Foster, and I've been hired by this station to talk to you for an hour. It's three o'clock in the morning, so God knows who I'm talking to. Maybe you have insomnia. Or maybe you're on the night shift and just got home from work. Or maybe you've been out partying all night, and you're just now getting ready for bed. Or maybe you're a black-robed vampire, killing time before the sun comes up. I don't know what you are, or who you are, or where you are, but you're now my audience, and I'll take what I can get."

Jeremy noticed that Mr. Whalen was several feet away from him, standing in the studio. "Go on, go on," Mr. Whalen whispered, smiling and motioning with his hands for him to continue.

"I'm going to make some promises," Jeremy said into the microphone. "I promise to be honest. The world has way too much distortion and dishonesty. So, for one golden hour, I'm going to give you a breather from all the lies. Yes, I'm going to give you a break. Second, I promise to do my best to entertain you. I'll give you my opinions, but I won't lecture you. No, there's nothing wrong with wanting to be entertained. Nothing at all. If I'm not entertaining you, then turn your radio off, or turn to another station, and there will be no hard feelings. Third, I'll always try to make you laugh. It's true what they say, that laughter *is* the best medicine, and God knows America could use a few yuks. Only after we stop taking life so seriously and learn to laugh at ourselves and one another will we have a shot at any kind of success. And I believe in success. I believe in it with all my heart. I'm all about each and every one of us being successful. Fourth, and finally, I promise to never stop promoting myself. Listen, I'm not going to be shy about this. I want to succeed. I've spent years trying to get a foothold in this business, and this is my one big chance. I want to be the most talked about talk show host on the radio. I want to be admired. I want to be quoted. So, if you like what you hear tonight, be sure to tell all your friends. And tell your enemies. And tell the strangers you pass on the street. Grab them by their arms and say, 'Listen to Jeremy! Listen to Jeremy! Damn it, my friend, turn on your cotton-picking radio and listen to Jeremy!'"

Well, maybe you've tuned in to his show and enjoyed listening to Jeremy, or maybe you've always thought he was kind of a jerk, but there's one thing you have to agree with, and that was that the man could attract listeners, especially conservatives. What's funny is that according to the article I read, he didn't start off wanting to be a conservative mouthpiece. He just wanted to speak his mind and let the chips fall where they may. But it was the conservatives who immediately identified with him. And they didn't just identify with him. They adored him. And because they adored him, they were even willing to forgive his occasional meanderings into enemy positions. For example, unlike many of his followers, he strongly believed in the legalization of marijuana. On his show, he said that, compared to alcohol, "marijuana was a pussycat." He said if people wanted to smoke a few joints rather than have a few Scotch and waters, that he saw no reason in the world why they shouldn't be allowed to smoke in peace. "There's only one reason why pot scares the daylights out of so many people," he said. "It's because law enforcement has labelled it as a gateway drug, a sure path to heroin, methamphetamine, and other killers. But the only reason pot has become a gateway drug is that people who smoke it are forced to buy it from criminals. If you take the drug dealers out of the equation, a couple ounces of marijuana will be no more of a gateway than the six-pack of Budweiser or bottle of Chardonnay you buy from the cooler at your local grocery store."

The weed issue really threw his detractors off guard. They didn't know whether they should applaud him or hate his guts. And this made his conservative followers like him even more. He was always a moving target. Trying to land a punch on Jeremy Foster was like trying to land a punch on the chin of a hummingbird. And this brings us to Billy Gabriel's story. Well, it almost of gets us there. First, there's Jeremy's stand on homosexuality to contend with. It was one of the deepest lines he drew in the sand. A lot of people hated Jeremy for his opinions. But a lot of people loved him for them, and I'm talking about both Democrats and Republicans. He was standing up and saying some things that many people felt needed to be said. It turned out that a lot of people were sick and tired of the media telling them that homosexuality was okay, that it was just fine and dandy.

I remember one of Jeremy's broadcasts on homosexuality that I listened to on the way to work. He had a guest in his studio who was there to promote something he referred to as the "Bill of Gay Rights for American Citizens." I had no idea who the man was, except that he had written a book about homosexuality, and this Bill of Rights was in his book. Jeremy let him talk. He had a friendly and calm way about him, and he expressed himself very well. In fact, he almost had *me* convinced that men loving other men, and women loving other women, was a perfectly normal and acceptable human behavior. Then Jeremy responded, and the world made sense again. "Listen," he said. "I love lots of men. I love my father, and I love my brother. I love my second cousin, Ralph. Seriously, the guy is one of the funniest men I know, and I love him to death. And I love my male friends, and there isn't much I wouldn't do for them. We go to baseball games, play poker together, tell lots of dirty jokes, and go camping and fishing. But I don't have any desire to bend any of these men over and stick my manhood into their bums, or put their filthy schlongs in my mouth, or kiss any of them passionately on the lips. And I certainly don't want them doing any of this stuff to me. It seems to me that people like you confuse love with sex. It's possible to love all kinds of people, but it's just wrong to go around molesting them like a horny dog who can't tell the difference between a bitch in heat and a man's leg. It's as wrong as putting ketchup on a Chicago hot dog."

I think there were a lot of men and women like me who liked listening to Jeremy's takes on homosexuality because it helped us maintain our sanity in a world that seemed to be going a little insane. We could hang onto his words like a life preserver and say, "Here's a guy on the radio with millions of ardent fans who is saying the same things that we've been thinking in private. Here is someone who agrees with us. Here's someone who gets it. And here's someone who is saying exactly what we would say if only we had our own radio show and his mastery of the English language."

But let's go back. Let's return to Paul, Mr. Edwards, Thomas the attorney, and Billy, the California surfer who didn't actually surf. We were waiting for Billy to start talking.

"He's going down," Billy said.

"Maybe he is," Paul said. "Maybe he isn't"

"Oh, he's finished."

"Just tell the story," Mr. Edwards said. "And try to stick to the facts. Paul and I are depending on you to be truthful."

Billy thought for a moment, trying to decide where to begin. Then he began by telling about himself. "I'm a gay man," he said. "It's no secret. I don't keep it to myself. I came out of the closet years ago, when I was a senior in high school. I didn't see the point pretending I was someone I wasn't. I took a lot of grief from the other kids, but I was glad I came clean. And I was glad that my parents finally knew the truth. Mom didn't seem surprised when I first told her, and she's been very supportive. But Dad was another story. It took him about a year to accept the idea. But he's supporting me now. He thinks I'm doing the right thing by coming to you about Jeremy Foster, even if it is a little embarrassing to him. I mean, my name is going to be in your paper, and everyone knows I'm his son. But he says he's behind me a hundred percent. He told me he'd have my back. That's why Thomas is here. Dad sent Thomas to look out for me. Am I right, Thomas?"

"So far, so good," Thomas said.

"So what exactly happened?" Paul asked.

"I'll begin at the beginning. This story begins on a Saturday night about a year ago, when I went to Chad's on Santa Monica Boulevard. Are your familiar with Chad's? It's a bar in Los Angeles where gays hang out. I used to go there a lot because it had a decent clientele. It wasn't low class or sleazy, and I liked most of the men I met there. On this Saturday night, I made the acquaintance of a man named Jim. I'll describe Jim for you. He was six-two or six-three, and I'd guess he was in his forties. He was very well-dressed in a suit and tie, and he wore a lot of jewelry. He had a solid gold Piaget Altiplano, a pair of diamond stud earrings, three or four rings on his fingers, and a thick gold chain around his neck. He smelled heavy of cologne, but I couldn't place the brand. His head was shaved, but he also had a closely cropped beard. He looked like some kind of Mafia character, or a foreign spy, or a bodyguard to some movie star. He was well put together, if you know what I mean."

"Did you think he was handsome?" Paul asked.

"Oh, yes, he was quite handsome. It was weird that he wanted to talk to me. There I was, dressed in worn jeans, a Hawaiian shirt, and leather sandals. I looked like I was going to a beach party, and he looked like he was going to an awards banquet. Honestly, it didn't seem like we'd have much in common, but he asked if he could buy me a drink. I said yes, and we sat down at the bar. Then he said, 'I have a proposition for you.'"

Front-Page News

Two weeks after Paul met with Billy Gabriel, his father's law partner, and Mr. Edwards, Paul's article was ready to publish. He called us the night before it was to appear in the newspaper. Paul told us to look at the paper's frontpage first thing in the morning, that we'd be in for a real treat. "It's big," Paul said. "It's going to knock your socks off!"

At the time, I knew nothing about Billy's story. Now Paul had me on the edge of my set, and I couldn't wait to see what my son had been up to. I don't usually get out of bed before eight, but the next day I got up well before the sun came up. I climbed out of bed, put on my bathrobe, and walked to the kitchen to make a pot of coffee. I clicked on the lights, so I could see what I was doing. Then I got the newspaper from the dark front yard and brought it into the house. I flattened it on the kitchen table and looked for Paul's article. Sure enough, there it was, printed on the front page just as Paul had said it would be. Paul's name was listed below the headline that read, "The Secret Life of Jeremy Foster."

I poured a cup of coffee and sat down at the table to see what this was all about. I read each word carefully, to be sure I wasn't missing anything. I read the article from its beginning on the front page, to its continuation on page three, to its conclusion on page five. In fact, I read the article twice.

Paul was right. This was big. It was the full story about Billy Gabriel and his experience with Jeremy Foster. Paul started the article by describing Billy as the son of a prominent Los Angeles attorney. Paul wrote, "You are about to read a story about this young man that you will find hard to believe, but it is a true story that needs to be told." The article went on to tell about how Billy had gone to a popular gay bar called Chad's, and how he was approached by a tall and well-dressed man named Jim. The man named Jim bought Billy a drink and then presented a most unusual proposition. Jim told Billy that he worked for a wealthy middle-age man who, for some personal and sensitive reasons, could not come to Chad's and make his request in person. Jim said the man he worked for was gay and looking for some male company. The man was willing to pay ten thousand dollars for the evening—five thousand up front and five thousand when the evening was over. "He's a good guy," Jim said. "He just wants some company. There will be nothing kinky involved, nor will there be anything strange or out of the ordinary. My boss is kind, bright, and generous. I'm confident you'll enjoy getting to know him and spending a few hours with him. I'll drive you to his house and then bring you back. You'll be free to leave whenever you wish. All you have to do is ask, and I'll take you home."

Billy said he had nothing better to do that evening and that the idea was intriguing. Who the heck was this mysterious gay man who Jim worked for? He wanted to meet him. Of course, the money was also an important factor. Ten thousand dollars was nothing to sneeze at.

Billy agreed to the offer, and Jim removed an envelope from his pocket and handed it to Billy. It contained the cash as promised. "You'll get the other half when I bring you back," he said. "It's all there, and you can count it if you wish." Billy looked into the envelope and said he didn't need to count it. The two men walked out to the parking lot, where they found Jim's car. The car was an old Rolls Royce Silver Wraith. They climbed into the car, and Jim started up the engine. "Put this on," Jim said, and he handed Billy a blindfold. Billy was about to say no this, but then he decided to play along and put on the blindfold. Billy said it was like a scene out of a film noir—the old Rolls Royce, a moonless night, and the bald-headed go-between named Jim. He thought about the man he was about to meet, wondering if he would look something like Robert Mitchum, or Van Heflin, or maybe even Peter Lorre. He had no idea what to expect.

They drove for about forty-five minutes until Billy guessed they had pulled up to a gate. Jim got out of the car, probably to open the gate, and then he climbed back in the car and drove up a crunchy gravel drive. Finally, the car stopped, and Jim turned off the engine. "You can remove your blindfold," Jim said, and Billy took it off. They were at their destination, a two-story English Tudor mansion, the sort of grand home one only saw in the movies or the pages of magazines.

It was the size of a hotel. The night sky was black and starry, and the surrounding grounds were blanketed in the darkness. But the brick porch was well lit by two large light fixtures, one on each side of the entry doors. They stepped up to the massive front doors, and Jim pushed one of the doors open. "Follow me," he said, and he led the way to a large room that was to the left of the foyer. "Take a seat and wait," Jim said, and he walked away to tell the owner of the house that his guest had arrived. Billy took a seat on one of the old couches, and he looked around. The room was filled with an amazing collection of antique furniture, lamps, oil paintings, statuettes, vases filled with fresh-cut flowers, and bookcases filled with old leather-bound books. Billy was no expert on antiques, but he figured the stuff in the room was probably worth a fortune. Everything looked authentic, and the authenticity alone meant this room full of junk cost someone plenty of money.

He didn't have to wait long. The mystery man appeared in the room out of nowhere as if he'd walked right out of a magician's cloud of smoke. He was suddenly standing about ten feet from Billy, dressed in an old-fashioned, silk-lined smoking jacket, leather slippers, and cotton slacks. In his hand he held an unlit meerschaum pipe. He set the pipe down on an end table and came closer. His stiff gait made him look older than he probably was, and he was not what you'd call a handsome man. He had puffy bags under each of his eyes like he hadn't been sleeping well for weeks. His hair was thick and unkempt, and for the most part gray. His bulbous nose was large and gnarled, like an old piece of tree root, and he had very thin lips, like twigs. When he smiled at Billy he revealed a mouthful of yellow and crooked teeth. The teeth were all there. None of them were missing, but they were yellow, probably from smoking that meerschaum pipe.

"I understand your name is Billy," the man said. "My name is John. I'm so glad you came. Your visit means a lot to me."

The man asked Billy if he wanted something to drink, and Billy said yes. The man stepped over to the liquor cart and poured each of them a glass of cognac. He brought the glasses to the sofa and sat down beside Billy, handing Billy his drink. It became clear to Billy that the man wanted more than just a night of sex. He actually wanted to talk. He wanted to get to know Billy, and he began asking a lot of personal questions. He asked Billy if he graduated from high school, and if he went to college. He asked if he got along with his parents, and he asked if he had any brothers or sisters. He asked what his favorite color was, who his favorite music band was, and what books he liked. He asked how long he'd known he was gay, and whether he had any boyfriends, past or present. He also asked if Billy was a surfer, noticing Billy's attire, and Billy told him no. He said, "If you gave me a surfboard and sent me out into the ocean, I wouldn't know which end of the board to aim forward." John got a kick out of this. He seemed to feel Billy was being honest with him, and he said he liked that. "You don't meet many people these days who are honest," John said. "Sadly, everyone wants to pretend they're something they're not. Or maybe that's just Los Angeles."

Billy liked John, and they sat together on the old couch and chatted for hours. John was a pleasant man and easy to talk to. They eventually drank the entire bottle of cognac. They didn't talk about John at all, only about Billy, for whenever Billy asked John a personal question, John would deftly change the subject. Billy stayed at the house for over five hours. During the last half hour, they were physically intimate. He said John was surprisingly sensuous, and he never felt like he was pushing himself on him or being aggressive. John was the oldest man Billy had ever been close to, and while the age difference made the experience a little weird, it was also strangely enticing. At the end of their lovemaking, Billy told John he was ready to leave. It was no problem. John shook Billy's hand and thanked him for the evening.

John called for Jim, who led Billy outside to the old Rolls Royce. Jim then proceeded to drive Billy back to Chad's, and when they arrived, he reached into his pocket. "Here's the rest of your money,"

Jim said, handing the second envelope to Billy. "No one can know about tonight. As far as anyone else is concerned, this evening never happened." Billy assured Jim he'd keep the night secret. Billy said goodbye and stepped out. He got in his car and drove home, thinking this was going to be the last time he would ever see Jim or John.

According to Paul's article, several months went by, and nothing notable happened. John became nothing more than a pleasant memory, and Billy turned his attention to other things. Then one evening he got a call from an old friend named Arnold Harvey. Arnold called Billy because an older friend of his was in trouble, and he wanted Billy to help. This friend was an elementary school teacher, and he was in hot water because he came out and told everyone he was gay. The school was in Los Angeles County, and Arnold thought Billy might be able to talk his dad into helping provide legal influence, being that he was such a well-known and respected attorney in the area. The situation was getting out of hand. Some of the parents supported the teacher, but many wanted him gone. To make things worse, several people called Jeremy Foster's radio show. They were demanding that the school board fire Arnold's friend, and Jeremy agreed with them. There were several things Jeremy did to stir things up. He gave out the phone number and email address of the school board over the air and told his listeners to complain. He also told them to contact the mayor and city councilmen, giving out their phone numbers and email addresses as well. "Let your voice be heard. Tell them you're mad as hell, and you're not going to take in anymore," he said, stealing the line right out of Peter Finch's mouth. Further, he told the parents at the school to pull their children out of the teacher's class until the matter was resolved. No thanks to Jeremy, this was turning into a very ugly battle, and Arnold learned that the story was now going to be on TV. He told Billy to watch the news, thinking it might motivate him to finally get his father involved. Billy did watch, but the last thing he thought about as he watched the TV was his father. He was stunned! They showed a recent photo of Jeremy Foster, and it was him! It was John, the very same John who lived in the English Tudor mansion. There was no doubt about it.

Billy immediately called Arnold and told him about his evening with John, who was Jeremy. He told him about the old Rolls Royce and the stupid blindfold. He told Arnold about the envelopes filled with cash, about the bottle of cognac, and about the time they spent in John's bedroom. "Jesus Christ," Arnold exclaimed. "Do you have any idea what this means? Listen, I know a guy at the paper. We've got to go to him."

Billy was furious with Jeremy, or John, or whoever the hell he now was. Imposter! Hypocrite! Hatemonger! He agreed without hesitation to go with Arnold and meet with his friend at the newspaper. The friend referred them to Mr. Edwards, Paul's boss, and it was then that Mr. Edwards assigned the story to Paul. Now the wheels were turning, and Billy told Paul and Mr. Edwards everything that had happened. Mr. Edwards then told Paul in private, "This is some great stuff. I always knew there was something wrong with that idiot. And we have our front-page story, but now you need to back the story up. Jeremy Foster is a powerful man, and we need to be sure we're on solid ground before we start shooting at the fool."

So far, it was Billy's word against the word of Jeremy Foster, the word of a kid who dressed like a surfer versus the word of a popular and beloved radio talk show host. So Mr. Edwards was right. Billy's story alone wasn't enough. Then it hit Paul. If Jeremy had used Jim to find Billy, then it was very likely that he'd used Jim to find other young men. Paul called the TV station that had the recent photo of Jeremy Foster, and he asked for a print of the picture. Once he had an eight-by-ten of Jeremy, he went to work. He made a list of the gay bars in the greater Los Angeles area, and he went to the bars with the photo in hand. He went from patron to patron, asking if they knew anything about the man in the picture. After several days, he found three men who not only knew who Jeremy was, but admitted to having the same experience as Billy. Paul was sure there were more, and maybe they would step forward at a later date. But for the time being, he had three men willing to back up the story. They were even more willing when Paul told them about Arnold's school teacher friend and everything Jeremy had been doing to him. It was all Paul needed. All three of the men gave Paul written and signed permission to include their names in his article about Billy and Jeremy.

I called Paul after I read the article, but he didn't answer his phone. So I left a message on his voice mail and asked him to call me back. On the way to work that morning, I tuned in Jeremy's radio show on my car radio. The show was on, but there was a guest host in his place. The explanation they were running with was that Jeremy had the stomach flu and would be back once he felt better. The guest host didn't even mention Paul's article; rather, he was talking about the future of terrorism and what citizens should be doing to prevent it. So what do you think? Was Jeremy down for the count? It looked like Paul had landed a blow on the hummingbird's chin.

Paul returned my phone call that afternoon while I was at work. I asked him what reaction he was getting to his sensational article. He said, "The phone has been ringing off the hook."

"Angry Jeremy Foster supporters?" I asked.

"A few of them. Mostly calls from people thanking me for writing the story."

"Gay people?"

"All kinds of people."

"Have you heard anything from Jeremy?"

"Not a peep."

"His lawyers will probably be calling."

"Mr. Edwards doesn't think they will."

"Seriously?"

"He thinks Jeremy is through. He says he's probably packing his things right now, getting ready to board the first flight to Buenos Aires."

I laughed at this.

"Have you heard from Jeremy's producer?" I asked.

"No, I'm telling you we haven't heard anything from anyone at all in his camp. I thought they would be firing their guns right away. I thought Jeremy would be ranting and raving on his show, defending himself, telling all his listeners what a crock of crap my article was and what a jerk I was for writing it. But we've heard nothing. This is not what I expected."

"It must make you feel good."

"To tell you the truth, I'm not sure how I feel."

"You nailed one of the bad guys."

"Did I?"

"Well, didn't you?" I asked.

There was a pause, and then Paul said, "I'm not sure what I did. I mean I know what I did, I just don't know *what* I did."

The next story the paper printed about Jeremy Foster appeared three days later. It was not written by Paul, but by one of the paper's other reporters. I was shocked. I honestly didn't think this would happen. Jeremy was found dead in his home office, slumped over his Louis XVI desk in a pool of his own blood. He had died from a self-inflicted gunshot to the head. It was done at night, and the article said his personal assistant, Jim, found his body the next morning. He left no will and no suicide note. There was no mention in the paper of Paul's article.

The day following the suicide, Paul stepped into Mr. Edwards' office to hand in his resignation. Mr. Edwards tried his best to talk him out of it, but Paul wouldn't have any of it. Just like that, he was willing to throw away all his years of education and experience. I thought I understood why he did this at the time, yet I probably didn't. But now I think I get it. There is currently a lot that I don't understand about my son, but I think I understand this.

Paul knew what he'd done, and it sickened him. He had destroyed a human life. He had stripped Jeremy of all his pretenses so that he was stark naked before the world. He had utterly destroyed a man who was lonely, confused, and misguided. He never did bother to talk to Jeremy, to warn him, to reason with him, or to love him. And aren't we all supposed to love one another? Aren't we supposed to give one another the benefit of the doubt? No, he had put the poison arrow in his bow and had taken aim. With a single fatal snap of the bowstring, he had sent the arrow flying and had done to Jeremy exactly what he prayed to God that no one would ever do to him.

The Waffle House

slept like a baby last night. If I was dreaming, I don't remember any of it. I feel like I had eight full hours of sound, uneventful sleep, the kind of sleep you get when you have nothing stressful or disturbing on your mind. I woke up at a little before seven, which was early for me. Now I feel refreshed, alert, and ready to face the day. And I'm starving.

We haven't lived in South Carolina long, and we have done a few new things here. But there is one thing we haven't done, and this morning I decide it's time to do it. Yes, we're going to go have breakfast at a Waffle House. These restaurants are all over the place around here, like magnolia trees and lawn mowers. We didn't have any Waffle Houses where we lived in California; in fact, before we moved out here, I didn't even know what a Waffle House was. There happens to be one not far from our house, right on Whiskey Road, and I'll bet I've passed it a hundred times while doing my errands. Well, maybe not a hundred times, but often enough to know where it is and to have heard its syrupy siren song. I'm going to take Veronica to that exact Waffle House, and we're going to order breakfast and eat like we mean it.

Right now, Veronica is in the kitchen making coffee, and she's about to prepare something to eat. "Whoa there, girl," I say. "Don't dirty any dishes. I'm taking you out to eat this morning."

"Where to?" she asks.

"To the Waffle House."

"Are you kidding?"

"No, I'm not kidding. Get dressed, brush your hair, and grab your purse. I'm starving to death. I need to get something in my stomach."

Veronica laughs and then realizes I'm serious. "You really want to go to a Waffle House?"

"Why the heck not?" I say.

Veronica thinks for a moment and then she agrees to go with me. So off we go. We hop into my car and drive down the country highway that leads us to Whiskey Road. When we get to the restaurant, the place is only about half full of customers, so we sit at a perfect little table by the front window. We watch the cars go by and wait for our server.

Half the fun of going to a restaurant like this is looking at the people who eat there. I notice that on one side of us there is a pair of construction workers. I can tell they're construction workers by the I've-seen-it-all look in their rheumy eyes and by the dark bristles on their unshaven faces. They appear to be in their fifties, but if they were shaved and dressed up they could easily look ten years younger. They're talking in low voices so that it's impossible to hear what they're saying. My God, they've ordered enough food to sustain an entire work crew for a ten-hour day. Their table is covered with plates, bowls, glasses of orange juice and milk, and mugs of hot coffee. If I ate and drank that much each morning, I'd weigh four hundred pounds in no time.

On our other side is a man eating by himself, looking out the window while he chews on a sausage. He is dressed in a suit and tie, but the tie doesn't go with his suit or with his shirt. He looks like he just got his hair cut, and his face is pink and painfully clean shaven. I figure he's a salesman. Being a salesman myself, I ought to know a fellow salesman when I see one, right? I'm guessing this guy sells residential floor coverings or window treatments to picky, cheapskate homeowners. He just looks like the type, like you could change your mind a hundred times, and he'd keep his cool and politely refuse to give up. The waitress steps up to him and refills his coffee, and he says, "Thanks, sweetheart." She winks at him and smiles, and says, "You're welcome, darling." Then she comes to our table with our menus, silverware, and paper napkins. I'm guessing she knows we're not native Southerners, because she is not as chummy with us as she had been with the with the salesman.

"Can I get you coffee?" she asks us.

"I'll have some," I say.

"Same here," Veronica says. Then just before the waitress leaves, Veronica asks, "Do you serve pancakes here?"

"No pancakes, ma'am."

"Just waffles?"

"Whatever you see on the menu, we have."

"I really feel like pancakes."

"Sorry, ma'am."

When the waitress walks away, I say, "What the heck? Why are you trying to order pancakes?"

"Because that's what I feel like having."

"We're at the Waffle House. Use your head and order a waffle."

"I can't believe they don't have pancakes."

"Waffles are good."

"I don't feel like a waffle. I was really looking forward to having pancakes for breakfast. Who ever heard of a restaurant that specializes in breakfast and doesn't serve pancakes?"

"I guess we're sitting in one," I say.

Veronica looks over her menu and says, "Maybe I'll get some scrambled eggs."

I look at my own menu and say, "I'm going to get the eggs over easy. And some grits. I've got to try their grits."

Veronica makes a face and says, "I can live without the grits."

"You're in the South, Veronica. Why don't you try the grits? You've got to have some grits. I haven't seen you order grits since we moved here."

"I'm just going to get some toast. And maybe a couple strips of bacon."

I continue to look over my menu. Then I say, "We should order at least one waffle. It's their specialty. We can share it, okay? You don't have to eat the whole thing."

"You can have a waffle if you want."

"You might like it."

"Listen, I don't feel like a waffle. I feel like a goddamn pancake."

"Okay, okay," I say.

Veronica realizes she might have come across a little harsh, and she says, "Go ahead and order a waffle. I'll try a bite or two. But what I really wanted was some pancakes."

When the waitress comes back to take our orders, we tell her what we want, and I order a waffle for the two of us to share. When the waitress leaves, Veronica says, "The prices here are certainly reasonable."

"They are," I agree.

The service is fast, and our food is delivered before we know it. I put the waffle in the center of the table, so Veronica can try it. She'll never admit this, but she just about eats the whole thing before she even touches her main meal. I notice this, of course, but I don't say anything about it. I know better than to bring it up since she's so touchy about her food. Instead I say, "Do you remember when we took Paul to Hawaii after he quit his job at the paper?"

"God, he was so depressed."

"That suicide really upset him."

"I was glad he agreed to come with us."

"So was I," I say. "He needed a change of scenery. It was the perfect trip for him. He needed a week to clear his head."

"Do you remember that girl at the hotel you tried to hook him up with?" Veronica asks.

"I do. What was her name?"

"Jennifer something."

"Yes, Jennifer. She was a nice girl. She was just sitting there at the pool by herself. She was thrilled that I asked her to join us."

"Paul liked her a lot."

"He did, didn't he? He didn't seem very gay then. I mean, he liked her, and she was a girl."

"Just because he's gay, it doesn't mean he doesn't like having girls as friends. It doesn't mean he doesn't like talking to them, or being with them, or doing things with them."

"No?"

"It just means he isn't sexually attracted to them."

"Okay," I say. "I guess that's the thing I really don't understand. And maybe I'll never understand it. I mean, I really don't get it."

"Of course you don't. You're not gay."

"Have you ever wondered what it's like?"

195

"Wondered what what's like?" Veronica asks.

"Have you ever wondered what it's like to be gay?"

"I can't say I have."

"I can remember when I was in high school, I used to test myself to be sure I wasn't gay. I'd try to imagine myself kissing another boy, not just as in a quick kiss, but a long and passionate kiss on our mouths like we were lovers. And I would see if it turned me on. I would see if the idea of kissing a boy made me feel excited or repulsed."

"And?"

"Well, obviously it was repulsive. In fact, it disgusted me. It made me feel like gagging and spitting, just thinking about it."

Veronica laughs and says, "I think it's funny you felt a need to test yourself."

"All boys do that, don't they? They just want to be sure. They want to be certain they're not gay."

"You'd think they already knew."

"Maybe they *think* they know. But it's just a matter of being sure."

"I guess I don't get it. When I was a girl, I knew I was attracted to boys. I never had to pretend I was kissing a girl to reassure myself. I didn't want to kiss girls. I wanted to kiss boys. Why would I even think I wanted to kiss a girl?"

"Well, I knew I wanted to kiss girls."

"But you pretended to kiss boys?"

"Only to prove I didn't want to do it."

Veronica laughs again and says, "That makes no sense at all. If you don't want to do something, you shouldn't need to pretend you're doing it just to prove to yourself you don't want to do it."

"I'm just telling you what I did. I wasn't asking to get psychoanalyzed."

"Can I make a suggestion?"

"Sure," I say.

"If you don't want people to think you're gay, don't go around telling them you used to pretend you were kissing boys."

I look at Veronica and sigh. I then look down at my eggs and say, "I give up."

We don't talk for a moment. I notice we're now both eating our eggs. Then Veronica says, "Do you happen to remember the Ambersons?"

"Hank and Martha, right?"

"That's right."

"Don't they have a daughter?"

"Her name is Isabelle."

"She's about ten years younger than Paul?"

"Yes, she's in college now."

"Last time I saw her, she was just a squirt. She was a cute kid, wasn't she?"

"Now she's a lesbian."

"Christ," I say.

"She has a girlfriend who's in the military."

"How are Hank and Martha taking it?"

"I heard they told Isabelle she wasn't welcome in their home until she came to her senses and got rid of her girlfriend."

"That's kind of harsh."

"They're very religious."

"Well, you might think *I'm* an old dinosaur, but at least I haven't told Paul to take a hike."

"Can you imagine disowning your own child?"

"No," I say.

"Neither can I."

I reach for my coffee, and Veronica is nibbling on her toast. I don't know why this pops into my mind, but I ask her, "Did you ever meet Adrian?"

"At your work?"

"Yes," I say.

"I think you introduced us at the last Christmas party. He's one of the salesmen, right?"

"Yes, and he's about our age. Did you know he already has three grandchildren?"

"How many sons and daughters does he have?"

"Just one son, like us. The kid got married right after he graduated from college. I've seen a picture of him and his wife. She's very nice-looking."

Veronica is serious when she asks, "Are you jealous of Adrian?"

"I probably am."

"You shouldn't be. I knew you would be, but you shouldn't be. Every family is different."

"Do you want to know the truth? I'm glad we have our son, and I love him to death, but I always wanted a daughter-in-law. I wish Paul had stayed married to Marie. I liked having a daughter-in-law, a young woman who was as fond of me as I was of her, who looked up to me and called me Dad. She could've been the mother of my grandchildren. I was always hoping Paul and Marie would give us at least two or three grandchildren who we could have stay at our house, play in our yard, eat meals with us, and sleep in our guest room. We could've tucked them in at night. We could've told them stories. I could've shown them stupid magic tricks and described what life was like before computers, cell phones, and video games. And while I watched a ball game on TV, you could've been in the kitchen with them, baking chocolate chip cookies. And we could've spoiled them. We could've bought them whatever they wanted at the toy section in Walmart, and we could've let them stay up way past midnight. And we could've let them sleep in until noon the next day. That's what I think about when I hear about Adrian's grandchildren. That's what I imagine when I see the photo Adrian keeps on his desk of his son and his family. But our son? Paul? He'll grow old with another man. Jesus, Veronica, I can't think of anything worse. Two men living together and growing old together. Two old homosexuals in a house."

"Can I taste your grits?"

"I thought you didn't like them."

"I just want a taste."

"Have at it," I say, and Veronica reaches to my plate and gets a small spoonful. She then pokes the spoonful into her mouth.

"I don't see what the big deal is with grits. They just taste like lousy mashed potatoes."

"You don't like them?"

"I mean, they're okay. But they don't have much flavor."

"I kind of like them."

"You know, Paul could get married someday, to a man. And they could adopt a child."

"That would be kind of weird."

"But it happens."

"Seems like that might be hard on their kid."

"Maybe not."

"Who would be the father, and who would be the mother?"

"They'd both be fathers."

"Don't you think a kid needs a mother in its life? I can't imagine being a kid who had no mother. Moms are so special. Moms do so much that fathers can't do. I mean, what the hell? It isn't right. A child should have both a mother and a father."

"It's a brave new world."

"It's a *what?*"

"It's a brave new world, like the title of the book. The times are a changing, like the song. I guess the answer is blowing in the wind."

"So you don't believe we're on the eve of destruction?"

"Barry McGuire?"

"You have a good memory."

We stop talking for a minute, and I finish up the rest of my grits. Veronica is still nibbling on her slice of toast. "Would you come here again?" she asks.

"To a Waffle House?"

"Yes," she says. "Would you come back?"

"I like my breakfast. Would you come back?"

"Probably not."

"Something wrong with your eggs?"

"No, they're fine."

"Then why wouldn't you come back?"

"Because if I'm going to eat breakfast out, I want to get pancakes. I never make them at home. I like having pancakes for breakfast, and the only time I can get them is when we have breakfast out."

"You could always make them at home."

"They're too messy."

"Too messy?"

"And they never come out right when I make them."

"Maybe you just need to learn."

"I'm almost sixty years old. If I haven't learned to make them now, I don't see myself learning to make them anytime soon. And if I'm going to learn to do something new, I'm not going to waste my time learning to make pancakes when all I have to do is go to a restaurant that serves pancakes. If I'm going to spend time learning something, I'd rather learn how to do something special, like play the piano."

"Learning to make pancakes is hardly comparable to learning how to play the piano."

"Whatever."

"But next time we'll go to a restaurant that serves pancakes," I say.

Veronica realizes she's been a little difficult, so she says, "But I enjoyed tasting your grits. I really did. I've never had them before. And I'm glad we got to try this place out."

"It isn't easy, is it?" I ask.

"What isn't easy?"

"Changing your ways. It isn't easy to open yourself up to new experiences, ignoring all your preconceived ideas of how the world should be, bending what you believe to be wrong into what's right. You know, as in eating breakfast at a restaurant that doesn't serve pancakes."

"You're talking about Paul, aren't you?"

"He's going to be here in three days."

Veronica takes a moment to think about this. Then she says, "Don't think it's easy for me either. I'm the boy's mother."

"That's all I wanted to hear from you," I say, and already I feel a little better.

The Great Years

They were the great years. They were the best years of my life. How old was I? Maybe six. Maybe seven. The world was a much different place in those days. It's so hard to believe how much has changed since I was a kid. There were no personal computers back then, and there was no Internet. Cell phones were still a Dick Tracy fantasy, and diapers were made of cloth and safety pins. Cars didn't come from Japan; they were marvelous American four-wheeled sculptures made of heavy steel and chrome. Looking for a place to live? A house would cost you less in those days than a car would set you back today. A Hershey bar was a nickel, a Coke was a dime. For under fifty cents you could ride your bike to the local five-and-dime and buy a kite and a big ball of string, and you could entertain yourself for the rest of the day by scraping the bottoms of the clouds with tissue paper and sticks. I remember my parents drove us around without seat belts or child seats, and we rode on bikes and steel-wheeled skates without helmets. Helmets were for mentally disturbed kids who beat their heads against tabletops and walls. Hell, hockey players didn't even wear helmets. Helmets were for sissies. Quality of life is supposed to improve over the years, but I swear it was better back then.

When I was a kid I had a mom and a dad—a dad who went to work each day to provide for us, and a mother who stayed home to raise me and my sister. I was a rough-and-tumble little bristle-headed boy who wore striped T-shirts, Fruit of the Loom underwear, a beaded Indian leather belt, and baggy blue jeans with perpetually grass-stained knees. I never forgot to put on the PF Flyers that Madison Avenue told me would make me run faster and jump higher than any other kid on our street. I always had a Band-Aid stuck to me somewhere, and there was always plenty of dirt under my fingernails and grime behind my ears. We climbed trees, shot squirrels with our slingshots, and captured snakes, frogs, and lizards with our bare hands. Every day was a marvelous adventure.

Like I said, I had a sister. She was older than me, and she was placed on this earth for one reason, and one reason only, to give me someone to tease, annoy, and insult. The poor girl. She should've been able to hold her own, being older. But I was relentless. I made the girl miserable every chance I had.

I remember Dad. He was *the* man in my life, and I'll tell you the truth, the guy scared me to death. I knew he loved me, and he wasn't mean or abusive. But he was an imposing figure, and he belonged to that secret adult club he met with every day. It was that dark and distant place away from home that he called "work." It was godless and merciless, and it caused him constant frustration, but it also provided us with food to eat, a roof over our heads, and clothing on our backs. Somehow going there each day gave my dad the inarguable right to punish me whenever I did or said something stupid. I always had that hanging over my head, and I was terrified of being whipped. Nice guy? Scary guy? I never knew which dad I was going to get, because I never seemed to know what dumb thing I'd do next. At least, that's how it felt.

Then there was Mom—lovely, glorious, understanding, and nurturing Mom. My mom was the prettiest of them all. My mom was the coolest. There were times when I would've traded Dad in for another model, given that such an option was given to me, but never my mom. I wouldn't have traded Mom for all the swimming pools in Southern California. I remember when I told my mom I was going to run away, I was six or seven at the time. I saw some kid on TV run away from home, and I wanted to be like him. I think it was on an *Our Gang* episode. I wasn't really upset with my family. I just thought I'd run away.

I remember that afternoon. It's funny the things we can remember, isn't it? I can recall everything I packed for my trip. I brought my slingshot, my Jew's harp, and a couple Spiderman comic books. I brought three Band-Aids and a plastic comb that was guaranteed to be unbreakable for as long as I lived. I packed my new stopwatch in case I wanted to time something. I was given the stopwatch last Christmas, and I got a kick out of timing things. I also brought my pocket knife, the little compass my dad gave me, and a box of crackers. I brought a can of Coke and a can opener. There was no such thing as pop-tops back then. I put everything on top of a red bandana and then pulled its four corners up. I tied the corners together so that it made a big red ball of junk. I then went to the garage and grabbed a wooden tree stake. Poking one end of the stake into the bandana knot, I was ready to leave with the middle of the stake resting on my shoulder. It was just like the kids in the comics, just like I'd seen the kid actors do on TV. And toward the front door I went, but not before Mom stopped me to find out what I was up to.

"Where do you think you're going?" she asked.

"I'm running away," I said.

"Did you clean your room?"

"I'm not going to clean my room. I'm running away, and don't try to stop me."

"Okay."

"And don't expect me to come back."

"Oh, I won't."

"And don't come to get me."

"I wouldn't think of it."

I looked up at my mom and asked, "Well, aren't you going to try to stop me?"

"You just told me not to."

"You'll never see me again."

"Will you write?"

"Write what?"

"Write us a letter now and again, to let us know how you're getting along."

"Don't hold your breath," I said. I'd heard Dad use that expression on my mom when she asked him when he was going to get her the new Chevy Parkwood station wagon she had her eyes on.

Anyway, you get the basic idea. Off I went with my possessions on the end of my stick. I had no idea where I was going. As I walked out the front door, Mom told me dinner would be ready by seven. "Try not to be late," she said. "We're having hamburgers."

I shut the front door. Then I walked down the street toward the end of our neighborhood. The street ended about ten houses down from ours, where it turned into a narrow dirt road that ran through a grove of orange trees. There was a sign posted at the side of the dirt road that said no trespassing, but none of us kids ever paid attention to it. Surely, it wasn't meant for us. Before I arrived at the grove, I came upon Nancy Winters, who was playing jacks by herself on the sidewalk. Her house was the last one on the street. Nancy was my same age, a cute little curly-haired girl who always wore homemade cotton dresses with flowers printed all over them. Today they were sunflowers. Her mom, who I knew as Mrs. Winters, was on her knees in the sunlight, wearing a big straw hat and working on a flower bed at the front of their house. She was snipping off branches from one of her rose bushes and tossing the thorny sticks into a pile on their front lawn. I looked at Nancy. She bounced her rubber ball on the sidewalk and grabbed a handful of jacks.

"Where are you going?" she asked me.

"I'm running away," I said.

"To where?"

"I don't know yet."

"Can I come?"

"I don't plan on coming back."

"I want to go with you."

"I guess it'd be okay." Nancy was alright for a girl, and I couldn't think of any good reason to tell her not to join me.

"Let me put my jacks away," Nancy said. She gathered them up and took them to her porch, dropping them near the front door. To her mom she said, "I'm done playing jacks. I'm going with Robert."

"Where are you kids headed?" Her mom didn't turn around when she asked this. It was like she was looking at Nancy with eyes she claimed to have in the back of her head.

"Robert's running away."

"Oh?"

"He said I could come with him."

"That's fine, dear. Don't go too far."

"We won't."

"Be back for dinner."

"Okay."

The next thing I knew, Nancy was at my side. We were soon on the dirt road. I was walking briskly, and she was skipping. For some reason, girls that age always liked to skip. As we made our way into the orange grove, I found the perfect tree. It had to be just the right tree. "This will be it," I said.

"Will be what?" Nancy asked.

"Our ship. Let's sit in the shade. Do you want to share a Coke? I'm getting thirsty."

"You have a Coke?"

"I do," I said. I untied the knot in my bandana and opened it on the ground. Nancy was interested in all the things I brought, and she was on her hands and knees, checking everything out. I popped open the can of Coke with the opener, taking a sip. I then handed the Coke to Nancy, and she took a couple swallows. "This is the main mast," I said, patting the tree trunk with my hand. "The branches and leaves are our sails. The oranges, well, I guess they're just oranges."

"What kind of ship is it?"

"It's an English ship of war, and I'm the captain. Everyone calls me Captain Robert. We've got eighty men, fifty cannons, and enough rum to swim in."

"And who am I?"

"I guess you're the princess."

"The princess?"

"My orders are to take you from England to the New World."

"Why am I going to the New World?"

"How should I know? I'm just following the king's orders."

"What's the New World."

"It's America, stupid."

"Am I pretty?"

"All princesses are pretty, aren't they?"

"What's my name?"

"We'll call you Lady Nancy.

"I'd rather be named Pricilla."

"Fine, we'll call you Lady Pricilla."

"Can I have straight hair?"

"If that's what you want."

"And blue eyes. I want to have blue eyes."

"Okay," I said. "You have blue eyes."

"What am I supposed to do?"

"You stay here. It's my job to protect you and make sure your voyage is successful. You can stand on the deck and watch me while I'm gone."

"Where are you going?"

"Do you see that tree way over there?" I asked, and I pointed to another orange tree. "Those are the pirates. They have a hundred men and sixty cannons."

"Pirates?"

"It's Blackbeard's ship. Have you ever heard of the famous pirate named Blackbeard?"

"No," Nancy said. "I don't know much about pirates or ships."

"Blackbeard is the most feared of all pirates, and he's after you."

"He's after me?"

"He plans to kidnap you and demand a large ransom from the king. It's my duty to stop him. My orders are to get you to America in one piece, even if it means risking my own life."

"But how will you stop him?"

"You wait here and watch me. I have a plan. A good captain always has a plan. When I'm done, Blackbeard won't even know what hit him."

"Be careful," Nancy said.

"I'm always careful," I said. I got down on one knee and kissed the top of Nancy's hand. I called her milady, and this made her blush for a second. I then grabbed my trusty pocket knife from my pile of things. I stepped to the edge of our make-believe ship and looked down at the water. I turned around at the last minute and told my imaginary first mate to wage war on the pirate ship if I wasn't back in an hour. Then I jumped off the bow of the ship and landed in the ocean with a mighty splash. The water was cold as ice, but I wasn't going to let that slow me down. I swam with the knife held in my teeth until I reached the slimy side of the pirate ship. My head was just above the water, and I could hear the pirates shouting at one another, preparing for battle. Some of the men were singing, and one of them was playing a concertina. There was a rope dangling down the side of the ship, and with my knife still in my mouth, I climbed the rope. Water was dripping off my soaking wet clothes, and it took every bit of strength I had to keep a firm grip on the rope with my slippery hands. When I reached to top, I peered over the edge of the pirate ship and saw what I was faced with. Pirates! A hundred of them, armed from the scabbards on their wide leather belts to their rotten teeth. Filthy, debauched, godless pirates! The importance of my mission was clear, and the danger was now imminent. And success was imperative. I, Captain Robert Ashcroft, held the fate of the beautiful Pricilla in my hands.

It was all up to me! Carefully and quietly, I climbed up over the edge of the ship and jumped down to the wooden deck. So far, so good. No one noticed me. Then a wild-looking fellow in a purple velvet shirt and tattered black trousers appeared from around a corner and drew his sword. He was coming directly at me, intent on taking my life. I had been discovered, but it was my good fortune that this crazy pirate was a deaf-mute and he said nothing to alert his fellow criminals. The closer he came, the worse he looked. He had the glow of burning sulfur in his eyes, a sign of the devil if ever there was one. He bared his brown, tobacco-stained teeth and raised his sword high over his head. He took a terrible swing at me. I ducked just in time, and I could feel the wind from his blade passing over the top of my head. I had to act fast before he made another attempt to strike me, so I lunged at him with my knife in hand. I went directly for his throat, and in one amazing motion, I cut him open from earlobe to earlobe. He dropped his sword and grabbed the fatal wound, his blood spurting from behind his hands, his eyes open wide, wild with fury. The blood was streaming down his velvet shirt and dripping in big red splats all over the ship's deck. He opened his mouth as if he wanted to yell, but no words came out of his mouth. Then he crumpled to the deck in a bloody, dying heap. *One pirate down,* I said to myself. *Ninety-nine left to deal with.* No way I could kill them all. But killing them all was not part of my plan. I was no fool.

For my plan to work, I had to employ the black magic I'd learned during one of my recent voyages along the coast of Africa. I befriended a sorcerer who lived inland from the port town where we docked. He taught me the magic of invisibility. It required a dead man's blood, a lock of his hair, and a swatch of his clothing. And there were the three Swahili words I had committed to memory. I took what was needed off the dead pirate, and I said the magic words. I watched my feet dissolve, and then my hands, and then my arms, belly, knees, and legs. Within seconds, I was completely gone. The only thing visible was the bloody knife I held in my hand. It looked like the knife was floating in the air. Ha, a floating knife, like it was in the hand of a ghost! I climbed over the rigging to the upper deck. None of the pirates could see me, and they were not noticing the knife. There were weapons and knives all over the place. What was one more, floating or not! Then a chill suddenly ran up my spine. There he was! It was the famous man in the flesh, smoke curling up from under his hat like his hair was on fire. It was the mighty Blackbeard! He was standing like a six-foot marble statue of himself, watching his men prepare for the attack. From head to toe, he was every bit as intimidating as his awful reputation had promised. I ran up behind him, invisible to everyone, and quickly put my floating knife to this throat, firm enough against his flesh to draw blood. "Tell your men to stop," I said. "Or I'll slice you open like a pig."

"Who the hell are you?" he asked.

"I'm Captain Robert. You have five seconds to do as I say." For a couple seconds he thought it over, and then with a thunderous voice, he instructed his men to stop what they were doing. They all looked up at him, astonished. The floating knife was still pressed against his throat. One of the men said, "By God, it's a ghost!"

"Aye," another said. "He's right about that. It's a bleeding ghost!"

"A ghost?" Blackbeard said. He turned around to look at me,

and when he saw no one was holding the knife at his throat, his eyes opened wide and his face turned white. "Great Davy Jones's locker!" he shouted to his men. "Sail us the hell away from here! This place is haunted!" His men then went to work, turning the pirate ship around and with their sails full of wind they sailed away without my Lady Pricilla. And that, my friend, is the true story of how I single-handedly defeated the notorious Blackbeard and saved Princess Pricilla. Once I was sure the pirates were on their way, I jumped back into the ocean and swam to my ship. The invisibility spell washed off while I was swimming, and by the time I reached my ship, I was fully visible. Nancy was waiting on the bow, under the shade of the orange tree. "We're safe now," I announced, climbing back aboard and drying myself with an imaginary towel. "That's the last we'll see of Blackbeard."

Nancy and I spent the rest of the afternoon eating crackers, sipping Coke, and goofing around. I taught her how to play my Jew's harp. I let her use my comb to get some tangles out of her hair. We climbed the orange tree and picked some oranges. We peeled and ate a couple of them. When we were done with the Coke, we set the can up about twenty feet away and threw dirt clods at it. Nancy was the first to hit it. The girl had a pretty good arm. We both got home in time for dinner, and when I stepped into my house, Mom made me go to the bathroom to clean up. She also made me change my clothes. "God knows what you kids do to get so dirty," she said.

Like I said, those were the great years. I had no idea what a homosexual even was. Hell, I don't think I even knew how babies were made. And while I like my life a lot now, and while I love being an adult, and while I sure wouldn't want to be a child again, I have to say that ever since the afternoon I saved Nancy from Blackbeard and his pirates, it's all been downhill. It seems the more you learn, the worse it gets. Do you get what I mean by that? And you can't put the cork back in the bottle, or so they like to say.

Paul's New Job

D o you know who Elbert Hubbard is? I'm going to quote him for you. Not yet, but shortly, as soon as I tell you about Paul's new job.

To say that Paul was a little excited was like saying a South Carolina summer was a little humid. He came over for dinner at our house that night and told us all about the job interview. It was the first time since the Jeremy Foster suicide that Veronica and I had seen Paul feeling jovial and upbeat. His spirits were optimistic. He was smiling and laughing, and there was a glint in his eye we hadn't seen for a long time.

He had been interviewed by Charles Day, the founder and president of a public relations firm that called itself The Heartfelt Team. Their office was in Santa Monica, not far from where Paul already lived. Heartfelt had been in business for twenty-two years and served charity and nonprofit groups in Southern California. Charles Day was a good-natured man in his late fifties. Paul told us his sandy hair looked like it needed combing and trimming, but that the man was also remarkably clean-shaven. While his hair may have been an unruly mess, there wasn't a speck of stubble on his face, as though the top half of his head was protesting the state of the bottom, or vice versa. Paul said Charles had intelligent green eyes and wore a pair of wire-rimmed spectacles. While he talked, he rubbed the glasses clean on his shirt over and over. Paul figured this was a nervous habit because of the number of times he did it for no apparent reason.

According to Paul, Charles didn't delegate the task of staffing his office. He interviewed every single person who applied for a job at Heartfelt personally, and Paul was no exception. Paul said the interview lasted for over an hour. Charles was especially interested to learn about Paul's experiences at the newspaper, and he also wanted to know why Paul left. "You had a stable job," Charles said. "I need to understand why you quit. Public relations is a difficult game requiring a lot of grit and determination, and I don't need quitters joining our team. What I really need are go-getters."

"Oh, I'm not a quitter," Paul said.

"But you did quit your job."

"I didn't quit because I was a quitter. I didn't quit because the kitchen was too hot. I quit because I didn't like the food they were serving."

Charles liked Paul's response. In fact, he laughed and said, "That was the perfect answer." He spent the rest of the interview describing what Paul would be doing at the firm if he was hired. He said there would be a lot of writing involved, and Paul said he liked to write more than just about anything. Most importantly, however, Charles told Paul he would be helping people. Unlike much of the work he did at the newspaper, he would be building people up rather than tearing them down. "The pay isn't quite as good as what you were getting from the paper, but the rewards will more than make up for it. This is very gratifying work. You will go home each night knowing that you have done something positive with your time and energy. I've been doing this for twenty-two years, and I don't regret a single second of it. No, I don't live in Beverly Hills, drive a Porsche, or vacation in the south of France, but over time I've become rich beyond my wildest dreams."

Two days after Paul was interviewed, Charles offered him a job. It was true that the pay was less than he'd been getting at the paper, but it was enough to live on. Paul immediately accepted the offer. In his position, he would be reporting directly to Charles, which he liked. It made him feel important, reporting directly to the top man. He discovered after a few days at his job that everyone in the office except for the secretaries reported directly to Charles, but no matter. He still liked the idea of working closely with Charles. He liked the man a lot, and he felt that Charles liked him. It wasn't like the daily grind at the newspaper, where he felt like a cog in a big media machine.

Charles didn't waste any time acclimating Paul to his new position. His first assignment was to take charge of the Lighthouse account. Paul knew nothing about Lighthouse when he first started, so he spent the next two days and nights learning all there was to know. Lighthouse was an orphanage in LA County, although they didn't refer to themselves as an orphanage. They liked to call themselves a "children's opportunity home." Whatever euphemism they wanted to employ was fine with him. Paul was determined to be the best PR professional they'd ever had.

Zach Tanner was the director of Lighthouse, and Paul drove over to their offices and introduced himself to Zach as the new account executive. The first thing Zach said to Paul was, "Are you ready for the initiation?" Paul didn't know if he was serious or joking.

"The initiation?" Paul asked.

"It's a Lighthouse tradition."

"I don't understand."

"We've been doing things a certain way for the past fifteen years. It works for us. I'm surprised Charles didn't tell you about your initiation."

"He didn't say anything."

"You can look at it this way; it's like putting your money where your mouth is. That's about the best way I can describe it."

"It's a bet?"

"No, nothing like that."

"Then I have to do something?"

"Yes, you have to do something. I mean, you don't *have* to do it. But if you want to work for us, it's highly recommended."

"What am I supposed to do?"

"Charles tells me you're a baseball fan."

"Yes, I like baseball."

"You played a lot when you were young?"

"Yes, I did."

"And you're an Angels fan?"

"I've been an Angels fan since I was a little kid."

"I've got a pair of tickets for you. They're supposed to be great seats. They're for Sunday's game against the Yankees."

"Okay," Paul said.

"I'd like you to go to the game."

"You're going to give me the tickets?"

"I am," Zach said. "But there's someone I want you to take with you."

"A woman?" Paul asked. He was used to people trying to set him up with dates.

"No, no, not a woman. A boy, actually. His name is Kevin Smart. He's thirteen years old, and he's currently staying with us at Lighthouse. His mom passed away three years ago, and his father is in prison. He's a baseball fan, and I think you'll have a good time with him. He's a little rambunctious, but he has a good heart. It would be good for you to spend some time with one of our kids. It would give you a better feel for the kind of work we do here."

"I guess I can do that," Paul said.

"Good, you won't regret it."

"Are you sure he even wants to go with me?"

"Trust me, you two will get along great."

When Sunday came, Paul drove over to the Lighthouse facility in East Los Angeles to pick up Kevin. Zach introduced Paul to Kevin. Paul told me the kid looked as normal and innocuous as a warm bowl of Quaker Oats oatmeal. He was dressed in a T-shirt, a clean pair of Levi jeans, and a pair of Nike athletic shoes. He looked like every other adolescent boy in America, complete with a slight case of acne and a scrawny caterpillar of unshaven hair on his upper lip. Certainly, there was nothing in his appearance that spelled trouble. It was not like his face was full of piercings, or like his arms and neck were covered with weird tattoos. Paul led Kevin to his car in the parking lot, and the two of them climbed in. Kevin looked around inside the car and said, "So this is actually your car?"

"Yep," Paul said. "It's my car."

"How old are you?" Kevin asked.

"I'm twenty-six."

"You're twenty-six, and this is the best you've been able to do?"

"You don't like my car?"

"How much money do you make?"

"That's kind of a personal question, Kevin."

"Well, when I turn twenty-six, you sure won't find me struggling to make monthly payments on a piece of crap like this. I'm going to buy a *real* car. Maybe a Mercedes or a Jaguar."

"Well, I hope you get what you want. If you work hard, you should get it."

"You're fucking right," Kevin said.

Paul ignored the unnecessary profanity, and he said, "It's good to have a dream. I think everyone should have a dream."

"Dream, shit," Kevin said. "I know what I want out of life, and just as sure as my name is Kevin Smart, I'm going to get it. It'll be no dream. No lame-brain job for me, working nine to five for a handful of pennies. I'm going to be raking it in. I'm going to be a multimillionaire before I'm old enough to go into a liquor store and legally buy a six-pack of beer."

It's fair to say that the boy took Paul by surprise. He wasn't sure what to expect when he agreed to take Kevin with him, but he was definitely not as anticipated. He was brash, a little rude, and was fond of foul language. Paul wondered if the boy talked this way in front of Zach. It was hard to imagine. A lot of people would probably be put off by Kevin, but Paul found the boy's honesty refreshing. He actually liked the kid.

When they arrived at the stadium, they parked Paul's car and walked to the building. They then made their way through the crowds, found their seats, and sat down. The seats were good. In fact, Paul said they were great. It was like they could reach out and touch the infield grass with the palms of their hands. They were a little early, and Paul was struggling a little, trying to think of something to say.

"What do you think of these seats?" Paul finally asked. "They're pretty good, no?"

"They're good," Kevin said. "Do you have any money on you?"

"I have a credit card."

"I don't have any money, but I feel like getting something to eat. I haven't had any lunch today. Will you buy me something to eat?"

"What do you want?"

"A couple hot dogs."

"Sure, we can get some hot dogs."

"And a beer."

Paul laughed. "You're only thirteen. They're not going to sell you a beer."

"But they'll sell you one. You can buy it for me, and then I can drink it when they're not looking."

"I don't think so."

"Why not?"

Paul laughed at this. "Because you're too young," he said. "You're not supposed to be drinking alcohol."

"My dad used to buy me beer."

"And you're dad's in prison."

"But not for buying me a fucking beer."

"I'm not going to buy you a beer. I'm not even going to buy myself a beer."

"Fine," Kevin said. He pouted for a moment and then said, "I guess I'll have a Coke."

Paul sighed. The game hadn't started yet, and already Paul had to argue with the boy. "Like I'm going to buy him a beer," he said under his breath.

"What'd you say?" Kevin asked.

"Nothing," Paul said.

"I thought you just said something."

"It was nothing. I was just talking to myself. I was thinking about something that happened yesterday."

"Well, can we go now? I'm starving."

"Sure," Paul said. The two of them walked up the stairs to the concession stand. Paul ordered three hot dogs, two for Kevin and one for himself. He also ordered two Cokes and a bag of peanuts. He paid for the order with his credit card, and they carried the goods back to their seats. "I got some peanuts," Paul said. "You can have some if you want."

"Peanuts are for monkeys."

"Well, they're here if you change your mind."

Kevin was now watching the game, eating his hot dogs. After swallowing the last bite and washing it down with a couple gulps of Coke, he spoke up again. Now he was telling Paul how he was going to buy a baseball team of his own someday and how he was doing to move the team to Las Vegas. "I'm going to call them the Las Vegas Hard Eights," he said. "You know, like a craps game. And they're going to wear solid-black leather uniforms. Head to toe, they'll wear all black leather. And I'm going to put together a *real* fucking team. Not a bunch of losers, but a clubhouse full of home run hitters and big-time playmakers. No expense will be spared. We're going to have the best team in the league. And we'll travel and kick everyone's ass from California to Montreal. There won't be one fucking team in the big leagues that can beat us."

"That'll take a lot of money," Paul said.

"Nothing to it," Kevin said. "By then I'll have more money than I know what to do with."

"Where's all this money coming from?"

"From my music. I'm going to be a world-famous rapper. The money is going to come pouring in from record sales and concerts faster than I can spend it. Rappers rake it in. Do you know how much those fuckers make these days?"

"No," Paul said.

"Billions. They get paid a fortune just for talking. Billions of dollars for making up some bullshit lyrics and talking. People are eating this shit up. They can't get enough of it."

"There must be more to it than that."

"Like what?"

"I don't know. I don't listen to rap music."

"You see? Now you sound like Zach. You don't even know what you're talking about. Trust me, I'll know exactly what to do."

"It sounds like you got it figured out."

"Fucking right I do."

Paul and Kevin were quiet for a while and watching the game. The Angels were behind by two runs. Then Kevin told Paul he had to use the restroom. "I'll come with you," Paul said.

"I think I can manage."

"Do you know where the restrooms are?"

"I can find them."

"I don't want you to get lost."

"Like I'm going to get lost. I'm not a fucking six-year-old."

"No, I suppose you're not," Paul said. "But you'll come right back?"

"Of course I'll come back. Where else am I going to go? Just stay here and enjoy your game. Mike Trout is coming up next."

"Okay," Paul said.

Kevin walked up the stairs. Paul said he began to grow nervous. Was it a mistake letting the boy look for the restrooms on his own? Paul honestly didn't know. He'd never been in charge of a thirteen-year-old boy before. And he was now responsible, wasn't he? Maybe this whole idea of him taking Kevin to the ballgame was some kind of test, to see how he'd handle the situation. And what if Kevin got into some kind of trouble? What if he tried to talk someone in line at the concession stand into buying a beer for him? And what if some idiot said okay, and Kevin was caught with the beer? Maybe going to the restroom was just a ruse so that he could get a beer. On the other hand, Kevin said he didn't have any money, so how could he buy a beer without any cash? Paul told himself, *Don't worry, don't worry.* The boy was probably in the restroom right now, standing in front of a urinal. No, there was nothing to worry about. Nothing at all. Mike Trout was now in the box, and Paul would concentrate on that instead. Maybe he'd hit another home run.

Then *crack!* Trout knocked the ball sky-high, and the crowd jumped up and went crazy. But Paul just couldn't get into it. Yes, it was a home run, but as the game went on, he kept checking his watch. Five minutes passed. Then ten minutes. Then it was fifteen minutes. When Kevin finally returned, Paul was a nervous wreck. Kevin was all smiles as if nothing at all had happened. But there was clearly something different about him. Paul couldn't figure it out at first, and then he said, "You got a cap?"

"You like it?" Kevin asked.

"Where'd you get it? I thought you didn't have any money."

"I found it."

"You found it?"

"It was on the floor. Someone must have bought it and then dropped it."

"The price tag is still on it."

Kevin removed the cap from his head and looked at it. He pulled off the price tag and tossed it away. "Like I said, they must have just bought it."

"Those caps are expensive," Paul said.

"Tough luck for someone."

"Are you sure you found it on the floor?"

"Where else would it be?"

"In the team store."

"Are you accusing me of stealing it?"

"No, I guess not."

"I found it on the floor. It's a case of finders keepers. It's not my fault some absentminded idiot dropped his hat."

Paul thought for a moment. Then he said, "Look, if you did take the hat from the store, we need to return it. It isn't cool to steal."

"I found the fucking hat on the floor. I don't know what you think I'm going to tell you."

"I was just saying."

"I know what you're saying. You're saying you don't believe me. No one ever believes me."

"I'm sorry," Paul said. "I just wanted to be sure. I don't want you to get in trouble. If you say you found it, then you found it."

"I *did* find it."

"Fine, then. It's a nice cap. And it looks good on you. So I guess today's your lucky day."

"Yeah, I'm real lucky."

Paul laughed. He realized he was indeed fond of the kid. Who knew why? Maybe it was because he knew what it was like to have the odds stacked against you. Or maybe he just had a weakness for thirteen-year-old boys with foul mouths and the chutzpa to say exactly what was on their minds, not caring what the world thought of them. Paul said, "You missed all the action, Kevin. Trout hit a home run."

"I heard the crowd," Kevin said. The cap was still in his hands, and he was looking at it. He was obviously very happy to have it. He then put it back on his head, adjusting it so it was just right.

They watched the rest of the game. The Angels lost by a run. Paul said it was a weird game. The Yankees fans at the stadium were actually louder and more vociferous than the Angels fans. It was like they'd been watching the game in New York.

When Paul and Kevin returned to Lighthouse, Zach was waiting for them. The first thing Zach noticed was the cap on Kevin's head. "I see you got a new cap," Zach said to Kevin.

"I bought it for him," Paul said.

"You didn't have to do that."

"We saw it in the team store. He really wanted it, so I figured what the hell. It was no big deal."

To Kevin, Zach said, "Did you enjoy yourself?"

"It was alright," Kevin said.

"We had a great time," Paul said. "Kevin is a good kid. It was a pleasure to take him with me."

"I heard Trout hit a home run," Zach said.

"It was great," Paul said. "He knocked it a mile out of the park."

"Out of the park," Kevin said, thinking.

"Well, very good. It sounds like you two got along well."

"We're friends," Paul said, and he patted Kevin on the back. Kevin smiled just a little.

And now for the Elbert Hubbard quote I promised you. He wrote, "A friend is one who knows you and loves you just the same." I think it's a good quote. When I first read it, I chuckled.

Paul understood. I'm not sure if Kevin would have had any idea what Hubbard was saying. But Paul got it.

Several Toasts

t was about two years ago when Veronica and I decided we would move to South Carolina, and it took us a while to actually make the move. But here we now are, living with the feral pigs, armadillos, whip-poor-wills, and John Deere tractors. I've wondered over the last several days whether it was this move from Southern California that prompted Paul to tell everyone he was gay. Did he need us to be two thousand miles away before he told the truth? If we hadn't moved, would things be different? If we were still in the old neighborhood, would he have kept everything under his hat? I think these are valid questions. Sometimes a child needs his parents to be gone before he feels it's okay to be honest. And as hard as it may be for me to believe, that's what he's is doing, isn't it? At least that's what he thinks he's doing—being honest. After all these years of pretending, he can now stand tall and tell the world what he's made of.

Setting Paul free to be honest with the world was not our intention when we moved. In fact, Paul was one of the primary reasons we had *not* to move. We didn't want to be far away from our only son, but honestly, we'd had all of Southern California we could take. We'd lived our entire lives in the lower half of the Golden State, and it was time to move on.

When we tell people around here where we're from, many of them say things like, "Oh, I've always wanted to go to Southern California. I have a sister who lives there. I have a cousin who lives there. Someday I'm going to pack up my things and move out there." I look these people in the eye and tell them, "If you like sitting in automobile traffic for hours and hours every day, then you're sure to love Southern California. If you like fires, earthquakes, and droughts, you'll love Southern California. If you like people who are rude, angry, arrogant, and more than just a little full of themselves, and if you like being tailgated when you're driving the speed limit, you're going to love the Golden State. And if you like being cut off or honked at every time you change a lane, and if your idea of an ideal home is living in an air-conditioned stucco box three feet from your noisy neighbors, then make the move. And if your idea of a fun weekend is waiting in lines, and if you get a thrill out of smog, crowds, concrete, and asphalt for as far as the eye can see, you're going to love the place. As for me? And as for Veronica? No, thank you. Now we live on five acres of fenced-in land among fields of grass, thick woods, dilapidated barns, and a network of two-lane country roads that will take you wherever you want to go, and we couldn't be happier.

I have many friends in California who think we were crazy to move here. I've heard it all. "There's nothing to do. The people are all racists. The summers are hot and unbearable. Hurricane season is awful. And there are no good restaurants anywhere." Some of this nonsense is partially true, but most of it is crap. We love it here and seriously can't think of another place we'd rather be living.

So here we are in our new digs, and Paul is back where we came from, telling everyone who'll listen that he's gay and proud of it. The days have gone by quickly since his initial phone call to us, and tomorrow he'll be here with his friend, Terrance, seeking our love and approval. So what do I now think? I know what I *should* think, but what I should think and what I actually do think are, well, what the heck are they?

Now Aloysius Czchnick pops into my head. Yes, good old unlikely Aloysius. Good old bald-headed, tall, gum-chewing, black-as-coal Aloysius. I remember the day they hired him at the dealership.

We knew they were bringing someone new aboard, but he was not at all what we expected. His arrival reminded me of that scene from *Blazing Saddles* when the new sheriff is riding into town. He's a what? He's a what? He's a near? To get what I'm talking about, you have to understand where I lived. You have to know the demographics of that place we all fondly called Orange County. We were chock full of white people and Hispanics with a large and growing third-place Asian population. But blacks? Not so many. Finding a black in Orange County was like finding a rabbi in a Joel Osteen audience. Black people accounted for only a meager 1.6 percent of our population.

Then in rode Aloysius, as black as any black man I'd ever seen. He was black and as bald as a bowling ball, as tall as a eucalyptus tree, and he was the newest addition to our sales force.

Behind his back, we placed our ten-dollar bets. The bet among us salesmen was: Precisely how long do you think it will be before this character named Aloysius gives up and turns in his resignation to the sales manager? There were four of us. Jeff said one week, Harry said three weeks, and Abe said two months. I figured a month and a half. Whoever was closest to the actual time would win the forty-dollar pot, ha, ha. Of course, Aloysius knew nothing about our wager. It was our little secret, an agreement between the four of us, just a harmless bit of fun we were having at the expense of the new guy. Besides, we knew the hire wasn't serious. We knew what was going on. Aloysius wasn't hired because he was a crackerjack salesman expected to sell tons of cars. He was hired because the dealership wanted to prove it was an equal opportunity employer and have a black man on its payroll.

Well, the first month went by, and then the second, and then the third, and then an entire year passed, and Aloysius had no intention of giving up. In fact, when I left for South Carolina, he was still there selling cars. It's funny, but the three guys I made that ten-dollar bet with—Jeff, Harry, and Abe—no longer worked there. Hell, they'd all given up themselves and moved on to do other things ages ago.

When I announced my retirement, Aloysius invited me to have dinner with his family. I accepted the invitation, and Veronica and I went to their home in Tustin on a Saturday evening. When we got there, Aloysius introduced us to his wife and two lovely daughters. Don't you think it's interesting that this was the first time we'd met any of them? As we sat down to eat salads, it occurred to me that this was the first time I'd ever have had dinner with *any* black family. It was the first time I'd ever been in a black home, the first time I'd eat black people food, and the first time I'd use black people plates and silverware, and the first time I'd drink black people wine. All my life I never once thought of myself as a racist, not even obliquely, yet I suddenly realized that maybe I wasn't all as open-minded and virtuous as I thought. Then there was a *ring, ring, ring* as Aloysius tapped his wine glass with his spoon. "I'd like to make a toast," he said, and he raised the glass up toward the center of the table. We all raised our glasses along with him. "To Robert, my mentor and best friend," he said.

I admit this toast really threw me. I mean, I liked Aloysius, and I had taught him a thing or two. But a best friend and a mentor? "You're being way too kind," I said, and I meant this.

Aloysius's family was staring at me, his wife, Yvette, and his daughters, Sasha who was eight and Serena who was ten. I think they were expecting me to say more, but I just couldn't think of anything else to add.

"Do you remember the man with those trucks?" Yvette asked Aloysius. "I think his name was Chuck. I don't recall his last name."

"Of course," Aloysius said. "His name was Chuck Harvey."

"Yes, that's right. His last name was Harvey. I remember now. He saved our tails."

"He did," Aloysius said. "And that was all thanks to Robert."

"Thanks to me?"

"Don't you remember? It was my second month at the dealership, and I was having a tough time getting the ball rolling. I was working on a few promising deals, but nothing was closing. Yvette and I were running out of money to pay our bills. We were two months behind on our mortgage, and they were about to turn off our phone service. Yvette and I didn't know what we were going to do." Aloysius looked at his daughters and said, "Along came Robert to save the day."

"What'd he do?" Sasha asked.

"He was selfless as always. He was working with this guy named Chuck Harvey, who owned a large landscape and maintenance company. Chuck was at the dealership to buy a new sedan for his wife, and he'd been working with Robert, and knowing that I needed desperately to sell something, Robert referred the gentleman to me. Chuck wanted the car sold to him at cost, and in return for the favor he said he'd buy several trucks for his business. So I sold him the car at cost. We didn't add anything to the price. I didn't even get a commission out of it. Then sure enough, later that week we closed a deal with Chuck to lease twelve new flatbed trucks. The commission from that truck sale paid all our past due bills with enough leftover for us to go out to dinner and celebrate. I owed all that to Robert. He saved our tails, without a doubt. And it wasn't just that the bills got paid. The truck sale did wonders for my self-confidence. For the first time since I'd been hired, I knew I was in the right business."

"Yes, I remember Chuck," I said.

"That was so nice of you," Veronica said.

Nice of me?

I need to come clean here by telling you a couple of things. First, I had no idea that Aloysius was having any difficulty paying his bills. It wasn't my intention to help him out of a jam. Second, I do remember Chuck Harvey, and I remember I thought the guy was a first-rate liar. I always had guys coming in and trying to get a great deal out of me, promising me more lucrative sales down the road. It was a common ploy, asking for a great deal and claiming to make it worth my while later on. So when I referred Chuck to Aloysius, the truth was that I thought Chuck's promise to buy a bunch of trucks was bullshit. If I'd known for sure that Chuck was actually going to buy twelve trucks, I certainly would never have passed his name along to Aloysius. I would've handled the sale myself and taken the big commission. I had helped Aloysius, but it was by accident, but at the dinner table, with everyone looking at me and thinking I was such a great guy, I said, "I'm glad that deal worked out for you."

"It saved my tail," Aloysius said.

"Is everyone done with their salads?" Yvette asked, and we all nodded our heads. Then to her daughters she said, "Give me a hand bringing out dinner, girls."

"I can help," Veronica said.

"No, no, you just stay right there. You're the guests of honor."

"More wine?" Aloysius asked. He was holding up the bottle. Both Veronica and I said we were fine. "We're having pork chops," Aloysius said. "Yvette prepares the best pork chops this side of the Mississippi."

"Sounds good," I said.

"Sounds delicious," Veronica said.

The food was brought out, and when Yvette and the girls were sitting down again, everyone began to eat. No one was talking, and suddenly Yvette tapped the side of her wineglass with her spoon. *Ring, ring, ring!* She wanted to make another toast, and she was looking at me. "Here's to the black guy," she said.

"Hear, hear," Aloysius said. "Yes, here's to the black guy." He too was looking at me, holding his drink toward mine.

Were they calling *me* the black guy? I didn't get it. Aloysius's entire family was looking at me. "Ask for the black guy," Yvette said, and Aloysius laughed.

"What's so funny?" I asked.

"It was your idea," Aloysius said. "Don't you even know what we're talking about?"

"I guess I don't."

"Don't you remember when I first started working at the dealership, when everyone was having so much trouble with my name? I'd hand out my business cards, but when customers called for me, they didn't know how to pronounce my name. So they wouldn't ask for me. Who knew how many sales I lost because of my crazy name? I was talking to you and the other salesmen about it, and I told you guys I was thinking of changing my name. You said, 'Hell, you don't need to change your name. Just tell everyone to call and ask for the black guy.' It was pure genius, wasn't it, Yvette?"

"It was," Yvette said.

"Of course, I was the only black guy working at the dealership. All they had to do was ask for the black guy, and there I was. Then I had it printed on my business cards. The cards had my name on them, then just below my name it said, 'Ask for the black guy!' Now everyone was coming into the place and asking for the black guy. Do you remember the ad? I ran a small ad in the newspaper that listed the dealership and our phone number, and it said, for the best deal, call and ask for the black guy." Heck, the phone rang off the hook for weeks. Everyone wanted to cut a deal with the black guy. Everyone wanted to ask for me."

Veronica and Yvette agreed with Aloysius that it was a bit of marketing genius on my part. But do you want to know the truth? When Aloysius told me and the other three salesmen about the trouble he was having with his name, I did say to have people ask for the black guy, but I was only trying to be funny. I didn't think he'd actually print it on his business cards or in a newspaper ad for crying out loud. It was just a joke. That's all I meant it to be.

Ring, ring, ring! Yvette was tapping her wine glass again, and we all looked at her. "Here's to Veronica," she said. "Behind every great man is a fine, fine woman like Veronica."

"Hear, hear," Aloysius said.

"Correction," I said. "They say behind every great man is a woman rolling her eyes."

Everyone laughed except for Sasha and Serena, who were too young to get the joke.

It was weird being toasted. The only other time I'd been toasted by anyone was when Paul raised his glass to me at my fifty-third birthday dinner. We were at a restaurant in Newport Beach, the three of us. I remember exactly what I ordered. I had scallops and polenta, accompanied by a pile of greens on a bed of pureed peas. It was a little strange, but I liked it a lot. I remember what Veronica ordered. She was torn between the beef tenderloin and the swordfish. This evening, she chose the swordfish, and when I asked her how it was, she said, "I don't really like seafood. I don't know why I ordered this. I should have ordered the beef." She only took a couple bites of it and then pushed her plate away from her. Paul then raised his glass and said he wanted to make a toast.

"I want to toast Dad," he said. "To you, Dad, the man who taught me to be true to myself."

"I taught you that?"

"Of course you did."

"Maybe I did," I said, thinking. I wasn't sure what Paul was talking about.

"When I was in grade school, when we were driving to one of my baseball games, you quoted Shakespeare to me in the car. You said he wrote, 'To thine own self be true,' and then you asked me what I thought it meant. I don't remember what I said, but I remember you told me never to forget the line. You told me to think about it once or twice a year, to apply it to my life. You said, 'You'll be amazed how many ways this simple line will clear things up for you.' Those were your exact words. I had a feeling you were telling me something of great importance, so I committed the line and your words to memory. And as you can see, I haven't forgotten them."

"I don't remember any of that," I said. Honestly, I had no idea what he was talking about.

"You don't remember us in your car?"

"I remember we were in the car a lot, driving to baseball games. But I don't recall quoting Shakespeare to you. How old were you?"

"Nine or ten."

"I'll be damned," I said.

"So here's to you, Dad." Paul raised his glass again, and he smiled.

I thanked Paul for the toast. It was a nice thing for him to do. But last night before going to bed, I got to thinking. I asked Veronica if she ever thought about all the things she did that impacted the lives of others. "We go through life like we're lone meteors in space," I said. "Yet the truth of the matter is that we alter, hurt, and improve people's lives with every word we say, with every action we take, and with every little thought we have. Who knows what effects we have on others?

"Are you thinking about Paul again?"

"Maybe," I said.

"Are you thinking there was something we did that made him gay?"

"Do you think it's possible?"

"I suppose anything is possible."

"I keep looking back. Did I say something dumb? Did I make an errant move? Did I breathe too fast or too slow? Did I forget to tell him I loved him when he needed to hear it? Did I miss a chance to pat him on the back? Did I let him get away with something he should've been punished for?"

"I've wondered the same about myself."

"And?"

"I think most things just are what they are. Some days are cloudy, and some days are clear. Some flowers are red, and others are white.

Some bugs fly, and some bugs just crawl. Some children have freckles, and others have none at all. It's true that we affect the world, and we greatly affect one another, but in the grand, grand scheme of things, we are just actors in a play that has already been written."

"Nicely said."

"Thank you. Of course, the trick isn't being able to put it into words. The trick is in getting yourself to believe it."

The Dad-Blamed Trial

I t's my dream, and seemingly real. But just as with all my dreams, I have no control over it. For the time being, I'm a spectator, keeping quiet and watching the dream unfold. My lips are chapped, my throat is parched, and I'm about to drink from a warm glass of sarsaparilla. I am dusty and exhausted, and my horse is tied to the hitching rail in front of the saloon. Christ, it's as hot as the inside of a pot-bellied stove. It is hot, dusty, and bone dry, but it's nice to be inside the saloon and finally out from the desert sun. I raise the glass of sarsaparilla to my mouth, when I'm startled by a shouting man.

"All rise! All rise! Court is now in session. Your honorable Judge Roy Bean be presiding." This announcement comes from a twisted sidewinder of a man called Halfwit, the judge's bailiff. He pulls his six-shooter out from its holster and fires a couple rounds up toward the ceiling to get everyone's attention. The reports from his gun hurt my ears and make them ring for a moment. "I said court's in session, goddamn it," he shouts. "Get up on your feet and show the judge some respect!"

Everyone in the room stops talking and stands up. The judge is standing behind the bar with a glass of rotgut whiskey in his hand. He gulps down the whiskey and makes a face, then wipes his lips with the back of his free hand and slams the empty glass down on the counter. "I want everyone to finish off your dad-blamed drinks," he says. "You know the rules. There's no drinking of alcohol during any of these proceedings. If you have a drink, finish it now and set your empty glass down so Halfwit can collect it." The judge glares at the patrons as they follow his order and finish their drinks. He tells Halfwit to gather up the empty glasses and to put them in the sink behind the bar. Halfwit clomps around on the wood floors with his heavy boots and jangling spurs. He picks up the glasses one by one, setting them onto his tray. Then, once his tray is full, he makes his way to the back of the bar.

"Where do you want them?" he asks the judge.

"In the sink, you idiot. Wasn't you listening?"

"Sorry, Judge."

Speaking to me, the judge says, "I got to get me a new dad-blamed bailiff. This knucklehead is driving me out of my dad-blamed mind."

"I said I was sorry, Judge," Halfwit says, having heard what the judge just said to me.

"Hell, you're always sorry," the judge says. "Just put the glasses in the sink. And try not to break them. Them glasses cost me a dad-blamed fortune. They come all the way from St. Louis, and there's no telling when that good-for-nothing peddler will be by here again."

"Yes, Judge," Halfwit says. He carelessly dumps the tray of empty glasses into the sink. Remarkably, none of the glasses break.

"Where's my book?"

"It's right below the bar, Judge, where you always keep it."

"All I see is my bartending guide."

"Try the next shelf down."

"Oh, yes, yes, here it is." The judge pulls a thick legal book out from below the bar and slams it down on the counter. He blows the dust from the face of the book and then puts his hand on it, saying, "By the powers vested in me by the great state of Texas and by our quaint locality of Vinegaroon, I hereby and temporarily and legally shut down this drinking establishment and commence this here court of legal justice, *modus operandi*. I do also hereby swear to act as this court's judge, and I will be firm, fair, and impartial to the best of my ability. And I also promise to shoot or hang any low-down snake-in-the-weeds who opens his dad-blamed yap and interferes with the due process of this proceeding. In other words, speak when your spoken to or keep your dad-blamed yap shut. Do you all understand the rules?"

The judge looks at everyone in the room, and they are nodding their heads, men and women alike. "Is there going to be a hanging?" one of the men asks. He is a scruffy old codger wearing a gigantic cowboy hat. His eyes are open wide and he's smiling, like he's looking forward to seeing someone hang.

"That'll depend on what the defendant has to say for himself, and it will depend upon what the witnesses have to say. Are our witnesses all here and accounted for?"

"They're all here," Halfwit says.

"Are they all sober?"

"Every one of them."

"And well-fed?"

"They had a big meal this morning. Miss Archibald had breakfast ready for them at her hotel at six o'clock. She served them buttermilk pancakes, scrambled eggs, bacon, sausages, and toast."

"Good, good. I don't want anyone testifying on an empty stomach."

"There'll be no empty stomachs."

"I've always found that hunger distorts the truth."

"Yes, Judge."

"Do you agree?" the judge asks me.

"Yes," I say. "I can agree with that."

"Did you get something to eat?"

"Yes, I did."

"How was it?"

"It was fine," I say. "There was plenty of food for everyone, and Miss Archibald is a terrific cook."

"Good, good, so now we can get down to brass tacks. Tell me, son. How do you plead?"

The question takes me by surprise. I didn't realize I was the one who was being tried. This is upsetting news. "Am I on trial?" I ask.

"Dern right you're on trial," Halfwit says.

"Shut your yap," the judge says to him. "I'll do the dad-blamed talking here." Then he turns to me and says, "Tell us, how do you plead, son? It's important that we know."

"What am I being charged with?"

"You need to plead first, and then we'll come up with the charges."

"That doesn't make sense," I say.

"This is a court of law. It isn't supposed to make any dad-blamed sense. Are you really that naïve? Since when does a court of law have to make any sense? I'll ask again, how do you plead?"

I stare at the judge, and he's serious. His eyes are a steely gray color, and they give me a chill. I can hear my voice wavering as I speak. "Well, I guess I have to plead innocent."

"Aha! Did you all hear what he said? The kid pleads innocent! Yes indeed, a likely story, coming from the boy caught with his hand in the cookie jar."

"What cookie jar?"

"Oh, we'll get to that soon enough. Just be patient. They say patience is a virtue, right? Just hold on to your horses. Good things come to those who wait. Hold on to the wheel and keep her steady as she goes. And don't take any wooden nickels. Do as I say, and not as I do. Are we on the same page?"

"I suppose so," I say. I have no idea what the judge is talking about, but I don't want to make him mad by crossing him.

"State your full name for the record." Halfwit now has a notepad and a pen, ready to write down what I say. Apparently, he is also the court stenographer.

"My name is Robert Ashcroft."

"And your current address?"

"I live at 364 Richmond Drive."

"In Anaheim?"

"Yes, in Anaheim."

"What's your phone number?" I give the judge my phone number, and then he asks for my social security number. I give him that too. Then he asks, "What's your favorite color?"

"My favorite color?"

"Come on, now. We haven't got all dad-blamed day."

"Blue, I guess."

"What's wrong with purple?"

"Nothing is wrong with purple."

"Then why didn't you say purple?"

"Because it's not my favorite color."

"Ah, good answer. Now see if you can answer this one. I am the beginning of everything. I am the end of space and time. I play an essential role in life. The earth is not the earth without me. I am not God. So what the heck am I?"

I laugh and say, "You're the letter e."

"You've heard it before?"

"I have," I say.

"Well, here's a tougher one. If God is all-powerful, can he make a stone so dad-blamed heavy that even he can't lift it?"

"The answer is that there is no such thing as a being who is all-powerful."

"Oh? You don't believe in God?"

"I believe in God. I just don't believe he's all-powerful."

"So you're an atheist?"

"That's not what I said."

"Write that down, Halfwit. The defendant is a self-admitted atheist."

Several women in the saloon gasp.

"I have one final question for you," the judge says. "This is very important, and I'll bet you haven't heard this one before. What's the difference between your pecker and your jokes?"

"I don't know," I say. "What's the difference?"

"No one laughs at your jokes."

There is a moment of silence, and then everyone in the saloon busts out laughing. The judge lets them laugh for a few seconds, and then he runs his finger across his throat, and they all shut up.

"Are you ready for the first witness?" Halfwit asks. "He's ready whenever you are."

"Bring him forward," the judge says. Halfwit has ahold of a man by his elbow, and he leads him up to the bar to face the judge. He is a plump, short man wearing a crooked hairpiece, dressed like a waiter with a red jacket, black bow tie, and baggy cotton trousers. The judge looks at the man with one eye squinted, sizing the little fellow up. "You can begin by stating your name for the record," the judge says.

"My name is Omar."

"Your occupation?"

"I'm a waiter, sir."

"A waiter where?"

"At a restaurant called The Salty Dog. On the island of Barbados."

"Put your hand on the book," the judge says, and Omar places his hand on the judge's book. "Now repeat after me: I am Omar, and I will tell the truth or hang by the neck until I die."

Omar takes the oath and then removes his hand from the book like he is pulling it off a hot burner.

"Good, good, you're sworn in. Did you have breakfast this morning? Is your stomach full?"

"Yes, sir."

"Do you know the defendant?"

"Yes, I do."

"Can you tell us how you know him?"

"He and his wife were at my restaurant."

"When was this?"

"A little over thirty years ago."

"What did they have to eat?"

"He had a hamburger, and she had the halibut. She couldn't make up her mind between the pork chop or the swordfish, and then she ordered the halibut."

"Did they talk while they ate?"

"They did," Omar says.

"Did you hear what they talked about?"

"Yes, I heard some of their conversation. I wasn't eavesdropping. It's a small restaurant, and it's easy to hear what others are saying."

"Anyone could've heard them?"

"Yes, sir."

"Go on."

"Well, they were talking about their future. And then they began talking about having a baby. I don't think the defendant's wife was pregnant yet, but they were talking about the baby's sex when she did get pregnant. He said it didn't matter what sex the child was, so long as it was healthy. That's exactly what he said. It was over thirty years ago, but I remember that quite clearly. He said it didn't matter."

"Did *she* have a preference."

"She didn't say so."

"So neither of them showed any concern over the sex of their child?"

"Didn't seem so, sir."

"One final question for you. Did they leave you a decent tip?"

"Oh, yes, they were very generous."

"I see, I see," the judge says. Then he turns to me. "Do you want to cross-examine?"

"What for?" I ask.

"To defend yourself, of course."

"Defend myself from what?"

"From the testimony we just heard. It was pretty dad-blamed incriminating, I'd say. It's not looking very good for you, and we're only on the first witness."

"What questions would I ask? I still don't even know what the charges are. What *are* the charges?"

"All in due time."

"Can I be excused?" Omar asks.

"You can step down," the judge says. Then to me he says, "If I were you, I'd start taking this trial a little more seriously. You're not an ignoramus. Maybe you are only a car salesman, and maybe you're not overflowing with talent, but you're not a dad-blamed ignoramus. From what I've heard, you have a pretty decent cerebrum between your ear holes. Your words with your wife at The Salty Dog were clear and precise, and our waiter friend has recounted exactly what you said. You said you weren't concerned with the sex of your child. You just wanted your kid to be healthy. Those were *your* words, not ours. So now here you are thirty dad-blamed years later, and you have your healthy child. He's grown up to be a strapping young man. He has his arms, legs, fingers, and toes. His heart beats as steady as a marching-band drum, and his vision is clear and unclouded. It's hard to fathom all this angst, regret, and frustration you're feeling when you got exactly what you asked for. God gave you your wish. He was much kinder to you than he is to most of us. The way I see things, you should be on your knees saying thank you, as grateful as hell."

I stare at the judge. He has surprised me. I didn't figure him to be quite so insightful, and I have no good response. "Who's going to be your next witness?" I ask. I can't think of anything else to say.

"You don't want to ask Omar anything else?"

"You excused him, didn't you?"

"Well, I can bring him right back up here. I'm the dad-blamed judge, and I can do any dad-blamed thing I want. Do you want to ask him a question? He's still under oath, so he has to tell the truth."

"What would I ask?"

"I can think of a few things. Maybe you could ask if he heard you say you didn't want a gay son. When you were having dinner with your wife, did you say you didn't want a gay son?"

"No, of course not."

"Of course, if you didn't want a gay son *before* he was born, it would mean you didn't want him after. *Ipso facto*, you don't want your son. But you do still want your son, don't you?"

"Yes, I do."

"Then that line of questioning won't help."

"I guess you're right."

"You could ask if the hamburger meat he served you really came from their local island cattle. Isn't that what he claimed when you ordered your dinner? He's under oath now, so he'll have to tell you the truth. Or forget about the hamburger. You could also ask him if he really liked you and your wife, or if he was just pretending to like you so that you'd leave him a big tip. I always wonder about that when I have dinner at a restaurant. I wonder if those smiling food jockeys really think so much of me, or if they're just acting friendly to butter me up so I'll leave a big tip."

Roly-Poly Babies

"Bring up Dr. Stanley," the judge says. "Let's see what the doc has to say."

"Here he is," Halfwit says. He's holding the doctor by the arm and leading him to the judge. When they get there, Halfwit puts the doctor's hand down on the old law book.

"You promise to tell the truth?" the judge asks.

"I do," the doctor says.

"You know if we catch you lying, you'll be hung by the neck until your tongue turns black?"

"Yes, I understand."

"Did you eat a hearty breakfast with the others this morning?"

"I certainly did. It was a breakfast feast fit for kings. I especially liked the buttermilk pancakes. The best darned buttermilk pancakes I've had in years. And the maple syrup was out of this world. It tasted like it oozed straight out of a tree."

"Good, good."

"No complaints here."

"Please give us your full name for the record."

"Doctor Eugene Seymour Stanley, MD."

"What kind of a sawbones are you?"

"I'm an obstetrician."

"So you deliver a lot of babies?"

"I do. Don't even ask me how many. I used to keep track, but I lost count of them years ago."

"And you delivered the defendant's son?"

"Yes, I did."

"Can we assume that you're competent? Do you know what you're doing? You know, a lot of doctors these days are flakes. It's a wonder how a lot of them ever made it through medical school."

"Yes, I know what I'm doing. I've been pulling babies out from between women's legs for sixteen very busy years. It's my calling and my passion. Some people devote their time to painting landscapes, some people play Bach and Mozart on the piano, some people devote hours to reading classic literature, but me? Well, I deliver babies. Can't think of anything I'd rather be doing, morning, noon, and night. Boatloads of roly-poly blue-eyed newborn babies. It excites me just talking about it."

"Do you have a favorite color?"

"A favorite color?"

"Yes, what's your favorite color? Everyone has a dad-blamed color, don't they? I've never met anyone who didn't have a favorite color."

"I guess it's orange."

"Orange, orange, orange. So I take it you eat lots of oranges?"

"Actually, I'm a carrot man."

"Ah, a carrot man. I had an uncle in Louisiana who was a carrot man. He was a highly respected blacksmith. He was always eating carrots like the dad-blamed things were made of candy. He ate so many carrots that the palms of his hands turned orange. But he was also an honest man. Honest as the day is long. Never told a lie in his life. Are you like him? Can we depend on you to tell us the truth?"

"You can depend on me."

"Tell us about your experience with gays."

"With gays?"

"How many gay babies do you think you've delivered over the past sixteen years?"

"I'm not sure what you mean by gay babies."

"I'm talking about little babies who grow up to be big gay adults. How many have you delivered?"

"I have no idea."

"No idea, eh? Okay, then let me ask you this. How many babies have you delivered that grew up to be town drunks?"

"I don't know that either."

"How about babies who grew up to be arsonists? Or babies who grew up to be preachers, or communists, or kleptomaniacs?"

"I honestly don't know. I just help bring the little bundles of joy into the world. I don't follow them around after they're born and check up on what they're doing with their lives."

"I see. So you're like the Oliver Winchester of the maternity ward."

"The rifle manufacturer?"

"Yes, the rifle guy. From what you're telling me, I'd say you don't know any more about your babies than he knows about the disposition of the rifles he sells."

The doctor stares at the judge for a moment and then says, "I suppose that's true, but I don't think you should compare babies to rifles."

"No?"

"No, I don't think so."

"Your objection is overruled."

"My objection?"

"I overrule your objection to my analogy. That's my prerogative as the judge of this here court. And my ruling is final, so don't waste any of your dad-blamed breath arguing with me."

"Okay," the doctor says.

"Listen, I like you, and I'm not saying what you do is wrong. I'm not saying there's anything rightly wrong with delivering babies. And maybe babies aren't rifles, but in the long run, they're just as dangerous. So I'm just trying to present an accurate description of what you do for a living. Although, now that I think about it, none of this has anything to do with the charges made against the defendant, so you can forget I even brought it up. Now, why don't you tell us about Robert and Veronica? Actually, never mind Veronica. She isn't the one on trial here, so just tell us about Robert. What was he like?"

"I only met with him once."

"Did you like him?"

"He seemed nice enough."

"Did he make eye contact with you?"

"I think he did."

"Did he appear to be well-groomed?"

"He was clean, and he was dressed nicely. His hair was kind of a mess. But it was windy outside that day, so I suppose that accounted for it."

"Did he seem obsessed with his son-to-be? He did know the baby was going to be a boy, right?"

"Yes, he knew."

"Most dads go a little crazy over their sons, don't they? It seems only natural to me that a father would be thinking a lot about how his son was going to turn out, whether he was going to get along with other kids, whether he was going to do well in school, whether he was going to be handsome, whether he was going to be shy or outgoing, whether he was going to score high on an IQ test, or whether he was going to be able to dance with his girl at the high school prom without looking like Jerry Lewis on Adderall. Tell us about Robert, Doc. How did he seem to you?"

"He seemed very rational."

"Rational?"

"And I would say mature."

"So what does that mean?"

"It means that in my opinion, he had all the makings to be a good father. How can I best explain this? To be a good father, you have to understand that having a child is a lot like playing poker here in your saloon. You shuffle the cards and deal them to the men. Some cards you draw will make your heart skip a beat or raise your eyebrows, while others will make you frown. Some bets have great potential payoffs and others get you nothing. Every time you bring a kid into this world, you're drawing cards and playing poker. It can be thrilling, rewarding, and fun. And if you're smart about it, you don't play until you lose your shirt, nor do you count on being a big winner. You just play for the fun of playing, day after day, night after night, until God finally says it's time to stop and step away from the table. I think that Robert understood this. Like I said, I only met with him once, but I got the distinct impression that he had what it took to be a good father. You'd be surprised how many men don't get any of this at all. They have all sorts of expectations and make all kinds of bets on their kids. Then they draw a few bad cards. They're confused, frustrated, and disappointed when they discover the world isn't going to cooperate with the plans they had."

"When's the last time you saw Robert?"

"Thirty years ago."

"Would it surprise you to learn that his son has greatly disappointed him?"

I step forward toward the judge and raise my hand. "Objection!" I say.

"Overruled," the judge says. He glares at me for a moment. Obviously, he does not like being interrupted by a defendant.

"But it's not that I'm disappointed. That isn't the real issue."

"Blah, blah, the real issue," the judge says. "We all know what the real issue is." Then he turns back to the doctor and says, "So are you surprised at the defendant's disappointment or not?"

"No, nothing surprises me. I wouldn't say that it surprises me at all. If Robert is disappointed in Paul, I'd just say I'm saddened."

"That he let you down?"

"That he let himself down."

"Ah!" the judge says. He looks over at me and says, "And *that's* coming from your own doctor. You didn't see me twisting his arm, did you?"

"Hear, hear," a man says.

"According to his own doctor," another man says.

"He's got you there," Halfwit says to me. "Looks like you've been foiled by your own medical professional. A doctor you picked and paid for."

Suddenly there's a lot of murmuring in the room. The people in the saloon are shaking their heads and talking about me, but I can't make out what they're saying. But I'm sure it isn't good. Some of them are looking at me like they can't believe what jerk I am. The old codger with the big cowboy hat smiles and says, "Leave it to old Judge Bean. The man sure knows what he's doing. By God, we're going to have a hanging."

Everybody laughs.

The judge, who is also laughing, steps to the man and puts his arm around him. "Not quite yet, old-timer," he says. "This trial isn't over until I say it's over. I am the law, and the law is fair. And I don't want it said anywhere in Texas that a man tried in my court doesn't get the benefit of a fair shake. Let's see what our friend has to say for himself before we go all cactus crazy and slip a noose over his head. Maybe there's another side to the story."

"We're all ears, Judge," a man says.

"I'd like to hear more," a woman says.

"Dang it all," says the old codger. Then he decides to put on a show. He pretends to hang himself from a tree with an imaginary rope, rolling up his eyes and sticking out his tongue like he's choking to death.

Ignoring the man's antics, the judge looks at me. "Do you have any questions for the doc?" he asks. "If you do, now's the time to ask them. I'm turning the questioning over to you."

"Yes, I have a few questions," I say. I am trying not to look at the old codger who is still sticking out his tongue and pretending to choke. I'm really beginning to dislike this man.

"Well, go on," the judge says.

"First, I'd like to compliment the doctor," I say. "I think he's been answering the questions put to him honestly and intelligently."

"Thanks," the doctor says.

"Oh, brother," the judge says. "What a load of steer dung. I suppose I could object to this blatant flattery, but who would I be objecting to but myself? And it would hardly be fair to ask me to hand down a ruling on my own dad-blamed objection."

Everyone laughs.

I try to ignore the laughter. I try not to let it get to me. Instead, I direct my attention to the doctor and say, "I'd like to ask you some questions that are general in nature. Here's what I'd like to know. Isn't it true that there are proven ways couples can learn a lot of critical information about their babies before they're born?"

"Yes, of course."

"Can you give an example?"

"They can learn if their child has Down syndrome."

"So it's possible to detect Down syndrome prior to giving birth to the child? In fact, early on enough to have an abortion?"

"Yes, that's true."

"Do women usually have an abortion when they discover their baby has Down syndrome?"

"I think a majority of them do."

"Isn't Down syndrome a genetic thing?"

"That's one way of putting it."

I pause for effect. Then I place my hand on the bar and lean toward the doctor to pose the critical question. "Doctor, I ask this. Do you think homosexuality is also a genetic thing?"

The doctor stares at me without answering. The judge says, "Go ahead, Doc. He's just on fishing expedition, but you should answer the question."

"Yes, that's my opinion. Same sex attraction does not appear to be learned behavior, and it isn't just a choice or lifestyle. It appears to be genetic."

"So is there a way of detecting whether an unborn child will grow up to be gay, the same as we can detect Down syndrome?"

"No, obviously not."

"What if there was? What if we could find out if our baby was going to be gay before it was born? Do you think mothers would opt to abort?"

"Some of them probably would."

"Do you think they'd have the right?"

"You're now talking about abortion, eugenics, and gay rights all rolled into one. We could talk about this all day and night. The implications are huge. The arguments for both viewpoints are compelling. All kinds of factors are involved. In other words, I don't have time to discuss this with you here."

"Then let me put it this way. I'll make the question easier and simpler. Do you know of any heterosexual couple anywhere on earth who would deliberately bring a gay baby into the world?"

"There probably are some."

"But do you *know* of one? I'm talking about a couple that you know. Not two or three. Just one single couple that you know personally."

"No, not really."

"Aha!" I say. I then look around at the others in the room, and they all look bewildered. It's like none of them has a clue what I've been talking about.

"Are you quite done with this?" the judge asks. He looks a little annoyed with me. "As much as I don't want to interfere with your attempt at a defense, you're putting us all to sleep. So you say most parents don't want to have any gay children. Why don't you tell us something we *don't* know? I think now's a good time to move on to the next witness. We've taken up enough of the doctor's valuable time. Do you have any objections to me excusing the doctor?"

"No," I say. "I guess I'm done with him."

"You can go now," the judge says to the doctor. Then to me the judge says a little angrily, "What in tarnation were you trying to prove?"

"I'm not sure," I say.

"Can I make a suggestion?"

"Sure."

"Stick to fighting the charges."

"But I still don't know what the charges are."

"You pleaded innocent, didn't you?"

"I did," I say.

"Well, how could you plead guilty or innocent if you didn't know the dad-blamed charges?"

"I pleaded innocent only *because* I didn't know the charges."

"That doesn't make any sense."

"Exactly," I say. But the judge isn't listening to me. He's paying attention to Halfwit.

"Your next witness is ready," Halfwit says.

"Who is he?"

"He's a she."

"Well then, who is *she?*"

"She's an old friend of the defendant and his wife. Her name is Amber. She's here with her husband, but her husband doesn't want to testify."

"Well, bring her up."

Halfwit escorts Amber up to the bar and places her small hand on the gigantic book. "Do you promise to tell the truth?" he asks.

"I do," Amber says.

"You know you'll hang if you lie."

"I understand that."

Halfwit takes her hand off the book. "Okay, she's all yours," he says to the judge.

The judge squints his eye and looks over the witness. "So you're Amber," he says.

"Yes, that's me."

"It's nice to finally meet you in person. It's my understanding that you have a few choice words to say about the defendant."

"Oh, do I ever," Amber says. Then she sneers at me. I swear she wants to tear me limb from limb, and I wonder what I did to make her so mad.

Amber's Eyes

A mber is sitting on a bar stool while Halfwit is standing with his back against the wall, ready to write everything down, his pen and notebook in hand. "I'm glad you made the trip out here," the judge says. "Will you please state your full name for the record?"

"My name is Amber Ellen Manning."

"You live on the same street as the defendant?"

"I used to. We moved five years ago."

"Where do you live now?"

"I live in Oceanside with my husband, Jeff. We moved there when Jeff retired because he wanted to be closer to the beach. We found a little rundown bungalow about three blocks from the ocean and did some work on it to make it livable. Jeff never goes to the beach, but it makes him feel content to be close to it. He says he likes knowing that he can drop everything and walk to the beach, and I'm thinking maybe someday he'll actually go there. Me, I go there often. I especially like going on overcast days when the sky is soft and the air is cool. There are fewer people then. I like to walk along the shore. I like the way the sand feels on my bare feet, and I enjoy listening to the seagulls. They remind me of how lucky I am to be alive, living close to the beach, living the California dream. It helps take the pain away. I suffer and cry my eyes out every day, but the ocean helps."

"What your new address?"

"We live at 3654 Seashell Lane."

"What's your favorite sport?"

"My favorite sport? I'm not really a sports fan, but I like watching

246

baseball occasionally. I liked it when the Angels won the World Series. I'd like to see that happen again."

"Your favorite singer?"

"Frank Sinatra. Or maybe it's Tom Waits. That's a tough one. I like Frank because he's such a fixture of the establishment, and I like Tom Waits because he's such an individual."

"Your favorite movie?"

"*The Wizard of Oz.*"

"I should've guessed. Didn't those dad-blamed flying monkeys freak you out? What kind of drug was L. Frank Baum on when he came up with those things?"

"When I was a young girl, that monkey scene gave me the worst nightmares. I kept dreaming over and over that the monkeys were attacking me and pulling straw out of my breast. I kept wondering, 'Am I really made of straw?' and 'Why didn't anyone warn me about this?'"

"Who was your favorite character?"

"The Tin Man. I felt so sorry for him, not having a heart."

"*My* favorite character was the Lion. He reminded me of my deputies, as yellow as that dad-blamed brick road. Which brings me to my most important question."

"Which is?"

"What's your favorite color?"

"That's easy. It's definitely pink."

"Pink, pink, pink. We haven't had anyone partial to pink here for quite some time. But I have to ask. Pink like a Renaissance cherub's cheeks in an oil painting, or pink like cotton candy?"

"Pink like a flamingo."

"Ah, of course."

"I love flamingos. The first time I saw them, I was a little girl. Have you ever seen them in numbers, preening themselves and standing on one leg? Seeing them can make you believe in God."

"And you believe in God?"

"I do, with all my heart."

"Go to church?"

"Every Sunday. We haven't missed a church service for years. Well, we go so long as we're in town. We don't go to church when we're on vacation. But that's only once a year, and we usually only miss one service. We vacation for a week at a time.

"Where's your favorite vacation spot?"

"Oh, that's easy. We go to a little-known resort in Costa Rica, in the middle of their rain forest. We've been going there for years. It's such a welcome relief from our dry Southern California climate. It's out in the middle of nowhere, deep in the Costa Rican jungle where it *rains*. I mean, it rains all the time. That's the one thing we don't like about living in Southern California. It hardly rains at all, and when it does rain, it's just a big nuisance. But deep in the rain forest, it rains every day and night, and the vegetation is thick and green, and streams and waterfalls are constantly spilling from mountains. The creeks and rivers are always overflowing with cool, clear water, and the ground is always slippery, soggy, and fertile. There's just something I love about rain, the way it washes everything clean, the way it purifies the air, the way it douses everything in sight. I love the way it hoses down the tree leaves, dirty streets, and filthy rooftops. And we love the sound of it, splashing and dripping, sometimes even roaring like a raging river, absorbing every other sound in the rain forest as if there were no other sounds. And then when it lets up for a few hours, the sun peeks through the clouds, the birds and frogs sing a symphony, and the sunbeams turn the humid air to steam. The world tries to dry out before the next impending deluge."

"I'd like to go there," the judge says. His eyes are closed, and he is imagining the place. "You make it sound so dad-blamed enticing."

"You'd like it."

"It would be a nice change from this hot, stinking desert we live in."

"I can give you the phone number of the resort."

"Do they have a website?"

"Yes, they do. I can also give you their Internet address."

"By God, we're due for a little rest and relaxation, aren't we, Halfwit?"

"Sure as sand," Halfwit says.

"Maybe we'll go there, alright," the judge says as he's looking at Amber. "Maybe we will pack up and go. Maybe if things settle down here so I'm not needed for a week. This desert gets ahold of you. Once you've lived here a few years, it's like you grow dad-blamed roots deep in the dry ground and can't get yourself to leave. I don't know what it is. Maybe it's some kind of subliminal heatstroke that gets to you gradually. You get to thinking subconsciously that there is no other way of life in the world. You get to thinking that this desert is all there is to life, all this dust, cactus, and the scorching sun. You accept all these buzzards, jackrabbits, and disgusting snakes as your friends. I'd *like* to go where it rains seven days a week, like you say. I'd really like to visit a rain forest. You know what I'd do if I went? I'd bend my head all the way back and let the rain land on my face and fill my mouth with water. I'd let it soak into my hair and run down the middle of my back and right into my pants, into my drawers. I'd like to be soaking wet. Yes, I'd like to be wet to the bone, cold and wet and squeaky clean."

The judge is staring at Amber, daydreaming about his visit to her rain forest. He's off in another world. It's the same silly way he gets when he daydreams about Lillie Langtry.

"Remember me?" I say. The judge snaps out of it. He, Halfwit, and Amber turn look at me. "Can we move things along?"

"In a hurry to be hanged?" the judge says.

"No, I'm in a hurry to be found innocent," I say. "I'd like to get the heck out of here."

"You'll have to excuse our defendant," the judge says to Amber. "I told him patience was a virtue. I guess he didn't hear me."

"I'm sure you've done everything you can with him," Amber says. She is glaring at me again. Then she puts her hand on the judge's arm and says, "But I suppose we should get on with my testimony. After all, that is why I came. I feel like I have a lot to say. Are you going to ask me the questions, or shall I ask them?"

"You can do the asking," the judge says. "It will probably be more efficient that way, since you already know the questions you came here to answer."

"That suits me."

"I'm ready whenever you are."

Amber gets off her bar stool and turns around, facing the spot where she sat. Then she begins talking. She says to her imaginary self, "I understand you have two sons. Can you tell us something about your boys? What are they like? What are their names? How old are they?" She then sits down on the barstool and replies to her own questions. It is kind of weird the way she does this. In fact, I think it's silly, but the judge is impressed. She says to herself, "I'm glad you asked me those questions. Yes, we have two sons. They're both grown men. Adam is thirty-nine, and Taylor is forty. First let me tell you a little about Taylor. Over the years, he's grown into a fine man with a good work ethic, a strong moral compass, and a great sense of humor. He's a wonderful husband and father, and he takes good care of his family and himself. Everyone likes Taylor when they meet him, and he has a lot of friends. Now, I'm not going to tell you that he's perfect, because nobody goes through life without having their fair share of problems. But when problems have surfaced in his life, he has always met them face-to-face, and toe to toe, and he's dealt with them honestly. Does he have his faults? Sure he does, but who doesn't? There are days he can be a little sarcastic and times when he settles for too little. I think he underestimates his potential. But I can tell you, the positives far outweigh the negatives. A younger friend of mine who just gave birth to a boy told me that she hoped her son would grow up to be just like Taylor. And that's about the best compliment a mother can get."

Amber stands up, looking again at her imaginary self on the barstool. "What does Taylor do for a living?" she asks herself. Then she sits down to answer. "Taylor is an English literature teacher at our community college. He doesn't make a great deal of money, and his father and I think he'd be better off teaching at a real university. He'd make more money at a university. He's also a very bright man, and we think he'd be challenged more if he was teaching more serious students. But like I said, he tends to settle for less. And it really doesn't matter, does it? He's very happy where he is, and he loves his job at the community college. We did such a good job raising him. He truly is a good, good man. If you want to know what a good man looks like, you need not look any further than our son Taylor."

Amber stands up again to ask a question. She says, "So can you tell us about your other son? What is his name? What's he like? What does he do for a living?" Amber then sits down and sighs. "Oh yes, our other son," she says. "His name is Adam, and he's a year younger than Taylor. Poor, troubled Adam. We used to wonder where we went wrong. It really used to bother us. He's caused us so much grief and so much soul-searching over the years. Yes, I'll tell you all about Adam. Ever since he was a small boy, Adam was the sort of kid who, when faced with two roads, a straight road and a crooked road, would take the crooked one. It was the story of his life, always taking the wrong road, always finding himself in hot water. It was cute when he was a small boy, the funny predicaments he would get himself into. But the cuteness soon wore off, and we began to worry. He was shunning our love and concern, never heeding our warnings or taking any of our advice. It was one thing after another, all through his school years. I guess the worst of it started when he broke a boy's arm at school over a drug purchase that went sour. That was just the beginning. School soon became a nightmare. There were detentions, suspensions, clashes with the law, and finally he was expelled. He never did bother to finish high school, and he never did get his diploma. So now, at the age of seventeen, our son was a high school dropout and a juvenile delinquent. He lived with us at home, but he was seldom there. God knows where he was or what he was doing. We lost control of him. Then when he turned eighteen, my husband told him he had to find his own place to stay and figure out a way to support himself financially. Then there were even more serious problems. He started to get into more trouble with the police. I remember they'd come over to our house looking for him, and we wouldn't know what to tell them. We had no idea where he was or what he was doing. By the time he was twenty, he was locked up in the county jail on a burglary conviction. We had hired an attorney to defend him, but he'd been caught in the act, and there wasn't much our attorney could do. Then it went even further downhill from there. There was one crime after the other. We lost contact with him for about eight years, and right now he's serving a sentence in the state prison for an armed robbery conviction. He won't be up for parole for another four years. I've left out a lot of his story, but I think I've told enough to paint a clear picture. This boy broke our hearts. We still love him dearly, but words can't explain to you the pain he has inflicted on us. It's so hard to fathom that this is our son, our flesh and blood. We've had people tell us to forget about him, to put him out of our minds, but he's our son. Forgetting about him is out of the question."

Amber stands up and talks to herself again, saying, "I'm sorry to hear all of this. You and your husband have obviously been through a lot. But can you explain what all this has to do with the charges the defendant in this courtroom is facing? What does the story you've told us about your troubled son have to do with Robert and his son, Paul?"

"I reckon I'd like to know that myself," the judge says.

"I'd like to know too," I say.

Amber sits down on the barstool. She looks up at the ceiling to collect her thoughts, and then she speaks. The men and women in the saloon are hanging on her every word. "There is no love more powerful than the love a mother has for her child," she says. "Despite all of Adam's missteps and problems, I have always loved that boy with all my heart, more than I love myself. I go see him on visiting days at the state prison, and do you want to know who I see when I go there? I see that little bright-eyed boy in jeans and a T-shirt who would come to me with a scuffed knee when he fell off his bicycle, the boy who wouldn't eat his vegetables, the boy who would gulp down every ice-cold glass of milk you gave him without taking a single breath. He was the little boy who'd play with his Hot Wheels in the backyard and make motor and skidding tire sounds with his mouth. That's who I see, and that's who I'll always see. I can't help it. I'm the boy's mother. He grew inside me, and we faced the world together, so what went wrong? I don't know what went wrong. But it hurts. The pain is so sharp and profound that I can't even describe it. I would rather have my arms and legs broken or have bamboo shoot pushed under my fingernails. I would give anything to see Adam living a good life, working at a good job, meeting a nice girl, and living in a decent neighborhood. I hate seeing him in prison more than you can imagine. But the good things life has to offer will probably never be his. There is no light at the end of the tunnel. There is only blackness and the bleak, humid air of a tunnel leading nowhere except deep into the bowels of nowhere. My dear, sweet son. He's the boy I gave birth to, raised, fed, and loved. My son—forever lost in the darkness of that

God-awful tunnel. I can't tell you how much it hurts, how it rips my heart into pieces, how it weighs on me every night that I lie in bed and think of him."

Amber stops talking, and she begins to sob. I reach to put my hand on her shoulder, to comfort her, but she swats it away. "Don't touch me," she says. Then she glares at me with her watery eyes. My God, those eyes! They are on fire with anger, burning into me. "You!" she says. "You and your scientific testing, Down syndrome, and elective abortion. You and your foolishness. You and your stupidity. Can't you see how utterly wrong you are? And you call yourself a father, and you think you understand what love is? You consider yourself to be a man? What kind of spoiled and self-centered monster are you? *You* have a son. You have a good and remarkable man. He is honest, bright, hard-working, loyal, well-meaning, giving, loving, and brave. I'd give up everything I own for Adam to have a tenth of your boy's good qualities. Yet here you are, questioning your love for him. So what if you were able to know he was gay before he was born? Would you seriously give up on him just to avoid being embarrassed, or frustrated, or angry, or whatever it is you're feeling because he's born to love a little differently? Years ago, I thought I knew you, Robert, and we were friends. But now just the sight of you sickens me. You're unfit! No, Paul isn't an unfit son. You're an unfit father. And I pity Veronica. And I pity Paul. And I pity anyone else who has sadly made the mistake of loving you or depending on you for anything."

Amber bursts into tears. I feel so guilty. I want to hold her, but this time I keep my distance. "Now, do you see what you've done?" the judge says. "You're a dad-blamed piece of work, you are."

One of the other women in the saloon puts her arms around Amber and helps her up from the barstool. "Come with me, sweetheart," she says. "Let's get out of this place."

"Take her to the hotel," the judge says. "Take her back to her room."

"I'll make her some tea," the woman says.

"Poor kid," one of the men says.

"I wish there was more we could do," a woman says. "Such a pity."

"Listen up," the judge says to everyone. "We've still got more witnesses. Each of you who came here as a witness will get your chance to testify, but I need you to line up. You need to form a single-file line. Doesn't matter where you are in the line. I promise that each of you will get your chance."

I look at all the people forming the line, and I say to the judge, "This could take days."

"It'll take as long as it takes. We're going to get to the bottom of this if it takes a dad-blamed month and a half. We're going to have a verdict that *no* court will overturn."

My Friggin' Sister

A s I wake up, my head is spinning like I've been on a wild amusement park ride. Judge Roy Bean? A silly sidekick named Halfwit? Flying monkeys, favorite colors, and buttermilk pancakes? I think I've been watching too many late-night movies before going to bed. Yes, way too many movies. It isn't good for me to provoke my imagination into giving me such weird dreams. I jump out of bed and get dressed, putting on a pair of sweatpants and an old Hard Rock T-shirt. Then I go directly to the kitchen to make a fresh pot of coffee. Veronica is already up. In fact, she has already left the house to do her horseback riding at the stables. She told me last night she wanted to get an early start today because she still needed time to get the house ready for Paul and his guest. They're arriving at the airport tonight at nine-thirty. In just a matter of hours, we'll see, won't we? We'll see what kind of father I am.

The phone rings. Should I answer it and see who it is, or should I let the thing ring? I can't make up my mind.

Who in the world would be calling this early in the morning? I look at the kitchen clock, and it's a little after nine, not nearly as early as I thought. I yawn and rub my eyes, then pick up the phone and say hello. Christ, I haven't even had my first cup of coffee and already I'm on the phone. It's my sister, Alex, asking how I'm doing. She's asking how I'm doing, not because she wants to know how things are going in general, but because she wants to know if I'm surviving Paul's coming out. She just found out about it last night. Our father is the one who told her. According to her, no one ever tells her anything. "Why

255

didn't Paul call *me*?" she asks. I say I don't know, and she says, "I just happened to be talking to Dad about something else, and he asked me what I thought of the big news. Well, I said what news? And when he told me what Paul was telling everyone, well, you could've knocked me over with a friggin' feather. My dear little nephew? My sweet little Paul? Tell me it isn't true."

"It's all true," I say.

"What are we going to do about it?"

"Do about it?"

"It was Marie, wasn't it?"

"What about Marie?"

"He should never have married that girl. I knew that friggin' marriage was a mistake from the very first day they announced their engagement. I knew in my heart of hearts there was something terribly wrong with that girl. She was too good-looking. That's what it was. You can't trust girls who are too good-looking. I wouldn't trust a girl like Marie any further than I could throw her. Did she cheat of him? What do you know about it? No one ever tells me anything. She cheated on him, didn't she? She broke his heart and made him hate all women, so he turned to men. That's what happens, isn't it? These poor men go after beautiful women and get their hearts broken in two, and then they turn to men because they think all women are impossible to love, impossible to live with. Is that what happened? Do you know what happened?"

"I don't know for sure."

"The same thing happened to little Sarah Avery. You remember her, don't you? She was Gladys and Henry Miller's daughter. Surely you remember Gladys and Henry. You met them when Jack and I had you, Veronica, and Paul over for dinner. Sarah got married to that handsome boy Roger Avery, and they were together for five full years. Roger turned out to be a regular Bill Clinton. He couldn't keep his hands off the other women. It was one trollop after the other until Sarah finally came to her senses and divorced the jerk. Then the next thing you know, Sarah is living with a girlfriend. I mean, not just a friend who happened to be a girl, but an actual girlfriend, as in that the two of them were lovers. Can you believe it? Well, I'm telling you that you could've knocked me over with a friggin' feather. That dear, sweet little girl announced to the world that she was a lesbian, and Gladys and Henry were fit to be tied. I can't tell you how many hours I spent with Gladys on the phone, trying to calm her down. Dear God, she was so upset. Her little girl, now in the arms of a woman. She may as well have stuck her mother in the heart with a butcher knife."

"I do remember," I say.

"And it was all because that overly handsome husband of hers couldn't keep his friggin' hands to himself. You can't trust overly handsome men, and you can't trust overly pretty girls. It's a fact of life."

"I'll try to keep that in mind."

"By the way, Jack did some research for you last night."

Well, this was great. This was just what I needed, to get good old Jack involved. Jack was my idiotic brother-in-law, Alex's husband. He fancied himself as the family's go-to guy for vital information. Unfortunately, Jack got all his information off the Internet, and he had no fact filters. By fact filters I mean the rational ability most of us have to discern between information that is true and useful and information that is crap. The weirder the claim made on a website, the more likely Jack was to fall for it. I'll give you a few crazy examples. Jack believed there *was* a cure for cancer, that it was being withheld from the public in a plot by drug companies to profit from selling their current inventory of drugs. And Jack believed the US government had captured flying saucers from outer space and was keeping the them and their alien pilots under wraps at certain top-secret airfields. And Jack believed Elvis was alive and well, living in Argentina. And Jack still had faith in the rumor that Paul McCartney was dead, that the guy who was going around claiming to be Paul for all these years was actually a British impersonator who had been put in his place a long time ago by John, George, and Ringo. And to top it off, Jack believed without a doubt that the monkey, Curious George, once had a tail, that the bears so many of us loved to read about were the Berenstain Bears, and that James Earl Jones said, "Luke, I am your father." Perhaps you've heard of this. They call it the Mandela Effect.

Alex wants to fill me in on what Jack learned about homosexuality. "He found the perfect place for Paul," she says. "It's a clinic in

Mazatlán, Mexico. It's right on the ocean, just like a five-star resort. It has a swimming pool, tennis court, café, and gift shop. They call the clinic New Beginnings, and it was founded by an American sexual behavioral expert named Ernest P. Gladwell. This Dr. Gladwell went to medical school at Harvard, and he did all his undergraduate work at Princeton. And he's no phony, Robert. This doctor is the real McCoy, and he's come up with a treatment that works. When Jack read me their current success rate, you could've knocked me over with a friggin' feather. Eighty-nine percent, Robert. That means eighty-nine out of a hundred patients that go to the clinic for a couple of months of his intensive care walk out just as normal as you or me. All these years I thought it was impossible for gays to turn it all around, but it turns out I was wrong. It turns out we've been hoodwinked."

"Well, I have a question," I say. "Why isn't this clinic better known? And if it's legitimate, why is it down in Mexico?"

"The press, Robert," she says. "Jack says the press has an agenda, and I believe him. Think about it. I mean, let's be real about this. The press has always been a big supporter of gay rights. If you're in the public eye, you don't dare say anything bad about homosexuals, or the press will tear you apart and feed you to the lions. This is our American press. And this is the same press that refuses to print anything good about Dr. Gladwell because he's proven their position on gays is untenable. They don't dare say one good thing about him. One positive word about his work, and they'll have every queer, lesbian, and cross-dresser in the country camped on their doorstep. Talk about bullies. And they are bullies, Robert. They want everyone to agree with them, or else. That's why the doctor's clinic is in Mexico, to keep his work out of the spotlight. He doesn't want to be famous. That's not why he does what he does. He just wants to help people learn how to lead clean and normal men-love-women lives. Jack sent away for some of the literature. He'll probably hear back from them soon, and we'll forward the literature to you, so you can share it with Paul."

"I'm not sure Paul will be interested."

"He might pretend not to care, but trust me, he'll be interested. No one really wants to be gay. That's what you have to understand, Robert. That's what it says on Dr. Gladwell's website.

"Isn't there a chance this doctor is wrong?"

"He does this for a living. He's devoted his life to this clinic. He knows what he's talking about. To be gay is to be unhappy."

"Paul seems quite content to be exactly what he is. You obviously haven't talked to him."

"He never called me."

"I'll ask him to give you a call."

"You know, I can't imagine why he didn't call me. He used to call me all the time. We've always been able to talk. I always had the impression we were close, and that he was comfortable talking to me about anything. Remember when he called me about that girl in grade school? What was her name? I think it was Becky. He was embarrassed to talk to you or Veronica, so he called me."

"That was almost twenty years ago."

"Do you remember that little girl? Paul didn't know what to do. The poor girl had a gigantic crush on Paul, but he couldn't stand her. He told me she made his skin crawl. He said she made him want to gag. Paul had done everything he could think of to get the girl to leave him alone, but she kept coming after him. Whatever he tried to do to push her away, she just interpreted it as him playing hard-to-get. And she'd just try harder. The girl was a force to be reckoned with. You know how girls that age can get. Anyway, I told Paul what to do."

"I remember that."

"'No more Mr. Nice Guy,' I said. I told him to wait until a time when they were in front of lots of other kids and then read her the riot act, loud and clear, so that everyone could hear what he had to say. I told him to tell her he thought she was ugly and obnoxious, and that she smelled bad, and that she had bad breath, and that whenever he saw her it made him want to vomit. I told him to tell her he wouldn't have her as a girlfriend even if they were the last two people on earth. And sure enough, he did exactly as I advised, and that was the last time the girl ever even thought about pestering him."

"He was also sent to the principal's office. The girl was so humiliated that she had to go home."

"She left him alone, didn't she?"

"Veronica was furious at you."

"Sometimes you just have to get tough with others and stand up for yourself. I'm sure in the long run Veronica knew I was right. People these days are afraid to stand up for themselves. They're afraid to stand their ground and put their foot down. When we were kids, people said what had to be said. Now people are all afraid of hurting one another's feelings. I mean, look at you and Paul. You can't honestly tell me that you're okay with this gay thing. You can't honestly tell me your happy he's bringing his little pal to your house for Thanksgiving. What's this guy's name, anyway?"

"It's Terrance."

"Are you telling me you're really okay with Terrance being in your house? Where are they going to sleep? I suppose they're going to be in the same room, in the same friggin' bed. Jesus, Robert, what if they kiss in front of you? Then what are you going to do? Have you thought about any of this? Have you and Veronica really thought it through? If Paul was my son, I'll tell you exactly what I'd do, and I'd do it right away. I'd put my foot down and say, 'Enough of this nonsense. This is unacceptable. This isn't going to happen, not so long as I'm your parent, and not so long as you're here visiting in my house.' That's what I'd say if I was you. That's what our dad would've said if you came home one day and said you were gay. Can you even imagine it? Do you think our dad would've let you bring a friggin' boyfriend over for Thanksgiving dinner, to a family gathering? He would've thrown Terrance out on his ear."

"Times change," I say.

"Only if you let them."

There is a pause, and then I decide I need to change the subject, so I say, "Isn't it awful? What did you think about that earthquake in Iraq and Iran? They say it was a 7.3, that it killed over five hundred people."

"Iraq and Iran?"

"They say it left over seventy thousand homeless. Can you imagine it? It won't be long before you have a big one in California. Are you and Jack prepared for it? When we lived in California, I put together an earthquake survival closet in our garage."

"You're so obvious," Alex says.

"Obvious?"

"You're just trying to change the subject."

"Well, *are* you and Jack prepared?"

"Who cares if we're prepared? And who the hell cares about Iraq and Iran? Those people are all nuts anyway. And you live in South Carolina now, so what do you care if California gets shaken to pieces by an earthquake? You and Veronica will be two thousand miles away."

"We have family and friends in California. We care about them."

"If you cared so much about them, then why did you move away? You have a very strange way of showing you care."

"We needed a change of scenery. And we don't have to live next door to everyone in order to care about them."

"I never did understand why you and Veronica felt it was necessary to move clear across the country. When you told us you were moving to South Carolina, you could've knocked me over. I didn't see it coming. It wasn't even on my radar. Heck, Robert, you were born here, and you've spent your whole life here. And your family is here, and all your friends live here. What were you guys thinking? What were you trying to run away from?"

"We weren't trying to run from anything."

"And see what happens?"

"What do you mean?"

"See what happened to Paul. You've barely been gone a few months and look what happened."

"I've thought about that."

"And?"

"I don't think it had anything to do with us moving to South Carolina. Well, maybe it would've taken him a little longer to tell everyone if we'd stayed in California, but he would've eventually had to say what he did. I think it was something he had to do, whether Veronica and I were living nearby or not."

"Well, that's your opinion."

"Yes, it is."

"It makes me think of Dad."

"What about him?"

"Did I ever tell you about the time Dad caught me smoking?"

"I haven't heard that one."

"You know how Dad hates cigarettes?"

"I know," I say.

"When I was a teenager, I bought a pack of cigarettes from the vending machine at the Sambo's restaurant when no one was looking, and I snuck the pack home in my purse. I wanted to smoke a cigarette, so while Mom was busy in the kitchen and Dad was watching a boxing match on TV, I lit one up behind the house. I just wanted to see what it was like. I took a few puffs, and I didn't think it was that big of a deal. I sat there, puffing away. Well, like an idiot I was smoking the cigarette right under the family room window, and Dad had the window open. The smoke from my cigarette went right up through the window, and Dad noticed it right away. He came to the backyard and found me smoking, and I thought, *Oh, boy, now I'm in for it.* I really thought I was in big trouble. But Dad didn't get angry at all. Instead he sat down next to me and said, 'I'm going to help you with this. You're not doing this right. You need to learn how to inhale.' And Dad taught me how to suck the smoke into my lungs. It made me cough the first few times I did it, but then I got the hang of it. Finally, I finished off the cigarette, and I began to feel dizzy. 'Let's light up another one,' Dad said, and he pulled a second cigarette out of the pack. He lit it and handed it over to me."

"Dad was letting you smoke?"

"He wanted me to smoke. By the time I was done with the second cigarette, I was even dizzier. And I noticed that my stomach was a little upset. 'Have a third one,' Dad said, and he pulled a third cigarette out of the pack and lit it for me. When he handed it to me, I told him I'd had enough, but he insisted that I smoke it. So I smoked the third cigarette, and then I smoked a fourth, and a fifth, and a sixth, and halfway through the seventh my head was spinning something awful. God, I was as sick as a friggin' dog. I told Dad I couldn't take it anymore, and I ran into the house to use the bathroom. I got on my knees and puked my guts out. When I finally came out of the bathroom, I was drenched in sweat and my head was still spinning. Dad had the pack of cigarettes in his hand, and he offered them to me. 'You want the rest of these?' he asked, and I said no. I told him to throw them away, that I didn't want to see another cigarette for as long as I lived. 'Didn't think so,' Dad said, and he threw the cigarettes in the trash. That was the first and last time I ever smoked a cigarette. I haven't had a single cigarette since that day. I can't even stand to be near anyone who's smoking. The smell makes me sick to my stomach."

There's a quiet lull in our conversation. We are both thinking instead of talking. I have no idea what Alex is thinking about, but I'm thinking about her story. I'm not sure what the story has to do with Paul being a homosexual. Finally, I break the silence and say, "I never knew about the cigarettes, but we were talking about Paul, and unless I've completely misunderstood you, I think you're comparing apples with oranges."

"That's because you lack insight," she says. I hold the phone away from my ear for a moment and make a face. What's that they say about the pot calling the kettle black? I probably should've said something like that to her, but I didn't.

My conversation with Alex lasts for well over an hour. It's nearly ten-thirty when we finally say goodbye. I'm hanging up the phone just as Veronica returns home and steps into the kitchen. She's done riding her horses, and she sees me hanging up the phone. "Who were you talking to?" she asks.

"Alex," I say.

"You called your sister?"

"She called me."

"What did she want?"

"We were talking about Paul and about fruit."

"About fruit?"

"Apples and oranges, you know. By the way, I have a favor to ask. Next time she calls, if you happen to answer the phone, just tell her I'm out somewhere."

"You don't want to talk to her?"

"No, not for a while."

Imposserous!

When I retired, the sales manager at the car dealership I worked at was a man named Eric Connors. Eric was about eight years younger than me, and he was promoted to the managerial position four years earlier. He used to be an ordinary salesman like me. I could've had his job if I wanted it; in fact, the position was offered to me before it was offered to him. But I didn't want to be a manager. I was happy being a salesman, and I liked my job. The money was good, and I truly enjoyed what I was doing day in and day out, selling cars. What's that they like to say? "If it ain't broke, don't fix it." My job was good for me just the way it was. It wasn't broke, so I didn't try to fix it.

Eric was married to a woman named Brenda, and they had a son a few years younger than Paul named Rick. Like Paul, Rick was an only child, but unlike Paul, Rick died several years ago. It was a tragic event, and it took Eric time to get over it. It was really awful for him, and he still probably hasn't freed himself from the pain. But he did eventually learn to put it behind him, at least so far as his work went. He became as gung-ho as ever, like his son had never died. He was not one of those people who brood forever and let the darkness of a tragedy hold him back. He didn't waste a lot of time feeling sorry for himself, and I think he was proud of the fact that he knew how to move forward. I don't say this to knock the guy or say that he was shallow. In fact, I admired him. We all have unique tragedies in our lives that try their hardest to knock us down, but, seriously, if we all dwelled on them forever and let them overwhelm us, the whole world would be such a miserable place and none of us would be getting anywhere.

I saw Eric's son, Rick, several times before he died. The first time I met him, he was a senior in high school. He was tall, good-looking boy who looked a lot like his mother. I saw him again after he had graduated from high school, the day after he had enrolled in community college. He wasn't sure what he wanted to do with his life but thought he might discover something that interested him in school. I saw him again when he was a fire fighter. Yes, he had found his calling. He wanted to put out fires and help others. He had come to the dealership that day to say hi to Eric, and the two of them went out to lunch. He seemed like a great kid, polite and full of life, and Eric was especially proud of him. He used to brag about him to the rest of us every chance he had. It didn't bother me, listening to Eric brag. The truth is, I loved hearing proud fathers talking about their sons. And I liked seeing sons who did their best to live up to their fathers' expectations. To my way of thinking, a healthy and loving relationship between a father and son was not a corny thing to be belittled, dismissed, or laughed at. Heck, I used to brag about Paul all the time. I bragged about his skills at baseball, writing, investigative reporting, his job at the newspaper, and most recently, his new job at the public relations firm. Believe me, if you were anywhere near me for any amount of time, you'd learn all about my Paul and everything he was doing.

Some people say Rick was a hero on the day he died. Others say he was a fool.

It was a hot day in September, and the Santa Ana winds were kicking up. Rick was on duty with his fellow firemen at their station in Norwalk. At a house about two miles from the station, a man named Harvey Spangle was helping his wife clean the house and yard. Harvey was married to a woman named Mary Ann. They had a four-year-old daughter named Britany and a female cocker spaniel named Daisy. Britany was upstairs playing in her room, while Mary Ann was mopping the kitchen floor. Harvey was cleaning up the yard, which included cleaning out the BBQ. He had dumped all the ashes into a plastic bag, placing the bag next to the trash cans at the side of the house. He went to rake the leaves from the front yard lawn. The winds made raking impossible, so Harvey gave up on his leaf raking chore and went to put the rake away in the garage. And that's when he noticed the flames. The ashes he had put alongside the house were still smoldering from the night before, and the winds had fanned them into a roaring fire. The fire was crawling up the side of the house and in through an open window. In no time, it seemed, the side of the house was engulfed in flames.

Watching a fire grow in the Santa Ana winds is like nothing else you'll ever experience. It was like the house had been soaked with an accelerant. The fire was whipping about, burning like crazy and igniting everything within its reach. Curtains were now on fire, and the furniture was beginning to burn. The carpeting and the bookshelves burst into flames, and smoke began to billow. The flames were crackling and popping, and the walls were beginning to creak. Harvey immediately ran up the stairs to get Britany while Mary Ann called 911. Harvey quickly came down with their daughter in his arms. You'd think it would've taken longer, but it was amazing how quickly the fire engines arrived. Fireman were running all over the place, doing their jobs. It seemed like mayhem, but they knew exactly what they were doing. Eric's son, Rick, who was one of the firemen, led Harvey, Mary Ann, and Britany into the street where it was safe. "Daisy!" Mary Ann suddenly cried. "Where's Daisy? Is she in the house?"

"Who's Daisy?" Rick asked.

"She's our dog," Mary Ann said. "Our cocker spaniel." Then she looked at Britany and grabbed her arm, "Where's Daisy? Was she playing with you?"

"She's in my room," Britany said.

"She's in Britany's room!" Mary Ann cried. "She's trapped in the house!"

"Where's her room?" Rick asked. Mary Ann was now sobbing, and she was too distraught to answer.

"Her room is upstairs," Harvey said.

"You folks wait here," Rick said. "I'll see if I can get your dog."

"It's the first room on your left," Harvey shouted as Rick ran toward the house.

Without even putting on an oxygen mask, Rick ran to the front door and then into the burning house. "Where the hell is he going?" the captain shouted.

"Jesus," another fireman said.

"Christ, goddammit!"

They all waited for him to come out. It seemed like Rick was in the house forever, but he finally appeared at the front door. He was holding Daisy in his arms and about to step out of the house. He had a big smile on his face, and the family was cheering. But suddenly the roof over the porch collapsed. It didn't land on Rick and Daisy, but it did startle the dog so that she jumped out of his arms. And rather than run outside, the dog hightailed it right back up the stairs. The poor dog was terrified and had no idea where to go. Rick turned around and went after her.

"What's that idiot doing?" the captain said.

"Look!" one of the other men exclaimed.

Everyone looked up, and as they did, the roof of the house collapsed, falling in on the second floor. Smoke and flames were now pouring out of the rubble and swirling in the winds. "Jesus!" the captain exclaimed. "Does anybody see him?"

Everyone was squinting their eyes, looking at the burning mess, but then they were shaking their heads in disbelief.

"What do we do?" one man asked.

"Nothing," another man said.

By the time they got the fire to subside, and by the time they dug Rick out of the rubble, he was gone. The dog's burnt body was about ten feet away. It was horrible, but there was nothing they could've done.

"For a fucking dog," the captain said.

Eric and his wife found out about Rick's fate an hour later. Eric told me when the captain called him with the news it was like being hit in the head with a sledgehammer in a bad dream. It couldn't be real! It couldn't be real, but it was. His son was gone. Just like that. He was just a kid.

Ernest Hemingway wrote that courage is "grace under pressure." Do you think this is a fitting definition? Or is it lacking? Do you think Rick was courageous? Do you think his demise was graceful?

Do you know who Dan Bullock was? Like Rick, he left this world when he was very young. When he was alive, he wanted to be a marine. When he died, he was even younger than Rick. He's considered courageous by a lot of bright and well-intentioned people. So who is he? Dan Bullock is the youngest soldier to die in the Vietnam War. He was fifteen when he was shot dead. At the age of fourteen, he doctored his birth certificate and fooled the marines into letting him sign up for duty. He went through bootcamp and was flown to Vietnam, where he stayed alive for less than a month, quickly becoming a casualty of enemy fire. They sent him home in a pine box and put him in an unmarked grave. Years later people caught wind of his story, and they gave the kid a headstone. They also named a couple streets after him. "The youngest patriot to die in the war," they now like to say, full of pride, honoring his bravery. But was the boy brave?

How brave was he? And what are your feelings about Hanoi Jane? That's what they like to call her, the spoiled Hollywood brat who had the nerve to oppose our involvement in the war and pander to the enemy. What the heck was she thinking? The point of the war was clear, and a line had been drawn. These gooks didn't look like us, or think like us, or go to the same churches as us, but by thunder they were going to do as we said and run their government as we saw fit. I ask you, now that this war is in our rearview mirror, which took more courage—lying to the marines about your age and obediently following their orders or standing up against a bully? I know people still hate Jane's guts with a passion. But was she truly a traitor, or was she just brave? Or was she a fool?

Do you remember a man named Lenny Skutnik? Lenny was honored with medals and lots of news coverage. Now do you remember this guy? Air Florida Flight 90 crashed into the frozen Potomac, and a helicopter dropped a rescue line to the river. One woman was too weak to grasp the line. She kept falling back into the water, over and over, until Lenny jumped into the icy water and swam out to save the woman. He dragged her to safety. It was a miracle he didn't succumb to the freezing water himself. It was a true act of courage, and yes, he was a hero, but you have to ask yourself what the heck was this guy even thinking? He could easily have died along with the woman.

Was that courage that he showed? Or was he just being foolish? Or here's something to think about. Maybe raw courage and foolishness the very same thing.

Have you seen the old Stanley Kubrick movie *Paths to Glory*? It's a great war movie. It's a film about courage and cowardice, told from the French trenches of World War I. The generals get together and decide they have to seize an enemy position that they call the Ant Hill. The odds are next to impossible, and they know the casualties will be ridiculous, but they go ahead with the attack. Well, they *think* they're going ahead. A few of the soldiers do climb out of the trenches, but most of them stay and refuse to fight. Long story short, the generals are appalled at this mutinous behavior, and they convict three random men for cowardice in the face of the enemy. They want to set an example for the others, so the three men are shot to death by a well-organized firing squad in front of all the other soldiers.

I have a question for you. Were these soldiers really cowards, or were they just smarter than the generals gave them credit for? If they were smart, then what's the difference between a hero and an idiot? And what did I now want for Paul? Did I want to be proud of him for jumping out of the trenches and marching proudly toward his own Ant Hill? Or did I want to be proud that he had a prudent head on his shoulders?

When Paul called me earlier this week to give me the news that he was gay, I wasn't available at first. He left a message on my voicemail. While he was waiting for me to return his call, he called others. When I did get ahold of him, and after he gave me the news, I asked him who else he'd told. I wanted to know if he was telling everyone or just a few select people. "It's out there," Paul said. "I'm telling everyone. No more pretending."

"Does Mom know yet?"

"Yes, I told her. I asked her not to say anything to you until we talked."

"Did you tell your grandfather?"

"I did."

"What'd he have to say?"

"At first, nothing. There was a long pause over the phone, and then he said, 'You're pulling my leg, right?' It took me a couple minutes to convince him that I was serious."

"Then what did he say?"

"He was quiet at first. Then he just said, 'Uh, okay. Are you going to be alright?' I said of course I was going to be alright, then he asked me what you had to say. I told him I hadn't talked to you yet, and he said, 'Uh, okay,' again. I think a really took him by surprise. He was kind of speechless. I'll call him again after he's had a chance to mull it all over. I think he just needs a little time."

"How about Aunt Alex?"

"I haven't called her."

"Why not?"

"You know how she is. She's probably the last one I'll tell."

"Have you told your friends?"

"Most of them already knew."

"How long have they known?"

"I don't know. Some of them for years, I guess."

"How about Marie?"

"I told her after we were married. She didn't take it well. It's the reason we got divorced. I know what I did was wrong, not telling her until after we were married, but it wasn't that I didn't love her. I loved her, just not the way she wanted me to love her. It was complicated. I probably shouldn't have married her. But like they say, hindsight is twenty-twenty."

"How about Kevin?" I knew Paul still saw Kevin, the kid at the orphanage, who was now living in a foster home. Paul took Kevin out every couple months. They had become good pals.

"I told him. It didn't go well. I told him in person the last time we went out, and he told me I was a phony and a liar. I tried to make him understand, but he was pretty upset with me. When I dropped him off at his foster home, I asked him to call me after he had a chance to think it over, but he hasn't called me. It's been over two weeks since I saw him. I think he may still call. At least I hope he calls."

"I can see why he's angry," I said.

"I guess I can too."

"Did you tell your employer?"

"I did. He said it was no problem."

I asked about a few more people. It seemed Paul had everyone covered. It was then he told me about Terrance and about how he was coming with Paul to our house for the Thanksgiving holiday. I was surprised at this, but I said it was okay. Seriously, what was I supposed to say? It was so weird how I now seemed to be taking part in this circus. It wasn't until after I hung up the phone that I realized what had happened. My heart was pounding like a drum. My head felt a little dizzy. Honestly, there were so many emotions in me that it's hard to say exactly what I was feeling.

But that was then, and this is now. Today is the day, and now that I've had seven whole days to think about it, and sleep on it, and dream about it, I know what I'm going to do. I won't let anyone stand in my way. My dad can't stop me, and Alex can't stop me. Veronica can't stop me. Not even Paul or his friend can stop me.

Paul showed me what it means to be brave. I'm going to show him I can be just a brave, maybe even a little bit braver.

Less Than a Dollar

t's time to leave for the airport. I've locked all the doors, but I left the TV on to make it appear someone is home. We haven't had any problem with burglars since we moved here, but you never know. Better safe than sorry, I always say.

Veronica is standing by the door that goes into the garage. "Are you ready?" she asks. "We should get going." She has her hand on the door knob like she's going to walk out with or without me.

"I have one last thing to do," I say.

"We should leave now."

"I know, I know. I'm coming."

I go to the bookshelves in the family room, and it's still there. It's right where I left it, next to the photo of Paul and Veronica at Disneyland. I'm talking about the little blue whistle. If it worked for Paul, it ought to work for me, right? I grab the whistle and stuff it into my pants pocket. "Why are you bringing that?" Veronica asks. She saw what I just did.

"It's for luck," I say.

"You're being ridiculous."

"Maybe, maybe not."

"Well, now are you ready?"

"I'm as ready as I'll ever be," I say. Veronica is still there at the door, as pretty as ever, ready to lead the way. We go out through the door and step into the cold garage. We climb into my car, and I back out of the garage and into the driveway. Then off we go. It's an hour-long drive to the airport, and most of the drive is along a two-lane country highway.

I drive carefully, and I turn on the high beams so that I can see ahead. Sometimes deer run cross the highway, and the last thing we need to do is to hit a deer. I've heard it happens often around here. Fortunately for us, at this time of night, there aren't many cars on the road, so the traffic is light. It looks like it's going to be an easy drive. "I'm going to take a nap," Veronica says. "I'm exhausted. It's been a long day."

"Go ahead," I say.

Veronica leans her head against the side window and closes her eyes. "What do you suppose he looks like?" she asks with her eyes closed.

"What who looks like?" I ask.

"This boy Terrance."

"First of all, he won't be a boy."

"Boy, man, whatever."

"I have no idea what he looks like. He could look like Elton John, or he could look like Rock Hudson. Take your pick."

"I wonder if we'll like him."

"We'll find out soon enough."

"What do you think he does for a living?"

"I don't know anything about him. The only thing I know is that his name is Terrance and that Paul thinks a lot of him."

"Do you think he likes horses?"

"Horses? How should I know? I suppose he might like horses. Would you like him more if he did?"

"Maybe I would. Lots of gay men like horses. Do you know where Paul met him? Paul didn't tell me where they met."

"No, I don't where they met. I told you, I don't know any more than you do. And what's with all the questions? I thought you were going to take a nap."

"I am," Veronica says.

She finally stops talking, and after a couple minutes I turn to look at her. She is frowning, but she is also sound asleep. I reach to the dashboard and turn on the car radio. I set the volume down low enough so as not to disturb Veronica while she's sleeping. Then I think back, and I fall into a daydream of sorts. I am daydreaming and driving at the same time. I'm imagining that I'm in my early forties and that the car is filled with eleven-year-old boys. Paul is sitting in the passenger seat, and in the back are his friends Spencer, Bret, and Johnny. We are driving to Knott's Berry Farm on a summer afternoon. "Roll down the window this time," Bret says. "They can't see you with the window up."

"Like this?" Spencer asks.

"Yeah, now do it to the blue car."

"Yeah, do it," Johnny says.

"Pull up closer to him, Dad. He can't see us from here."

"There, that's good. He's right next to us. Now go ahead and do it." The boys all laugh.

"Did you see his face?" "Ha, ha, he looked pissed. He looked like he was going to blow his top."

"Did you see his wife"

"What are you boys doing?" I ask. "I'm not looking at them because I'm paying attention to the road."

"We're flipping people off."

"Did you see that guy?"

"Don't do that," I say. I am laughing slightly when I say this. Then I suppress the laugh. It's funny as hell, but I don't want them doing it, and I don't want them thinking that I think it's funny."

"Pull up," Spencer says.

"Get this lady."

"She's not looking over here. She's got both hands on the steering wheel, and she's looking straight forward."

"She's trying to drive," I say.

"Pull up closer."

"Honk your horn, Dad."

"No," I say. "I'm not going to honk my horn at the poor woman."

"There, she's looking at us! Get her now."

"Ha, ha, did you see that?"

"Man, she looks pretty mad."

"That's enough, you guys," I say. "Think of something else to do. You're going to get me in trouble."

"Hold on," Bret says. "It's coming."

"What's coming?" Spencer asks.

"Roll up your window."

Spencer rolls up his window. "So I rolled up my window, now what?" he asks.

"Breathe in through your nose," Bret says.

There's a loud fart from the back of the car, which I assume came from Bret. "You're an ass," Spencer says.

"Dude, that's gross."

"It sounded like an elephant."

"Roll down all the windows," Spencer says.

"God, we're dying back here."

"Dad, roll down your window," Paul says. He is laughing, and it makes me laugh.

"That's so sick," Spencer says. "What the heck did you have for breakfast?"

Bret sniffs the air. "Smells to me like scrambled eggs, toast, and bacon."

Everyone laughs.

"You're such a fag."

"*You're* a fag."

"If I'm the fag, then why are you the one who hangs out with Henry Murphy at school."

"I don't hang out with him," Bret says.

"I've seen you eating lunch with him."

"The booger eater," Spencer says.

"Dude, that was so funny."

"What was so funny?" Paul asks.

"In our class, Henry sits next to Marsha Powell. The teacher was talking, and Henry was picking his nose like he always does. I mean, he was really digging into it, and Marsha saw him. Then Henry pulled his finger out of his nose, and he had a big green booger on it the size of a maraschino cherry. He stuck the booger in his mouth, and Marsha practically screamed bloody murder right in the middle of Mr. Windom's lecture. You'd think a lizard just crawled up her leg and into her panties. Then she told Mr. Windom she wanted to change seats."

"Marsha Powell? That *is* funny!"

"Mr. Windom told her to stay in her seat. Then he told Henry to quit picking his nose."

"That dude is a freak."

"Why *do* you eat lunch with him?"

"His mom and my mom are friends," Bret says. "I have to be nice to him, or my mom will get mad at me."

"Sucks to be you, I guess."

"He might be a freak, but he can hit a baseball," Paul says. "He was on my team last year, and he hit six or seven homers."

"I heard he can hit, but that he can't throw."

"He couldn't throw his grandmother out," Spencer says. "Not even if she was in a wheelchair."

"You guys want to know who can throw a ball? Jake Mills can throw like there's no tomorrow."

"Gary Paxton can throw like there's no tomorrow."

"Jake can outthrow Gary."

"I don't think so."

"They can both throw like there's no tomorrow."

"I heard Jake was going steady with Susan Baker," Spencer says. "She's such a dog."

"I don't think she's so bad."

"You'd go steady with your mom's German shepherd if she wasn't already so attached to your mom. What's that dog's name? I keep forgetting."

"Her name is Lucy."

"Lucy, Lucy, Lucy," Bret says. He puts one hand over his heart and waves the other like he's a lovesick stage actor. "Let me take you away from this life, girl. Let's elope."

"Screw you."

We come to a stoplight, and I pull up behind a line of cars. It's time for me to have a little fun. "I have a puzzle for you guys," I say.

"A puzzle?"

"Let's see how smart you are."

"My dad has good puzzles," Paul says.

"Let's hear it," Bret says.

"Okay, pay close attention," I say, and I turn my head so I'm looking at the kids. "There's an old man driving a delivery truck down a street. His headlights are off, and there is no moon out. And there are no streetlights. In fact, there are no lights anywhere. A woman dressed in black begins to cross the street. She has black hair, and she is wearing a black hat. The driver suddenly puts on his brakes for her. The question is, how did he know to stop?"

There is silence while the boys think it over.

"He saw the whites of her eyes," Spencer suddenly says.

"Let's say she's wearing sunglasses," I say.

"I know," Bret says. "He sees her white teeth."

"Let's say her mouth is closed."

"I know, I know," Johnny says, raising his hand. "He smells her perfume."

"No, she isn't wearing any perfume."

The boys are quiet again, thinking, and I'm enjoying the silence. "Ten bucks to whoever gets the right answer," I say.

"Maybe he hears her footsteps," Spencer says.

"His truck engine is very noisy," I say. "He can't hear anything except for the motor."

There is silence again.

"Here comes another one," Bret says, interrupting the peace and quiet. He makes a face like he's bearing down on a bowel movement. The boys hurry to roll down the windows, but no fart is forthcoming. Bret then says, "Sorry about that, boys. I guess it was a false alarm."

"You're a dick," Spencer says, rolling his window back up. But once the windows are back up, Bret finally does break wind. It's a blast of air about twice as loud as his previous fart, and it's three times as foul. Spencer punches Bret in his shoulder.

"Must be the orange juice," Bret says. "This one smells like orange juice."

"I've got it," Paul says.

"Got what?"

"I know the answer to the puzzle."

"What is it?" I say.

"Yeah, what is it?" Spencer asks. I look in the rearview mirror, and Spencer's eyes are actually watering from the fart.

"It was daytime," Paul says.

The boys think about this. "I thought your dad said it was night," Spencer says.

"He didn't say it was day or night. He didn't say either way. So I say it was day."

"You're absolutely right," I say.

"Do I win the ten bucks?"

"Dude, why didn't I think of that?" Bret says.

"Because you're a retard."

Everyone laughs.

"I got it, right?" Paul is looking at me with his big, needy eyes. I think he wants me to tell him how smart he is in front of the other boys. I reach over with my free hand and squeeze his shoulder.

"You did it, kid," I say.

Then *poof!*

I snap out of the daydream. The boys are no longer in the car, and we're no longer in California, on our way to Knott's Berry Farm. Veronica is still sleeping, and we're driving toward the airport. But I can remember the boys. Those were such good times, good years. Life was so simple then, wasn't it? But it is like they say. Nothing lasts forever.

As I'm driving there's a gas station up to my right, and I pull up to one of the pumps. This wakes Veronica, and she lifts her head and asks, "What are you doing?"

"We need gas," I say.

"How far to the airport?"

"About fifteen more minutes."

"I fell sound asleep."

"You did," I said.

Once I step outside, I poke the gas nozzle into the side of my car and swipe my credit card. I then select my grade of gas and get it flowing. I'm thirsty, so I go into the convenience store to get a Coke after asking Veronica if she wants anything. It takes me a while to find the Cokes. Then there's a line at the register, and I take my place at the end of it. When it's my turn, the cashier calls me sweetie and asks if the Coke is all I want. I tell her the Coke is it. She's about my age, a little on the plump side, and I wonder about her. Is she married, and does she have any children? Does she have a son Paul's age? Is she still with her husband, or are they separated? What's her son like? Does her son have a girlfriend? Or a wife? Or a boyfriend? I pay for the Coke and leave the store. When I return to the car, my tank is full, and I hang the handle back on the pump, tearing off my little paper receipt. When I get in the car, Veronica asks for a sip of my Coke. "I asked you if you wanted anything," I say. "You should've told me you wanted something to drink. I would've got it for you."

"I just wanted a sip."

"You can go back to sleep now."

"I can't. Now I'm wide awake."

I start up the car, and we pull back onto the highway. We don't talk much the rest of the way. We're both just thinking quietly. I am thinking about Paul, and Veronica is probably doing the same. When we arrive at the airport, I follow the signs to the short-term parking lot. I find a place to park, and the two of us walk to the building.

We step inside and walk to the large hall where the arriving passengers will soon be. I look out the window, and I can see the plane that flew in from Atlanta. "They should be in here any minute," I say. "I can see their plane outside. They've already landed."

Just as I say this, the people begin to appear in the hallway. Some look tired, and some look excited. They are walking, talking, and carrying all their junk like refugees who've just landed in America. They all look like they're glad to be off the airplane.

"There he is!" I say.

Yes, I see Paul. In fact, I see him *and* his friend. And they are holding hands. Can you believe it? They're actually holding hands in public! I reach down to be sure the whistle is still safe in my pocket.

Veronica sees what I'm doing. "Is it still there?" she asks. She is smiling at me.

"It's there," I say.

"So are you ready for this?"

"As ready as I'll ever be," I say, and we step forward to greet our son and his friend. And I can feel it. I can feel the whistle's astonishing power.

"Dad!" Paul says. He lets go of his friend's hand and walks quickly toward me. We embrace, and then I pat his back.

"It's so good to see you, boy," I say.

Paul lets go of me and goes over to Veronica. He hugs her and kisses her on the cheek. When they're done, Paul steps aside and says, "This is Terrance."

"So you're Terrance," I say. I reach out to shake Terrance's hand. He seems a little nervous. "Any friend of Paul's is a friend of ours. Welcome to our neck of the woods. Honestly, we're glad you're here. We've been looking forward to meeting you all week."

Don't ask me where I got the courage. My voice was calm and unwavering. Maybe it *was* the whistle, that dumb grocery store toy that, if I remember right, cost me less than a dollar. Or maybe I just wasn't such a bad father. Maybe I should give myself more credit. After all, it's kind of silly for a grown man to attribute magical powers to a plastic toy.

Or is it?